*"Awake! 'Ware foes! 'Ware blood!
'Ware ruin in the night! Awake, Earl of Night!
To arms, Keep of Winds!"*

All through the New Keep the gargoyles sprang fiercely into life, yammering out her call to arms in a wild clangor that went on and on and did not stop. Malian heard the shouting and clatter of weaponry, the war cries and the rush of running feet as she swept through the darkness like a flame.

"Awake, Nhairin!" she commanded. "To arms, Asantir! Treachery and blood! Awake, Earl of Night!" she cried again, and felt the flash of her father's mind, like a blade being drawn to cross hers before she sprang away. She heard the sudden outcry, and the clash of steel on steel, and knew that the intruders had been discovered at last.

" 'Ware foes!" Malian shook the keep with one last call. She felt weary now, ready to return through the Old Keep to its heart, her place of safety.

Something caught at her mind and held on; a suffocating darkness coiled itself around her. Malian felt a terrible hunger that sought to drain her soul and her power with it, down to the marrow—and realized that she had forgotten the Raptor of Darkness . . .

By Helen Lowe

The Wall of Night
HEIR OF NIGHT

THORNSPELL

HELEN LOWE

THE
HEIR OF
NIGHT

THE WALL OF NIGHT
BOOK ONE

eos

An Imprint of HarperCollinsPublishers

EOS
An Imprint of HarperCollins*Publishers*
10 East 53rd Street
New York, New York 10022-5299

Copyright © 2010 by Helen Lowe
Cover art by Gregory Bridges
Map by Peter Fitzpatrick
ISBN 978-0-06-173404-5
www.eosbooks.com

First Eos paperback printing: October 2010
First Eos special paperback printing: May 2010

HarperCollins® and Eos® are registered trademarks of HarperCollins Publishers.

Printed in the U.S.A.

10 9 8 7 6 5 4 3 2 1

In memory of my parents,
Malcolm and Esther Lowe

Contents

PART I: *The Wall of Night*

PART II: *Storm Shadows*

PART III: *Jaransor*

THE
HEIR OF
NIGHT

WINTER COUNTRY

JARANSOR

WILD LANDS

R. WILDENRUSH

TELUMBRAS GORGE

CNKOT TOWN

TERENANTH

AR

THE RIVER

ACRIS

WESTERN MOUNTAINS

EMER

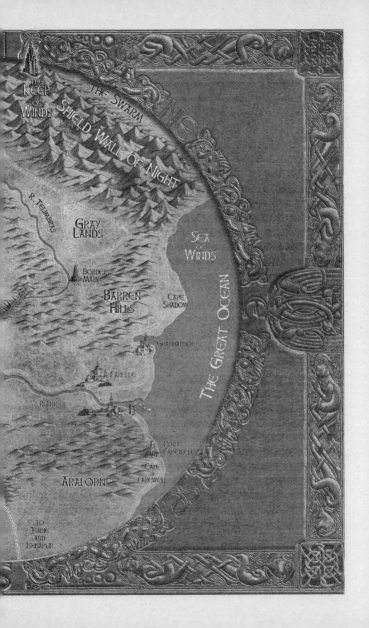

PART I

The Wall of Night

1

The Keep of Winds

The wind blew out of the northwest in dry, fierce gusts, sweeping across the face of the Gray Lands. It clawed at the close-hauled shutters and billowed every tapestry and hanging banner in the keep. Loose tiles rattled and slid, bouncing off tall towers into the black depths below; as the wind whistled through the Old Keep, finding every crack and chink in its shutters and blowing the dust of years along the floors. It whispered in the tattered hangings that had once graced the High Hall, back in those far-off days when the hall had blazed with light and laughter, gleaming with jewel and sword. Now the cool, dry fingers of wind teased their frayed edges and banged a whole succession of doors that long neglect had loosened on their hinges. Stone and mortar were still strong, even here, and the shutters held against the elements, but everything else was given over to the slow corrosion of time.

Another tile banged and rattled its way down the roof as a slight figure swarmed up one of the massive stone pillars that marched along either side of the hall. There was an alarming creak as the climber swung up and over the balustrade of a wooden gallery, high above the hall floor—but the timbers held. The climber paused, looking around with satisfaction, and wiped dusty hands on the seat of her plain, black pants. A narrow, wooden staircase twisted up toward another, even higher gallery of sculpted stone, but the treads stopped just short of the top. She studied the gap, her eyes narrowed as they traced the leap she would need to make: from the top of the stair to the gargoyles beneath the stone balcony, and then up, by a series of precarious finger- and toe-holds, onto the balcony itself.

The girl frowned, knowing that to miss that jump would mean plummeting to certain death, then shrugged and began to climb, testing each wooden tread before trusting her weight to it. She paused again on the topmost step, then sprang, her first hand slapping onto a corbel while the other grasped at a gargoyle's half-spread wing. She hung for a moment, swinging, then knifed her feet up onto the gargoyle's claws before scrambling over the high shoulder and into the gallery itself. Her eyes shone with triumph and excitement as she stared through the rear of the gallery into another hall.

Although smaller than the High Hall below, she could see that it had once been richer and more elegant. Beneath the dust, the floors were a mosaic of beasts, birds, and trailing vines; panels of metal and jeweled glass decorated the walls. There was a dais at the far end of the long room, with the fragile remains of a tapestry draped on the wall behind it. The hanging would have been bright with color once, the girl thought; the whole hall must have glowed with it, but it was a dim and lifeless place now.

She stepped forward, then jumped and swung around as her reflection leapt to life in the mirrored walls. A short, slightly built girl stared back at her out of eyes like smoke in a delicately chiseled face. She continued to stare for a moment, then poked her tongue out at the reflection, laughing at her own fright. "This must be the Hall of Mirrors," she said, pitching her voice against the silence. She knew that Yorindesarinen herself would have walked here once, if all the tales were true, and Telemanthar, the Swordsman of Stars. But now there was only emptiness and decay.

She walked the length of the hall and stepped onto the shallow dais. Most of the tapestry on the rear wall had decayed into shreds or been eaten by moths, but part of the central panel was still intact. The background was darkness, rimmed with fire, but the foreground was occupied by a figure in hacked and riven armor, confronting a creature that was as vast as the tapestry itself. Its flat, serpentine head loomed out of the surrounding darkness, exuding menace, and its bulk was doom. The figure of the hero, dwarfed beneath its shadow, looked overmatched and very much alone.

The girl touched the battered figure with her fingertips, then pulled back as the fabric crumbled further. "The hero Yorindesarinen," she whispered, "and the Worm of Chaos. This should never have been left here, to fall into ruin." She hummed a thread of tune that was first martial, then turned to haunting sadness as she slid forward, raising an imaginary sword against an unseen opponent. Her eyes were half closed as she became the fated hero in her mind, watching the legendary frost-fire gleam along her blade.

Another door banged in the distance and a voice called, echoing along silent corridors and through the dusty hall. "Malian! Mal—lee-ee—aan, my poppet!" The Old Keep caught the voice and tossed it into shadowy corners, bouncing echoes off stone and shutter while the wind whispered all around. "Where are you-oo-oo? Is this fit behavior for a Lady of Night? You are naught but an imp of wickedness, child!"

The door banged again, cutting off the voice, but the damage was done. The bright figure of Yorindesarinen faded back into memory and Malian was no longer a hero of song and story, but a half-grown girl in grubby clothes. Frowning, she smoothed her hands over her dark braid. The hero Yorindesarinen, she thought, would not have been plagued with nurses when she was a girl; she would have been too busy learning hero craft and worm slaying.

Malian hummed the snatch of tune again and sighed,

walking back to the stone balcony—then froze at a suggestion of movement from the High Hall, two storeys below. Crouching down, she peered between the stone balusters, then smiled and stood up again as a shimmer of lilting sound followed the initial footfall. A slender, golden figure gazed up at her through the twilit gloom, his hands on his hips and his sleeves flared wide, casting a fantastic shadow to either side. One by one the tiny golden bells on his clothes fell silent.

"And how," asked Haimyr, the golden minstrel, the one bright, exotic note in her father's austere keep, "do you propose getting down from there? Just looking at you makes my blood run cold!"

Malian laughed. "It's easy," she said, "especially if you've been trained by Asantir." She slid over the balustrade and made her way back down the finger- and toe-holds to hang again from the gargoyle. She grinned down at the minstrel's upturned face while she swung backward and forward, gaining momentum, before arching out and dropping neatly to the stairs below. The staircase swayed a little, but held, and she ran lightly down, vaulting up and over the second balcony, then scrambled through its wooden trusses to descend the final pillar. The minstrel held open his golden sleeves, scalloped and edged and trailing almost to the floor, and she jumped the last few feet, straight into his arms. He reeled slightly, but kept his balance, catching her in a brocaded, musical embrace. A little trail of mortar slid down the pillar after her.

"I had no idea you were due back!" Malian exclaimed, her voice muffled by the brocade. "You have been away for*ever*! You have no idea how tedious it has been without you."

Haimyr stepped back and held her at arm's length. His hair was a smooth curve along his shoulders and no less golden than his clothes, or the bright gleam of his eyes. "My dear child," he said, "you are entirely mistaken. I have every idea how tedious it has been, not to mention dull and entirely unleavened by culture, wit, or any other redeeming quality.

But you—I go away for half a year and you shoot up like a weed in my absence."

She shook her head. "I'm still short, just not *quite* as short as I was."

"But," he said, "every bit as grubby and disheveled, which will not do, not if you expect to embrace me in this wild fashion." He looked around with the lazy, lambent gaze of a cat. "This is a strange place for your play, my Malian—and what of the danger to your father's only child and heir, climbing about in that reckless manner. What would any of us say to him if you were to fall and break your neck?"

"Oh, he is away at present, riding the bounds and inspecting the outposts," said Malian. "You would all have time to run away before he got back."

Haimyr regarded her with a satirical eye. "My dear child," he said, "why do you think your good nurse and the maids are all out hunting for you, high and low? Your father is back." Mockery glinted in his smile. "On the whole, my Malian, I think that it would be better for you and your household if you were on time for his returning feast."

Malian pulled a face. "We all thought the patrols would be away another week at least," she said, with feeling. "But thank you for coming in here after me. You're right, I don't think anyone in my household would brave it, even to prevent my father's anger." She grinned again. "That's why I like it, because no one else ever comes here and I can do what I want. They think it's haunted," she added.

"I know," said Haimyr. "They have been telling me so since before you were born." He shrugged, his tall, fantastic shadow shrugging with him on the wall. "Well, folk have always liked to frighten themselves, by daylight or by dark, but they may be partly right about this place. The shadows of memory lie very thick here."

"It is a strange place," Malian agreed, "but I don't think it's dangerous. It seems sad to me, because of the decay and the silence, rather than frightening. And the memories, of course, are very bitter."

The minstrel nodded. "All the histories of your people are tragic and shot through with darkness. But the memories here must rank among the darkest."

"You are not afraid to come here, though," she said.

Haimyr laughed, and the sound echoed in the high stone vault overhead. "Afraid? Of the past's shadows? No. But then, they are not my shadows. They are your blood heritage, my Malian, not mine."

Malian frowned. "I am not afraid either," she declared, and Haimyr laughed again.

"Of course not, since you choose to come here," he said. "And rather often, too, I suspect."

Malian smiled in response, a small secret smile. "*Quite* a lot," she agreed, "especially when you and Asantir are away." She drew a pattern in the dust with her foot. "It has been very dull without you, Haimyr. Six months was far too long a time."

He smiled down at her. "I apologize for condemning you to a life of tedium. Will you forgive me if I say that I have brought back something you value, to make up for my neglect?"

Malian considered this. "New songs and stories?" she asked. "Then I may forgive you, but only if you promise to teach me every one."

Haimyr swept a low, extravagant bow, his sleeves tinkling and his golden eyes glinting into hers, one long slender hand placed over his heart. Malian smiled back at him.

"Every one, remember," she said again, and he laughed, promising nothing, as was his way.

It was only a few hundred paces from the old High Hall to the gate into the New Keep, which was barred and soldered closed, although there was a locked postern a few yards away. Malian's customary means of coming and going was a narrow gap between the apex of the gate and the corridor's arched roof, but she was resigned, rather than surprised, when Haimyr took the postern key from his pocket. "Oh dear," she murmured, "now I am in trouble."

Haimyr slanted her a mocking smile. "Didn't you hear poor Doria, calling to you? She summoned the courage to put her head around the postern for love of you, but even a lifetime's devotion wouldn't take her any further. Nhairin, of course, is made of sterner stuff, but we agreed that I was better suited to hunting you out."

"Because you could hope to catch me if I ran?" she inquired, with a smile as sly as his. "But I cannot see you scaling the walls, Haimyr, even to save me from my father's wrath."

He closed the postern behind them, locking it with a small, definite click. "You are quite right. Even the thought is an abhorrence. The ghosts of the past are one thing, but to scramble through the rafters like an Ishnapuri monkey, quite another. I would have absolutely no choice but to abandon you to your fate."

Malian laughed aloud, but sobered as they turned into the golden blaze of the New Keep. Darkness never fell in these corridors and halls where jewel-bright tapestries graced the walls and the floors were patterned with colored tiles. Pages sped by on their innumerable errands while soldiers marched with measured tread and the vaulted ceilings echoed with all the commotion of a busy keep. Malian's eyes lit up as the bustle surged around them. "It's always like this when my father comes home," she said. "He sets the entire keep in a flurry."

Haimyr's laugh was rueful. "Do I not know it? And now I must hurry, too, if I am to prepare my songs for the feast."

"Everyone will be eager for something new," Malian agreed. "But only after you have sung of the deeds and glory of the House of Night—for are we not first and oldest?"

"Oldest, first, and greatest of all the Derai Houses on the Wall, in deeds and duty if not in numbers," a new voice put in, as though reciting indisputable fact. A spare figure rose from an alcove seat and limped forward. She was as dark and reserved as the minstrel was golden and flamboyant, and her face was disfigured by the scar that slashed across it from temple to chin.

"'For it is the House of Night that holds the Keep of Winds,'" Malian chanted in reply, "'foremost of all the strongholds on the Shield-wall of Night.' It was you who first taught me that, Nhairin."

The newcomer's dark brows lifted. "I have not forgotten," she said, taking the postern key from Haimyr. She had soldiered once for the Earl of Night, until the fight in which she gained both limp and scar, and she liked to say that she soldiered still in the Earl's service, but as High Steward of the Keep of Winds, rather than with a sword. "I do not forget any of the few lessons that did not have to be beaten into you," she added meditatively.

"Nhair-rin!" said Malian, then a quick, guilty look crossed her face. "Have I caused you a great deal of trouble, having to look for me?"

The steward smiled, a slight twist of her mouth. "Trouble? Nay, I am not troubled. But I know who will be if you are not clean and in your place when the feast bell strikes." The smile widened at Malian's alarmed look. "That bell is not so very far off, so if I were you I should be running like the wind itself to my chamber, and the bath that is waiting there."

Haimyr clapped Malian on the shoulder. "The good steward is right, as always. So run now, my bold heart!"

Malian ran. Her father held strict views on the conduct appropriate to an Heir of Night, and exacted the same obedience from his daughter as he did from the warriors under his command. "We keep the long watch," he often said to Malian, "and that means we are a fighting House. The Wall itself is named for us, and of all the fortresses along its length, this one stands closest to our enemy. We cannot let our vigilance or discipline waver for an instant, and you and I must be the most vigilant of all, knowing all others look to us and will follow our example, whether good or bad."

Malian knew that upholding discipline included being on time for a formal Feast of Returning. Her nurse and the other maids knew it, too, for they did not stop to scold but descended on her as one when she ran through the door, hustling her out of her grimy clothes and into the tepid bathwater. Nesta, the most senior of the maids, caught Malian's eye as she opened her mouth to complain, and Malian immediately shut it again. Nesta came of a family that had served the Earls of Night for long generations, and she held views on the value of discipline, tradition, and truancy that were remarkably similar to those of Malian's father.

Doria, Malian's nurse, was more voluble. "An imp of wickedness, that's what you are," she said. "Running here, and running there, and never in sight when wanted. You'll be the death of me yet, I swear—not to mention the wrath of the Earl, your father, if he ever finds out about your expeditions."

"We'll all die of fright on that day, sure enough," said Nesta, in her dry way, "if nothing worse happens first. But will our fine young lady care, that's what I ask? And none of your wheedling answers either, my girl!" She struck a stern attitude, with arms akimbo, and the younger maids giggled.

"Well," said Malian meekly, "it hasn't happened yet, has it? And you know I don't mean to be a trouble to you, Doria darling." She hugged and kissed her nurse, but poked her tongue out at Nesta over Doria's shoulder.

The maid made a snipping motion with her fingers, imitating scissors. "Ay, Doria knows you don't mean to cause her trouble, but it won't stop trouble coming—especially if we don't get you down to dinner on time." She held up an elaborate black velvet dress. "It had better be black, I suppose, since you welcome the Earl of Night."

"Black is good, thank you," agreed Malian, scrambling into it. She waited, as patiently as she could, while Doria bound her hair into a net of smoky pearls.

"You look just like the ladies in the old tapestries," the nurse sighed, as her fingers twisted and pinned. "You are growing up, my poppet. Nearly thirteen already! And in just a few more years you will be a grand lady of the Derai, in truth."

Malian made a face at the polished reflection in the mirror. "I do look like a scion of the oldest line, I suppose." She kicked the train out behind her. "But can you imagine Yorindesarinen wearing anything so restrictive?"

"That skirt would make worm slaying very difficult," Nesta observed, and Malian grinned.

Doria, however, frowned. "Yorindesarinen is nothing but a fable put about by the House of Stars to make themselves feel important." She sniffed. "Just like the length of their names. Ridiculous!"

"They're not all long," Malian pointed out. "What about Tasian and Xeria?"

The nurse made a sign against bad luck, while Nesta shook her head. "Shortened," the maid said. "Why should we honor that pair of ill omen with their full names?" She pulled a face. "Especially she who brought ruin upon us all."

Doria nodded, her mouth pursed as if she had filled it with pins. "Cursed be her name—and completely beneath the attention of the Heir of Night, so we will not sully our lips with it now!" She gave a last tweak to the gauze collar, so that it stood up like black butterfly wings on either side of Malian's face. "You look just as you should," she said, not without pride. "And if you hurry, you'll be on time as well."

Malian kissed her cheek. "Thank you," she said, with real gratitude. "I am sorry that I gave you all so much trouble."

Nesta rolled her eyes and Doria looked resigned. "You always are," she said, sighing. "But I don't like your gallivanting off into the Old Keep, nasty cold place that it is. Trouble will come of it—and then what the Earl will do to us all, I shudder to think."

Malian laughed. "You worry too much," she said. "But if I don't hurry I really will be late and my father will make us all shudder, sooner rather than later."

She blew a butterfly kiss back around the door and walked off as quickly as the black dress would allow, leaving Doria and Nesta to look at each other with a mixture of exasperation, resignation, and affection.

"Don't say it," the nurse said to the younger woman, sitting down with a sigh. "The fact is that she is just like her mother was at the same age—too much on her own and with a head filled with dreams of glory. Not to mention running wild, all over the New Keep and half the Old."

Nesta shook her head. "They've been at her since she was a babe with all their lessons, turning her into an earl in miniature, not to mention the swordplay and other skills required by a warrior House. I like it when she acts like a normal girl and plays truant, for all the anxiety it causes us."

Doria folded her arms across her chest. "But not into the Old Keep," she said, troubled. "That was her mother's way, always mad for adventure and leading the others after her. We all know how that ended." She shook her head. "Malian is already too much her mother's daughter for my comfort."

Nesta frowned. "The trouble is," she said, pitching her voice so that no one else could hear her, "does the Earl realize that? And what will he do when he finds out?"

Doria sighed again, looking anxious. "I don't know," she replied. "I know that Nhairin sees it, plain as I do—and that outsider minstrel, too, I've no doubt. It's as though the Earl is the only person who does not see it."

"Or will not," Nesta said softly.

"Does not, will not," replied Doria, "the outcome is the same. Well, there's nothing we can do except our best for her, as we always have."

"Perhaps," agreed Nesta. Her dark eyes gazed into the fire. "Although what happens," she asked, "if your best is not enough?"

But neither the nurse nor the fire had any answer for her.

2

Heralds of the Guild

The High Hall lay some distance from Malian's apartments, and like its counterpart in the Old Keep it was an enormous chamber of stone, with soaring pillars and a high, vaulted roof. The hall, like the keep corridors, had no windows onto the outside world but was lit by lamps and chandeliers of jeweled glass that shone like a thousand stars. Huge fires blazed in the many fireplaces set along the length of the hall, warming the vast space and casting a further glow over the walls. Banners floated down, long and bright from the ceiling vault, and the walls were hung with tapestries and heraldic shields. But there were no weapons to be seen anywhere. They were not displayed on the walls or stored by the doors for ready use, a prohibition that was enforced in every stronghold along the Derai Wall.

Malian knew the story, of course. Every Derai child was taught it young. It had happened at the end of the civil war, nearly five hundred years before, at the feast intended to confirm a lasting truce. The cup of peace had gone round, but rather than drinking, some of those present had snatched up weapons instead, cutting down their guests. The shadow of that night of death still lay over the Derai Alliance, haunting the nine Houses with its legacy of blood feud and mistrust.

The divisions had been passed down from one generation to the next, setting House against House, warrior against priest, kin against kin.

Malian saw that she had beaten her father's party, after all, and stopped in the shadow of the hall doors, studying the great banner that hung directly above the Earl's empty chair. The winged horse device of Night, depicted in the moment of springing into the air, had been worked into the black fabric with silver and diamond, and the unfurled wings gleamed where it caught the light. Malian's heart quickened as it always did when she saw the banner of her House, knowing that the same ensign had led the Derai Alliance from the beginning, for the threads of the old standard were always painstakingly unpicked and rewoven into the new cloth. The heroes Telemanthar and Kerem had fought beneath its shadow and this same winged horse would have followed Yorindesarinen when she led the Derai.

Quietly, Malian made her way to the Heir's Seat, set on its own canopied dais halfway down the long hall. The warriors and retainers of Night began to crowd in around her and the buzz of anticipation grew. There were no clerics, of course. The Keep of Winds had its Temple quarter, but those who served there were forbidden the everyday life of the keep—as they had been for five hundred years.

It was five hundred years, too, since the walls of the keep had last flared with the Golden Fire that had once been the heart and strength of the Derai Alliance. The loss of the Fire was not much talked about now, except in whispers, although some said that it still slumbered, deep in the heart of the nine keeps, and would reemerge in the hour of the Derai's greatest need.

It was a comforting story, but Malian's doubts had grown as she became older and learned that the Golden Fire could only be summoned and wielded by those Derai known as the Blood. The Blood comprised the Earls of the nine Houses and their blood kin, but their numbers had diminished generation by generation since the civil war, eroding the Derai's ability to command the Golden Fire—should it ever return. Malian's uneasiness had only deepened on those nights when she lay awake, listening to her guards and servants talking in the outer room. "What if the Fire doesn't slumber at all?" they would ask each other, fear in their voices. "What if it burned to gray, cold ashes on the Night of Death? What will become of the Derai Alliance then, when the Swarm rises again and the tide of their darkness comes flowing in, strong and cold across the Wall?"

"What indeed?" Malian asked herself now, and shivered. The conflict between the Derai and the Swarm had been in stasis ever since their arrival on this world, but she knew from history that such stalemates never endured—and she had seen the reports from Night's scouts that suggested the Swarm's dark power was stirring again. Yet the stasis had lasted so long now that there were many in the Alliance who questioned the very existence of the Swarm. The darkness along the Wall, these Derai claimed, was simply a phenomenon natural to this world of Haarth. Similarly, the foul creatures that dwelt amongst the passes and ravines of the Wall must also be natives of Haarth and not the scavengers and foragers of the Swarm. The real problem, according to the doubters, was not these infestations, but the internal enmities that had preoccupied the Derai Houses since the civil war.

It was Malian's father who had explained this situation to her, on one of the few days that was calm enough for them to walk on the pinnacled battlements of the keep. Malian had stared out across the great expanse of the Wall, range on towering range of jagged peaks as far as the eye could see— and wondered if their long history of struggle was truly only a myth. She had wondered, too, how the Derai could possibly hope to withstand a renewed onslaught by the Swarm, if so many in the Alliance had lost faith in their ancient vigil.

The Earl had nodded when she shared this thought, chill humor touching his eyes. "Ay, the Derai who promote these claims tend to live in those strongholds that sit far behind the outer Wall—and we slay the Swarm skirmishers before they breach their borders. Yet every report I get suggests that incursions are on the increase. We should be strengthening our Alliance and our vigilance, not turning our backs on the Wall."

Malian mulled over this discussion again while the life of the hall swirled around her. She sat at Night's council table and knew it was her duty as Heir to understand the perils that beset her House, even if many still treated her as just a child. Yet she longed to prove her worth, to perform some great deed or face down a dire foe, so that all knew she was the Heir of Night in truth, not just in name.

A gong sounded, clear above the din, and the gathering fell silent as Nhairin stepped through the great double doors. She paused, surveying the throng with her somber gaze, then cried out, in a voice that filled the hall: "The Earl of Night comes into his High Hall! All rise for the Earl of Night!"

The gathering rose and Malian, too, turned toward the doors as her father walked through. He was a dark man, tall like all their kin except Malian herself, and walked with the trained grace of a swordsman. But his expression was shuttered—cold, even, thought Malian: he holds the whole world at arm's length, including me. But then her eyes slid to the woman at his side. Almost the whole world, Malian amended, keeping her expression neutral.

She knew the rest of the Earl's household as well if not better than her father. Gerenth, the Commander of Night, strode in first behind the Earl, with Asantir, the Captain of the Earl's Honor Guard, at his side. Teron, the senior squire, walked behind them, but checked his brisk stride to remain in step with Jiron, the Earl's scribe. Jiron, Malian observed with an inward smile, looked as disheveled as ever, with ink stains on his fingers and his russet cloak slipping half off one shoulder. Haimyr brought up the rear of the immediate household and fell in beside Nhairin, just ahead of a small army of squires and pages, all wearing the black uniform and winged-horse badge of the House of Night.

Malian watched their progress up the hall and was struck again by how alien her father's consort, the Lady Rowan Birchmoon, looked amongst the Earl's dark-clad, dark-visaged household. Her skin was almost as white as the snows of her own Winter Country, her eyes gray and clear beneath slim brows. Pale brown hair hung down her back in a long braid, with pieces of shell and small feathers plaited into it; her long tunic and leggings of supple white leather were embroidered with beasts and birds. There was usually a white hound running at her heels, or a spotted, tuft-eared hunting cat pressed against her legs. Tonight, Malian saw with a pang of envy, it was one of the feather-footed hounds.

She did not, however, envy the ripple of disquiet that followed Rowan Birchmoon down the length of the cheerful hall. The scandal of her coming, three years before, had rocked the Derai Alliance to its foundations. It was unheard of, completely unthinkable, for any Derai, let alone an Earl, to take an outsider as the companion of his body and his hearth. Yet here she was, Rowan Birchmoon of the Winter people, bearing the unprecedented title of Lady Consort and sitting at the Earl of Night's side in the High Hall, as well as sleeping in his bed. At least he had not married her, the whispers ran, and given her both the title and full powers of Countess of Night—at least he was not so bewitched as that.

How many Derai, Malian wondered, still believe she is a witch and my father ensnared in her spells? She sank into a deep curtsey as the Earl's party stopped at the Heir's dais, but although her father's eyes met hers as she rose, he did not smile.

He never smiles, Malian thought. "Welcome again to this hall, Father," she said, initiating the formal exchange that convention required. "The Heir rejoices in the Earl's safe return."

"The welcome is warmer for the Heir's presence, honoring this High Hall." The Earl's voice was cool in the listening quiet, his expression austere.

"The Heir's first duty is to uphold the honor of the Earl and of this House," Malian responded.

The hall murmured its approval and Malian turned to Rowan Birchmoon, but her greeting was forestalled by the hound, which thrust a cold wet nose into her hand. Malian laughed, stroking the silky head, and the Winter woman smiled. "Falath is remiss in matters of tradition," she said, in her clear voice, "but very attentive in friendship."

"I'm glad he remembers me," said Malian, but felt her father's eye and added quickly, "I am glad, too, for your continued health and safe return."

"Ay," said the Earl, less formally. "We saw few signs of any enemy and lost no riders to either skirmish or accident. Our only injuries resulted from the journey itself, a sprained ankle and a fall from a horse. Still, we were glad to see the Gate of Winds again." He inclined his head, formal again, before moving on to his own chair. The white hound wagged a polite farewell to Malian and trotted after its mistress.

The Earl did not sit, but remained standing beneath the great banner of Night. He held his right hand up, palm facing out toward the waiting hall, and when he spoke, his voice was strong. "House of Night, whence came we and why?"

The gathering, led by Malian, raised their hands in response and replied with one voice: "From the stars we came, where we fought the long war against the Swarm of Dark. In battle after battle we fought them, in victory and defeat, until the great portal opened and we came through into this place."

"And what do we do now, on this world of Haarth?" the Earl asked.

"We garrison the Shield-wall of Night," they replied. "We keep the long watch for that hour when the Swarm of Dark will rise again and seek to overrun this world, as it overran so many others beyond the stars. When that day and that hour come, we will stand forth against the power of the Swarm, as we have always done."

"Why, then, do we call ourselves Night, who oppose the

Swarm of Dark?" The Earl's voice carried the length of the hall.

"The Swarm rose and spread across the face of the stars," they answered him. "One by one it blotted them out, sucking all light and life into its maw. The great darkness stole night's beauty and replaced it with fear and dread. We were the first to stand against it, taking the name of Night in memory of what had once been beautiful and without fear."

"We are first," the Earl said, slow and sonorous. "First of all the nine Houses to serve in this cause, just as we stand foremost on the Wall of Night, keeping the long vigil. I charge you, House of Night, to neither fear nor falter, but hold to the Wall."

"We will not falter!" Their roar filled the vaulted roof. "We shall keep faith!"

"So be it," the Earl replied, "until our vigil is done."

How stirring it is, thought Malian, with the thrill that always coursed along her veins when she spoke Night's creed. Surely we shall not fail in our duty, even if those in the other Houses waver?

The feast was brought in with a clatter, and the hall soon became filled with an ocean of noise as Night celebrated the safe return of friends, comrades, and kin from the dangerous boundary patrols. Even the Earl and his household, generally more reserved, seemed relaxed. Nhairin smiled her twisted smile at some joke of Haimyr's; Gerenth, overhearing, brayed out a laugh.

Malian watched them wistfully from her place down the hall. Derai custom demanded that the households of Earl and Heir be kept separate: *'Ware to those who lose Earl and Heir in one night*, the proverb ran, and history had proved its truth. Even before the civil war, Derai annals had been full of assassination attempts by the Swarm, with its tracking sorceries and insidious, creeping magics. Since the Night of Death, the Derai had added their own record of blood feud and knives in the dark to that bitter history, and the custom of separate households was strictly enforced. Once the Heir would have been surrounded by siblings and Blood kin, but Malian was the only child of the Blood of Night born into her generation, so her household comprised Doria, the maids, and various tutors, with no friends or companions her own age. She had been told that the Earl of Blood had a daughter of similar age and knew she had second cousins in the Sea Keep. But sometimes she longed to be like Yorindesarinen, growing up Heir of Stars in a citadel where Blood kin were as numerous as the constellations—although that hadn't helped the hero when she faced the Chaos worm. Yorindesarinen had fought and died alone, all the stories agreed on that.

The first course was being cleared away when Malian heard a distant tolling from the keep gates. She saw Haimyr's head lift, and her own surprise was mirrored in the faces around her. It was late for anyone to come beating at the Gate of Winds and there were no visitors expected from Night's outlying holds, or emissaries from the other Houses.

Odd, thought Malian. She knew that no traveler would be turned away, here at the Wall's farthest bounds, although the Lieutenant of the Gate would also never let any visitors proceed further until satisfied of their good faith. So she was not surprised that some time elapsed before the hall gong sounded.

"Tarathan of Ar and Jehane Mor, heralds of the Guild," one of Nhairin's stewards roared out, above the hubbub. "From Terebanth, on the Great River."

Absolute silence crashed down as every face turned toward the man and woman who stepped through the door. The man had multiple braids of chestnut hair flowing below his shoulders, while the woman was fair, with a single plait twisted around her head like a crown. They were both of middle height and clad alike in gray, their long cloaks cast back. A badge pinned each cloak on the left shoulder and a dagger was sheathed at their belts. Both their faces were drawn and weary, their clothes mired from the road, but they walked steadily through the watching, silent hall until they stood before the Earl's chair. There they stopped as one and bowed, first to the Earl and then, slightly lower, to the woman at his side. Malian's eyes widened, and she saw the faintest of mocking smiles on Haimyr's face, but no one else appeared to have noticed the graded courtesy.

The heralds straightened. "Hail, Earl of Night," they said, their individual tones weaving together as if they had only the one voice between them. "Honor to you and to your House."

"And light and safety on your road," the Earl responded. He did not seem surprised that they knew the Derai greeting. "What brings heralds of the Guild so far into the Wall of Night?"

"We are charged with a message for you," they replied. "It is held under sigil of silence, so you alone may hear it or know the sender, and no other may command it to be spoken."

There was a collective hiss of breath, but the Earl held up his hand, commanding silence again. "Indeed?" he said. His dark gaze measured the two before him, who simply waited. Malian leaned forward, fascinated: heralds of the Guild actually *here*, on the Derai Wall! For a moment she even thought her father might break tradition and leave the feast. She held her breath, but released it, half disappointed, when he spoke again.

"You have traveled a long, hazardous road and I will hear you, but not now. This is a Feast of Returning, which our custom demands should not be broken unless we come under attack. Besides, you are weary." He raised his voice so everyone in the hall would hear. "Heralds of the Guild, I welcome you as guests of Night. Eat now, and then rest. I will hear your message in the morning."

The heralds bowed and spoke again as one. "As the Earl wills, so shall it be. For Night's hospitality, we thank you."

The watching Derai sighed and turned back to their feasting, while a page led the heralds to a place by one of the fires. The Earl and his household, too, resumed their conversation as though nothing unusual had happened. Malian pushed a piece of dried fruit around her plate. Open curiosity would be beneath her dignity as Heir, but she could feel the surreptitious intensity of the hall's interest, matching her own, and was sure that the heralds must sense it as well.

Even on the Wall there were a great many stories told about the heralds of the Guild. According to the legends heralds rarely failed in their duty, no matter what difficulties were encountered, and would only reveal a message to the designated recipient. It was said that heralds had died rather than break that trust. The message must be of considerable importance then, to justify sending a herald pair so far from the cities of the River—but the Derai had their own messenger corps, so the message must also have been sent by an outsider. Malian's eyes narrowed, full of speculation, for the Derai had few dealings with outsiders.

She glanced at her father who was listening to Gerenth, his expression courteous but unrevealing. He looked as though he had dismissed the heralds from his mind, although Malian was sure that he had not. Almost against her will, she found her eyes drawn to the gray-clad figures sitting by the fire. They looked ordinary enough as they concentrated on their food, but Malian suspected that appearances were deceiving. As if in answer to her thought, both heralds looked up before she could glance aside. Their eyes met and held hers, keen-edged as lances.

Malian wanted to wrench her eyes away, except that would suggest she was afraid of the power in their gaze. So she made herself bow instead, a grave inclination of the head that they answered as gravely. Yet Malian could not shake that suggestion of power. She wanted to know more, to speak with them herself—but right now the gathering was calling for Haimyr. The clamor fell into an expectant hush as he rose to his feet.

Malian—looking from the corner of her eye—saw that even the gray-clad heralds were leaning forward as the minstrel waited, holding the hall in his silence. Then his hand touched the strings and the golden voice soared, sweeping them into the old, old tale of Kerem the Dark Handed and Emeriath of Night. Kerem was one of the elder heroes of the Derai, a solitary hunter and warrior who wreaked great havoc amongst the Swarm and rescued Emeriath from the Maze of Fire. It was a dark story, like all the great hero tales, but with a rare bright ending, for Kerem and Emeriath won clear of the Maze, despite desperate odds.

Malian found herself caught up in the emotion and power of the tale, even though she had heard it many times before. When it was done, everyone cheered and clapped, calling for more, but Malian found herself yawning. She was tired from her explorations in the Old Keep, and one benefit in being underage was that she need not remain at the feast until the Earl left. Malian caught his eye and he nodded, half raising a hand in salute as she stood up to make her formal bow. Teron said something and her father turned, allowing Malian to slip away while the hall's attention was focused on Haimyr.

She did not think that anyone else had noticed her departure, unless it was Asantir, who noticed everything. Yet when she paused by a side door, she saw that both the heralds were watching her, their faces colored by the fire. Again, their light-filled eyes held hers and Malian paused—but a page bowed, offering the heralds more food, and the moment was broken. Malian turned and left the hall.

Despite her earlier tiredness, Malian could not shake the memory of the heralds' eyes. She stood quietly while Doria helped her out of the black dress and combed out the cloud of her hair, but her thoughts were busy, circling the puzzle of the gray-clad strangers.

I should go to the old library, Malian told herself. The records there are bound to hold something about the heralds and their guild.

She waited patiently after Doria left her, letting the comings and goings in the outer room die away and watching until the last light was extinguished. Eventually, she heard a chorus of gentle snores from the nurse's chamber and slipped out of bed, pushing a pillow down under the covers so it would seem that she slept—at least so long as the room remained unlit. The legend of Kerem claimed that he could see in the dark, and Malian longed for the same ability as she groped for her clothes, bruising her shins against a chair. She made her way by feel to the back of the room, moving her fingers carefully across the wooden panels until she found the place she wanted, and pressed. The panel swung silently back and she felt the cool air from the narrow passage beyond, which led into the maze of spyruns that crisscrossed the keep.

Malian had discovered the maze long ago and like the Old Keep it had become one of her favorite places. She had scored trails along the different routes with her dagger so that she could find her way by touch, even in the dark. She had never met anyone else traversing its secret ways and so had come to think of it as hers alone. Now she clicked the hidden door closed behind her and moved along the narrow route, her fingers tracing her blazed trail, to enter the library by another concealed door.

The chamber was disused and dusty, with books and parchments crammed from floor to ceiling around all four walls. The first thing Malian did was light a lamp, which cast a small circle of golden light and threw mysterious shadows over the bookshelves. The library was so rarely used that she was sure that no one else would come in, especially not tonight, but she locked the door into the corridor anyway. She took off her jacket as well and pushed it into the crack between door and floor, because it would only take one overly zealous guard to investigate the light and find her out. Then Doria would scold, and Nesta would frown, and Nhairin would talk sternly about the responsibilities of being Heir. Her father would punish her, too, if they told him, for disobeying those he had set in authority over her. Malian pulled a face and checked the bolts on the inside of the door a second time.

It took some time to find a book that held any reference to heralds and she judged, from the mildewed cover and archaic hand, that it was very old. She ran her forefinger under the thin, spidery writing, working out the sense of the words, and realized that it must have been written in the early centuries of the Derai arrival on Haarth.

> *"As for the peoples beyond the Wall, although diverse in their ways they remain united in their hostility to our Derai Alliance, with its great fortresses and vigilant watch against an enemy that they do not yet perceive. Doubtless, too, they fear our strength on the borders of their own divided realms. Recently, however, they have sought to know more of us, and sent emissaries from the caste or society they call "heralds." These are of some interest to me, for they are always sent in pairs and function in a form of symbiosis that we cannot yet fathom, but is demonstrated most overtly through their habit of speaking in unison. We wonder, too, about the exact nature of their power, for even the strongest and most subtle of our mindspeakers cannot read them. I find this alarming, but our adepts seem convinced that it is simply that their minds are still alien to us. After all, we have never before encountered another people with powers to match our own—except for the Swarm of cursed name, and its minions cannot be termed "people." Still, I wonder—and believe that we must learn more about these heralds."*

The writing continued, but the remaining entries were all of Derai life on the Wall; eventually the handwriting changed, as though someone else had taken over the record. Heralds were never mentioned again in any detail, although Malian pored over the faded pages and tried several other volumes. It was tedious work and soon she was yawning steadily. Her eyes grew heavy and she kept jerking her head back up after it nodded forward, thinking that she would read just a few more pages and then return to bed.

Malian woke to pitch darkness, lifting her head from where she had slumped forward over the book, and realized that the lamp must have burned out while she slept. Her heart was fluttering, high and hard in her breast, and the night was pressing in. She strained her ears, but there was nothing to hear, only a silence comprised of musty air and the tiny noises of the library. And then she did hear it, the thing that had roused her from deep sleep to instant, heart-pounding wakefulness. It was not an external sound but a voice, clear and certain in her mind. The voice spoke just one word, dropped like a stone into silence: *"Flee!"*

3

Whispers in the Dark

Kalan was hiding from his fate in the broom cupboard on the lowest level of the Temple quarter. News of the Earl's successful expedition had run through the keep and Kalan had wanted, suddenly and quite desperately, to be part of the camaraderie of the High Hall. He could not bear to sit down to his usual plain meal with the other novices and then return to an evening of dusting books in Brother Selmor's study. His heart was hot with rebellion when he thought of the laughter and storytelling that would fill the High Hall—and that he was excluded simply because he had been born with the old powers. He had had to get away, to escape the everyday sameness of his peers; and although the cupboard, with its jumble of mops and brooms and buckets, was a poor alternative to the Feast of Returning, at least he could brood over his wrongs in peace.

"It isn't fair!" Kalan whispered, striking one fist hard against his leg. "Everyone else can go the feast, no matter how low their place, everyone except us!" He sat with his chin pulled up to his knees and stared hot-eyed into the darkness. It wasn't as though he had ever wanted to be a priest. He came of the House of Blood, one of the great warrior Houses and Night's long ally—and all of his family without exception, for generations beyond count, had been warriors. As a very young child he had wished for nothing more than to grow up and join their ranks.

Kalan's face darkened at the thought of his family. He had been the youngest of seven children, somewhat lost underfoot but well loved enough until the old power emerged during his seventh year. Kalan still remembered the cold, closed look on his father's face, and his siblings' hostility as they performed the ceremony that had declared him dead to his family, shutting him out from the mainstream life of the House of Blood. The quiet click of the door to his family home, closing behind him when the ritual ended, had been absolute in its finality.

Even now, that memory hurt. It did not matter that Kalan knew this practice was common amongst the warrior Houses and that his family had not turned him out to starve. Word had been sent to the priest in his hold, and when the door swung shut behind him Kalan had found guards waiting to escort him to his new life. The realization that his siblings' hostility sprang from fear that they, too, might carry the priestly taint did not help either. Seven years on, the unfairness still cut deep and a slow, hot anger, against it and them, smoldered in his heart. "Unfair," he said again, as he had thought it so many times before. His jaw set and his fists clenched. "Unfair, unfair!"

The word struck a chord in his memory: Sister Korriya, the temple's senior priestess, looking down her aristocratic nose at him the first time he had dared to say that he thought his fate unfair. "Unfair?" she had rapped out. "Unfair? I daresay it is. And so is a great deal more in this life, as you'll find before you are too much older. You had best accustom yourself, young man!"

She was right, Kalan thought, but he still loathed the turn his life had taken. The House of Blood was the most extreme of the warrior orders, exiling all but a bare minimum of those with the old powers—usually to one of the priestly Houses. There were days when Kalan was grateful that the Temple of Night had been short of novices and so he was still part of the forbidden warrior world, even at a distance. But at times like this it made his lot seem that much harder.

At first, his resentment had taken the form of pranks, or absconding from lessons and chores—and he had incurred his fair share of punishment from Sister Korriya, who had a sharp eye for novice misdeeds. Yet Kalan sensed sympathy in her as well. She had overlooked the stolen hours that he had spent with Brother Belan, listening to tales of the great Derai heroes. Belan, the oldest of the priests, had known all the stories of the priestess Errianthar and her twin, Telemanthar, and how they had beaten back the Swarm of Dark. Telemanthar, the old priest would mumble, had carried a hero's sword, but Errianthar had called the Golden Fire with her mind and hurled it against the onslaught of the Swarm. Belan could recite the Saga of Yorindesarinen, too, despite his faded voice, and would whisper that Kerem the Dark Handed, Kerem of the subtle mind, had also wielded the old powers as well as a sword.

Back in the good old days, Kalan thought bitterly, when warriors had the old powers and priests trained in the fighting arts—before the civil war and the schism between the Houses.

Brother Belan had died three years before and his stories, the brightness and solace of Kalan's life, had died with him. Since then, Kalan had retreated further into his own company, exploring the less-used parts of the Temple quarter and discovering the warren of storerooms at its lowest level. The warren made it easier to absent himself at will, although he tried to time his disappearances to avoid unwelcome attention. But lately, Kalan had found his moods of despondency becoming more frequent. It was not just his exclusion from the life of the wider keep, although that galled him deeply, or even the tedium of temple life. Soon he would complete his seventh year as a novice and be required to take the initiate's vow; after that, there would be no going back.

Until recently, Kalan had indulged a fervent hope that his powers might disappear again as suddenly as they had emerged. Dogged but determined, he had continued to practice the beginnings of the warrior training, learned in his father's house, in secret. But as his fourteenth birthday drew closer he had begun to despair, knowing that he was bound, whatever his personal aspirations, into a life that promised to be narrow, circumscribed, and dull. He did not know if he could bear it.

Kalan knew from Sister Korriya's lessons that there had been other temple dwellers who felt they could not bear it. Some had taken their own lives while others sought to flee the Wall. It was not easy, however, to hide the old powers from other Derai. Most were returned to the temples, sometimes with the "R" for renegade branded into their forehead or cheek to prevent further escape attempts.

As if we were criminals, Kalan reflected angrily. Or slaves.

The Earls of Blood were renowned for their implacable pursuit of such renegades, and Kalan wondered whether the Earl of Night would be similarly relentless. Even in the Temple quarter, the current Earl was known for his justice, but there were some nasty stories told about his father, the Old Earl. And the schism between priest and warrior ran very deep in Night, which Kalan found strange, because in all the long history of the Derai, only the House of Stars had produced more heroes with the old powers.

Sister Korriya had shaken her head when he shared this thought. "Strange," she replied, echoing his word. "Perhaps. But then again, perhaps not. The line between love and hate can run very fine, as we have seen time and again in our history."

Kalan had not been quite sure what she meant, and he still wondered why the temples were so feared when most clerics only had minor powers. Once, Derai temples had housed sibyls, with their talent for prophecy, and mindspeakers who could communicate across vast distances, as well as those like Errianthar, whose powers allowed them to move objects and to bring fire with the touch of their minds. Such powers were difficult to hide, particularly when the one bearing them was startled or threatened, although temple tradition held that with training, natural instinct could be overruled. Even so, there were stories . . . Kalan had heard that there were weather workers in the Sea Keep who paced its walls in savage weather, their physical forms fraying into the elements. Behavior like that drew attention, but it might be possible for those with lesser powers to survive undetected, even amongst other Derai.

Kalan sighed again and shifted, trying to find a comfortable position in his hiding place. It was probably time to start back anyway. There was no way that he or any other priest would see anything of the Feast of Returning, and a longer sojourn with the mops and brooms would not change that. Easing himself to his feet, he peered into the hallway.

The sound was fainter than a whisper, but Kalan tensed instantly. Then he heard it again, the suggestion of a nearly silent footfall or the slither of a cloak against wall. Its stealth made him freeze, his heart beating a sudden, sharp tattoo. Kalan eased backward, retreating into the broom cupboard.

The whisper sounded again, resolving into a definite footfall—and then more than one. It came from the maze of unused corridors and storerooms, rather than the stairway to the upper levels, and this made Kalan doubly cautious. He crouched low, trying to blend with the deeper shadows and the angles cast by the stacked mops and brooms. He had discovered, over years of playing truant, that if he kept very quiet and still, emptying his mind of everything except the image and texture of his surroundings, people tended to overlook his presence. Kalan had never discussed this aptitude with anyone, not even Brother Belan, but he found it very useful, especially when he wanted to avoid unwelcome attention.

The footsteps drew closer and Kalan saw the first shadowy figures file past the cupboard entrance. They were clad in black, but he could make out sword hilts at their sides and the keen, flame-shaped heads of spears in their hands. They carried no lights, but could apparently see clearly in the unlit hall.

And that, Kalan knew, ruled out any possibility that they were a patrol of keep guards who had gotten into the Temple quarter by mistake.

Besides, there were too many of them, far more than in any guard patrol—upward of a hundred at least, he estimated, swallowing hard. Their silence exuded menace and their helms were crowned with horn and talons like werebeasts, quite unlike anything used by the Derai. Kalan could almost remember seeing something similar in one of Brother Selmor's books, but the exact detail eluded him. He pressed further back, holding his breath as the lead warrior halted.

The warrior's grotesque helm peered this way and that, like a hound questing for scent, and Kalan thought desperately of stone, cold and still and rough-hewn all around him. He *became* stone, forgotten in the darkness. The voice that spoke was cold, too; sibilant and metallic, rasping against the silence. "I thought I sensed something, another presence." The words sank slowly into Kalan's consciousness, filtering through the weight of stone. They were strangely accented, but he found he could understand them. "Just for a moment . . . But now there is nothing."

"This is a temple," another voice replied, dispassionate as iron. "Even at this level it will echo power. If you cannot sense anything more, an echo is all it will have been."

The first speaker did not move. "Still nothing," he said, after a long moment.

"We must go on," the iron voice said. "The others will be in place soon. We must not fail in our part." He paused. "What of our . . . ally? Do you have it safe?"

"For now," the other replied, a thread of tension in the sibilant voice. "But I do not know how long I can contain it."

The darkness thickened as he spoke, and Kalan felt a rapacious, insatiable will striving to push through. It hungered, that will, famished and thirsting; the sweep of its power was like a dark wing brushing across Kalan's mind. Desperate, he clung to the roughness of the surrounding stone. The first speaker grunted, as though lifting a weight, and the warriors stirred, their hands shifting on their weapons. The warrior with the hard voice cursed under his breath, then gestured the advance, and they moved forward as one, flowing silently up the stairs.

Kalan's whole body was shaking, cold and sick from the brush of the deadly will across his mind. Cautiously, he released his hold on the image of stone, letting out his breath with a gasp when he realized that the blood was hammering in his ears. "Darkswarm," he whispered. There could be no mistaking that dark will. For the first time in his life he wished he was a mindspeaker and could raise an instant alarm.

The intruders must have come through the Old Keep, he thought. Brother Belan had always said that there were secret doors from the abandoned fortress into the temple quarter.

"But how," Kalan whispered, "would the Swarm know that?" He shook his head, still trying to take in what was happening, to think out what he should do. "I have to get ahead of the warband somehow," he told himself sharply, "warn Sister Korriya and the others." But the only other way up was a service stair that had fallen into disrepair and the attacking warriors could already have sent another warband by that route. And who knew what other dark powers they might possess?

I don't know, Kalan thought, and clenched his fists until the nails cut into his palms. But I have to try and do something.

Carefully, he checked the hallway again and then hurried toward the service stair, keeping as close to the wall as he could and straining both eyes and ears for hidden enemies. The distance to the second stair seemed further than he remembered, and Kalan gradually picked up speed. Rounding a corner fast, he slid to an abrupt halt, staring at a large door of black metal where he had never seen anything but blank walls before. "So they did come through the Old Keep," he muttered, realizing that he had not quite believed it before.

The door had been jammed open. Kalan could see a stone landing through the gap, and a stair twisting down into darkness. He peered through, thinking that if anything it seemed sadder, colder, and more derelict than his side of the door. But even with his keen sight, the absolute blackness beyond the landing was frightening. Kalan shivered, almost glad to have a reason to turn away and start running again. Caution made him slow before he reached his destination, hugging the wall again and creeping along the last half corridor to the foot of the staircase. He craned to look, and saw a bar of light across the first landing and booted feet beneath long black cloaks.

Lookouts, Kalan thought grimly, and retreated as quietly as he had come. He frowned, trying to come up with some way of getting past unseen. But there were too many rearguards posted and the stair was too narrow, with too few places to hide if they came after him. The only option he could think of now was to try the Old Keep. The staircase he had seen twisted down, but it might lead to a landing where another stair led up—and Belan had said that there was more than one secret door. Kalan suppressed the thought that the invaders might know of those doors as well; that he might already be too late. "I can't just give up," he whispered. "I have to keep trying."

But he still hesitated when he reached the iron door, wondering what might be waiting inside that profound dark. He could not help remembering all the ghost stories told about the Old Keep—but every moment he hesitated was taking the intruders further into the unarmed temple quarter. "You wanted adventure!" Kalan told himself sternly, and stepped through the door.

The stairs wound tightly down and the blackness was intense. The silence, too, felt tangible, pressing in on Kalan as though the Old Keep itself were aware of him. The muted echo of his sandals on stone sounded frighteningly loud, and Kalan tried to step and breathe more quietly. As he descended, the darkness grew thicker, even to his catlike vision; he listened intently to compensate, his neck and shoulders tense with strain. But there was no sign of any other route leading upward again, let alone back into the New Keep. Eventually, Kalan stopped.

"This is hopeless," he muttered. He would have to go back, see if he could slip past the intruders' rearguard somehow. But Kalan remembered their bright, bitter weapons, and the way the one with the sibilant voice had quested after his presence, and was not sure how it could be done. He closed his eyes, trying to think—then opened them again as a sense of light penetrated his lids. All he could make out was the stone floor and rough block walls on either side, yet the impression of light, pale as honey, teased at the corners of his eyes.

Kalan turned his head quickly, trying to catch it out, but there was nothing there. He shook his head, but the light flickered again at the periphery of his vision and this time it persisted, enticing him further down the stairs. Kalan resisted, trying to turn back, but the light twisted and danced, beckoning him further into the dark. Fear touched his spine with a cool finger as he strained to hear something—anything at all—but only silence answered. "Nine take it!" Kalan muttered, and swung around, determined to return to the iron door.

Far above him, a voice howled. The drawn out, ululating wail made every hair on his body stand straight up. Even as he shuddered, it was answered by another eerie, mournful cry and then another, like an unearthly pack baying for the scent. The surrounding darkness was filled with urgency and fear.

"Danger!" The whisper brushed the surface of Kalan's

mind. *"Make haste!"* Light glimmered again on the downward spiral, a compelling flicker. Above him, the hunting cries rose, ululating to banshee pitch.

"Hurry!" the voice in his mind commanded. Kalan hesitated a moment longer, then turned with a curse, plunging further into the dark.

4

Call to Arms

The light in Malian's mind, which had flooded in with the voice that bade her flee, had almost gone out. It had led her through the spyruns and then down, deep into the Old Keep and well beyond the places that she knew. Now it had grown dim and the surrounding darkness was so thick that Malian felt it might swallow her.

There was humor in that, she supposed, the Heir of Night being devoured by night itself. She wondered if Yorindesarinen had felt something similar when she stood alone, abandoned by her comrades and her kin, to face the Worm of Chaos. The stories said that the Worm's vastness had blotted out the constellations, but that Yorindesarinen had blazed in answer—like a star fallen from heaven to pierce the Darkswarm murk. Malian found the thought comforting and tried to imagine herself as the hero, blazing like a comet across the darkness of her age. Immediately, the light in her mind caught fire and sprang up again, white and clear and brilliant.

A cry split the silence of the Old Keep, rising on a long, ululating note until it was almost a shriek before dying away again. Another cry followed, melding into a wild clamor of howling voices. Malian's heart leapt into her throat, then came thudding down again into her stomach. *"Flee!"* her mind commanded, but night blindness betrayed her. She had only taken a few hasty steps when her front foot came down onto nothing.

"Nine!" Malian flung out both arms to steady herself, but there was nothing to grasp and she pitched forward, tumbling head over heels to the next level. For a long moment she lay completely still, flat on her back and trying to decide whether she was still alive. When she finally decided that she was uninjured, she had to fight back a wild desire to laugh.

"Now that," said a boy's voice, "was impressive. Do you always go down stairs that way?"

Malian turned her head carefully and decided that the patch of deeper blackness crouched a precautionary spear's length away, could—just possibly—be a person. "Not usually," she said. She sat up, tentatively, and confirmed that yes, her body did seem to be intact. "It's just that I can't see a cursed thing in this darkness."

"Can't you?" the boy asked. He paused, then continued slowly: "Because the light burning in you could illuminate the entire keep."

Malian wondered if the fall had done more damage than she realized, or whether the boy she was talking to was hallucinating. She hesitated and the hunting cries rose again, far away still, but coming closer.

"I think they can sense it, too." The boy spoke again, and she felt rather than saw the jerk of his head toward the cries. "The light. I think that's how they're tracking you."

Malian shivered, peering at him through the darkness. "Who *are* you?" she asked. "What are you doing down here?"

"I'm Kalan," the boy replied. "But we don't have time for that now. We have to run!" He paused again. "Are you sure that you can't see anything at all?"

"Not a thing!" said Malian. "I can't even see you. Not really. Unfortunately, I am no Kerem to see in the dark!"

"Kerem?" Kalan echoed, an odd note in his voice. He cleared his throat. "Well, I can. See, that is, so I'd better lead you." She sensed his sudden doubt as the clamor rose again behind them, louder now. "I don't suppose you've any idea which way to go?"

Malian stood up, steadying herself against the rough stone of the wall, and forced herself to think coolly. "I don't know these regions at all," she said. "Certainly not well enough to play hide-and-seek in the dark. But it's too risky to double back, or to try and dodge them on this level. We'd better keep going down or find somewhere to go to ground."

"Down, then," Kalan agreed. His hand reached out and closed over hers, reassuringly warm and real, but his voice was rough with anxiety. "You're going to have to do something about that light, though." The dark outline of his head turned toward the wailing cries. "They aren't even hesitating," he whispered. "They know exactly where you are. If you don't do something now, we're lost."

Malian concentrated, responding to the raw certainty in his voice. She thought about the path of light she had followed, and how it had faded when she grew weary and flared up when she thought of Yorindesarinen—just as it ignited again now at the memory. Beside her, Kalan flinched and Malian quenched the thought hastily, transforming the image of blazing fire into a candle flame cupped between her two palms. Carefully, she visualized the hands closing together, so that not even a chink of light escaped.

"Nine!" Kalan's relief was palpable. "That's so much better! We might even have a chance, so long as we get going." He started down the next curving flight of stairs, murmuring cautions to guide her, but still descending far more rapidly than Malian could have managed on her own. There was frustration in the ululating cries behind them now, like a pack that circles after a lost scent.

The stairs leveled and Malian hesitated, sensing the size of the space around them, but something tugged at her awareness, a tiny flicker of light that was not her own. It hovered like a will-o'-the-wisp at the corner of her eye, pulling her attention back to the staircase they had just descended.

"I wonder," she whispered, thinking of the spyruns that riddled the New Keep—and perhaps the Old, too, since Night had built them both.

The will-o'-the-wisp danced, an imperative flicker. "Over there!" Malian whispered to Kalan and pointed. "Can you see what's there?" She didn't want to ask outright whether the light was visible to him as well.

"I see something," Kalan muttered, peering toward the wisp. "There's a recess under the staircase. But we don't have time to explore it. We've got to stay ahead of the hunt."

"Or find somewhere to hide," she whispered back. "This reminds me of places in the New Keep, where the entrances to secret ways and bolt-holes are concealed." She glanced over her shoulder. "We should have time if we hurry."

Kalan hesitated, then led her closer to the recess, a darkness beneath the curved base of the staircase. "You're right," he said, after a moment. "There is an opening here. It's very narrow," he added, turning his body sideways and edging forward. "But—we should—just—be able to—squeeze through." Malian crawled through after him and began to search the interior walls, her fingertips seeking for concealed triggers like those in the New Keep.

"Whatever you're looking for," Kalan whispered, "you'd better find it soon. They're coming!"

Malian's hands trembled in nervous haste, then she sighed as the first stone shifted and a whole section of wall slid aside. She slipped through the gap and Kalan followed, helping her ease the secret door back into place.

"They're here!" he muttered. Malian could sense it, too, like a stifling closeness in the air. But if this was like the New Keep, there should be a spyhole . . . After a moment her fingers found it and she peered through, catching the first uneven leap of torchlight across floor and walls. Jagged shadows loomed and Malian held her breath as the first of the hunters padded into view.

One by one, four more hunters crept down the stairs to join the first, their heads moving constantly as they turned and quested, checking everywhere for the prey. Their headgear was horned, bestial. Masks? Malian wondered, staring intently, then swallowed hard as she realized that the grotesque beast shapes were neither masks nor helms. Were-hunters, she thought, her eyes dropping to the raking claws that served them instead of hands. She and this boy, this Kalan, could never have outrun these pursuers; they had found their hiding place just in time. Even so, they were still far from safe, for she knew that were-hunters used Darkswarm sorcery to enhance the sharpness of their beast senses.

Silently, Malian motioned Kalan to look and felt the sudden, rigid tension in his body the moment he set his eye to the spyhole. He reached out an arm and drew her close, placing his hand over her mouth as though to prevent even a whisper. For a moment she resisted—and then felt a wall close around the remaining spark of fire in her mind. It was like being encased by stone: cold, rough-hewn, and dry with the undisturbed dust of centuries. She could almost see it closing over the narrow opening beneath the stairs as well, impenetrable to searching eyes. The flaring nostrils and bestial heads swung from side to side, baffled by the silence and sense of nothing-there-at-all in a place where they had expected prey.

Gently, Malian eased away from the boy and he lifted his hand from her mouth, moving to let her look through the spyhole again. A light flickered on the far side of the landing now, a tantalizing firefly spark, and the bestial heads turned toward it as one.

It's drawing them off, Malian thought, just as it showed me this hideaway. She could sense the were-hunters' wariness and doubt, almost tangible in the air, but they followed the will-o'-the-wisp anyway, padding out of sight. There were no more hunting cries, but both she and Kalan remained very still for some time, watching and listening. "I think they're gone," Malian murmured at last, daring a whisper.

Kalan shifted. "For now," he said. "But with were-hunters you never really know."

Malian shivered. "You did something, didn't you?" she said. "I could feel you blocking them with your wall of stone, turning their eyes and minds away."

I would never have escaped them without you, she added silently.

He shifted again, as if uncomfortable, and was close enough that she could feel his focus, intent on her. "So what is your name?" he asked. But she could imagine the unspoken questions, too: The *"Who are you?"*; and *"Why are they hunting you?"*

Malian frowned, and for a moment considered not telling him, but then she shrugged. "It's Malian," she said.

"Malian," he repeated, but not as though the name held any significance for him. Malian suppressed a wry grin, mocking herself.

"We should go," Kalan continued, sounding worried. "Before they come back."

Malian nodded and let him lead her away from the spyhole and the secret door, deeper into the maze that ran through the walls of the Old Keep. After a time, she whispered that they should keep bearing to the left, that doing so should bring them to a concealed safehold. "If," she added, "this place works the same as in the New Keep."

"How—" Kalan began, then broke off, apparently thinking better of whatever question he had been going to ask.

They went on in silence, following the secret way for what seemed like a very long time. In one part, the roof curved in so low that they had to crawl on hands and knees. Eventually, the passage opened up again and they were able to stand upright, only to find their way blocked by a steel door. "Is this your safehold?" Kalan asked, keeping his voice low, but Malian shook her head.

"All the doors into the safeholds are wooden," she murmured. "I've never encountered anything like this before."

Kalan put his ear to the door and appeared to be listening. Finally, he eased it open, just wide enough to peer through—then stopped. "The room's not large," he whispered after a moment; he must have remembered that she couldn't see. "But it has twelve sides and twelve doors, one in the center of every wall. The walls look rounded, as though they're curving into the roof." Kalan took a step forward, into the room, drawing Malian after him. "And the roof's arched."

"It's very quiet," Malian whispered back.

"But peaceful. Not threatening at all. Not like the silence in so much of this place." Kalan took another step forward. "I don't think these walls are made of stone either. The surface looks very smooth."

"This bit feels like glass." Malian snatched her hand back as light flared beneath her touch. The initial spark brightened to a soft glow and she blinked at Kalan in astonishment. Then she looked again, absorbing the detail of a square face beneath rough tawny hair, gold-flecked gray eyes, and the spattering of freckles across a straight nose. He was stockily built and slightly taller than herself, and the mouth below the freckles was wide—with a quirk, Malian thought, that might mean humor. She noted the gray-blue robes of a temple novice, robes that were patched and far too short at wrist and ankle. Her eyebrows went up when she realized that he was surveying her every bit as critically as she was studying him: A second later, as though reaching some unspoken consensus of approval, they looked into each other's tired, grime-smudged faces and smiled.

"I like the light," Kalan said, "even though I don't need it to see by." He reached up and touched the glass panel, but the light didn't change. "How did you do that?"

Malian ran her hand over the glass and the light faded until they stood in darkness once more. When she touched it again, the light returned. She shook her head. "I don't know." She looked around at the white, gleaming walls and saw more glass panels spaced at even intervals. "What a strange place this is. It feels as though we've been drawn here, but to what end?" She slanted a look at Kalan. "And what brought you down here, out of the Temple quarter?"

His eyes held hers, his expression curious, assessing. "I thought you'd know, since those were-hunters seemed to be after you. They're not the first Swarm minions I've seen today: The keep's been invaded." Quickly and quietly, he told her about seeing the company of black-clad warriors pass, bringing some sort of Darkswarm demon with them. "I was trying to warn the temple," he said at last, "to get around the invaders somehow. But I just got drawn deeper and deeper into the Old Keep, until I met you."

Malian felt sick, almost dizzy. "So it's not just an assassination attempt," she whispered. "This is a major attack. Even now, our people may be dying in their sleep!" Her hands shook and she curled them into fists. "We must find a way to warn them, to save them!"

"What can we do, just the two of us?" She saw her despair reflected in Kalan's face. "We're not armed and there are were-hunters after us. Or after you," he amended, with that same measuring look.

Malian ignored his unspoken question and began to pace. "I was asleep," she said, half to herself, half to him, "and when I woke it was to a voice in my mind, telling me to flee. The warning was so compelling that I didn't wait to ask questions; I just did as it said. I ran." Her fingers opened, then closed again. "Unlike you, I didn't even think about warning anyone else."

Kalan was frowning. "It's probably just as well since the were-hunt was after you. Brother Selmor's books are full of warnings like that." A thread of excitement crept into his voice. "All from the old days, of course, when we were strong in the powers and the Golden Fire burned in every keep. Some stories claim that the warnings came from the gods, some say from the Fire. But they almost always came to the Blood alone, usually when they were in very great danger." He nodded, as though a puzzle had clicked into place. "I knew your name seemed familiar, although mostly people just say 'the Heir' or 'the Heir of Night.' But it certainly explains why they're hunting you."

"I suppose it does. But otherwise—" Malian shrugged. "I don't think it matters that much who I am, not right now."

Kalan rolled his eyes. "Of course it matters! You're the Heir of the House of Night, by all the Nine Gods! There *are* no other children of your Blood—you're the only heir that Night has. You of all people have to know how important that makes you."

Malian sighed. " *'If Night falls, all fall.'* They say that prophecy is as old as the Derai Alliance itself, but that its true meaning has been lost over time."

Kalan's lip curled. "Brother Belan always said that the prophecy means exactly what it says; that belief in it is the only thing that's been lost. But you do see," he added, stumbling a little over the words, "that it's my duty to help you, and to try and protect you and all that other stuff, now that I know who you are?"

Malian grinned. "You've already helped me," she pointed out, "and not because you knew I was the Heir of Night." The grin faded. "Can you understand how I feel, though, knowing that I fled when it was my duty as Heir to warn and protect my House?"

"I can," Kalan said slowly, "except that you were told to flee. And in the old stories, it's always disastrous to ignore warnings like that—to set your own will against that of the gods, as it were. No good ever comes of it."

"Wise boy." The whisper seared the quiet air with light and heat and both Malian and Kalan jumped, staring around the twelve-walled room.

"Who are you?" Malian demanded. "What do you want?"

"You, Heir of Night." The will-o'-the-wisp danced at the edge of her vision.

"Well, I'm here," she said, as boldly as she dared. "Now— who *are* you?"

"Do you not know me?" asked the voice, a rumble of muted thunder. *"I and my fellows are in all the histories of the Derai, your long allies and your friends in the age old war against the Swarm of Dark."*

Malian pushed a hand through her hair. "Then I do know you," she said, and heard the wonder in her voice, "although you have been gone a long time. Most believe that you died, along with so many others, on the Night of Death."

"Died?" mused the voice. It was warmth, light, heat, all shimmering together. *"No, we did not die, but we came very close when Xeriatherien broke the first law and called down our fire against the Derai. That dealt us a soul wound, striking at our very essence, and we fled from it and the horror of her deed. And then the Blood, who should have been most diligent in seeking us out and aiding our recovery, abandoned us instead. The Old Keep and I have become ghosts together, neglected and forgotten by all but a very few. You, child, were one of that handful, creeping through to play your games and breathe a little life back into the old halls. You were not aware of me, but I learned your voice and your heart, which is why I could reach out to you and warn you of your peril. I cannot rouse anyone else. I have tried, but though some few may have stirred in their sleep, none have woken. The House of Night, it seems, has grown both deaf and blind!"* The voice paused, as though recollecting itself. *"But you, child—it may be that you can reach them, for you know the New Keep as I do not, and they know you. You may even be in time to save many, for the enemy have delayed and dispersed in hunting you. Much of the keep still sleeps on, unaware of the attack."*

Malian stood straighter. "Tell me what I must do," she said.

"First you must come into the heart of my power," the voice replied, *"so I have some hope of protecting you, while you may draw on my strength. It is imperative that we work together, for you are young and untrained and I am weaker than I used to be. But together, and with the boy's help, we may do what needs to be done."*

Kalan was frowning. "Rouse the keep?" he asked. "Is that all you mean to do? Or is there something more?"

Fire crackled through the air, like the dry summer lightning that scoured the heights of the Wall. *"There is,"* said the voice of fire. *"The Child of Night must mindspeak the New Keep, rousing the alarms that the invaders have silenced. The alarms are tuned to the Blood of Night, so she can override the Darkswarm binding. You must help by anchoring her to this physical place and adding your strength to hers. But as soon as she touches the alarms, the enemy will become aware of her presence and then she will be in deadly danger. For they have brought an ally with them, a Raptor of Darkness, and even now it hunts in the New Keep."*

Malian looked at Kalan. "A Raptor of Darkness?" she asked, and saw him shudder.

"It must be the darkspawn I sensed when they passed by me in the Temple quarter," he replied, low voiced. "It was terrible, like an all-devouring darkness brushing against my mind."

"You did more than well," said the fiery voice, *"if you felt its presence but it did not sense yours. It is an eater of souls and hungers most for those who are power wielders, which is why they loosed it in the Temple quarter. There is no one there now, alas, who is a match for it. But the Darkswarm minions have overreached themselves, for to get the Raptor through they had to bring down the psychic barrier that Night erected between the Old Keep and the New, in order to wall out the ghosts of their dead. Those same walls have kept me out as well—but now the wards are down."*

"Does this mean that you can fight the demon and defeat it?" Kalan asked, the eagerness clear in his voice.

"It means I will try, but I, too, am not what I was. And since I cannot be sure of success I will need an edge, something to distract the Raptor's attention so I can take it by surprise."

Malian swallowed. "You plan to use me as bait," she said.

"No!" exclaimed Kalan. "You cannot risk the Heir of Night!"

The room was silent, and after a moment Malian nodded, understanding that it was to be her decision. "The enemy is loose in the New Keep," she said quietly, "and once this

Raptor of Darkness is finished in the Temple quarter, it will hunt us out anyway. We have to do this, Kalan, take the risk." But inwardly, she mocked her brave words, wishing that she did not feel so afraid.

Kalan looked bleak. "It's '*Yorindesarinen's Choice*'," he said somberly, "from the saga."

Malian shook her head, thinking that Yorindesarinen's choice had been far more bitter, her hour more desperate. She drew a deep breath and spoke to the quiet room: "Tell us how to come inside your power."

"Close your eyes and empty your minds and hearts, then open them again to me."

Malian exchanged an uncertain look with Kalan, then closed her eyes, striving to let all thought and emotion drain away and fix her mind on emptiness. Gradually, she was filled with an immense golden light that intensified until she flinched away from its brilliance. The muted thunder rumbled in her head. *"Fear not, I will not burn you. Now open your eyes."*

Malian obeyed and saw her own awe and wonder mirrored in Kalan's face. The room's twelve walls remained, but now the roof was far overhead and points of fire glimmered in the arched dome.

Like stars, Malian thought, staring up—or meteors burning through space.

The twelve doorways, too, had grown tall, stretching toward the distant roof. Each frame was outlined in golden flame and the solid wooden doors had been replaced by shimmering mist. *"You may not look through them yet,"* the fiery voice said. *"For now, turn your eyes to the table."*

Malian blinked at the circular table that had appeared in the center of the room. Its circumference was vast and supported on what looked like a massive tree trunk, rooted into the stone floor. She moved closer and saw that the table was divided into twelve equal parts, each one separated by fiery lines. The surface was cloudy, filled with moving shapes that she could not make out.

"No child of the Blood of Night has stood at this table in over five hundred years," the Fire said. *"But if you look closely, you will see your place."*

Malian looked again and saw that one of the twelve sections was growing clearer. As she watched, it became a field of gold with a glittering horse flying across it, its wings cleaving heaven.

"Touch it with your hand and mind at the same time, and join with me," the Fire commanded. *"As you do so, let the boy take your other hand. He will anchor you here, for that is part of his gift. But be careful, boy, not to touch the table yourself, for only the Blood may do so and live."*

"I was born to the House of Blood," Kalan said, but he sounded uncertain.

"It is not the same, alas," the Fire replied. *"Your House has named itself for the blood of battle and war, at which it excels, whereas I speak of* the *Blood, the kin bound to us since the beginning of the Derai Alliance. Now, Heir of Night, are you ready?"*

"I am," said Malian and placed her right palm on the table. The surface was cool as flowing water, and she could feel the contrasting warmth of Kalan's right hand, clasping her left. Her whole being was infused with light; she felt intensely and gloriously alive with it and could sense the Old Keep, with all its silent levels, rising above her. She shot up through them like an arrow burning through darkness, past the enormity of empty rooms and vast echoing corridors. The chill of long neglect numbed her but she forced herself on, coming at last to the tiled halls and wooden galleries of the upper levels. From there, it was only a very short journey into the New Keep with its lights and warmth and life, a life that was muted now in sleep.

Too much sleep. Malian could feel the silence of death and smell congealing blood. She was aware, too, of the dark malice of her enemies, regrouping now from the hunt and preparing to attack again.

The Fire in her mind drew her attention to the bronze gargoyles that leered down from every major door and gateway in the New Keep, forgotten through the long years and unseen by those who passed by every day. Now their leers had grown tortured, contorted beyond the grotesque into silent screams. Malian let her awareness settle on a verdigris-rimed gargoyle that crouched above the main entrance into the High Hall.

"'Ware," she whispered to it. "'Ware foes, 'ware terror, 'ware treachery by night!" She felt it shudder, heard the faint shiver of sound that ran through it, but nothing more happened.

"You must try harder, Child." Malian felt the urgency of the Fire in her mind, and also its fear, matching her own. *"They are slaying your clan and your kin. Do not whisper the alarm—thunder it through the keep! It is in your hands, and yours alone, Heir of Night!"* The Fire's power burned along her veins, searing every nerve ending and flaring from her mind into the gargoyle, wreathing it in golden flame. Far down in the Old Keep, Kalan threw up his free arm to protect his eyes from the light that snapped out of her.

"Awake!" Malian cried at the top of her voice. "'Ware foes! 'Ware blood! 'Ware ruin in the night! Awake, Earl of Night! To arms, Keep of Winds!"

All through the New Keep the gargoyles sprang fiercely into life, yammering out her call to arms in a wild clangor that went on and on and did not stop. Malian heard the shouting and clatter of weaponry, the war cries and the rush of running feet as she swept through the darkness like a flame.

"Awake, Nhairin!" she commanded. "To arms, Asantir! Treachery and blood! Awake, Earl of Night!" she cried again, and felt the flash of her father's mind, like a blade being drawn to cross hers before she sprang away. She heard the sudden outcry, and the clash of steel on steel, and knew that the intruders had been discovered at last.

"'Ware foes!" Malian shook the keep with one last call. She felt weary now, ready to return through the Old Keep to its heart, her place of safety.

Something caught at her mind and held on; a suffocating darkness coiled itself around her. Malian felt a terrible hunger that sought to drain her soul and her power with it, down to the marrow—and realized that she had forgotten the Raptor of Darkness, was not even thinking of it as she turned away. It would have leached her to a husk in an instant if she had not been filled with raging wildfire and linked to Kalan in the heart of the Old Keep. Even so, she felt the protective link waver as darkness dragged at her soul, inexorable as an ebb tide.

Malian screamed and fought back, struggling to sear the engulfing darkness with fire while holding on to the link to Kalan. She heard Kalan scream, too, pouring his strength into hers and pushing back against that terrible, draining force. For a moment their resistance held, but Malian could feel the Raptor's satisfaction and its greed beating in on her, and knew, in a blinding flash of terror, that it was far, far stronger than she was. Struggle though she would, she could not break free, and already her strength was fading. Kalan was cursing; she could hear him far down in her mind, while the darkness crept in and her last defences crumbled.

Is this how Yorindesarinen felt at the end, Malian wondered, with the Worm's venom in her veins and her lifeblood draining away?

The thought of the hero rallied her, like a star blazing in darkness, and she clung to it like a spar. She felt her attacker pause, its malice and hunger hesitating for a single instant, and a new voice, calm and yet compelling, spoke in her head: *"Hold on. Help is coming!"*

Fire snapped back into her mind, flinging the darkness back. There was someone standing in the heart of the fire, Malian thought dizzily, as the image of a man scored itself into her brain; he seemed made of flame and lightning coruscated around him. Someone else stood in his shadow, as deep and cool as he was bright, but Malian was dazzled by the flames and could not see either figure clearly. The Fire roared, assaulting the Raptor's power, and its voice rang out like a thunderclap: *"Begone, Raptor of Darkness!"*

There was more than one voice bound into that thunder, weaving in and out of each other and the Fire. Malian reached out to them through the conflagration and felt a touch on her mind that was gentle, luminous, and clear, like light dancing on water. Through or beyond it she sensed a hotter, deeper blaze, and then another touch that was cold, gray steel. There were other minds there, too, paler and dimmer again, but all were bound up into the Golden Fire, joined in battle against the Raptor of Darkness.

Malian exerted herself for one last effort, joining her strength to theirs and pushing back hard against the Raptor's mass. It was still frighteningly strong and she could feel it hunting for weaknesses to exploit, but the Fire, too, was relentless. Slowly but inexorably, the Raptor was driven back. Gouts of golden flame burned into its darkness until it was in full retreat, dwindling before the onslaught and hunting for escape.

Done, thought Malian—and faltered, falling away from the firestorm. Out of control, she plummeted headlong, down through the Old Keep toward her crumpled body and the pinprick of light that she recognized as her own dwindling consciousness.

Collapsing in on myself, she thought with mild hilarity. She knew that she was falling much too fast and should feel frightened, and part of her did, but mostly she was too exhausted to care. Her body and the tiled floor were rushing up to meet her and she could hear Kalan cursing again.

The light—which Malian had thought entirely gone out—sparked, and she felt the touch of another mind, the one that was cool and deep as water, joining with hers. It held her up and slowed her headlong descent so that she was floating rather than falling, sinking gently back into her body. "Who?" Malian asked in bewilderment, but even that last touch was gone. Kalan's frightened, tear-tracked face blurred above hers for one brief moment, then all light flickered and went out.

5

The Broken Gate

Nhairin limped toward the frontline of the battle that had raged throughout the night, rubbing at the tight scar on her face and cursing the bad leg that had prevented her from playing any real part in the fighting. A troop of the keep garrison doubled past without speaking. For all the attention they paid, she might as well have been invisible.

Useless! Nhairin derided herself, but pressed stubbornly on, her thoughts circling back to what could have gone so hideously, disastrously wrong. She had stumbled from her bed when the alarms rang out, echoing the imperative cry that had snapped like a lightning crack into her head: *"Awake! 'Ware foes! 'Ware blood! 'Ware ruin in the night!"* Like half the keep, it had sent her grabbing for clothes and weapons even as she struggled to throw off sleep. She remembered cursing everything: the darkness, the confusion, and especially the lameness that had meant that she could not keep up with the running melees being fought along corridors, up stairwells, and through room after room. She had, Nhairin reflected bitterly, simply been in the way.

It was Asantir who had finally yelled at her to get back. The captain had come charging past with half the Honor Guard behind her, torchlight leaping wildly across her inlaid helm and along the naked blade of her sword. She had cursed Nhairin for a fool, demanding whether she wanted to get herself killed, before sweeping on and up the central stairs with the guard baying at her heels. They had met a wedge of the black-clad intruders on the first landing—and the rest had been a reeling, thrusting, cut, and slash of bloody ruin. Nhairin, accepting at last that she would be more hindrance than help, had gotten back as ordered.

She had done what she could to rally those behind the fighting lines, forming the stewards and any others who were willing into squads. Those with weapons and some ability to use them she sent forward to support the guards while she, together with the rest, organized medicine, bandages, and a place to tend the wounded. They had been more than busy as the long hours dragged by and the High Hall became a nightmare of blood and gaping wounds, voices that cried ceaselessly for aid, and the groans of the dying. And there had been too many for whom nothing could be done, except to send their cloak-covered bodies on to the Hall of Silence.

It was dawn, a gray creeping dawn, before Nhairin had time to take stock of the battle's bloody aftermath. Now she picked her careful way along a corridor strewn with splintered wood and broken doors that marked where Asantir and the Honor Guard had hacked and fought their way forward. Debris and bodies were piled on either side, and Nhairin's heart sank as she realized that the wreckage was growing worse as she approached the Heir's quarter. The floor was sticky with blood and there were far too many of their own amongst the black-clad bodies of the intruders. The faces of the guards standing watch over the Heir's rooms were drawn in the pale light; they turned their faces away as she limped up, avoiding her gaze.

It should have warned her. It did warn her. Even so, Nhairin staggered, her stomach heaving, when she saw the carnage in the Heir's chambers: Doria and Nesta with their throats torn out, the dismembered bodies of the pages, the blood sprayed across every wall and soaked blackly into furnishings. She could see how those of the household who had not died immediately must have stumbled and crawled to dodge blows, although it had not saved them. Nhairin rested one hand against the wall for support, closing her eyes against the horror. Blood roared in her ears like the ocean, but finally she found the strength to grate out the one, vital question: "Where is the Heir?"

The guards exchanged a look, their expressions bleak. "Not here," one told her, anger and the echo of her own horror in his voice. "Nine knows, we've searched, but there's no body with the dead and no word of her amongst the living."

"But given the night's events," the other added, "we fear the worst."

Appalled, Nhairin sought out Asantir, finding her amidst the wreckage of the invaders' last stand. The Honor Captain was surrounded by a tattered remnant of her guard and what seemed like a small army of the main keep garrison. One guard was binding up a bloody wound to the captain's shoulder while a sergeant pored over plans spread out on the floor. Asantir leaned over his shoulder and nodded as his finger stabbed from one corridor to the next. The grim and weary troops surrounding them were either watching, too, or occupied with their own hurts and battered gear.

Nhairin hesitated as Asantir turned away from the plans to deal with fresh dispatches coming in. Sarus had secured the Temple quarter, one runner reported, but it was very bad there, as badly hit as the Heir's quarter, or worse. The attackers had been determined and merciless, despite nearly all those they killed having been unarmed. Worse, though— and here the whites of the runner's eyes showed—there had been some kind of demon loose. Mind and soul, it had sucked its victims dry.

A low, disturbed murmur ran through the surrounding guards, but Asantir held up her free hand, checking them. "The point," she said calmly, "is that it has been driven off. Does Sarus need more troops?"

The runner shook his head. "He said it was not essential, Captain, although more would be welcome if you could spare them."

Asantir nodded, turning to one of the guards beside her. "Kyr, take another twenty and reinforce Sarus. Tell him I'll be along myself as soon as I'm done here."

She turned immediately to the next runner, who gasped out that he came from Lannorth, who was with the Earl. Asantir's brow cleared a little. "How goes it there?"

"Lannorth reports that the fighting has been fierce," the runner replied, "but they've driven the invaders back and the Earl is safe."

"And the Heir?" Nhairin put in sharply. "What news of Malian?"

Asantir looked around. "None," she said wearily. "We're looking, but we have to secure each area as we go through and it all takes time."

Nhairin limped over to her. "What of the Old Keep?" she asked.

Asantir's mouth set in a grim, hard line. "That," she said, "is where the enemy came through—and it's the bolt-hole they've retreated into as well. We can't pursue them in there, not until we have the New Keep secure. And that's not yet done."

Nhairin frowned, biting her lip. "What of Gerenth?" she asked. "Perhaps he could free up more troops from the main garrison?" Her voice faltered as she saw Asantir's expression. "Dead?" she whispered.

Asantir nodded. "The invaders rigged an ambush and Gerenth's troop bore the brunt. I've taken command of the keep in his stead, but there are no troops to be spared, Nhairin."

"But what if Malian's been captured?" Nhairin protested. "Even now these invaders may be bearing her away, or worse."

The Honor Captain shook her head. "It's possible, but so far not many intruders have actually lived to escape. Most fought on like cornered rats, rather than fleeing. Even at the last they were still trying to cut their way forward into the New Keep, as though hunting for someone or something more vital than their own lives. Such behavior," she pointed out, "doesn't fit with an enemy who has a hostage like the Heir of Night to bargain with. And they took no other prisoners, quite the opposite in fact."

Given these circumstances, Nhairin conceded silently, it was unlikely Malian *had* been captured—although her whereabouts remained as great a mystery as the identity of whoever had sounded the keep's alarms. Ornorith, the goddess of Luck, had shown both of her two faces to the Derai that night: Many had died in the unexpected attack, but warning had been given before it was too late.

It did not pay, thought Nhairin, to underestimate the enigmatic, two-faced deity. And was the vanished Heir further evidence of Ornorith's influence, or had some other power come into play?

The steward shivered. Too many unanswered questions, she said to herself. But it's unthinkable that the Heir of Night should simply disappear. She must be found, and quickly. *Quickly*, before it's too late!

She must have spoken the last words aloud, because Asantir nodded. "I agree. But we must secure the New Keep before we venture into the Old. We are doing our best, Nhairin."

"I know you are." Nhairin looked around as another guard troop tramped in. "What can I do now to help you here?"

"Here? Nothing," said Asantir. "But if you could accompany Kyr to the Temple quarter, see what aid they need there and do something to organize it, I would be grateful."

It was not far to the Temple quarter, but the way was strewn with battle debris and Kyr and his fellow guards moved cautiously, checking every side corridor, alcove, and stairwell. When they did finally arrive, Nhairin was dismayed to see that the great iron gates, which had been sealed shut for five hundred years, were wrenched nearly off their hinges and slewed sideways at a drunken angle. Beyond them, she could see a wreckage of timber, stone, and bodies spread out across the concourse into the first of the nine temples.

Nhairin steadied herself against the still intact stone of the gatehouse, reluctant to proceed any further. She could hear activity at a distance, voices and shouted orders and the sounds of debris being cleared, but here all was silent. There was an eerie quality to the air—as though, Nhairin thought, remembering the runner's story, all the life had been sucked out of it. A shudder crawled across her skin, but she supposed that she had better follow Kyr's troop in. She straightened, gathering herself together, and realized that someone was watching her.

The watcher, swathed in a gray, hooded cloak, was concealed in the shadow of the gatehouse opposite, on its temple side. The cloak blended with the surrounding walls and the watcher stood so still that for a moment Nhairin thought the silent figure *was* stone. Her skin prickled, sensing a keen scrutiny from within the shadowing hood. "Who are you?" she demanded. "What are you doing here?"

"I might ask you the same questions," the watcher replied, in a woman's voice. "Except that I know the answers to both, Steward Nhairin." As she spoke, the watcher lifted the hood back, revealing a face of indeterminate age. Deep lines tracked the corners of eyes and mouth, and like every face that morning, the watcher's was etched with exhaustion.

Nhairin's brows rose. "Korriya," she said, then cleared her throat. "But that still doesn't answer my second question. What are you doing here?"

"In the Temple gate, do you mean, or what is left of it?" asked the priestess Korriya. Her voice was low pitched and slightly husky. "Officially, watching to ensure no stragglers slip through this way. Unofficially, I am waiting for someone like you, who is close to Tasarion."

"Why?" Nhairin asked bluntly.

The priestess gathered her cloak and picked her way

across the debris until she stood barely an arm's length from the steward. She did not, however, cross the line of the broken gates, nor did Nhairin step closer to her. "I need to speak with him, Nhairin," she said. "Urgently."

Nhairin shrugged. "The keep has been invaded and the Heir is missing. He will say that he has no time for Temple quarter nonsense."

Korriya's eyes searched Nhairin's. "Is that what you say as well?"

"I only tell you what he will say." Nhairin fingered the scar on her face. "It might help, I suppose, if he knew *why* you want to see him?"

Korriya shook her head. "This is for his ears only. You could," she added, her tone as devoid of expression as her face, "try telling him that the Temple quarter received special attention in this attack and has paid a bitter price for that distinction."

"And so he owes it to his honor, as Earl, to hear you?" said Nhairin. "I don't think that will help. There are too many others who have suffered, too many matters demanding his attention right now, not least his missing heir."

"I see." Korriya cast her eyes down, her lips compressing, and then she drew herself up so that she stood straight as a spear. Her gray eyes were stern, her voice sterner when she spoke. "Then tell the Earl of Night that I do not ask. Tell him that I name him First Kinsman and call on the Right of Blood to speak with him *now*. He may speak with me here or I will come to him, if he grants permission for me to pass the gate."

Nhairin took a step back and almost lost her balance on the rubble. Her breath hissed out. "Is this wise?" she asked, recovering.

"It is necessary." The priestess was unyielding. "I am not asking, Nhairin. By the Blood, I bid you go!" She did not wait for a reply but put up her hood and turned, stalking back into the concealing shadows. Nhairin cursed under her breath, but she too swung away.

It took her some time, after a terse conversation with Asantir, to find the Earl, and then she dared not disturb him. He was in the Hall of Silence, walking the long lines of their dead, his black armor hacked and dented and the pressure line from his helmet still livid across his forehead. His expression, as he walked the silent rows, was forbidding. Lannorth, the lieutenant of the Honor Guard, paced a careful distance behind him. Otherwise even Teron, the senior squire, hung back by the door, clutching the Earl's visored helm and black shield.

Nhairin surveyed those present with a fleeting but comprehensive look from beneath lowered lids. Jiron, the Earl's scribe, stood beside Teron, but both Haimyr and the Winter woman were absent. Nhairin shrugged inwardly. One could expect no better of outsiders: They were not Derai, after all. She moved to stand at Jiron's shoulder and he turned his head with a quick, unhappy smile.

"Not good?" she murmured, and he shook his head.

"Very bad," he replied, equally softly. "We have won the battle it seems, but at a bitter cost—and he knows now that the Heir is missing. There's to be a council of war as soon as he's paid his respects here."

"Unfortunately, it's going to get worse," Nhairin muttered. Jiron looked reproving, and Teron scowled. She shrugged and folded her arms, wondering how to deliver what she knew would be a far from welcome message. Another thought intruded and she leaned closer to Jiron's ear. "Where is the Winter woman? Surely she's not been . . . ?"

Jiron shook his head. "No. She was with the Earl throughout the fighting and did considerable damage with her bow and her beasts." He shuddered, dropping his voice lower still. "Apparently there was a were-hunt with the attackers and her beasts took them on. Four hounds were slain and a wildcat badly wounded. She tends to it now but will join us for the council."

Nhairin frowned sharply at Jiron's mention of a were-hunt, but the Earl had turned and was striding toward them before she could ask more. She shot one quick look at his face and decided that her unwelcome message could wait; there was nothing worse than being the bearer of unwanted news. She limped in the Earl's wake instead, trying to catch his conversation with Lannorth.

"I want Asantir here. Now! With Gerenth gone, we must have the Honor Captain at council."

"I'm not sure—" Lannorth began, but the Earl cut him off.

"Find her, Lieutenant. And get her here. That's all."

Nhairin caught Lannorth's eye as he summoned a runner. "She's in the halls above the Heir's wing, or gone on to the Temple quarter. They were hit hard there," she added, watching for the Earl's reaction, but his expression did not change although he lengthened his stride. Nhairin cursed silently, struggling to keep up.

The Earl's private council chamber, like the larger and more formal Great Chamber that had once hosted conclaves of the nine Houses, adjoined the High Hall. The Great Chamber glittered with inlaid metal and precious gems, and gleamed with rare woods. The Little Chamber was plain by comparison, with a long table scarred by centuries of use and chairs that were worn and comfortable. It was also one of the few places in the keep with glazing, long skylights that looked directly onto the iron skies of the Wall. They were veined with metal and protected from the Wall's blasting winds—and whatever rode them—by elaborate steel grilles, but still let in more natural light than was usual in the keep. Now a pallid daylight illuminated the faces of the Earl and his companions, showing up lines that had been graven overnight and the shadows left by too much horror and death.

The table was strewn with plans of both the New Keep and the Old and the Earl leaned both fists on the tabletop, studying them with a deep frown between his brows. There was a fire on the hearth and food set out on a side table, but nobody ate. Instead they gathered round the table, their frowns matching the Earl's. Nhairin was the only one who went to warm herself by the fire, studying the room as guards came and went and the councilors gathered.

The chamberlain looked like he had not slept in a month, and the Master of Night's messenger corps was staring woodenly at the tabletop. Khorion, the Lieutenant of the Gate, simply looked bleak. It must be hard, Nhairin supposed, when one expected to bear the brunt of any attack, to be tied to the main gate while a major battle was being fought inside the keep itself. She shrugged, turning away from the faces around the table and holding out her hands to the flames, which danced rose and orange in the grate.

"They are beautiful, are they not?" The voice that spoke was low, but very clear, and Nhairin looked around into Rowan Birchmoon's face. The Winter woman's expression was calm as a winter's morning, but Nhairin noticed that she still carried her bow over one shoulder. A hound stood in her shadow, gazing at Nhairin with dark, warning eyes.

Nhairin shrugged again, a little sourly, because she had not noticed either the woman or the hound come in. "Very beautiful," she said mechanically, although inwardly she did not think it mattered whether the flames were beautiful or not. Her own voice sounded harsh as a crow's and seemed to distract those around the table.

The Earl looked up, but his gaze went straight to Rowan Birchmoon, its dark austerity softening into something close to warmth. "How is your beast?" he asked.

Rowan Birchmoon shook her head. "She may live, if the gods are kind."

"Ay." His voice was somber. "It has been a night for the Silent God. We must trust that the day will belong to Meraun, the Healer." His dark gaze thrust past her. "Nhairin," he said, a recognition but also a question, as if wondering why she alone had nothing to report.

Now, thought Nhairin, would be the time for me to speak up, deliver Korriya's message. She began to marshal her words, but before she could speak there was a sudden clamor from the hall outside. A moment later the doors swung wide to admit Asantir, her helm tucked under one arm and blood staining the rough wadding on her shoulder. Haimyr the Golden slipped through in her wake as the Earl's dark, measuring gaze swung to meet his Honor Captain. "At last!" the Earl said.

The chamberlain leaned forward. "Ay, your report is vital, Captain. There's so much we need to know. Is the keep yet secure? And the Heir—has she been found?"

"The New Keep," Asantir said, speaking to the Earl, "is secure. The invaders were cleared from the Heir's quarter by dawn and we've now been right through the Temple precinct and the surrounding areas as well. Only a handful of the attackers survived to flee into the Old Keep, but what reinforcements they may have there, I cannot say." She made to shrug, then stopped as fresh blood seeped through the wadded bandage. "We have secured every portal between the two keeps, but our losses have been heavy. There are just no troops to spare for the Old Keep yet." She paused, her eyes steady as they met the Earl's. "You received my dispatch regarding Commander Gerenth's death?'

The Earl nodded. "I did. And I endorse your decision to take command of the keep garrison." His fingers rapped on the tabletop. "We have much to thank you for, it seems, not least that you had the Honor Guard out on special maneuvers last night."

Nhairin's brows rose, for she had not known this, but Asantir shook her head as though disclaiming any special merit. "It helped, my lord, that we were on the ramparts, rather than in the barracks asleep. But the ramparts are too far from where the invasion occurred. If the alarm had not been given, the fact that we were armed and wakeful up there would not have mattered until it was too late." She paused again. "Given that we were the first to respond, the toll on the Honor Guard has been heavy. In the short term, we may have to augment your guard with troops from the keep garrison."

The Earl nodded. "Do whatever you think necessary, Captain." His gaze grew hard again, searching hers. "But you have not mentioned the Heir. Does *no one* have any idea where she is, or might be?"

Not "Malian," thought Nhairin, or "my daughter," but "the Heir." She bent to rub her aching leg, concealing her expression.

"We have scoured the New Keep, hunting out enemies and searching for Lady Malian." Asantir's gaze never left the Earl's. "She is not here, my lord. I believe she is in the Old Keep, that she fled there during the attack."

"Under the circumstances," Haimyr murmured, "not good news." He was standing with one golden shoulder propped against the wall and the Earl shot him a brief, cold glance before swinging back to Asantir.

"Fled, or been taken forcibly," he demanded, "since all reports suggest that the intruders came via the Old Keep?"

"My lord, I don't believe she has been taken prisoner." Carefully, the captain repeated the arguments she had advanced to Nhairin amidst the wreckage of the invaders' last stand, but the Earl's frown did not lift.

"Nevertheless," he said finally, "we must find out for certain what the facts are, whether the Heir has fled or been taken prisoner—" He paused. "Whether she is alive or dead. We must locate her—and quickly. I am relying on you, Asantir!"

The Honor Captain nodded. "I have already sent to Storm Hold for wyr hounds," she replied. "But it will be days before they arrive. Malian cannot wait that long, not if she is in the Old Keep with what's left of the attackers. And we cannot leave you and the New Keep unprotected." She frowned. "In the end, we may not have the numbers to do more than scout out the Old Keep. We also risk losing those scouts, if the enemy has anything in reserve."

The Earl studied her, his black eyes unreadable. Nhairin cleared her throat. "What I don't understand," she said, her voice harsh again as all the faces around the table turned in her direction, "is how they could have gotten into the Old

Keep in the first place? It's supposed to be the very heart, the most unassailable source, of Night's power. Yet these intruders came through it unscathed. No alarm was sounded until everyone in the Heir's quarter, and a great many in the Temple precinct, were already dead. But who were, or are, these intruders? How could this possibly have happened? And who did finally activate the alarms?"

"All good questions," said Asantir, "but we, it seems, have too few answers."

"I cannot answer your questions either, Nhairin," Haimyr put in lazily. "But I can tell you all that Malian is not in the Old Keep's High Hall, or in the Hall of Mirrors above it. They have been her favorite hideaways of late, but there is no sign of her in either place."

The Earl's brows had drawn together while Haimyr spoke. "Of late?" he inquired ominously. "What do you mean, 'of late'?" His terrible stare shifted to include everyone in the room. "Am I to understand that my daughter has been going into the Old Keep, which is forbidden, and that some or all of you knew yet did nothing about it?"

Only Haimyr and the Honor Captain seemed unperturbed by his wrath. The minstrel was concentrating on brushing dust from his golden cuff, but Asantir met the Earl's stare, her gauntleted hands resting quietly on the buckle of her sword belt. "I think we all knew it, myself included," she replied gravely. "Yet every keep child and new recruit has to go there at least once as a rite of passage—and Malian is your daughter, after all."

Nhairin shook her head, watching the Earl and remembering how they had run wild in the Old Keep when they were children, laughing at the rumors of ghosts.

The Earl drew a deep breath and the hard-won control closed down over his face again. "It seems," he said, his voice devoid of expression, "that there is much I do not know, even in my own keep." He studied the minstrel again. "So you went in there alone, with the attack barely over and the garrison still standing to arms?"

The chamberlain clicked his tongue. "Individual hero-ics!" he said, only half beneath his breath.

The minstrel glanced at him, a sideways look that was hard to read. "It seemed like a good idea at the time," he said, with the faintest of shrugs.

Asantir shook her head. "It was bravely done, but not wise. Those intruders showed no mercy to anyone else; they would not have spared you."

The minstrel smiled at her. "But they did not find me, my careful Captain, so all is well. And now I have reduced your search area, if only by a little."

"So you have," she agreed, turning back to the Earl. "But not, alas, by much. My lord, we will do all that we can, and more. But the Old Keep is a vast place and a thorough search will require numbers, which we do not have."

The Earl looked bleak and the room was silent except for the fire's hiss and the moan of the wind outside.

"What we need," Jiron murmured, "is a seeker." He looked up from the scroll he was unrolling, then rerolling again, to find them all staring at him. "Well," he said, half shamefaced, half defiant, "it is what we need. You can't deny it."

"Well, we don't have one," the Earl said shortly. "We haven't had any seekers for generations."

"Besides," said Khorion, speaking for the first time, "half the Temple quarter is dead now anyway, from what I hear, and the rest in no condition to use whatever old powers they still have."

Silence fell again. Everyone in the room had heard the stories from the Temple quarter and now they avoided look-ing at each other. Although there would be some, Nhairin knew, who secretly considered what had happened there a good thing. She looked up and met the Earl's eyes.

"Nhairin?" he asked, for the second time that morning.

There could be no more delaying. Nhairin relayed Kor-riya's demand, without trying to soften the words, then waited for the Earl's explosion of wrath. She was more than surprised when it did not come. The Earl merely sat down, looking thoughtful. "Korriya, eh?" he said eventually, in a tone that matched his expression. Teron, standing a few paces behind him, looked outraged, and the councilors around the table disapproving.

"Right of Kin and Blood," the Earl said, as though thinking aloud. "If she has gone that far, it must be important. I cannot refuse, in any case."

"My lord Earl!" the chamberlain protested, "surely you will not let her come here. The Blood Oath, the law!" He shook his head in dismay.

"The gate," the Earl said dryly, "is already broken, from what I hear, and I am certainly not going there so that my First Kinswoman can shout at me across its ruin. It is my decision," he added softly, "and does not breach the Oath, that I can recall."

"But tradition—" the chamberlain began, then fell silent at the look in his Earl's eye.

"She has claimed Right of Kin and Blood," the Earl repeated, "and that lies at the heart of both our law and our traditions."

"First and oldest," Asantir murmured, into their silence. Everyone stared at her and she shrugged, wincing slightly at the movement. "Well, it's true, is it not?" She turned to the Earl. "I was going to the Temple quarter anyway, so after Nhairin spoke with me I took the liberty of escorting your kinswoman here. It seemed to me," she added deliberately, "that if the matter was that important it should be expedited, and if you did not wish to see her, well then"—she gave another, very small shrug—"the priestess could be escorted back again just as easily. She is waiting outside now."

So the clamor in the hall had not just been for Asantir's arrival, after all. Nhairin shook her head as the councilors gaped at the Honor Captain. Even the Earl's face was a mask as he studied her, but finally he gave a short nod. "You are bold, Asantir," he said, "but that, after all, is one of the reasons I made you Honor Captain." His fingers drummed briefly on the table. "You had better show her in, then." He spoke calmly, as if it was an everyday occurrence and not the first time such a thing had happened in five hundred years.

As if, thought Nhairin, the world hasn't been turned upside down enough! She felt the ache in her leg again, sharp and bitter, as she looked around the room. The chamberlain still looked outraged, Khorion was frowning, and Teron stared glumly at his feet as Asantir went to the door. Jiron looked down at the table, and Antiron at the wall. Haimyr lifted his brows in delicate inquiry but otherwise looked unperturbed—as he would, being an outsider. Nhairin did not even bother looking at Rowan Birchmoon, knowing that the Winter woman would distance herself from such events, as she always did.

The door reopened to admit Asantir and Korriya's tall, robed figure. The priestess lifted her hood back as she entered, her exhaustion and grief plain for all to see. Nhairin could not entirely repress a flicker of admiration for her straightness and calm in that circle of hostile eyes, and the austere dignity of her bow as she greeted the Earl of Night.

"Korriya," said the Earl of Night, although he did not return her bow. He paused, then added, "It has been a long time."

The priestess inclined her head. "I would not impose on you now," she replied, "except that necessity demands it."

The Earl's eyes narrowed. "Claiming Right of Kin and Blood generally suggests necessity. Anything less would be unacceptable given the circumstances." The flick of danger was there beneath the quiet tone, but Korriya remained calm.

"It is also," she said, "a Matter of Blood."

There was an instant outcry but the Earl made a sharp gesture, quelling the raised voices. "Those you see here, Priestess Korriya, are my household and my councilors. It is their right to advise me."

"I speak of a Matter of Blood," Korriya repeated, "and that is the first and oldest right amongst the Derai."

When the Earl spoke his voice was reflective. "And who

will uphold any other law or right if I, who am Earl of the first and oldest House, will not uphold you now?" But his look, measuring her, was not friendly. "You were always clever, Korriya. I remember it well. But do not push me too far."

She said nothing, simply waited, and after a moment he nodded. "So be it. I accept your Matter of Blood."

Teron sprang forward. "My lord, no! The raiders *must* have had inside help to traverse the Old Keep—and I say that aid came from the priest kind! Now she seeks to slay by treachery where the sword has failed."

"Peace!" the Earl commanded. "Be silent! Only the Blood may hear matters of Blood, Teron."

"My lord," the chamberlain objected, "this is not wise. I implore you—" Once again, he broke off. "Is there no other way? Must you hear her alone?"

"There may be another way," said Asantir unexpectedly. "While only the Blood may hear a Matter of Blood, my predecessor told me that the Honor Captain may be counted, de facto, as one of the Blood if no one else is available."

The Earl looked surprised. "I had forgotten that," he said, and looked at Korriya. "You don't dispute this claim?"

"No," said Korriya. "The captain is right. It is indeed the law, although an obscure point."

"Very well," said the Earl, "Asantir shall remain." He turned to the others. "I apologize for the discourtesy, but our law gives me no more freedom than you in a Matter of Blood. We shall resume our councils as soon as possible."

Nhairin caught the Earl's eye and thought better of protesting further, but she noticed several resentful glances toward the priestess as the councilors filed out. Only Haimyr and Rowan Birchmoon seemed unconcerned, the minstrel departing with a deep flourish divided evenly between Earl and priestess. The Earl, however, rose to his feet as Rowan Birchmoon passed. "I thank you," he said, gravely formal, "for your forbearance, particularly given your losses in our cause last night."

She smiled faintly. "How can I be offended," she replied, "when I am neither Derai, nor of your Blood?" Her fingers touched his, lightly, and she bowed to Korriya as she left. Nhairin limped out after her and Teron, scowling furiously, brought up the rear, closing the door behind him with a vicious click.

6

Matters of Blood

*A*santir spared a raised brow for this muted rebellion, but otherwise her attention was on the two faces studying each other across the table. They were almost mirrors of each other: They had the same lines, the same sculpted bones and shadowed eyes. The only difference lay in coloring and that one face was cast in a male mold, the other female. They reminded her of the old depictions of Ornorith of the Two Faces, each carved mask a reflection of the other except that they faced in different directions.

The two faces of Luck, thought Asantir, the dark and the light, which reflect the two faces—dark and light—of the Derai.

The Earl's fingers beat another tattoo on the scarred tabletop, breaking their silence, and Korriya moved to a chair opposite his. The Earl's expression, regarding her, was as hard as his voice. "Well?" he said. "Time and events are both pressing. Speak to me of this Matter of Blood!"

"Matters," she replied calmly. "There is more than one." She studied her hands, as though reading some detailed story there, before raising her gray eyes to meet his darker gaze. "As you know from our childhood together, I have always loved puzzles and riddles." She smiled faintly when he nodded. "The answers to last night's riddles are my Matters of Blood, Earl of Night."

He leaned forward, the winged horse device on his breastplate catching fire. "Unfold me these riddles, then."

Korriya spoke slowly, every word precise. "Who attacked us and why? Who woke the alarms and roused the keep? Who drove off the Swarm demon that hunted in the Temple quarter last night? And how did the attackers breach the Old Keep?"

The Earl leaned back. "Do you claim to have answers to these questions?"

"I have some certainties," the priestess replied, "and some surmises. But if I am right—" She broke off, looking at him intently. "You should be aware of what I suspect, at least."

"Very well," he said grimly. "I'm listening."

"Firstly," she said, "I have already heard speculation that the attackers must have been our Derai enemies pursuing blood feud and vendetta. Yet even if the foul sorceries they used did not point to the Swarm, a Raptor of Darkness must remove all doubt."

"I have heard the rumors," the Earl said carefully, "but what exactly is a Raptor of Darkness?"

"It is a psychic vampire," Korriya told him, "a powerful and terrible manifestation of the Swarm that sucks out the mind and soul of anyone insufficiently powerful to withstand it. Those with the old powers are its particular prey, for the Raptor increases its own strength by feeding on ours." She closed her eyes briefly. "It feasted well last night, before it was finally driven off."

"And how was it driven off?" the Earl asked quietly.

Korriya's smile was bitter. "Not by us. It entered the Temple quarter with the first wave of intruders, and the souls of the weak and the unwary were sucked into it like a vortex. None of us would have survived if we had not managed to barricade ourselves into the temple of Mhaelanar, the Defender, where the psychic barriers are strong and kept it at bay. But even they would not have held forever, since we no longer have the strength within ourselves to defend against such an attack. We knew it was only a matter of time before the Raptor prevailed." She paused briefly. "And so I come to the second and third riddles."

"Who woke the alarms and roused the keep?" Asantir spoke from her post by the door. "And who drove off the demon that hunted in the Temple quarter? They are good questions, Priestess."

"Ay," Korriya replied. "The one who raised the alarm was a mindspeaker of very great power, far stronger than anyone in our temples. She woke the keep alarms to life, but her power drew the Raptor of Darkness like blood to a kill. Even she was no match for its malignancy. She would have fallen, if she had not had aid."

Korriya closed her eyes momentarily, then opened them again, looking intently at the Earl. "At one moment, all I could perceive was a roiling darkness with the mindspeaker trapped in its heart, but I was powerless to help. The next moment the world was ablaze with golden fire. My whole mind was flooded with it; it called to me. Nay, it *commanded* my aid against the Raptor. Everyone barricaded into the temple of Mhaelanar was caught up in it, mind and spirit, from the greatest amongst us to the weakest. I sensed other powers there as well, powers that I did not recognize—but all that mattered was that together, bound into that golden conflagration, we were strong enough to cast out the Raptor of Darkness."

The Earl was on his feet. "The Golden Fire!" he exclaimed, sheer wonder in his voice. "Can it be possible?" He checked, frowning at Korriya. "Do you know what you are saying? Are you sure of this?"

"I am sure," Korriya answered steadily. "As sure as anyone can be when we have not encountered its like in five hundred years. The Golden Fire woke in this keep last night, my Kinsman and my Earl. It fought with us against the Swarm."

The Earl shook his head as though unable to credit what he heard. "This is news indeed," he said at last. "News to set the entire Derai Alliance alight! But if it is true, where is the Golden Fire now? Why is the keep not infused with its light, as it used to be? And why does it not speak directly to me, who am Earl and therefore first of our Blood, rather than to you?" There was sudden, sharp suspicion in his voice.

Korriya shook her head. "It did not speak to me as such. I saw it and heard its voice, I was caught up in it, but there was no direct speech as reported in the histories. I do not know why, for we understand so little about the Golden Fire now, after so long. I only know that it was real and it was here, if only for a very short time."

"When the need was greatest," Asantir observed thoughtfully. "That is not entirely unprecedented, I believe."

"But only when it aided Derai outside the keep itself," the Earl replied. "Within the keeps, the Fire was always a constant and visible presence."

Korriya nodded. "I have read those same records but even so, the more I think about it, the more I believe that last night's need *was* the key. First there was our own great need in the Temple, as we fell before the Raptor's onslaught. I also assume that the Raptor's presence itself would be anathema to the Golden Fire. Finally, there was the Raptor's attack on the unknown mindspeaker, which is when the Fire counterattacked." She paused, watching the Earl carefully, but he said nothing.

"I heard that mindcall, Tasarion," the priestess continued quietly, "and it spoke three specific names: the Earl of Night, Nhairin, and Asantir, which implies that the speaker was either of this keep or knew those who dwell here." She leaned toward the Earl. "As you know, the bond between the Golden Fire and the Derai was always strongest with those of the Blood. Now the Fire appears to have roused itself to protect the same unknown mindspeaker who called the keep to arms—and there is only one other in the House of Night, besides ourselves, who is of the Blood."

The Earl had gone white. "Malian," he whispered, and then his face contorted and he struck the table hard with his clenched fist. The blow was loud in the silent room, but the Earl did not seem to hear it, or feel any pain in his hand. "No!" he said, his voice so full of rage and revulsion that Korriya flinched. The Earl caught himself, exerting control with an obvious effort, and stood for a moment, his fist still clenched and his head bent. "No," he said again, his voice very quiet but with a deliberation that was more terrible than his rage. "I will not have it. Not again."

Korriya looked at him with compassion. "Tasarion, it is only surmise, but still—"

"I must prepare myself for the worst," he finished harshly, "given your impeccable reasoning. And do not remind me that no reasoning, however impeccable, is infallible and that we can be certain of nothing until the Heir is found. Not," he added bleakly, "that she will be able to remain Heir if your suspicion is correct." The face he turned toward her was bleak as his voice. "Is there more, Kinswoman? You had one more riddle, I believe?"

"How did the attackers breach the Old Keep?" murmured Asantir, and the priestess nodded. The lines of exhaustion and strain on her face were very marked now.

"I think," she said, "that you will find my suspicions in this case the least palatable of all."

The Earl seated himself again, his face grim. "Another Matter of Blood?" he asked. She nodded and he made a brief, impatient gesture. "Speak, then. You need not spare me."

"Indeed," she replied quietly, "I do not think I can. Your squire spoke of treachery and I believe that he is right. I do not believe that we are so weak, even now, that the Swarm could penetrate the Old Keep unaided. Only one of the Blood, or a very great power indeed, could set aside its in-built wards. When the attackers first poured into the Temple quarter there was a hint of something, a signature or seal on the spells they were using, that I recognized. It was elusive but familiar, although I could not name it. Then, of course, the Raptor came and there was no time left for naming things." She paused, almost visibly gathering her strength. "Since then, however, I have returned again and again to that elusive familiarity and finally a name has come to me. Yet it seems unthinkable."

"Except," the Earl said sharply, "that you are thinking it. No more riddles, Korriya. Name me this name!"

She raised her eyes to his. "Nerion," she said.

He recoiled as if she had struck him. "How can that be?" he cried. "They told us she was dead!"

"They said!" Korriya returned, with fine scorn. "She was exiled amongst those who have no cause to love this House—yet who, here, asked after the manner of her death, or sought her body for burial when they said that she was gone? We were all too ready to accept their word that she was dead. But if she was still alive, if she had not died but fled, then she might well seek revenge."

"And so," said Asantir, "by way of the fourth riddle, we come back to the first, at least in part. They did seem to be seeking something, or someone, even to the extent of leaving it too late for retreat."

"What are you suggesting?" the Earl asked her. "That the mother seeks the daughter?"

"It fits a part of the picture," Asantir replied, "although the attackers may well have had several objectives." She frowned. "It does not tell us why they attacked now, however."

"But Nerion," said the Earl, shaking his head, "alive and gone over to the Darkswarm? How can that even begin to be possible?"

Wearily, the priestess leaned back in her chair. "You are thinking of the Nerion we both knew. Now think of her fate: cast out, exiled, abandoned. And the fact remains that someone led our attackers through the Old Keep, someone who knew it very well."

"And Nerion, more than any other, ran wild there when we were young." The Earl thrust to his feet again, stalking back and forward between table and fire. "Now Malian is believed missing in the same place. If Nerion is in there—" He shook his head. "If only I could place more confidence in your report of the Golden Fire, but a five-hundred-year-old memory is a slender thread on which to pin Malian's life and the future of Night."

"We cannot afford to wait for the worst to happen," Korriya said urgently. "We must act."

"What can we do," the Earl returned, "except what we already intend, to regroup and then search the Old Keep, room by room, floor by floor? But we *must* have wyr hounds, for by the Nine, that place is an absolute warren and Asantir is right—we no longer have the numbers to take it on."

"Or the powers," said the priestess, under her breath. She straightened, speaking carefully. "If it is simply a matter of numbers, then despite last night's losses there are still those in the Temple quarter who can aid the search. . . . If you will allow it."

"But is it simply numbers?" asked Asantir, before the Earl could reply. "What of the Raptor of Darkness? Is it dead, or simply fled? And if it has fled, then where is it? We also know that at least some of the invaders retreated into the Old Keep. What we don't know is how many others remained there as rearguard, or what Darkswarm sorceries they may still unleash against us. We do not know who leads them, or what their objective is. As for those from your Temple quarter, do you have any idea how they will react under pressure, let alone under fire?"

Korriya held up one hand, color tingeing her tired face. "I did say if it was *only* numbers, Captain," she said. "As for the rest, I do not think that the Raptor is dead. It fled and it was badly weakened by the Golden Fire, but I cannot swear that it is incapable of troubling us again. Nor can I be certain that we would fare better against it wounded than we did against its full strength. It is likely, however, that we could at least detect its presence—and that of any other darkspawn in the Old Keep."

"But not," said Asantir, "protect us against them, I think?"

The priestess shook her head. "Our powers of protection are limited, as we discovered last night when we were so direly overmatched." Grief and shame flicked for a moment, raw in her expression.

"We were all overmatched last night," the Earl told her. "Our wards failed, we were taken by surprise, both by the attack and its execution, and the cost in beating it back was very high. And it will be higher yet. The morale of Night will suffer, our prestige in the Derai Alliance will be affected, and we will not be able to say that we have finally defeated our enemy until we can secure the Old Keep as well as the New, which may take years."

Korriya looked from his grim, weary face to Asantir's impassive one. "I see," she said. "Then it is even more important that I offer help, however limited our powers."

The Earl shook his head. "The offer is meaningless, given the Oath that binds us all and cannot be undone. The gates between the Temple quarter and the main keep may be broken, but it will take a far greater power to bridge the schism that sealed them fast, separating Temple from keep and warrior from priest."

"To our bitter cost," she replied, "as last night proved."

"Perhaps," he said, but he was looking at the fire rather than at her. "Nonetheless, my duty now is to rebuild the strength and confidence of Night, not undermine it further."

"There is no greater threat to Night, in this moment, than not finding and securing the Heir." Korriya's voice was low but edged. "You are a fool, Tasarion, if you will not see it!"

The Earl did look at her then. "Do not presume too far, Priestess," he said, bleak as the day. "The Blood Oath binds us all, exactly like the Right of Kin and Blood that brought you here today. Given your news, I am not ungrateful that you invoked that right and I am aware that your advice has merit. But make no mistake, you are still here on sufferance. It is I, together with my councilors, who weigh threats to Night and decide on them, no one else."

There was stark silence while their eyes held, the one cold and dark, the other gray and measuring. Then Korriya sighed and rose to her feet. "You are right," she said quietly. "Given the Oath, my only claim on you is that of Blood. But we are very nearly the last of that Blood. Perhaps, in my anxiety to preserve it, I spoke intemperately. Yet I was born to the House of Night as well as to its Blood, and I am not the only one behind the Temple quarter gate who still cares deeply for both." She paused, her eyes still locked on his. When she spoke again, her voice rang in the quiet room. "But I, my First Kinsman and my Earl, care at least enough to make you this pledge: my blood for the Earl of Night, my blood for his Blood, my life for his life, my heart only for this House and the Derai cause."

She did not wait to see the effect of her words, but simply bowed, turned on her heel and stalked out past Asantir, who saluted her and held open the door. The priestess met her eyes briefly, before nodding a curt acknowledgment and walking through. The Earl remained silent, frowning into the fire's heart, while Asantir stared straight ahead. Eventually, the Earl looked up. "I never thought that you were a priest lover, Asantir."

The Honor Captain put up her dark brows. "A priest lover? I? She is quite right, though. We need the Temple quarter now, whether we like it or not."

"My father," the Earl said, "would have called those traitor's words."

"But you," Asantir pointed out, "are not your father. Besides, traitors do not give the pledge that we just heard."

The Earl looked grim. "No. Although I was referring to you, not Korriya."

"Traitor and priest lover," Asantir replied. "It is fortunate, then, that I serve you and not the Old Earl. Still"—she smiled slightly—"if one did wish to overturn custom and tradition, what better time than when people are already reeling and so more likely to accept that extraordinary events require out-of-the-ordinary responses?"

The Earl gave a sharp bark of laughter. "You should have been born to the House of the Rose! You have exactly their double-edged, devious mindset and are quite wasted as a blunt warrior." Swiftly, his face grew serious again. "I promise to think about the Temple quarter, but that is all. As for the other matters Korriya spoke of, we must not mention them again—not until we are sure of all the facts."

"Not even the Golden Fire?" asked Asantir.

"That least of all," he said, "until we know that it is real." He shifted, as though his armor had grown suddenly heavy. "But Korriya was right about the Heir. We must find her, and quickly. *Quickly*, Asantir."

Her gaze met his, grave and steady. "All that can be done, shall be done. And more."

He nodded, both assent and dismissal, but before she could turn there was a crisp knock and a guard entered the room. "My lord Earl. Captain. The two heralds who arrived last night are here and say that they wish to deliver their message. They say that they were charged to give it to you without delay, my lord." He hesitated, seeing their resigned exchange of glances. "I have tried to send them away, but they won't go."

The Earl steepled his fingertips together. "As it happens, I had not forgotten our heralds of the Guild, whom someone has seen fit to send all the way from the River. Their timing, though, is hardly good."

"There will be no good time," Asantir murmured, "not in the days ahead. And you will have to see them at some stage, my lord."

He sighed, looking grimly resigned. "You are right, of course, although it's unlikely their message will seem significant beside last night's events. But even so—Show them in, Garan." The grimness deepened as he turned back to his Honor Captain. "I believe that they mentioned a sigil of silence yesterday. You had better stay a little longer, after all."

7

The Tower of the Rose

Nhairin paused outside the Little Chamber and surveyed the mix of guards, councilors, and the two young and plainly ill-at-ease priests standing at a distance down the hall. There had been no fighting in this area but guards were present in force, both outside the Earl's chamber and at intervals along the wide corridor. The majority were from the keep garrison, although there were honor guards at the Little Chamber door—drawn from those few, Nhairin surmised, who had survived the night unwounded. But she saw the same deep weariness in every face, however watchful their expressions.

Most of the Earl's councilors either ignored the waiting priests completely or stalked past them with a sidelong glance of distaste, but Teron stopped beside Nhairin and glared, his clenched fists on his hips. "What are they doing here, Garan?" he demanded, scowling at the guard standing next to him.

The guard's dark, mobile face was carefully neutral as he looked from Teron to the nervous priests. "Captain's orders," he replied. "She seemed to think the priestess was entitled to a tail."

"That is true enough," Nhairin agreed reluctantly. "Priestess Korriya is of the Blood of the House of Night and the Earl's First Kin."

Teron did not quite dare to switch that scowl onto her. "She's a priestess," he protested. "Kin or not, she shouldn't be allowed near the Earl at all, at least not without more of us to guard him!"

Haimyr laughed. "I don't think that the Earl is greatly at risk, even without your saving presence, sir squire."

"You don't know the priest kind, minstrel," the youth replied ominously. "They are devious and treacherous."

"Is this something you know from your own experience?" Haimyr inquired lazily.

"I? No!" Teron looked affronted. "We follow the House of Blood's example in our hold and will not suffer priests within our walls, given their past betrayals. Speaking of betrayal," he added darkly, "how do we know that last night's attack was not some conspiracy between the Temple quarter and the priestly Houses?"

"We do not, of course," Haimyr replied. "But from what I understand of last night's events, and the number of priests that lie dead, it seems unlikely."

Teron's scowl did not lift. "What would you know anyway?" he muttered. "You're only—" He broke off at the sudden glint in Haimyr's golden eyes. The minstrel's tone, however, remained light.

"An outsider?" he inquired. "Why, so I am. All the same, I try to use my eyes and ears—and at least a little of what lies between them as well."

Nhairin snorted and Teron glowered at the minstrel, clearly biting back a reply. The guards looked openly amused but made no move to send him away, while the two priests retained their cautious station down the hall. Their faces had remained expressionless throughout, but the young woman was flying two spots of color high in her cheeks. Teron's belligerent stare shifted back to them. "I still say they shouldn't be here," he said loudly.

Garan's amused expression did not change, but there was

a warning note in his voice. "Captain's orders, young Teron, which means yours, too. So pipe down like a good lad, else I'll have to send you packing."

Teron flushed crimson from his collar to the roots of his hair, but remained silent. After a tiny pause, Haimyr turned back to Nhairin, but his eyebrows flew up when he saw her expression. "Ah," he said, drawing her away down the hall, "another sour face, I see. Surely *you* do not think that the priestess means the Earl any harm?"

Nhairin's mouth twisted. "No," she replied shortly. "It just galls me that Korriya calls on Right of Kin and Blood to speak privately with Tasarion and so I am sent away— but Asantir remains. Yet I am the friend and playmate of their childhood while Asantir is what? A one-time levy who came to us from the boundary holds." She snorted again. "The boundary holds that never send their best when the keep calls. Instead we get their leavings, those too old for active service and the half-grown younglings. That is all As-antir was, when she first came to us!"

The faintest hint of a frown pulled at Haimyr's brows. "Then, perhaps, but not now. Besides, I understand there are good reasons for that practice, since those who are well trained and in their prime can never be spared from the boundary watch. Just as the reasons why Asantir remained behind seem plain enough. Given your Derai law, no one else could do so."

Nhairin shrugged. "Because the former levy, the nobody, is now Honor Captain. Oh, I know it is foolish of me to feel excluded, doubly foolish even, since Asantir *is* the Honor Captain and so best qualified to protect Tasarion." She paused, her mouth a thin, sharp gash in her scarred face, and folded her arms across her chest. "I resent it sometimes, that's all," she muttered, not looking at him.

Haimyr rested one hand on her shoulder. "I know," he said, "for unlike Teron, I am not blind. It must be difficult indeed to watch your former comrades run and fight while you wait safely behind the lines, wondering whether or not they will save you. And hard, too, however much she is your friend, to see the comrade of your soldiering days promoted in honor while you must follow a path where glory is, at best, unlikely."

Nhairin uttered a short laugh. "Very unlikely, as last night showed. And you are right, both that Asantir and I are friends and that it doesn't make our relative situations any easier to accept." She stared down the hallway with bleak eyes then gave a quick shrug, as if to throw off her mood. "But this is all folly, as I have already said, and does me no credit. We must all make the best of what we have and who we are."

"And at least," Haimyr said, "you need not take your exclusion from the Little Chamber to heart. Even Rowan Birchmoon was turned out."

The flash in Nhairin's eyes came and went in an instant. "She is not—" she began, then quickly bit off the words.

Haimyr shrugged, smiling. "Derai?" he finished for her. "No, of course not." Nhairin flushed and looked away. "But speaking of being Derai," the minstrel continued, "we need to talk more of something that Jiron raised, this matter of seekers."

"Seekers?" Nhairin echoed, still uncomfortable. "What is there to talk about? As Tasarion said, we have none."

"But what," said Haimyr the Golden, "if I knew where to find one?"

"What?" exclaimed Nhairin. "But that's impossible!"

"Perhaps, perhaps not," murmured Haimyr. "But let us not discuss it here." He strolled away and Nhairin limped after him.

"What do you mean by this?" she demanded. "There are no seekers, Haimyr, not in the House of Night anyway."

He raised his brows slightly. "What should I mean by it, except a better chance to find our Malian? But first, I must speak with the chamberlain."

They found him back in his office, still muttering about the disruption of the council meeting. "No good will come of it," he said, as soon as he saw Nhairin. "The Earl should not put aside the counsel of his tried advisers to listen to the ranting of a priest, First Kin or no First Kin. Especially," he added gloomily, "at a time like this."

"Kin and Blood," said Nhairin, seating herself and easing her leg with a small sigh. "He had no choice."

The chamberlain looked peevish. "It's the old law, I suppose, but I still say no good will come of it. No good at all." His expression sharpened as he looked at Haimyr. "And what do you want?"

"Such courtesy," said Haimyr. "I came, good chamberlain, to inquire after our guests of yesterday evening, the heralds of the Guild. How do they fare in the aftermath of last night's battle?"

"Better than most," the chamberlain replied, still sharp, "since they are housed in the guest wing, which escaped last night's fighting. Now, of course, they are persistent in wanting their audience with the Earl." He held up his hands. "The Earl, I ask you! They must wait their turn like everyone else, and so I've told them."

Nhairin nodded, keeping her expression sympathetic. "Do you know where they are now?" she asked.

"Where they should not be, I have no doubt," the chamberlain replied shortly. "I asked that they await the Earl's summons in their guest suite in the Tower of the Rose. Yet now I hear that they've gone down to the stables, to see to their horses or some such thing. Just as if we don't have grooms enough!"

"Well, that is not entirely unreasonable," Nhairin pointed out, but the chamberlain shrugged.

"They should not be roaming the keep at will, not at a time like this! And I have better things to do than hunt them out once the Earl does eventually decide to see them. If he does," he concluded under his breath.

They left the chamberlain to his papers and Nhairin waited until they were out of earshot before detaining the minstrel. "What are you up to, Haimyr?" she demanded.

"And what have these heralds to do with it? Surely you are not suggesting that they are seekers?"

Haimyr's only answer was a hooded look and she stepped away from him. "But that's impossible!" she said incredulously. "Only the Derai priesthood has such powers!"

"Nhairin, Nhairin," the minstrel chided her, "you are becoming as Wall-bound as Teron. It is said, on the River, that the heralds of the Guild can seek out the hidden and find the lost. They are quite famous for it, in fact. So evidently it is *not* only the Derai who have that particular power."

The steward shook her head. "How can that be?" she whispered. "Such a thing has never happened before, even beyond the Gate of Stars. Forgive me, but I find it difficult to believe."

Haimyr smiled. "I must prove it to you, then. We shall find these heralds and see whether or not they will assist." He quirked a golden eyebrow at her. "Their assent should be proof enough even for you, my doubting Nhairin."

She drew herself up, flushing a little. "First we have to find them. The Tower of the Rose is on our way to the stables; we should try there first."

The Rose was the tallest tower in the complex of barbicans and galleries that formed the guest wing of the keep, located not far from the Gate of Winds. There was a time when the whole wing would have been overflowing with guests and envoys but now, when the Derai had grown mistrustful even of each other, the Tower of the Rose was the only part of the complex still in use.

There was romance in the name, Nhairin supposed as she limped up the steps to its double doors, as well as in the legend that it had been built by a long-ago Earl of Night to house his lover from the House of the Rose. Lover or no, it had been a considerable time now since any one from that House had sojourned in the Keep of Winds, although the rose vine was still carved around the tower entrance and stamped in silver on its doors.

No one would think, coming here, that battle had raged

through most of the keep last night. Everything was quiet, peaceful, calm, and yet—the tower had an abandoned feel, Nhairin thought, then instantly derided herself. But she could not quite shake the feeling that there was a focused quality to the silence, as though the tower itself was listening. She was annoyed to find herself keeping her voice low. "Do you think there's anyone here? It's very quiet."

Haimyr was standing in the center of the entry court with his head tilted, listening. "Oddly enough, given their calling," he murmured, "heralds have something of a reputation for silence." He gazed at the wooden paneling and mosaic floor as though seeing them for the first time. "But from what the chamberlain told us, they are probably not here."

"We should check," said Nhairin, and they mounted the stairs to the suite of rooms where the heralds were staying. Haimyr raised his hand to knock, the shadow of his sleeve casting a fantastic silhouette across both door and floor— but before his fist could fall, the door swung wide, as though inviting them to enter.

A coincidence, wondered Nhairin, peering around the minstrel's shoulder, or something more?

The room seemed ordinary enough, with rich yet somber furnishings, a bright fire in the grate, and a tumble of traveler's gear, including saddlebags, cloaks and bedrolls, strewn over chairs and sideboards. There was no sign of the two heralds, however, and the room was filled with the same listening silence as the rest of the tower. "Should we enter?" Nhairin asked.

"The door opened for us," the minstrel replied, as though that were invitation enough. "But to what purpose?" he added, half under his breath as he stepped forward. He looked around carefully, almost as though he expected to see the heralds materialize out of the shadows, but the room remained empty. Nhairin followed more slowly, casting a doubtful look at the closed doors on the far side of the room.

"They could be resting," she suggested, but without conviction.

Haimyr shook his head, although he seemed to be listening hard. Nhairin shrugged and drifted toward the fire. There was something strange about that, too, she thought, even as its warmth drew her close. It took her a moment longer to realize that the fire was burning without a sound. The blaze leapt up merrily, but there was no hiss or crackle of burning wood, no sudden snap of sparks. Nhairin moved closer still, fascinated by the clarity of the flames—then drew in her breath in sheer surprise as the patterns resolved themselves into a woman's face, looking back at her. The eyes, deep and cool, held Nhairin's gaze.

"Do not touch the fire!" Afterward, she could not be sure whether it was a voice in her mind that spoke, or Haimyr—sharply—from behind her. The minstrel's hands were hard on her shoulders as her head jerked back, away from the blaze. When she looked again the face was gone, although the silent, jewel-bright flames still burned.

"What happened?" Nhairin asked, shaken.

"You looked into a herald's ward fire," Haimyr said slowly, puzzlement banishing his concern. "It shouldn't have drawn you in like that, though."

"A ward fire." Nhairin frowned at the flames with distaste. "Is that what this is?"

"Ay. The silence, if nothing else, tells us that." Haimyr still looked puzzled. "Heralds use them to ward their camps when they are out in the lonely places of the world, and to watch over their accommodation from a distance. If they are staying somewhere dangerous. Given last night, I should have expected the fire or some similar device, but my eye slid over it, detecting no strangeness." He shook his head. "I had heard that heralds are masters at tricking the eyes and ears, but now I have proof!"

"I noticed its silence almost as soon as I came in." Nhairin remembered how first the fire and then the watcher's eyes had drawn her closer, and frowned more deeply. She wondered how much she should say about the face in the fire and decided to keep her own counsel, at least until she knew a little more. "So I take it they'll know we're here?"

"They will be aware that someone is here but beyond that—" Haimyr shrugged. "The door opened, so we cannot be entirely unwelcome."

"Perhaps," suggested Nhairin, "the fire drew me in because they wanted a closer look at us."

"Perhaps," said Haimyr, but his tone suggested doubt. "The question is, knowing someone is here, will they now return, or should we seek them out?"

He moved back toward the door in a soft chiming of bells, but paused by the table in the center of the room. It held a scattering of the small, personal possessions that Nhairin would have expected to find on any traveler: a compass, a pile of loose coins, and a book. She protested involuntarily when Haimyr's hand hovered over the book, and he flashed her a mocking smile. "I was only going to look at it, my Nhairin. If the legend on the cover is true, it is a rarity, an original work of J'mair of Ishnapur."

"It is not ours to look at," she said, "or even to touch. The door may have opened for us, but not to make free of the heralds' possessions."

"So very scrupulous," sighed Haimyr the Golden. "So very Derai. I will forgo looking more closely at this treasure, my punctilious friend, but we had best go before temptation proves too much for my slender virtue."

"Good," said Nhairin shortly, refusing to unbend as he bowed her out the door with a flourish. She limped down the stairs ahead of him, her boots heavy on the stone treads. "Who is J'mair of Ishnapur anyway?" she demanded, pausing in the tower door.

"Was," said Haimyr, coming to stand beside her. "He lived nearly a thousand years ago, but is probably the greatest poet produced by any of the civilized lands since the passing of the Old Empire. It may help you to understand my desire to look and touch a little better, my Nhairin, if I tell you that an original work of J'mair of Ishnapur is a treasure beyond price."

Nhairin recalled the slender volume's faded leather binding and shook her head in disbelief. "Beyond price," said Haimyr firmly, with a flash of mockery for her incredulity. "And that," he added, very softly, "makes me wonder how it came into the possession of a herald, when their kind are meant to forgo wealth and worldly goods."

Nhairin shrugged. "A gift from a patron," she said impatiently, "or a family heirloom? But these heralds—from whom or what exactly, are we seeking aid?"

"A fair question," replied Haimyr. "I will tell you as much as anyone knows, who is not themselves a herald." His voice took on the minstrel's lilt. "The Guild emerged out of the ruins of the Old Empire, when its last vestiges were swept away in fire and fear. But there were still some who sought to hold to their posts, to wrest some form of sanity out of the chaos of those times, which we now call the Anarchy. The old imperial posting corps was one group that clung doggedly to their duty. They strove to maintain communication, at first just between the cities of the River, but gradually along the roads to the north and south as well. The times were savage, though, and the members of the posting corps had to protect themselves. That is when so many of their uncanny skills, such as the ward fires, were developed. Eventually, when the world slowly widened again, they became the official couriers and heralds for all the new realms between Ij and Ishnapur."

"The Guild of Heralds," said Nhairin thoughtfully. "Fitting, then, that they should be housed here, given that the House of the Rose fulfills a similar function for the Derai Alliance. Or did," she added.

Haimyr shrugged. "The heralds, I suspect, are something other than the one-time diplomats and power brokers of your House of the Rose."

"So you are sure," Nhairin pressed him, "that one of these heralds is what we would call a seeker? We are not just chasing shadows?"

Haimyr shrugged again. "It is a skill they are said to have developed during the Anarchy, a knack for finding the lost. One of every herald pair has such powers."

A finder of the lost—and Malian was undoubtedly lost. Nhairin's hands clenched into fists at her side, flooded with shame at the thought of having to beg outsiders for help. Anger followed, deep and bitter, for once aid was accepted the Derai would owe the heralds a debt of blood and honor that must be paid, whatever the cost. Nhairin bit her lip, frowning darkly. "Yet the Heir must be found," she muttered. "That is all that matters, to find her!"

Haimyr rested his hand on her shoulder again, pulling her back from her dark thoughts. "Fretting and gnawing away at yourself will not locate her any more quickly, my friend."

She turned her frown on him. "But what if these heralds of yours will not help us? And can we rely on them if they do?"

"If they will not help us, then they will not." The minstrel's expression grew distant, considering. "Still, it is part of their code, to assist those in need. And the one thing that all the stories agree on is that heralds never betray a trust, once they have taken it on."

"Then we had better find them," Nhairin said. But her expression, as she shrugged off his hand and limped away, remained unhappy.

8

A Finder of the Lost

Nhairin grew unhappier still as the next hour passed. By the time she and Haimyr reached the stables, the heralds were long gone. A passing guard thought they had been seen in the Warriors' court, but a page said, no—the High Hall. Yet every lead proved empty. "Where can these heralds be?" she demanded. Haimyr shrugged.

"They went in to see the Earl as soon as the priestess left." Teron nearly bumped into them, more lists and maps piled in his arms, as he came around the corner. His scowl clamped down. "I was excluded from that meeting as well, but I heard there were some strange doings associated with it."

"The sigil of silence," murmured Haimyr. "It is as I told Nhairin here, heralds are queer folk."

Teron's scowl deepened. "The Nine know," he muttered, "we have enough queer folk of our own without importing any from outside."

Haimyr clapped the squire on the shoulder. "You are undoubtedly right," he agreed. "I have hopes of your wisdom yet, young Teron."

Nhairin shook her head, exasperated with them both. "Do you know where the heralds have gone now?" she asked.

"Of course I do!" Teron was indignant. "Apparently they intended to depart as soon as their message was delivered, as is their custom, but the Earl has closed the keep. No one," he said with gloomy satisfaction, "is to leave. The captain sent Garan to see them back to their quarters, but Kyr told me they went by way of the battlement towers."

"Near the main gate," said Nhairin, meaning: away from areas where fighting took place. She frowned. "But the battlement towers? Why would Garan take them there?"

"To keep them out of the way? Make sure they don't see anything they shouldn't?" Teron shrugged, then shivered. "There's nothing up there *to* see."

Haimyr looked thoughtful. "Perhaps not to those who dwell here. But there are so many tales told about the Wall of Night in the River cities, each one stranger than the last. To come so far and not see it, that is not the way of heralds."

Nhairin pulled a face, but said nothing until they had left Teron behind. "You'd think they'd be afraid, given last night's fighting and rumors of demons loose in the keep. Or alarmed, to find that they cannot depart at will. But instead they go to the battlements." She paused. "What if they're spies?"

She watched Haimyr closely but he only shook his head, half laughing at her as they began the steep, winding ascent to the battlements. It was difficult going but Nhairin gritted her teeth and persevered, wondering what the outsiders would make of the Wall's bitter peaks and razor-edged crags. Even on a good day the battlements were too windswept for the guards to do more than patrol at intervals. The main watch was undertaken from lookouts placed at strategic points along the keep's walls.

She had stood watch there herself in years past and knew that the gritty wind could turn knife sharp in an instant. And on a bad day—well, on a bad day no one even looked out onto the battlements, let alone walked them. The guards would batten the storm shutters closed and huddle in their cloaks, closing both ears and minds to the tempest's berserker voice.

Some claimed that voice could drive the unwary mad, and the wind itself was violent enough to flay flesh from bone.

Today, however, was mild and the storm shutters were open, allowing Nhairin to look out through reinforced glass, across the massive battlements, and up into gray, swirling sky. It was a gloomy, oppressive scene and she was not surprised that the heralds had not stayed.

"A forbidding place," Haimyr commented, but his tone was light.

"Yes." Nhairin turned to go, ignoring the knowing looks exchanged by the guards. She had given such looks herself once, but now she simply felt relief as the inner and outer doors of the watchroom thudded closed, shutting out the wind's low whine. Both she and Haimyr descended in silence, emerging into the network of galleries that ringed the Warriors' court.

It was here, finally, that they found Garan and the heralds, stopped to watch the hive of activity in the garrison's training hall. Weapons were being brought in and stacked along the walls, supplies sorted and packed, and guards allocated into squads. Nhairin glanced sidelong, wondering whether the heralds should be seeing all this, and saw that their attention was focused on a solitary figure on the training floor, immediately below. The warrior seemed oblivious to the noise and bustle, her expression remote as she flowed through the training forms. Every movement was smooth, powerful, and seemingly effortless, despite the bandage around one shoulder.

Asantir, thought Nhairin, recognizing the characteristic style even before she saw the warrior's face. The patterns were as familiar to her as breathing, but she too felt their spell as one form melted into another in a ritual that was at least as old as the Derai Alliance.

"Really," Haimyr murmured, "she is very good."

Nhairin hunched one shoulder, but it was Garan who answered. "Good?" he said, with friendly contempt. "She is the best of us."

The fair-haired herald looked up. "What does it take," she asked, "to be the best of you?"

Her voice was beautiful, like cool water running over stones, and Nhairin could not help looking to see if the face that went with the voice was the same as the one in the ward fire. She thought the eyes seemed alike, both luminous and deep—and difficult to meet. Nhairin let her own eyes slide away, focusing on what Garan was saying instead.

"Aptitude, of course, but that's not enough. You have to train relentlessly, every day from early childhood on. But that's not enough either." Garan paused, then shrugged. "She's the Honor Captain, that means she's the best. And if we didn't know it before," he added, half under his breath, "we do now, after last night."

"How so?" the other herald asked. He spoke quietly, but his voice was resonant and dark as the tone of a bronze bell, pulling Nhairin's eyes around to meet his gaze. His eyes were as dark as his voice, and clear and fierce as a falcon's. She stared, unable to look away until he shifted his attention back to Garan, who was speaking again.

"We all fought bravely last night, but that wasn't enough. We needed a strategist, someone who saw the patterns in the chaos all around us and made the right decisions at the right time." Garan rubbed a thumb along his shadowed jaw. "Commander Gerenth got himself and the keep garrison's vanguard cut to ribbons; Captain Asantir pulled the remains of his company out and regrouped our forces. The rest you know."

"Garan," Nhairin warned. Her tone said: *Be careful what you say;* she particularly meant, *before outsiders.* She caught the glint in Haimyr's eye that said that he at least understood her unspoken caution, but Garan met her eyes squarely. "It's no secret, Steward Nhairin. Everyone knows."

Nhairin bit back a tart rejoinder, to the effect that the heralds at least might not have known—and that to call the Honor Captain a strategist, setting her alongside the legendary Derai war leaders, was going too far. Garan held her gaze a moment longer, his humorous face unexpectedly serious; but after a moment, as if by unspoken agreement, they both turned back to the training floor.

"She trains in the old way," Nhairin said at last, grudgingly, as Asantir snapped through a series of movements that were clearly designed for combat at close quarters, then spun, somersaulted, and kicked from one side of the floor to the other in an explosion of power.

"What way is that?" asked the dark-voiced herald. With an effort, Nhairin remembered his name: He was Tarathan of Ar, that was it, and the woman was Jehane Mor.

She avoided his falcon's stare. "We call it the Derai-dan, the armed and unarmed combat forms that have been with our alliance from the beginning."

"But the old way," Garan added, when it was clear Nhairin did not intend to explain further, "is where will and intention are as integral to combat skill as ability with weapons."

"But a warrior's will and intention *are* weapons, are they not?" Tarathan of Ar replied. "Or so we believe."

Nhairin and Garan both looked around at him. "Do you have similar forms?" the guard asked, surprised.

The herald nodded. "Tradition says that our forms came down to us out of the Old Empire, but there are few, now, who keep the ancient skills alive. The assassins of Ij are amongst their number, and some say the Patrol also, although I cannot be sure of that."

"And parts of the old forms," Jehane Mor added, "are still taught in the temples of Jhaine and amongst the Shah's elite, in Ishnapur."

The flow of movement below had stopped and Asantir was standing on the edge of the training floor while others of the guard gathered around her. Tarathan of Ar's gaze shifted from Nhairin to Haimyr, and then back again. "But you have other matters to discuss with us, have you not?"

Nhairin was shocked into staring at him again, then looked as quickly away. "You gazed into the ward fire," Jehane Mor said quietly, "so we knew to expect you."

Nhairin frowned. "So it *was* you, in the fire."

The herald shook her head. "I cannot tell what you saw."

Nhairin flicked a quick look at Haimyr. "We should go somewhere private," she said. "Such talk should not be overheard."

The minstrel had been watching them with the familiar glint in his eye, but now he straightened. "Down first, I think. The captain needs to hear this, too. If you will," he added, with a bow sketched somewhere between the two heralds.

There were still guards around Asantir when they reached the ground, and Nhairin's lips compressed as several more moved out onto the floor to train. "I thought you were meant to be focused on finding Malian."

Asantir looked up. "We are," she replied quietly. "But we need numbers if we are to search the Old Keep effectively, and it takes time to assemble and equip numbers. We are doing that work now, as you can see if you look around. In fact, we are nearly done. But none of us are made of iron and the training floor helps us to relax—and to loosen up after last night's fighting." Her tone softened. "Trust me, Nhairin. The search will begin very soon."

Haimyr forestalled Nhairin's reply with a dramatic gesture. "It may be, Captain, that you will not need numbers, after all."

Asantir threw aside the towel she had used to wipe away sweat. "Why is that, Haimyr the Golden?"

"We need to speak in confidence," he told her more seriously. "You, Nhairin, and I—and these heralds."

Asantir raised one winged brow. "We should go to the Honor room, then. Garan, find Sarus and let him know that I'll be a little longer than expected."

The Honor Captain's room was located close to the training hall and was a well-worn space with not much furniture but an impressive array of weapons, including twin swords in unadorned black scabbards set on top of a battered war chest; an equally plain black spear was mounted on the wall above them. Asantir perched on a corner of her desk, swinging one booted foot, while the others disposed themselves on timeworn camp chairs and—in Tarathan's case—the war chest itself. A delicately carved silver lampshade, which was the only decorative element in the room, threw a filigree of light and shadow over them all.

"Now," said Asantir to Haimyr, "why may I not need numbers for the Old Keep, after all?"

" *'One to seek what is hidden, and to find; one to defend and conceal—both to bind.'* " Haimyr's gaze was enigmatic. "The rhyme is an old one, Captain, but it refers to the heralds of the Guild."

"He thinks," Nhairin interrupted, "that one of these heralds is a seeker who could pinpoint Malian's location."

"Ah." Asantir looked from Jehane Mor to Tarathan of Ar. "Is this true?"

"Yes," Jehane Mor replied calmly. "Tarathan is the seeker. I am the one who shields and conceals."

"I see," said Asantir. She drew a deep breath and ran a hand through her sweat-damp hair. "Indeed, I do see." Again she looked from one herald to the other. "I know little of your ways, except what I saw earlier today, but would it be possible to obtain your aid? For we, as you may know, need to find someone important to this House, who is also very dear to us all."

Jehane Mor nodded. "You seek the child who fell into darkness."

"What do you mean, fell into darkness?" Nhairin asked sharply. "What do you know?"

"We know many things," the herald said. "What is it that you wish to learn, Steward Nhairin?"

Asantir held up a hand, forestalling Nhairin's reply. "We seek the Heir of Night, the Earl's daughter whose name is Malian. What makes you believe that she is this child that you say fell into darkness?"

"We saw her for the first time last night, in your High Hall," Jehane Mor replied, "and felt the touch of her mind on ours, like a star in the twilight of this Derai Wall. We felt that touch again, last night, when the first alarm sounded and the demon hunted through the keep. They fought each other, the hunter-in-darkness and the girl."

Nhairin thought that Asantir seemed remarkably calm, despite this alarming speech. It was Haimyr who asked the question that burned in her own throat. "You said before that the child fell into darkness? Does this mean that she is dead?"

Jehane Mor shook her head quickly. "No, she lives. But she would have died if she had not had help, for the hunter's strength was terrifying and the child, although very strong herself, is untrained."

Asantir was watching both heralds intently. "Who helped her? Was it you?"

The herald inclined her head. "We did help, but even Tarathan and I could not have defeated the demon on our own."

Nhairin ground her teeth, wondering why they could not simply tell everything they knew without the need for these riddle games. If Asantir felt impatience, it did not show in her face or voice. "But," she said musingly, "you were not alone." Her keen gaze met the herald's luminous one and Nhairin could not help feeling that they understood each other in some way that was hidden from her. "And the child," Asantir continued, "what became of her?"

"She was not overcome by the hunter," answered Jehane Mor, "but she fell into a hidden place. I slowed her fall, but lost contact at the very end."

The others looked at each other. Nhairin cleared her throat. "So you don't know where she is."

"No," said Tarathan of Ar, speaking for the first time. "But we have both felt the touch of her mind on our own, so there is good hope that she can be found."

"*Hope!*" Nhairin exploded. "Do you have any idea how vast the Old Keep is? And how can we be sure that this child is Malian anyway, rather than some stray from the Temple quarter? Perhaps you're just saying what you know we want to hear?"

Haimyr touched her arm with light, restraining fingers. "Heralds do not lie, Nhairin. It is unwise to accuse them of deceit."

Nhairin folded her arms, held silent by Asantir's look. "Nhairin speaks sharply out of her fear for Malian," the Honor Captain said, "which reflects my own. We intend no discourtesy and ask your forgiveness if offence has been given."

"There is nothing to forgive," Jehane Mor said quietly, but the subsequent pause stretched, becoming awkward, before Tarathan spoke again.

"It may still take some time to pinpoint her location, if the Old Keep is as vast as the steward suggests. But once I do, I should be able to lead you directly to her, unless physically prevented." He shrugged. "Jehane will be able to conceal my seeking and can shield a small search party from another who seeks as I do. But it will not help if we come face-to-face with armed enemies."

"I'll deal with that," Asantir said crisply. She drew a deep breath. "But if you are quite certain of this, then Haimyr is right. It changes everything."

Nhairin could not keep silent any longer. "But why *should* they help us? What is Malian to them?"

"What indeed?" echoed Jehane Mor. She looked at Tarathan, an almost tangible silence flowing between them, and when she spoke again, her voice was reflective. "It is true that it is not the way of heralds to take on the troubles of others. We have our own sworn duties and must discharge those."

"But then," Tarathan replied, "the Earl of Night has named us as his guests and we must repay the sacred bonds of hospitality."

"Should we simply turn our backs and ride away," asked Jehane Mor in counterpoint, "because the lost child is Derai and has no claim on us?"

"That," said Tarathan with finality, "would be contrary to the code of heralds."

Nhairin folded her arms, refusing to be impressed. "And what is the price," she asked deliberately, "for your aid? Heralds of the Guild, I'm told, do not come cheap." She heard the jangle as Haimyr moved sharply beside her, but Tarathan spoke first.

"Everything has a price," he said. "But who can predetermine what the price will be or who will pay it?" The falcon's stare raked Nhairin and involuntarily she drew back. "We have already spoken of the terror that stalked these halls last night, but what if we should meet it again, or others of its kind? Then Jehane Mor and I risk being subsumed by the hunter-in-darkness, a worse fate by far than physical injury, or even death."

Asantir was frowning. "Yet knowing this, you are still willing to enter the Old Keep?"

"Life is a risk," the herald replied, "and so is death. One cannot hide from either, and if we turn away now we will only find some other terror waiting around the next bend in the road. You have asked for our help, and we have agreed to do what we can. That is all."

"I do not pretend to understand why," Asantir said, "but I offer you my heartfelt thanks. The Earl, of course, will offer far more, as befits a lord of the Derai."

"Even your thanks," Jehane Mor said simply, "are a great gift. But now, if you will excuse us, we need to rest if we are to draw on our powers again so soon."

The others all rose and bowed to them, even Nhairin, although she fixed her eyes on the scratched desktop as they walked past. She only lifted them, with considerable reluctance, when Jehane Mor paused in front of her. The luminous eyes seemed to search down into Nhairin's very soul as the herald's hand shaped, but did not touch, the scar etched into the steward's face. "The cut of the blade that maims flesh," Jehane Mor said, "need not scar the spirit, Nhairin of the Derai—unless you will it so."

Nhairin struck the hand away, bleak with anger and offence. "Neither my spirit nor my scars are any business of yours, Herald!"

Jehane Mor inclined her head. "As you say," she agreed, and walked out in a drift of gray cloak, Tarathan of Ar behind her. The door of the office swung shut in their wake and Nhairin put her hands over her aching face, her fingers pressed up into the line of her hair. "Who," she demanded tautly, "do they think they are, with their cryptic talk and cursed prying ways?"

Asantir's tone was even. "Nhairin, I can't even imagine what you were thinking, speaking to any guest like that, let alone those whose aid we need. Anyone would think you do not want their help."

"I'm not sure I do," muttered Nhairin. "What do we know of them, after all? They are outsiders and some sort of priest kind, too."

"Doubly damned, then," murmured Haimyr.

Nhairin lifted her head out of her hands. "I don't mean you, Haimyr, as you well know. It's their cursed uncanny ways that bother me."

Haimyr shrugged. "That is just the manner of heralds, my Nhairin. I think they must teach it in the Guild houses, the same way I learned to play scales at the college for minstrels in Ij."

Asantir grinned briefly, then shook her head. "We must be practical, Nhairin. We don't have a seeker and we need one. Should we refuse their help because their ways are strange to us?"

Nhairin folded her arms. "I suppose not," she conceded, "but I don't have to like it. It's obvious they're powerful, but we don't know their motives and they themselves said that everything has a price. We may not like theirs when we finally learn what it is."

Haimyr threw up his golden arms in exasperation. "Must you box at every shadow?" he demanded, amidst a cascade of bells. "There is a risk in everything, as they also said. But the danger of their unknown motivation seems far less, right now, than the risk of not finding Malian at all."

Asantir was still watching Nhairin. "I agree with Haimyr," she said quietly. "Their aid is invaluable, for it means that we no longer need numbers, which we don't have anyway—not enough, not after last night. With the herald Tarathan to seek Malian out, and Jehane Mor to disguise our presence, we can risk a much smaller, more mobile force that can get in and out of the Old Keep quickly. And with luck, without attracting unwanted attention."

Nhairin rubbed at her scar. "Does it not gall you, Asantir, that we must go cap in hand to outsiders and strangers for aid?"

The captain sighed. "Would you sacrifice Malian for our Derai pride, Nhairin?"

The steward shook her head, defeated, and Asantir nodded. "I didn't think so," she said. "Now I must speak with the Earl." Her departing step was lighter and brisker than it had been, and Nhairin grimaced before retreating into her own bleak thoughts.

Haimyr lingered, watching her. "Are you sure you are well?" he asked eventually.

Nhairin looked at him. "I was thinking," she said slowly, "that only yesterday what happened last night was unthinkable, but now everything that we thought certain is crumbling around us. Priests, outsiders, the Heir missing—I feel as though we are all poised on the edge of a knife, not knowing which way the blade will turn."

The minstrel reached out and took her hands, holding them between his own. "Malian will be found, Nhairin, I am sure of it. As for the rest, we must trust in those things that were as certain this morning as they were yesterday: the Earl, and Asantir, and every person in this keep, great and small, holding to your Wall."

"The path is dark," she said, avoiding his eyes. "I cannot see the way ahead."

He gave her hands a little shake. "Need we see it?" he

replied gently. "We are not the captains and commanders, Nhairin. All you and I must do is the thing in front of us that needs doing, the task that comes next."

"Our duty?" she inquired ironically. "Now you sound like a Derai, Haimyr the Golden."

He shrugged, smiling crookedly. "Well, I have lived amongst you a long time. But in this at least I am serious. We must remain of good heart and not give in to our fears."

"Bah!" she said, withdrawing her hands and rising to her feet. "You're only an outsider. What do you know?" They both laughed as he, too, rose, throwing a friendly arm around her shoulders. Yet the shadow remained in her eyes, despite the laughter, and she knew in her heart that she was still afraid, she who was never afraid, not even of the one who had lamed her and laid the bitter scar across her face.

9

The Twelve Doors

Malian floated in the middle of a vast, slowly spinning blackness. The world of light still pulled at her, but only pain lay in that direction and she fled from it, further into the dark. Yet even the darkness offered no respite. It was filled with movement, currents and eddies that swirled around her—and the echo of voices: *"We must find her, and quickly. Quickly, Asantir!"*

". . . the Heir must be found! That is all that matters, to find her!"

Her father's voice, and Nhairin's . . . but if anyone answered, Malian did not hear them. Instead she sensed minds, cold and hard, sifting through the layered dark: seeking, searching.

They were looking for her, Malian realized with a jolt, and would have fled again, except that she could not move.

"They were stronger than we thought." The first voice was a hiss deep in her mind, sibilant and metallic, but the one that answered it was ice.

"They had allies, that is all. Now we must do by cunning and stealth what we could not achieve by force of arms."

The third voice was smooth as obsidian. *"They have lost*

*their Heir, you say, so we have not failed yet. We must find
her before they do."*

"All that can be done, shall be done." The cold voice
was implacable. *"And they have no seekers, so we have the
advantage there. But what of the Raptor? Can we rely on it
now?"*

Once again, Malian heard no answer, but she felt the force
of their minds: questing, hunting. Their power was like their
voices, impervious but sharp edged, and they did not mean
her well. But still she could not flee. She remained frozen
in place, as though she were the center around which the
universe revolved, but no matter how deeply she lay hidden,
Malian knew that they would find her in the end.

Light grew slowly through the blackness, a ghostly star
that called to her, mind and spirit, even as she was repelled
by the same bitter chill that had characterized the unknown
voices. Tendrils of pale fire reached out and Malian could
only watch, detached, as her hand rose, seemingly of its own
volition, to grasp the nearest flame.

"Do not touch the fire!" The command was soft but clear,
sheering through the eldritch lure, and Malian pulled back
as though scorched. A will other than her own propelled her
toward a new light that had appeared far above. The spec-
tral glow dwindled as the second light strengthened, daz-
zling Malian's eyes and lancing into her head until the whole
world was a blaze of pain.

Eventually, the blaze resolved itself into a pale nimbus
around Kalan's head, and Malian realized that she was
lying on a hard, tiled floor. Her skull felt as though someone
had split it with an ax and her mouth was so dry that it was
difficult to swallow. She closed her eyes, then opened them
again, and this time Kalan's square face and gold-flecked
eyes sharpened into focus.

"Thank the Nine!" he said simply. "For a while there, I
thought that you had stopped breathing altogether." He studied her with obvious worry. "Are you really all right?"

It was hard to speak, but eventually she managed a whispered croak. "I'm . . . not sure." Malian tried to look around but there was too much pain. "What's happening here?"

Kalan grimaced. "I don't know. You've been unconscious for what seems like hours, and the Fire has disappeared, taking most of the light with it." He leaned down and spoke very quietly. "All the doors are impassable. I've tried every one but the mist filling them is impenetrable. Trying to step through feels like walking into glass—you can't see the barrier but it's there." He kept his voice steady, but Malian could hear the thread of fear. "We're trapped here."

She moved her head, trying to find a position where the pain eased. "You were cursing," she said. "I remember now."

She thought, from what she could see of his face in the dim light, that he looked embarrassed. "I was yelling at the Fire," he explained, a little stiffly. "I heard your mindcall to arms; I think both keeps must have rung with it! But then you started screaming and immediately after that it was as though you couldn't breathe. You were gasping for air and clawing at your throat—and your face turned blue." He paused and Malian realized that he was shaking. "I thought you were dying. And that cursed Fire had said it would protect you!"

Malian closed her eyes as the pain surged behind them. "Here," she whispered. "It said it could protect me here, but not necessarily in the New Keep."

And the Golden Fire *had* saved her. Together they had fought the Raptor of Darkness and won. She remembered the others that the Fire had pulled in to help them fight, and that last final touch of another mind, deep and cool on hers. "Do you have any idea where the Fire is now?" she asked.

"No," Kalan replied softly. "I think it said something about having to hide you before it disappeared, but I'm not sure. I wasn't thinking very clearly then myself."

So they were still in danger, then. But Malian had known that already, just as she had recognized the cold minds and voices in the darkness as enemies. She shuddered, remembering the eldritch light, and knew that she must think, make plans. The pain lessened if she kept her eyes closed and didn't move, but when she did that she felt herself slipping back into the tide of darkness—and there was too much danger that way. She had to stay conscious, despite the pain.

Malian struggled to lift her eyelids and focus on Kalan. "They are looking for us," she told him.

He frowned and she saw the deep weariness beneath his worry. "Who?" he asked. "Our friends or our enemies?"

"Both," she said. "I heard voices—our enemies were there, but I also heard Nhairin and my father. He was speaking to Asantir and saying that I must be found."

"The Honor Captain?" Kalan asked, and she heard the sudden hope in his voice. "Would she come after you herself, do you think?"

Malian dared not nod, but she reached out and touched his fingers with her own. "For me, yes," she said honestly. "And if anyone can find us, Asantir will."

"This is a very strange place." Gloom replaced the hope in Kalan's voice. "Maybe no one could find us in here."

Malian refused to be daunted. "The Fire may come back," she said. "If not— We must find our own way out, that's all."

Kalan grinned. "That's all," he echoed. "Well, perhaps we should expect to find a way, given everything else that's happened!" His expression sobered again. "And we've got no food or water, so we *have* to find a way out sooner rather than later. But you're hurt and I'm the expendable one, so I go first when we try those doors again."

Malian closed her eyes briefly, remembering that terrible force of will bent solely on finding her. Even thinking about it seemed to bring the danger nearer, as though she were drawing her enemies' attention. She forced herself back into the steady throb in her head. "We need to go together," she said, surprising herself with the clarity and strength of her voice. "I to find the way, and you to hide us from our enemies." Her fingers tightened over his. "Neither of us will make it on our own. And even if one did, there is no guarantee of finding the way back here again."

She felt the ring of truth in her words and saw the answering recognition in Kalan's face. "It seems very plain when you put it that way," he agreed, then looked away from her, frowning. "Truthsayer," he said under his breath, so low that she almost did not hear him.

Truthsayer. The word buzzed in Malian's head, sharper than the pain. Truthsaying was one of the old powers, like mindspeaking—and casting fire, although at least she hadn't done *that* yet. The other two powers were more than bad enough. Deliberately, Malian closed her mind to everything she had done—*was* doing—would mean once she returned to the New Keep. Right now, all that mattered was finding a way to return at all.

"Help me up," she said, grasping Kalan's arm. "I want to take a closer look at those doors."

The agony that knifed through her head as she rose was so intense that Malian nearly fainted again. She wavered, white faced, and Kalan supported her until the waves of pain and the accompanying nausea receded. His arm felt like rock, holding her up, but once her vision cleared Malian could see the fear and uncertainty in his eyes. She gave him her best attempt at a smile. "I'll manage," she said, trying to strengthen her voice. "Truly."

She circumnavigated the room with agonizing slowness, stopping at each of the twelve arched portals. It was exactly as Kalan had said: The veil of mist that had shimmered across each doorway had been replaced by a wall of impenetrable fog. The whiteness looked soft and yielding, as though she could put her hand into and through it easily, yet each time she tried the barrier was hard and cold as marble, repelling her touch. Malian peered at the detail of letters and symbols carved deep into the doorframes and realized that each door was different, as though every arch had a unique message to communicate—unmistakable as the distinct shock of power beneath her hand. At some doors, the primary feeling was one of indifference; at others hostility or a mix of emotions. But not one door would let Malian through.

"Twelve doors," she murmured at last, still leaning heavily on Kalan's arm. "And twelve sections to the table. But why twelve? If it had been nine the puzzle would be easy: one door and one section of the table for each of the nine gods, or the nine Houses, or both. But twelve?"

She heard Kalan's breath catch and felt the sudden tension in his arm. So he knew something, then, or was guessing at it. Malian waited, counting the tiles in the floor and keeping her own breath calm and steady to conceal her impatience. She felt rather than saw the turn of his head toward her, but kept her eyes down. "What if," he said, "there *were* twelve Houses, not nine?"

Her head jerked up, but the movement was too sharp and the pain bit deep. When she could speak, the words were gasped out. "But there's only ever been nine!"

Kalan looked unhappy. "I was told," he said, as though taking no responsibility for the veracity of his words, "that when the Swarm first rose and covered the heavens, not all Derai refused the lure of its power. It is said that there were those, even among our own people, who sought out the lightless dark and pledged themselves to its service— three of what were then the twelve Houses of the Derai, in fact. They became Darksworn, shadow warriors serving as the vanguard of the Swarm. Few know of it now and those who do are bound to secrecy with many oaths. But Brother Belan's wits wandered in his last years and he spoke to me of much that he should not have, including this. He even showed me the secret scrolls that record the story. It is called the Great Sundering and beside it, he said, even the Betrayal is as nothing."

Malian stared straight ahead with eyes that saw nothing. "How can that possibly be true?" she whispered. "If it were, then surely I, as Heir, would have been taught of it?"

Kalan shook his head. "It is forbidden," he answered. "The knowledge is permitted only to the very highest levels of the priesthood and possibly to the Earls—although I would not wager on that, these days. Brother Belan said that the truth, if widely known, would shatter the Derai Alliance. How could we continue to defend the Wall, believing that we alone have always stood against the Swarm of Dark, if we knew that Derai were also its foremost servants? How could we continue to believe ourselves the champions of the Nine?"

"How indeed?" echoed Malian, her tone hollow. She looked at Kalan intently. "And you really believe all this to be true?"

He shrugged, looking away. "Brother Belan used to be one of our greatest loremasters. And I have seen the records. I also saw the attackers when they first entered the Temple quarter last night." The glance he slid toward Malian was quick, uncertain. "At first, I couldn't recall where I had seen depictions of their armor before, but I remember now. They looked like us; not as we arm ourselves now, but as we used to do."

"They could have been our own Derai enemies," she said slowly, "from the House of Adamant or the House of Stars." But she remembered the were-hunters and the Raptor of Darkness and did not believe it herself.

"No," said Kalan. "I felt the Swarm taint, its mix of cold and evil that has been recorded so many times. The invaders were Darkswarm . . . but there was something of the Derai about them as well."

Derai amongst the Swarm. It was unthinkable—and yet Malian could not dismiss the conviction in Kalan's voice. Perversely, she could even be glad, a little, that the attackers were not from another of the nine Houses, particularly the House of Stars. Even the possibility of Derai amongst the Swarm was preferable to the heirs of Yorindesarinen, in their far-off citadel, plotting to kill her.

Malian stretched out a hand to steady herself against the nearest door arch, trying to think through the implications of what Kalan had told her. "Your Brother Belan was right," she said at last, her tone hollow. "This news would shake the foundations of the Wall itself." She wondered if that was part of what the attackers had intended—a strike at the Alliance on more than one level?

"Malian, look! Where your hand is!"

She saw the blaze of excitement in Kalan's face and realized that the doorframe had turned to gold beneath her hand. The script carved around the arch was alive with small, dancing flames and the symbol at the apex resolved itself into the image of a winged horse glittering with light. Puzzled, she looked more closely at the inscription and watched the letters waver, then shift, transforming into words that she could read.

"'I carry Night through void and flame,'" She murmured the words aloud. "'I move on more than one plane.' Of course!" She turned to Kalan. "What if we are on one plane here, but the keeps, both Old and New, are on another? That would mean that the Fire, if it is to protect us, would have to concentrate its presence on the plane where our enemies are located."

"And we have to get back to that plane if we are to have any hope of being found by a rescue party." Kalan studied the door uncertainly. "It's like the lights and the table, it seems to respond to your touch. But can we trust ourselves to it without the Fire actually being here?"

"We can't wait for the Fire to return," Malian replied soberly. "We don't even know that it will. We must find our own path—and I think it lies through this door."

Kalan shook his head. "I knew you were going to say that. Not that I have any better suggestions." He frowned at the wall of mist. "How to get through, though, that's the question."

"Mmm," agreed Malian. "But if the arch responds to my touch, like the table did . . . The Fire said that I must touch the table with both my hand and my mind and join my other hand to yours." She curled her fingers around Kalan's. "Well, my mind and one hand are on the door and we have each other. Shall we try our luck?"

He returned the clasp of her fingers, his frown lifting.

"Why not? Particularly given the unheroic alternative, which is to wait for something that may never happen!"

Malian smiled at him and the pain behind her eyes receded. "Waiting and staying alive can be heroic, if it thwarts your enemies. But dying slowly of starvation and thirst because you are afraid to act, is not. Now we must be bold."

"Then lead on," said Kalan. "I'm with you, Malian of Night."

10

In the Old Keep

"*T*here's something out there," Tarathan said, low voiced to Asantir.

They stared into the deep gloom of the Old Keep's lower halls and then back at the waiting file behind them: all black clad, with blacking on what would otherwise have been the pale blur of faces. There had been trouble over that when they set out, for not all those gathered behind them were Asantir's handpicked twenty, drawn from both the keep garrison and what was left of the Honor Guard. There were eight young priests, as well, all wearing the silver-gray robes of initiates—and their presence had caused quite a stir at the entrance to the Old Keep, both amongst the twenty and the few who had come to see them off.

Nhairin had been the first to protest. "You have the heralds," she had said sharply, but Asantir had remained firm.

"Two heralds," she had pointed out, "who have asked for the help, given what we may find in the Old Keep. You would not expect me to rely on just two warriors," she had added, with a touch of humor. She had leveled a dark, keen eye at Nhairin's frown and the disapproving faces behind her, her brows lifting a little. "They are coming with us," she had said, as cool and final as a steel blade.

No one seemed to have anything to say after that, except for Nhairin and even she was more guarded. "Initiates!" she had muttered, as she turned aside. "Green as grass and nothing more than a liability!" Most of the guards had looked as though they agreed, and the nearest of the priests had flushed deeply. But nothing more had been said until their small party reached the old High Hall and Asantir sprung her second unpleasant surprise—making it clear that she expected the priests to blacken their faces, too, and don the same garb worn by the warriors. Her sergeant, Sarus, had produced the required gear from his pack amidst a sudden, shocked silence.

It was Kyr who found his voice first. "This is warrior's gear. I know these heralds are wearing it, but priests? That can't be right, Captain, begging your pardon."

Even the slight, dark priestess who had accompanied Korriya earlier in the day, and who seemed to be the leader now, protested nervously. "Surely, Honor Captain, this is forbidden?"

"There is nothing in the Oath about clothing that I can recall, Initiate Eria." Asantir's sardonic gaze had swept the group. "And I'm really not prepared to have any of our number showing up like targets in the dark."

The warriors had exchanged reluctant shrugs and the priests, after a moment's hesitation, pulled off their full outer robes and replaced them with the black tunics and leggings. "Much more practical," Tarathan of Ar observed, to no one in particular, "if we have to run or fight." He, at least, seemed prepared for trouble, with the multiple braids of his hair clubbed into a knot and a pair of short, curved swords strapped to his back. Asantir's brows had risen again when she saw them, for swallowtail swords were a weapon of Ishnapur.

"And Jhaine," Tarathan had answered, when she said as much, "but they are popular now in the cities of the River." He had taken a blacking pot when Sarus handed them out and carefully spread the paste over his own face, before turning to help Eria with hers. It was plain that it was something he had done before, and equally clear that the young priestess had not. Asantir had shaken her head at her guards' expressions but said nothing, simply picked up a second pot and moved to assist another of the priests.

The guards had hesitated a moment longer before Garan rose with a shrug and went to help as well, closely followed by dark, silent Nerys. The blacking had been completed quickly after that, although in strained silence. They had then descended steadily through the Old Keep, scoring route markers into the walls as they went, and the only sounds were footsteps, breathing, and the occasional low-voiced conference between the heralds and Asantir. Tarathan had taken the lead from the beginning and led them unerringly, a file of shadows within shadow as the twilit gloom deepened toward full dark. Eventually, Asantir had given the reluctant order for light.

The young priests had exchanged glances as the guards unpacked storm lanterns, then Eria had brought out palm-sized cone lights that were secured by a strap across wrist and hand. Silently, she had offered one to Asantir. The cones had caps that could be flicked off with a thumb, emitting a shielded beam that fell no more than a few feet ahead of the holder. "Useful," was all Asantir said, but the look she had given Eria was very keen, and the storm lanterns were packed away again.

"Where do you think they got those?" Kyr had muttered to Garan. "They're plainly made for stealth work." But the younger guard just shrugged.

They walked on, light-footed and tense, hands resting on sword hilts and eyes seeking to penetrate beyond the narrow fall of light. The chill air seemed to thicken as they descended further, and every stumble or spurned pebble came back to them in eerie, hollow echoes. They were crossing a wide hall where all could sense, rather than see, the vast, soaring vault of stone above them, when Tarathan murmured his warning to Asantir.

They both listened intently. "There's another seeker," Tarathan said. "I can sense the power."

"Does this seeker know that we're here?" Asantir replied softly.

It was Jehane Mor who answered. "My mindshield holds—for now. But the closer we come to another seeker, the harder it will be to block the seeking out."

Asantir's gaze shifted back to Tarathan. "How close are we to Malian now?"

"Not close enough," he said slowly. "There is something strange at work, a sense that she is both *here* and *not here* that is difficult to resolve."

"But we are on the right track?" Asantir asked. Her frown lifted at the certainty of Tarathan's nod, but she kept her voice low. "What of these other seekers? Is one of them the Raptor of Darkness?"

"Last night's demon?" Tarathan's head moved in a quick negative. "I have not detected its presence. Whoever lies ahead is not someone I have encountered before."

"But even that," said Asantir, "is better than knowing nothing." She looked around. "Sarus, make sure the priests stay in the center, where they're protected, and strengthen our watch to the rear. I'll take the lead from now on. We can't afford to lose either of you," she added, turning back to the heralds.

Tarathan smiled slightly. "Can we afford to lose you, Captain?" he asked. "Besides, it is difficult enough to seek through this darkness without having either thoughts or jangling armor in my way."

"I'll try not to jangle," Asantir said dryly, "but we can't leave you unprotected." She glanced back at the main party where shields were being settled more firmly on arms and swords drawn. "It will definitely be close-quarters work down here," she added, and drew her own sword in a whisper of steel. She handed the cone light to Nerys, but Jehane Mor extended her hand before the guard could take it.

"Let me do it," she said. "I have to stay close to Tarathan

anyway, to shield his seeking most effectively. This way, Nerys will have two hands free to defend me."

Asantir nodded. "Try and keep the light angled so it falls just ahead of our feet. But make sure the beam stays low. We don't want to risk light blindness."

She looked over her armed and watchful party one more time, then gave the signal to move on. Every ear was strained, listening for any sound out of place, and the tension in the air was palpable. The priests drew in close behind Jehane Mor and the guards' eyes flicked to either side, while Kyr and the sergeant kept watch to the rear. Asantir walked catfooted at the front, her sword ready. No one spoke.

It was some time before the attack came. They had descended another long stair and come out into yet another hallway, where the walls were closer and the roof much lower overhead, when Jehane Mor gasped out: "Beware!"

Something streaked out of the darkness, straight as a flung spear. The attacker made no sound; there was just the sudden rush of air, an impression of driving wings and an outstretched, striking beak—and then Asantir's sword cut up, severing the creature's neck.

The attacker fell; the next moment a storm of the winged creatures hurtled along the low hall, attacking with vicious beaks and raking talons. Tarathan leapt to meet them, striking left and right with his swallowtail swords while Asantir's blade continued to bite, precise and deadly. "Draw in!" she commanded, her voice encompassing the entire party. "Shields up!" The guards obeyed, forming a tight circle around the noncombatants and clashing a shield wall into place.

"Roof's too low," Asantir remarked conversationally to Tarathan, holding her own shield to cover them both as they retreated, step by cutting step, into the circle of guards. "They can't get enough height to beat the shields."

The winged creatures seemed to prefer height, making no attempt to vary their pattern of attack, although they shrieked fiercely as they wheeled and dove. For a while their sheer numbers kept the battle even, but the shield circle held and the guard's swords continued to cut, disciplined and steady. The winged creatures either fell or circled sharply away from their blows. Then, as suddenly as the assault had begun, the remaining attackers wheeled around and sped back into the darkness.

"Hold your positions!" Asantir ordered. "Don't break formation! Anyone hurt?" she added after a moment.

A quick murmured response indicated that there were no serious injuries, although a few guards had sustained gashes from the slashing beaks and talons. "But what in Haarth were they?" someone asked in a shaken voice.

Asantir took the cone light from Jehane Mor and shone it onto one of the fallen creatures, illuminating a lizardlike body between long, leathery wings with sharp barbs at the end of each pinion. The head was bony, with a heavy, serrated beak, and the creature's short legs were razor taloned. "I've never seen them before," she said, "but I have heard them described. These are fell lizards, which some say are darkspawn but others claim are a Haarth creature corrupted by the Swarm. Either way, their presence usually means that other darkspawn aren't far away."

"Scouts, maybe," said Sarus.

Asantir stood up and handed the light back to Jehane Mor. "They could be hunting on their own, but we take no chances. I want a sharp watch kept while we see to these cuts. Give the alarm if you see or hear anything even slightly strange," she told the lookouts grimly. "Better that we jump at shadows before they jump us."

This got a general chuckle as the shield circle broke up and those who were not on lookout duty pulled out bandages and salves. Jehane Mor slid slowly down the wall to sit on the stone floor, her face drawn. Tarathan sheathed his swords quickly and knelt beside her, while Asantir squatted on her heels in front of the herald. "What's wrong?" she asked.

Jehane Mor shook her head. "I'm all right." But she spoke in a queer, slightly breathless way, like a person who has been running hard. She drew another, deeper breath before speaking again. "Something—a power—attacked hard just before the fell-lizards struck, so hard it was almost impossible for me to call a warning before it was too late."

"Was it the seeker?" Tarathan asked quietly.

"But in the moment that it attacked I felt something more, a flash of other powers out there." Jehane Mor's eyes met his. "Do you sense them?"

"Others?" Asantir said sharply.

Tarathan was silent a moment, as though listening. "I sense them. Their minds are cold, their purpose dark, and they, too, are hunting, seeking. I suspect that, like us, they hunt for your Heir."

"The psychic attack was designed to kill anything in its path," Jehane Mor said, speaking more easily. "But it also felt random, as though the attacker sensed another power but couldn't pinpoint our location or gauge our strength."

"A mindsweep," Tarathan said grimly. "But random or not, it's almost certain the seeker will have sensed your shield at work."

Jehane Mor nodded. "And will try and flush me out."

Asantir stared into the dark, her eyes narrowed. "Our enemies, it seems, still have teeth. Well," she added dryly, "if I had expected miracles, it would only be the three of us down here." She glanced around the small band of guards and priests, raising her eyebrows slightly at the sight of the initiate Eria helping Garan bandage his gashed forearm. "So long as you're sure that the concealing shield still holds, we'll push on. But we haven't had to contend with these psychic perils for many generations and I won't waste lives on a forlorn hope."

"There is another way of seeking," Tarathan said slowly, "but we will need to try it now, while Jehane's shield holds." He paused, but Asantir simply waited, her silence a question. "One can seek consciously on the physical plane, or one can seek through the psychic level by what we call mindwalking, which is what the shamans of the Winter people do when they dream through the smoke. But there are not many who have their skill."

"Or the strength to use it safely," murmured Jehane Mor.

Asantir frowned. "But surely the psychic plane is where the enemy threat is greatest?"

"It is," Tarathan agreed. "But my seeking will also be more powerful there, and swifter. And with other powers actively in play, we no longer have the luxury of time." He met Asantir's eyes squarely. "I will need Jehane to mind-walk with me, to shield me on the psychic plane. But given the danger here, the seeking will also have to be shielded in the physical realm."

"So we all bear the increased risk," said Asantir. "I suppose that's only fair." She looked around at the watching priests and guards. "But is it wise?"

Jehane Mor's eyes followed Asantir's gaze. "It is necessary, Captain. And although your priests are young and untried, there are eight of them. Together they should be strong enough to shield us on this plane."

"I'm not sure I like *should* be," Asantir murmured. But the heralds said nothing, simply looked back at her until she gave a short nod. "Then may Ornorith favor us, since she loves a risk taker. Tell me what we must do to make this mindwalking happen?"

Tarathan nodded, his gaze as dark as hers. "We must find a place where Jehane Mor and I can go into a deep trance. Somewhere defensible," he added, not quite as an afterthought.

Yet the further they descended the more of a labyrinth the Old Keep became. Every doorway was a lightless hole that opened into yet another corridor, or onto more narrow twisted stairs. Those rooms they did find were small, with only one door. "Deathtraps!" said Sarus. No one disagreed, although they were losing precious time and there was more than one sigh of relief when they finally found a chamber large enough for their purpose. It opened off one of the wider hallways and also had a second, smaller door leading onto the usual twisting stair.

Garan regarded both sets of doors, which were sagging off their hinges, with misgiving. "I don't like this at all."

"Rotten," said Sarus, rapping his fist against one of them. "We'll have to see what we can do, construct some kind of barricade."

The next few minutes were a flurry of activity as packs were swung off backs and Asantir split the guards into two groups. One team, under Sarus, was posted at the stairwell door while their main strength was with Asantir, at the larger entrance. The heralds gathered the priests together and Jehane Mor looked into each of their faces in turn. Some met her gaze, but others dropped their eyes or looked away. The herald's voice was even as she told the priests what she and Tarathan intended—and what was expected of them. All eyes flew back to hers then, wide with consternation, but no one spoke.

"Well?" Jehane Mor said softly.

The young faces looked at each other and then to Eria, as their spokesperson. The initiate shook her head. "We were proud to be chosen for this mission, Herald Jehane, and to be of service to our House. But now we are here and have seen what you do . . ." Her voice trailed away and she shook her head again.

"What have you seen?" the herald asked patiently.

"What real strength is," the young man beside Eria said harshly, bitterness stamped across his broad, blunt face.

"Hush," Eria said quickly, but the boy on her other side, who had narrow hazel eyes in a thin, clever face, spoke up impatiently.

"Torin's only saying what we all know, Eria—that Herald Jehane has been protecting us all."

"Ay," said Torin, still bitter. "We might as well not be here."

"Perhaps the High Steward was right," said the tall girl beside him. "Perhaps we are just a liability."

"We don't know why you asked for us at all," said another young woman, her eyes fixed on her feet.

"What is your name?" Jehane Mor asked.

The bent head lifted. "Tisanthe," she said, plainly shy.

"And you?" the herald asked the tall girl.

"Terithis," she answered, bolder than her friend.

"Var," said the priest with the thin, clever face, in answer to the herald's look.

"And you are Torin," the herald said to the young man on Eria's other side, with a small nod. She looked at the other three, who still remained silent. "Will you tell me your names as well?"

"Armar," said the lad beside Torin, with a quick bob of his head. Freckles marched across his beaky nose and he was all bony wrists and ankles in his borrowed black clothes. The youth at his shoulder contented himself with a swift upward glance out of eyes that were so darkly blue that they looked almost as black as his hair.

"Serin," he murmured, quickly lowering his eyes again, while the young woman beside him, who was similar enough in face and coloring to be his twin, spoke at the same time.

"I'm Ilor," she said.

"So," said Jehane Mor. She inclined her head gravely to all of them. "We would not have asked for you," she said simply, "if we didn't need your help."

Torin looked at her suspiciously. "You could just be saying that, to encourage us."

Jehane Mor smiled. "I could," she agreed, "but heralds of the Guild do not lie."

There was a brief, abashed silence before Eria, obviously pulling herself together, said, "We will do all that we can, but you must know by now that none of us is very strong in either seeking or shielding. Those particular talents have all but died out in the past century."

"We may," said Var, as ironic as Torin was bitter, "be amongst the best the Temple quarter has, but that—unfortunately—doesn't make us very strong."

"Individually, perhaps," said Tarathan, speaking for the first time, "but collectively your small abilities will amount to something far more substantial. You are no different, in that way, from any of the warriors here, who would all be hard-pressed on their own. Yet by standing and working together, they defeated the fell-lizard attack."

The circle of priests looked at each other, clearly taken aback.

"Tarathan is right," said Jehane Mor. "And I can teach you a shield form that will help you find your strength. It is very strong if all involved bind themselves to it."

The priests exchanged another swift look. "Show us," Eria said.

Jehane Mor reached out, holding Eria's eyes with her own, and shaped the outline of the initiate's face with her hand—and then all the young faces lifted as one as the herald's power rippled over them. "This shielding is called Eight," she said, her voice light on water. "To build the shield you must open your minds, first to me and then to all your comrades. The weave follows the pattern of the number, which is infinite, a flow without beginning or end. You must become one with that flow so that you are no longer singular and weak, but Eight and strong."

The herald looked from one face to the next, around their circle. "Can you see it?" she asked, very soft. "Can you feel the power?"

Eria drew in a shaky breath. "I feel it," she said.

"I feel like a mote," Tisanthe whispered, "a tiny spark in the middle of something vast."

"It's like floating in a river of light." Var was exultant.

"It is all those things, and far more," said Jehane Mor. "You must be part of it and it of you, but do not let it overpower you. You are neither the Eight's servant nor its master, but rather the fish, swimming in an infinite stream. You may swim with the current or against it, so long as it is you who chooses that path."

"If pressure is brought against you," said Tarathan, "then

you must pour yourselves, mind and spirit, into the Eight. No matter what else happens you must remain as one within the flow, in order to maintain the shield. Never forget that it is working together that makes you strong. The moment you allow yourself to be pulled out of the flow, you will be alone again and vulnerable."

"And those who remain," concluded Jehane Mor, "will no longer be Eight. You can reform as Six or Four, but the greatest power lies in the seamless infinite; anything less than an Eight will always be considerably weaker." She looked around at their serious faces and shining eyes. "Do you think you can do this, hold the shield?"

"We will try," Eria said, her expression serious, but Torin tossed his head.

"Of course we can do it," he said. "It doesn't seem that difficult."

"No-o-o," agreed Terithis, more cautiously. "But how long must we hold it?"

"Until we return," said Tarathan, with finality. "Time passes differently on the psychic plane and we don't know how long we will be gone. It could be minutes here, but it could also be hours."

"Not so easy after all," said Var. Eria squared her shoulders.

"We will just have to do the best we can," she said.

"No," said Asantir from behind them. "You are Derai and will do whatever it takes. You will hold this shield for as long as the heralds need it."

They all jumped, for none of them had heard her quiet approach. The keen eyes measured them and they flushed, shifting nervously. "Sister Korriya told me you are the best that the Temple has," Asantir told them, "and she chose you to serve your Earl and your House. There is no doubt in my mind that you will fulfill her trust."

No one spoke or even exchanged a glance but all the initiates drew themselves up a little straighter. Asantir, however, had already turned to the heralds. "We have this place as defensible as it can be. Are you ready for your mindwalking?"

"We are," the heralds said, speaking in their one, blended voice. They conferred briefly with the priests and then lay down, side by side, with Tarathan's head pointing toward the main doors and Jehane Mor's to the postern. Both heralds crossed their arms over their chests, but while Jehane Mor's hands were empty, Tarathan held a naked, swallowtail blade in either hand. The swords gleamed in the soft glow of the cone lights as the priests formed a figure-of-eight around the heralds and the guards watched with a mixture of curiosity and distaste.

Eria, Tisanthe, Var, and Torin took the inner positions, close to the feet and heads of the heralds, while Terithis and Armar, Serin, and Ilor formed the outer curves of the Eight. All their faces were subdued as they sat cross-legged, facing away from the heralds, and the light from the cone lamps spilled around them in an incandescent figure-of-eight.

Tarathan looked up at Asantir. "Be vigilant," he said, "for the enemy is very near."

She nodded and then both heralds closed their eyes, still as carven stone at the heart of the silence that emanated from the Eight. The Honor Captain studied them for a long moment, then called four of the guards to her. "This is your watch," she told them. "I do not want anyone to reach this Eight unless all four of you are dead." Garan nodded, his dark, mobile face serious, while his companions, Mareth and Korin, murmured their acquiescence. Only Nerys remained silent as she took up a position between Terithis and the postern, her hand resting on her sword hilt.

Asantir nodded, satisfied, then crossed to the main door and stared into the shadowed hall. "Oh, yes," she murmured, "they are close. It doesn't need a seeker to know that." She looked across the room to Sarus. "Keep a sharp eye out, old friend. It may be more than cold steel we have to deal with."

The sergeant grunted, settling his shield more firmly

on his arm, and she smiled slightly, as if that were answer enough. The guard, Soril, who was from the keep garrison, looked from one to the other doubtfully. "Are you sure there's something out there, Captain?"

"Ay," said Asantir, "and they know we're here as well. We are past seekers and shielding now, as far as that goes."

"How do you know?" asked Ber, another guard from the keep garrison.

Sarus chuckled from the other side of the room. "How does the raven scent battle? It's in the very air."

Kyr, squatting on his heels at the sergeant's side, had taken out a whetstone and was carefully honing his sword blade. "It's a matter of time, that's all," he said, without looking up.

"And time," murmured Asantir, with a quick glance back at the heralds, "is what we most need right now."

They waited, while the long minutes crawled by and became an hour. Tension coiled in the air, like the feeling of a storm about to break. The cone lamps burned on, clear and steady, and the guards settled and resettled their weapons. And then the attack came, a swift rush out of the dark.

Asantir saw the light first, a pale witch-glow that came streaming down the corridor with shadows running behind it. "Here they come," she said conversationally—and then the first wave was on them, a silent, snarling rush of warriors with the eldritch light spilling around them. Steel clashed on steel as Asantir shouted the battle cry of the House of Night and the guards to her left and right echoed it as they too leapt forward to engage the foe. For a moment, the witchlight wavered and drew back.

As swiftly as it had ebbed, however, it came flowing back and then the fight was on in earnest, a desperate reeling to and fro in the doorway with the attackers pressing fiercely forward and the defenders withstanding the assault. Shields pushed back against spearpoint and sword blade, the defenders' swords cutting and slashing in bitter answer. The narrowness of the door meant that only a few attackers or defenders could contest it at any one time, but there were always more attackers pressing forward over their fallen fellows and only a small number of defenders in reserve.

Nonetheless, the fight seemed very even, trampling back and forward across the threshold, which became slick and wet with blood. Asantir cut hard and fast with her sword, despite her wounded shoulder, and used her shield like a weapon, hammering it into her opponents' faces. Ber and Soril pressed forward on either side, supporting her, and there was no more breath for war cries. The attackers, too, fought in silence, fierce and deadly in their antique armor, with the black visors down across their faces, each helmet wrought into an alien and terrifying shape. The eldritch light billowed and ebbed around them, seeming to follow the success or failure of their attacks.

Behind the melee, one of the priests gave a terrible scream and collapsed to the floor. The pale light surged forward, up and over Ber like a wave that breaks against a cliff. He screamed, too, and flung up his hands to claw at his face, dropping his sword and letting his shield fall. An attacker followed through with a spear thrust to Ber's chest, then made to push on over the fallen body and into the room.

The guards behind pushed forward to close the gap—but the pale tide washed on over Mareth, who writhed and fell in his turn. His scream echoed that from another of the priests behind them, a woman's wail of anguish. "Stand firm!" shouted Asantir, as she and Soril struggled to turn the flank of the attack. "Defend, House of Night!"

Another guard sprang to aid them and Eria and the remaining priests shouted, as if in answer to the captain's call, a tremendous, unified cry that thundered in the chamber's low roof. The lights in their hands flared into columns of incandescent white, transforming almost instantly to a blaze of molten gold that hurtled outward like spears, straight into the heart of the eldritch light. The two fires clashed and twisted upward in a conflagration that echoed the cut and thrust of the battle, but the golden flame blazed hotter, towering to the roof. Gradually the pale light withered and shrank, dwindling until it was totally consumed.

The attackers broke and ran, leaving their dead behind them. The golden light flowed after them, crackling at their heels but neither consuming nor slaying as the witchlight had done.

"Hold!" commanded Asantir, for the second time that day. "Hold all positions! Our job is to defend this place, not pursue." Astonishingly, even the golden light seemed to heed her command: It retreated as swiftly as it had raced out, splitting into six streams again as it reentered the chamber. The streams flowed back into the palm lamps, which continued to glitter, luminous and golden. A faint golden glow remained in the air, casting a sheen across the six remaining priests. Their faces were remote and calm, lost in their trance, but all six were drenched in sweat.

"Well, I'll be damned!" said Sarus, but he sounded shaken.

Both Serin and Ilor were dead, their mouths stretched into a rictus, their beautiful, dark blue eyes holes that stared at nothing. They were both sprawled on their backs, Serin with his arms flung wide; blood had burst from their ears and nostrils, but was already starting to congeal. "Mind-burned," said Garan, kneeling beside them. "There was nothing physical for us to fight—nothing we could do."

"I know," Asantir said heavily. She rested a gauntleted hand briefly on his shoulder.

"Was that the Golden Fire?" Lira, one of the honor guards standing with Sarus, was staring at the cone lamps. "Has it come back?" Her voice was full of hope.

"Perhaps," said Asantir. "But it may simply have been some property of the lamps themselves. Do not hope too much, Lira. We need to be sure."

She returned to the door where the living guards were sorting out the wounded from the dead. Ber and Mareth looked much like the dead priests, their seared eyes still staring at some horror only they could see. Two others lay sprawled in death beside them, while Soril moaned on the ground, her intestines oozing from the terrible wound where a blow had cut clean through her mail shirt. Korin had removed her helmet, and Soril looked up at Asantir with pain-glazed eyes.

The guard's lips moved as though she were trying to say something, but all that came out was another agonized moan and a trickle of blood. Asantir knelt at her side, bending close to hear the words she was trying so desperately to say.

"Mercy . . ." The whisper was wrenched out, followed by another bubbling moan.

Asantir held Soril's eyes with her own, gripping the guard's hand. With her other hand, the one that Soril could not see, she slid a fine, slender dagger from its sheath in her boot and bent close. "Go well," she said and slid the dagger in under Soril's ear, into her brain.

Asantir continued to kneel, her head bent over the dead guard as she murmured the invocation to Hurulth, Lord of Death, the Silent God—and then she stood up, her mouth set in a hard line. "Lay our dead to one side," she said, "and cover them with their cloaks." She swept a cursory glance over the bodies of the attackers that lay across the threshold. "As for the others, make certain they're really dead before you get too close. Once you're sure, drag them well clear of the door and leave them. But they are Darkswarm, so best put them where we can still see them."

"Otherwise we wait and watch, is that it?" Sarus spoke from his post by the smaller door.

"As before," Asantir agreed, "until our friends here get back from wherever it is they've gone." She looked around at their reduced numbers, narrowing her eyes at the golden motes that still shimmered in the air. "Let's hope they don't take too long."

11

The Gate of Dreams

Malian was dreaming again, but this time her dream was not of darkness but of light. Light burned around her, as though she were standing in the heart of a fire, except that she felt no heat and the flames did not consume her. Voices murmured, but as with the hunters' cries in the Old Keep, Malian could make no sense of them: They hovered just beyond the boundaries of understanding.

The flames spiraled up, whirling around her in a white-gold conflagration and then separating to leave a clear space in their center—a window that Malian could peer through, into the room on its far side. A rose motif was repeated in the wall hangings and other furnishings, and a deep winged armchair had been placed before the fire, which burned silently in a small grate. A man lounged in the armchair, his long legs stretched out toward the blaze. His clothes were as golden as his hair and he was reading a slender book with a tattered cover. "Haimyr," said Malian, leaning forward, but a shadow moved in the corner of her eye and she drew back.

Haimyr looked up from the book, and Malian realized that the shadow must be someone entering the room in which he sat. "Nhairin," he said, in his golden voice. Malian could not see the steward but she could hear them both, as clearly as though she, too, stood in the room.

"What are you doing here?" Nhairin's tone was sharp.

Haimyr's answering smile was lazy. "Why, reading, my dear Nhairin." He had, Malian remembered, always enjoyed teasing the more serious and upright steward. "It's quite all right, this time I have asked permission, both to be here and to read the book. But I could ask you the same question." He laid the volume to one side and straightened a little in the chair. "Why are you here?"

Nhairin's voice was restless. "Looking for you, of course. It's been so long, half the day and well into the night already, and we've heard nothing. And I thought about this fire, that it might be possible to see through it the other way and learn something of what is happening." The shadow moved, unsettled as the voice, on the periphery of Malian's vision.

"The Old Keep's a vast place. We must expect them to be some time. But as for the fire . . ." The minstrel's voice was measured as he looked into the flames—and it was as though he gazed straight at Malian, through her window. His eyes flared, golden and lambent as the fire itself, and she was sure that he could see her. She stepped toward him, but before she could speak he bent forward, picked up a log, and tossed it onto the blaze. A shower of sparks, hot and fiery, flew up in Malian's face as the fire flared, licking across the window so that both Haimyr and the rose room disappeared. The last thing Malian heard was his voice, smooth as silk. "You know how it drew you in last time, in spite of yourself. Best not to meddle, lest we open ourselves to forces we cannot deal with."

What forces? Malian wondered, as the window disappeared. Couldn't he see it was me? She wanted to try and open the window in the fire again but something else was tugging at her attention, insistent as a tide. "What?" she demanded crossly.

The light in her dream contracted, the flames spinning together before gradually paling and drifting apart. She found herself in a dark forest where the crowns of the trees were so tall they hid the sky, and the moon and stars seemed to be caught in the net of their branches. Her feet brushed against long grass that was chill with dew, and tendrils of white mist swirled around her knees. She was standing on what appeared to be a small knoll above banks of white fog, with trees stretching away on all sides and a narrow path running down into the whiteness.

Malian shivered and wondered where her dream had brought her.

A slight sound made her spin around to see Kalan walking out of the fog, materializing first as a shadow and then as a creature of substance and life. "What are you doing here?" Malian asked. "Isn't this my dream?"

Kalan frowned. "I thought it was mine. I saw you walking away from me into the mist and thought I should follow. There didn't seem much point in staying behind."

Malian had a feeling there was more to it than that, but she couldn't quite remember what. She looked doubtfully at the thick, white fog lying between the dark trees. "Well, waking or dreaming, we're both here now. But there's something very strange about this place."

Kalan, too, was looking around uneasily. "I know, something uncanny. It feels as though it could be dangerous, but isn't. At least, not right now."

Malian felt the tug at her awareness again, steady and compelling. "Something's calling to me, pulling at me to follow the path into the trees. I'm not sure I should, though."

"Well, we can't just stay here." Kalan shrugged. "And if this is a dream, we'll probably wake up back where we started anyway."

"If it's a dream," Malian said thoughtfully. Memories of stepping through a golden gate into white mist were starting to come back to her and she tilted her chin at the dark forest. "So let's see where this leads us."

They walked down into the fog, which rolled up to meet them and was so thick and wet and eerily white that they could barely see the path ahead. But they had only covered what felt like a short distance when the whiteness began to lift, revealing vast trunks that soared skyward. The pattern of stars had shifted and the moon, too, had sunk deeper into the net of branches.

Malian sniffed. "Do you smell smoke?" she whispered.

Kalan pointed to a tendril of darker mist, curling through the trees. "There," he said softly. "Woodsmoke."

They continued on more slowly, peering around the dark trunks and into dense, tangled shadows. Initially, the scent of woodsmoke grew fainter as trees and undergrowth closed around them again, but it strengthened when the forest opened into a narrow, moon-washed glade. A fire was burning in the center of the clearing and a figure sat beside it, wrapped in a dark, hooded cloak. "You may come closer," the cloaked figure bade them, without turning around. The voice that spoke was a woman's, low and clear and pleasant. "It's quite safe."

The voice inspired confidence, but Malian and Kalan were children of the Derai and knew that enemies came in numerous guises, many of which could seem fair on the surface. They wanted to see the face inside the dark hood, if there was one, before they came too close. As though reading their thoughts, the woman reached up and pushed back the hood, revealing a face that was unmistakably Derai. A net of tiny white stars held the cloud of her black hair in place, while the moonlight revealed high cheekbones above a strong jaw, shadowed eyes, and a humorous curve to the woman's mouth. "Welcome to my fire," she said, and patted the ground. "Sit. I would speak with you a while before the moon wanes."

Malian sat down on the opposite side of the fire and Kalan squatted beside her, letting the rose and orange flames dance between them and this woman they did not know. "Will the moon wane?" Kalan asked. "I mean, isn't this a dream?"

"Is it?" the woman replied. "And if it is, is it impossible that dreams should have their own times and seasons?" She shifted slightly and Malian caught a glitter of silver beneath the black cloak.

"It feels like a dream to us," Malian replied. "But if it is a dream, are you in our dream or are we in yours?"

The woman smiled. "Well asked, my dear," she said. "The truth, as you are beginning to discover, is that the Gate of Dreams opens to many places and in more than one direction. But the two of you had the power to walk through and find your way to my fireside. I am impressed."

"Who are you?" asked Kalan bluntly. "How do we know that what you tell us is true?"

She grinned at him across the fire. "You can't know," she said, "either who I am or whether I speak the truth." Her smile widened as both Kalan and Malian blinked. "Not for certain. But you can learn to trust the judgment of your heart, both to discern truth and sift out falsehood." She paused. "Besides, you do know my name, Kalan of the House of Blood, just as I know yours—and that you have a true spirit."

Kalan flushed and looked suspicious at the same time. "How do you know that I'm from the House of Blood?" he asked. "Or anything else about me?"

"Dear lad," the woman replied, "it's obvious—as obvious as the fact that you are sitting at my fire with a child born into the House of Night, of the Blood itself if I'm not mistaken." She arched a slender black eyebrow in Malian's direction as if to say: *Am I not right?*

"Yes," said Malian, answering the unspoken question. She stared hard at the woman, frowning. "Your voice is familiar," she said slowly, "and yet I don't think we've met before." She continued to frown and then exclaimed, "It was *your* voice I heard, just before the Fire rescued me from the Raptor of Darkness! It was you who told me to hold on!"

"Yes," the woman replied gravely. "You were very close to me then, which is why I could speak to you directly and you could hear me."

Malian shivered, wondering if that was because she had

been close to death; the compassion in the woman's eyes confirmed her suspicion. "It was you later, as well," she said slowly, pushing away the horror of the Raptor's attack. "In the darkness, when the eldritch fire almost caught me. You told me not to touch it."

The woman nodded. "The limbo in which you floated was on a plane between worlds and time. It is connected to this place, which also lies beyond what we call the Gate of Dreams, so I could reach you quite readily—which was just as well, under the circumstances."

Remembering the pale fire that had reached out to entrap her, Malian had to agree. But that did not tell her who this woman was, or *why* she had helped. She studied the fire-tinted face opposite. "You said that we know your name, but not that we know you. And you may have spoken to me twice now, but I still don't think we'd met before that."

"Yes and no," the woman answered, smiling at her. "No and yes. It is true that we have never met before, but I am not unknown to you. And I have been waiting for you, my dear, for a very long time." She included Kalan in the smile, a hint of melancholy tingeing her expression. "You, however, I did not expect. And born to the House of Blood as well; now there's a mystery. Still," she added musingly, more to herself than to him, "I was promised that she would not be alone."

Malian's hands clenched into fists. "Who promised?" she demanded. "Why have you been waiting for me? Who *are* you?"

The cloaked woman picked up a stick and poked the fire into a flurry of sparks and flame that swirled into the night, revealing a long scar, which ran in a pale, jagged line down the right side of her face, from hairline to jaw. "Warrior kind," said Kalan, before he could stop himself. But the woman only smiled.

*"Warrior kind I am" she chanted, "and priest kind
    am I,
Born of the night and of the light,*

Sword wearing, fire bearing,
Who then am I, child of the Derai?"

Malian and Kalan looked at each other. "House of Stars!" they exclaimed with one voice.

Kalan grinned, but Malian continued to study the woman intently. Her mouth opened slightly as though to speak, then shut again. Eventually she swallowed hard and said in a sort of croak: "You said that we know your name . . . And the rhyme belongs to the House of Stars, but everyone knows that it particularly applies to the one we call the Child of Stars. Yet surely that's impossible . . ." Her voice trailed away.

The woman looked at her very kindly. "The rhyme is indeed mine," she said.

Malian swallowed again. "Then you must . . . Yet how can you possibly be . . . Are you—*Yorindesarinen*?"

The woman clapped her hands together in soft approval. "Yorindesarinen, I am," she said, "called by some the Bright, born of the House of Stars."

"Er, excuse me," said Kalan stiffly, when Malian remained silent, staring across the fire in amazement, "but didn't you, um, die?" His voice gained strength. "In fact, didn't you die a long time ago, before the Derai even came to this world?"

Wordlessly, she opened her cloak so they could see the mail beneath, gleaming silver in the moonlight. While they watched it became dull, hacked in a hundred places, with blood dried black around the wounds and in slow runnels across the armor's surface. "In the world beyond the Gate of Dreams," Yorindesarinen replied, "I did indeed die long ago, slain in my battle with the Worm of Chaos, even though I killed it at the last. We died for each other, that Worm and I." As she finished speaking, the hacked and bloodied armor transformed into gleaming silver again.

The hero grinned at Kalan's expression. "Are you afraid that I'm a ghost? I assure you, I am neither ghost nor ghoul.

If you know my story you will know that we nearly lost to the Swarm in that great battle, or series of battles as it actually was, because of the Worm of Chaos. It was huge, ferocious, and terrible; wherever it came, our forces broke and fled before it. It had to be stopped, but in the end only I was prepared to go against it. There was no one else left, either comrade or sword kin, willing to stand with me. So I fell. I died on that field before I could realize the destiny I was born to fulfill."

"You stood alone." Tears pricked Malian's eyes. "Yet even alone you defeated the Worm and so saved the Derai and all the worlds we fought to protect."

Yorindesarinen smiled sadly. "It sounds grand, does it not? Yet I hope that you will never have to know the loneliness that I knew then, or the dread that froze my blood, or the agony as I lay dying with the Worm's wounds on my body and the Worm's venom in my veins. And it should not have been so."

She lifted her face to the moon, caught in the net of tree branches. "It should not have been so," she repeated softly, "for I was born to unite the Derai and lead them to the final victory against our enemy. That was the destiny written in the stars in the hour of my birth—but the Swarm, too, can read the stars. It brought the Worm against us to thwart prophecy, so that I had no choice but to slay it or see the destruction of the Derai and all worlds." She paused. "Yet I was promised, even as I lay dying, that another would come to unite the Derai and that one would not have to stand alone—would not be alone. I was promised, too, that I might wait for the One-to-Come, for she would need my aid. So wait I have, and watched, all these long years."

"For me?" Malian asked faintly. "You can't possibly mean me."

"No?" inquired Yorindesarinen. "Why not?"

"Well, I'm just an ordinary person," Malian protested. "I'm not anyone special, a hero or an enchanter. I'm just myself."

"Just yourself," said Yorindesarinen musingly. "That can be a very large thing or a small one, depending on the person. And what does it mean in your case? Who are you, my dear? What is the sum of this ordinary self of yours?"

Malian drew herself up, straightening her spine despite the hero's kindly tone. "I am Malian," she declared, not without pride, "daughter of the Earl, Heir to the House of Night—the first and oldest of all the Derai Houses."

Yorindesarinen bowed, her dark head bending so that the starry jewels glittered and danced. "Greetings, Heir of Night," she said formally, and then her smile glinted, bright as the stars in her hair. "Yet is that not something more than ordinary, to be the Heir of Night? And clearly you have other powers as well, to have passed the Gate of Dreams and found me here."

"But," said Kalan, speaking up abruptly, "that doesn't make her the One of the old prophecies, which all say that the One-to-Come will be born of the Blood of the House of Stars." He grinned a little at Malian's surprised expression. "They make novices learn that kind of stuff. Besides, the prophecies are one of Brother Selmor's special studies. He said that no one bothers to learn them now, outside the Temple quarter, and even inside the temples most regard them as peripheral."

"Yet you know them," murmured Yorindesarinen. "So tell me what they say, Kalan of the House of Blood."

Kalan shrugged. "The promise of the One-to-Come is supposed to be our oldest legend, born in the time when the Dark first swarmed and the Derai alone stood against it. It is said that Mhaelanar promised that a champion would come, his shield born into the world, to turn back the Swarm. The prophecy says that the Chosen of Mhaelanar will be born of both the House of Stars and the House of Night, and will unite the Derai for the final victory over the Swarm." He looked at the woman across the fire. "You were—the hero, Yorindesarinen, that is—was born of the House of Stars, but her—*your*—mother was of the Blood of Night. But in the past five hundred years, with the schism between Night and Stars, everyone has rather given up hope of the prophesied champion."

Yorindesarinen looked at Malian. "Tell him who your mother was," she said.

Kalan rolled his eyes. "Nerion, daughter of Nerith of the Sea Keep. Everyone knows that!"

"They do," agreed Yorindesarinen. "What is not so well known is that Amboran of Night was Nerith's second husband. Her first was Serianrethen, who was the youngest son of the Earl of Stars. As it happens, it was a very short-lived union, since Serianrethen was killed on a Wall patrol. Nerith only discovered that she was with child after her return to the Sea Keep, but she chose not to tell the Earl of Stars because she wanted to keep the child for herself. She remarried quickly, to Amboran, so when Nerion was born everyone just assumed that he was the father and the babe had come early." She smiled at Kalan. "So you see, Malian does indeed come of both lines, Stars and Night."

"But why," Malian objected, "should having the Blood of both Houses make me this One you speak of? Surely Stars and Night must have intermarried many times in the past?"

Yorindesarinen nodded. "Not many times, but a few, until the civil war five hundred years ago. But since I died and you were born"—the hero's face grew grim—"no children of those few unions has ever lived to see adulthood. They died as babes or in early childhood, always from illness or by some accident."

"It could have been coincidence," Malian said. Yorindesarinen shrugged, her smile thin.

"A fortunate coincidence, for the Swarm. As for the secret of your heritage, it seemed well kept, but this attack can only mean that the enemy has learned of it at last. Make no mistake, the Swarm, too, believes that you are the One-to-Come." A flash of genuine humor replaced the thin smile. "The Darkswarm and I could both be wrong, of course, but you did wake the Golden Fire last night—or it roused itself to protect you—for the first time in five hundred years. That speaks of a very great power indeed, Malian of Night."

Malian shivered. "Even then, I nearly didn't survive."

Yorindesarinen nodded, grim faced again. "And now the Swarm will not rest until you are dead. This attack will only be the first and the Derai Alliance, after so many years of bloodletting, is no longer strong enough to protect you." She sighed. "Too late, the Derai will realize the bitter price of the folly that has allowed their once-great powers to wither. But you, my dear, must not be part of that bitter payment. You must flee the enemy and hide—and look outside the Derai for aid to develop your powers."

"To those like the Guild?" asked Malian. She remembered the power she had sensed in the heralds when she saw them in the High Hall, and the piercing light in their eyes.

"Perhaps," said the hero. "But there are more powers in this world than the Derai suspect—or the Swarm either, for all that they have begun sending emissaries with gifts and honeyed words to every city along the River."

Malian shook her head. "But to leave the Wall . . . And I don't know these other powers. How will I discern between enemies and friends?"

"You must learn to know them," Yorindesarinen said. "That is the point. For not all the forces that move and coalesce around you are enemies. There are many friends as well, some open and some still hidden from you. But you must remain well hidden until you have grown into your full power. Both of you," she added, looking from one to the other, "must remain hidden."

She fell silent, staring into the fire as though she had dismissed them from her mind. Malian, too, gazed into the fire and slowly she began to relax. Somewhere between walking through the golden door into the mist and emerging in the dark wood, the headache that had incapacitated her in the Old Keep had vanished. Now her weariness was lifting, too, and she saw the marks of strain in Kalan's face easing. She sighed deeply, her arms folded around her drawn-up knees.

The fire was not large but it burned very brightly, the weave of the flames fluid and constantly changing. Malian felt herself drawn to the pattern, white and lavender and palest saffron, that flickered in the fire's heart, gazing into its snap and brilliance until she felt made of fire herself. She let her awareness meld into the white-hot core—and just as in her dream, the flames burned fiercely but did not consume her and the fire became a window. But this time, instead of looking into a firelit room, Malian was gazing down, as from a great height, into a world she did not know.

The landscape was formed of low, rounded hills and jagged rock outcrops beneath a strange, bruised sky. A line of warriors rode in double column along a narrow defile, while the sky above them darkened from lavender to plum. Their attackers seemed to rise out of the ground itself, charging in to hack and slay. Swords rose and fell and Malian, unable to do anything but watch, could hear the cries of men and the screams of horses as they died. The riders tried to rally around their leader, to hold a path for his escape, but there were too many attackers. One by one the riders fell until the leader alone was left and his assailants closed in, yammering war cries and poised to cut him down. The next moment he vanished, winking out from beneath their blades. The attackers howled beneath the bruised sky and Malian, too, drew in a breath, sharp with surprise.

The flames swirled before her eyes, then parted again to show another scene, another place. A moon rose, pale as gold above a world of tiled roofs interspersed with graceful spires. Malian felt as though she were soaring above them, springing from rooftop to rooftop and filled with wild exultation despite being pursued. Yet she did not know who pursued her, or why.

The moon waxed to fullest gold, then waned, turning pale and cold, a wisp of its former self. Malian stood beneath it in a lonely place, waiting for something or somebody to appear; she knew that it was autumn, the dying season of the year. She called out, but only silence answered. A veil of mist drifted across the waning moon and swallowed it. When it rose again, it was a daylight moon sailing above a paved road that wound through gray hills. A long cavalcade of people and horses, carts and palanquins, crawled along the road; banners snapped bravely overhead and long narrow pennants furled and unfurled on the wind.

Malian recognized the significance of the pennants: This was a Derai wedding caravan, taking some scion of the Blood to meet his or her bride or groom. She noticed a wagon being dug out of the mud by cursing retainers and drifted closer. One of the guards, clad in quilted leather and a chain-mail shirt, frowned at the leaden sky, wiping his hands on his leather trousers.

Malian's eyes widened, for although a few years older and considerably grimmer, the warrior wore Kalan's face. She was so surprised that she shot back up and away from the road, and the fire wrapped around her vision again. When it drew away, she was standing in a room hung with crimson draperies in the Derai style. A young woman in jeweled crimson robes, with a shy, beautiful face, looked back at her in surprise. "Who are you?" she asked. "What are you doing here?" Her voice was steady, but Malian could tell that she was afraid.

She opened her mouth to answer but the flames snatched away the room and instead showed her a cobbled street, wreathed in mist. The body of a warrior was slumped facedown on the slick cobbles. His armor was bloody and he had lost his helmet. A cloud of black hair, matted with blood, fell around his shoulders and onto the path, pooling around his face. The prone figure called to Malian and she longed to lift back the concealing hair and see the hidden face. She extended a hand, eager for the moment of revelation.

The flames roared, fiercely bright, and raced over the cobblestones and the warrior, sweeping Malian along with them. The conflagration burned in her veins as well as in her mind and she feared that now, finally, she would be consumed. Yet she remained aware that somewhere she was still sitting by Yorindesarinen's fire, gazing dreamily into its heart. Malian tried to will herself back but the fire roared again, beating at her, and she closed her eyes against its scorching heat. Blindly, she extended her hands, trying to ward it off. She wondered, rather desperately, whether Kalan and Yorindesarinen would notice anything before it was too late—and then two hands gripped hers with reassuring strength.

12

The Hero's Fire

Malian's eyes flew open and down to the leather-gloved hands grasping her own, then up to the face that was emerging from the flames above them. It was a face she recognized—all lean, strong planes with darkly fierce eyes—even though she had only seen the newcomer once before. "What are you doing here?" she asked the herald, Tarathan of Ar.

The herald stepped fully out of the fire and gazed down at her. He seemed to have a measure of power over the flames for they subsided a little, drawing away from him. His voice, when he answered, was deep and calm. "Why, looking for you, Heir of Night."

Malian stared at him, the fire and her visions momentarily forgotten. "How did you find me?" she asked, trying to match his calmness.

"Last night, in the hall," he said, "I saw the light that burned in you, like a fire in your heart. It was not hard to recognize you again now, even on this plane. And I found you because I was searching for you." He paused. "There is a search party of your own people, as well, and Jehane Mor is with me."

She glanced round quickly, but the herald shook his head. "Only I have the power to walk into this fire," he said.

Malian shivered, remembering the feeling of being consumed. "I let myself be drawn into the fire's heart and now I'm lost. I can't find the way back."

"Looking deeply into such constructs can be very dangerous," the herald replied, "even for the strong; the weak and the unwary may be consumed by them. But you, I think, are neither weak nor unwary."

"Still," Malian pointed out, very reasonably she thought, "I cannot find my way back."

"Can you not?" he asked. "Yet I can see your path, stretching out behind you."

Malian turned and saw that what he said was true. There was a path now, where she had seen only fire before, leading back to the glade and a night filled with stars. She took one step along it, then a second—and then she was stepping back into the space behind her eyes with a jolt.

"Do not touch the fire," said Yorindesarinen.

Malian snatched back her hands, which had been extended toward the blaze, and looked around for the herald. "But—" she began, then stopped.

The hero smiled. "There are not many," she said, "who can look into my fire at all, let alone step into its heart."

Malian rubbed her hands up and down on her knees. "Is that what I did?" she asked. The look she cast across the fire was almost defiant. "And the visions that I saw? Are they usual for those who can look into your fire?"

"Not for all," Yorindesarinen replied gently, "only for those who have the gift of seeing."

"Or the curse," muttered Kalan.

Yorindesarinen shook her head at him. "Not so, if the gift can be properly trained and directed. The curse of the Derai, in these times, is that there is no one to teach such control."

Malian regarded her uneasily. "The visions that I saw, were they of the future or the past?"

"They could be either," the hero said, "or both, or even

another time and place in the present. The seer must learn to read his or her own visions."

Malian shivered. "Is that what I am?" she asked, not without bitterness. "A seer?"

"Amongst other things," Yorindesarinen replied, stirring the fire again. "You did very well, you know, finding your way back without my help."

"But I did have help," Malian said. "The fire nearly overcame me and I couldn't return until the herald came out of the flames. He held back the fire and showed me the path here."

"Now, that is impressive," murmured Yorindesarinen. She gazed into the darkness between the trees. "You may come out, my careful friend, now that you have found what you seek. My fire is safe enough."

Malian and Kalan both swung round, peering into the woods as a shadow that was darker than the tree trunks shifted, moving toward them. After a few paces they saw that it was not a shadow at all, but a man. A moment later and Malian recognized the herald, although he was clad all in warrior's black now, rather than Guild gray. His face, which had been clear to her in the fire, was blackened like a warrior's, too, but there was no mistaking the braided hair and the dark, penetrating eyes. Both she and Kalan watched intently as he crossed to the fire and bowed low to Yorindesarinen. His manner was contained, but he managed to look formidable nonetheless, even dangerous. "Hail, Great One," the herald, Tarathan, said, straightening out of his bow. "Honor on you and on your fireside."

"And light and safety on your path," Yorindesarinen replied. She smiled faintly, as though seeing or hearing something for the first time, and said: "Your friend is well concealed. Even I did not sense her until you drew near. Yet she, too, is welcome at my fire."

Again, Malian craned to look, but at first saw only moonlight and shadow, before finally making out another figure standing motionless in the wood. "Jehane is holding a mindshield to hide us from our enemies," Tarathan said quietly, "and would have to let it go to enter your enchanted circle. She is afraid that if she does so, she will not have the strength to build the shield again."

Yorindesarinen nodded. "Ay, your enemies are powerful, both on this plane and in the Old Keep." Her eyes were pools of night, unfathomable, as the herald squatted on his heels and held out his hands to the blaze, studying Malian and Kalan in turn.

"So," Tarathan said, "two of you." He inclined his head, very slightly, to Malian. "Well met again, Heir of Night. But who"—he quirked an eyebrow at Kalan—"are you?"

Kalan looked back at him, half defiant, half shy. "I'm Kalan, from the Temple quarter. Who are you? And how did you find us here?"

"All fair questions," murmured Yorindesarinen, and the herald nodded.

"They are indeed," he agreed. "I am called Tarathan of Ar and I am a herald from the Guild House in Terebanth, in the lands of the River. Amongst other things, I seek out the hidden and find the lost. It is difficult to hide from me, but you two have done well so far. Now, which of you, I wonder, was responsible for that?"

"Mainly Kalan," said Malian, and Kalan blushed.

"I stumbled into this by accident," he muttered, as though feeling an excuse was required. "Although I did help with hiding us both in the Old Keep. Mostly, though, I think it's been the Golden Fire and this lady doing the concealing." He bobbed his head at Yorindesarinen, who grinned at him.

"I called them here," she said, "but they found their own way through the mists, as must all who would pass the Gate of Dreams. But what of you? What brings a herald of the Guild beyond the Gate and into the heart of my fire, Tarathan of Ar?"

Tarathan's smile was a little grim. "The Heir of Night," he said, and told them about the search party that had gone into the Old Keep, the brush with the dark seeker, and the decision to look for Malian on the psychic plane. "But we never expected," he finished wryly, nodding to Malian across the flames, "to find you sitting at the Great One's fire."

"But, then," murmured Yorindesarinen, "so little in life is what one expects, after all."

The herald shot her a quick look and Malian thought there was a great deal of caution in his expression. "No," he said, then gave a sudden shrug and a half laugh. "No indeed. Still, some things are more unexpected than others, even when one passes the Gate of Dreams."

Kalan looked from one to the other. "Why do you call her the Great One?" he asked Tarathan. "How do you know her at all?"

"Say rather that we know of her," Tarathan replied, with a respectful nod to the hero. "Heralds of the Guild have known how to pass the Gate of Dreams for a long time. We also have some experience of the powers, some wise and bright, but many fearful and terrible, that may be encountered here. So we knew that one whom we recognized as great dwelt here amongst the folds and mists of time, on the threshold between worlds, but we did not know *who* she was."

"Or what," murmured Yorindesarinen.

Tarathan smiled, very slightly. "We did not know who you were," he reiterated firmly, "or that you were of the Derai."

"But how *can* you dwell on the threshold of Haarth?" Kalan asked Yorindesarinen. "You died long before we ever came to this world."

She smiled at him, her eyes kind. "So I did, my Kalan. But as the herald says, this place lies between worlds and time."

"So are we in a dream, after all?" he asked. "How can we all be dreaming the same thing?"

"Does this feel like a dream?" she asked him. He shook his head and the hero smiled again, but it was the herald who spoke.

"This place is called the Gate of Dreams because that is

the only way most people will ever access it. But dreams are haphazard and notoriously difficult to control, so most of those who wish to pass the Gate voluntarily do so by means of what the Guild calls mindwalking—spiritwalking to the Winter shamans. That is how Jehane Mor and I have come here now."

"But you seem substantial," Malian pointed out. She was remembering the strength in his hands as they grasped hers in the fire. "We all do."

Tarathan nodded. "A strong mindwalker can give him-or herself substance and form, while those who are weaker or less well trained often appear as shadows or wraiths, pale images of themselves. Yet mindwalking is not the only way to come here. There are some, a very few, who have the power to walk here in their physical bodies, traveling from one place and time to another." He paused, studying them, then continued quietly, "I believe this is what you and Kalan have done. You are both here in your physical bodies, which explains why I couldn't find you on the physical plane."

Malian and Kalan looked at each other. "Well," the boy said eventually, "that's a relief. I've been dreading waking up and finding myself back in the Old Keep, without food or water, in a room with impassable doors."

Yorindesarinen laughed, a sound so infectious that the others laughed with her, even the herald. "Fear not," she said. "I think you will find that there are few doors, on this plane or any other, that will prove impassable for the two of you. Particularly," she added, sobering, "when you come into your full strength." She looked up at the moon where it hung low amongst the trees. "But now you must go, before my moon sets, and find the friends who are waiting for you. I will provide a path back through the layers of the Gate, but you must remain watchful, for the mists can deceive the unwary."

She rose in one graceful, fluid movement and led them to the edge of the glade. The second herald retreated before their approach, a shadow amongst the trees, and Yorindesarinen's gaze pursued her. "It takes strength," she murmured, "to hold a shield beyond the Gate of Dreams, let alone when mindwalking." Her dark gaze shifted to Tarathan of Ar. "And you walked through my fire to find Malian, which also demonstrates considerable power." She paused. "You know that word of what you have done will get out, not only amongst the Derai but also amongst their enemies? The attention that draws to your Guild may be unwelcome."

Tarathan nodded. "Word always does get out, does it not?" he replied. "Jehane Mor and I considered this, but felt that our involvement was required, all the same."

"It was essential," Yorindesarinen agreed, "although not all would act as you have, if similarly placed." Her voice was tranquil, but the darkness in her eyes was vast and comprised both memory and pain.

Malian, knowing the old, grievous story, thought she understood that darkness, but she wondered if the herald did. To her surprise, however, he took the hero's hand and bowed over it, in what Haimyr had once described as the grand manner of the River; the hand, Malian saw, was crisscrossed with old scars.

"Life," said Tarathan of Ar, "is a risk and so is death and one cannot avoid either. Jehane Mor and I are one in believing that a time for taking risks, perhaps even great risks, is upon us all."

Yorindesarinen was smiling now. "It is a very long time," she said, "since anyone kissed my hand in that way. It is not a custom of the Derai. You are quite right, though, it is indeed a time for risks, both the great and the small—although your Guild may not see that as clearly as you and your comrade do. But see, here is your road." She pointed, and they all saw the path, silver touched, curving away between the trees.

The hero knelt and took Malian's face between her scarred hands. "I am glad, Child of Night," she said, "to have seen you at last. I believe we may meet again, but whether it will be soon or late, I cannot say." She rose to her feet, her dark eyes crinkling into a smile. "But you must not go without a gift, something to remind you of me in the times ahead." She unclasped a wide band of silver from her wrist and handed it to Malian, who turned it over in her hands. The armring was plainly wrought, except for a pattern of stars worked into a spiral around the band. "It will always fit you," said Yorindesarinen, "but wear it around your upper arm for now, under your sleeve where it will be hidden from prying eyes. When you come into your power, you shall wear it on your wrist as I did. I have kept it for you a long time, so bear it well, Child of Night."

"I will," murmured Malian. "Thank you."

The hero turned to Kalan. "And you," she said, smiling at him. "What gift shall I give you, my unexpected friend?"

The smile deepened when he shook his head. She tugged a ring off her finger and closed his hand over its three strands of black metal, plaited together around a misshapen black pearl. "A friend gave it to me, long ago," she said, "and he had it from another in his turn, down the long years. But you need not hide it as Malian must the armring: No one will remember it anymore."

Kalan flushed and nodded, looking as though he would like to say something but couldn't find the words, while Malian sank to one knee. "Farewell," she said. "Even if this meeting does turn out to be just a dream, I will remember it forever."

Yorindesarinen raised her up and kissed her on the forehead. "The path will become clearer, Child of Night, I promise you." She gave Kalan a quick, comradely hug before he could either kneel or bow in his turn. "Farewell," she said. "I will not say, 'stay with her,' for I think your two paths already lie together, without contrivance or encouragement of mine."

Kalan nodded, sliding the ring onto his finger, but it was Tarathan who spoke. "We must go," he said. "I fear for the safety of those we left behind."

Yorindesarinen nodded. "Go well, my bravehearts, until we meet again—and do not leave the path!"

"Farewell," Malian and Kalan called together, looking back as the mist thickened. "The Nine be with you!" The brume swirled higher, catching and echoing their words: "Farewell! Farewell!"

The hero turned and walked back to the fire, seating herself beside it again. She glanced up once at the moon, now very low amongst the tangled branches, but otherwise seemed absorbed by the play and flicker of the flames. If she noticed when the mist at the glade's edge coalesced into a ball of golden light and drifted toward the fire, she gave no sign. As the ball moved, it grew until there was a small cloud hovering above Yorindesarinen. It was only then that the hero looked up. "Welcome, old friend," she said. "It has been a long time."

"Greetings, Child of Stars," a voice of light replied, out of the cloud. *"I was worried when I saw that the children had been drawn this way, until I realized who was charting their path."*

"Oh, they found their way with little enough help from me," the hero said. "But you, my Hylcarian, have been busy as well. It gladdens my heart to see it."

"Ay, but I am weak, Child of Stars. I cannot do all that I would have done once, or wish to do now."

"You were hurt very badly on that night five hundred years ago, and then abandoned." Yorindesarinen shook her head. "It is little wonder your recovery has taken so long. And now, when the Derai need the Golden Fire as never before, there are too few of the Blood left to bring you back to your full strength. So you must strive to rebuild that strength on your own. That is not how it is meant to be, I know, but there is no other choice."

Hylcarian was silent and the hero's fire burned lower. *"You are sending the child away,"* the fiery voice said at last.

"She must go, old friend. You know that as well as I," said Yorindesarinen.

"You seem so sure," Hylcarian replied. *"You were always*

so sure . . . But who, beyond the keeps, can teach her what she needs to know?"

"Who can teach her in the keeps?" Yorindesarinen inquired dryly. "She must make her own way, find the allies that wait for her in the world beyond the Wall. That is her destiny—and the fate of the Derai Alliance, and of Haarth itself, is tied to it."

Silence fell again until lightning crackled through the golden cloud. *"Have you seen this, Child of Stars?"*

"I see many things," Yorindesarinen replied, "and understand only a few. But yes. I have seen it, both in the fire and in the stars."

"So much lost," Hylcarian murmured. *"So much broken or gone forever."* The light-filled voice paused briefly. *"The weapons of your power are lost, too. Sword, helm, and shield all vanished when you fell. Yet how can she hope to withstand the Darkswarm without them?"*

"There is always hope, old friend," the hero replied gently. "You should know that better than any. Just as you know that it is heart and wit that make the hero, not swords and helms, however powerful."

"All the same, the weapons of power would be very useful now. And they are her birthright, since it was for the benefit of the prophesied One that Mhaelanar sent them into the world."

"So legend says," agreed Yorindesarinen.

Again, lightning darted through the cloud. *"Do you, who bore them, doubt it?"*

The hero tipped back her scarred face and looked at the glitter of stars overhead. " 'Heaven's shield by the Chosen borne; Terennin wrought me in time's dawn,' " she chanted. "As you say, it was I who bore the weapons and I, too, who deciphered the hieroglyphs on the shield's rim. 'Terennin wrought me,' it says. There is no mention of Mhaelanar."

There was another silence. *"Terennin,"* Hylcarian said at last. *"The Farseer, Lord of the Dawn Eyes. He is also of the Nine, Child of Stars."*

"He is," Yorindesarinen replied. "And you're right, the weapons of power would undoubtedly be useful now. Unfortunately, there are still some things that are concealed from me, even dwelling here, and one is where those weapons are. They have been hidden well."

Tongues of golden flame flicked again. *"Their disappearance perturbed us greatly. Even before the Betrayal, it seemed that all had gone awry for the Derai Alliance since the time of your death and their loss. But our greatest fear was that they had been taken by the Swarm."*

The reflected firelight flared in Yorindesarinen's eyes. *"Not that!"* she said. Her voice rang out; cold, clear, and true. *"The Derai Alliance abandoned the Chosen of Mhaelanar in the darkest hour and so the god's gift abandoned the Derai, to await the coming of another One, as was promised. Just as the weapons are dispersed and broken, so also are the Derai—and will be until the new Chosen claims her birthright and takes up her fate. Only in that hour will the lost be found and return to the Derai fold."*

The fire died from Yorindesarinen's eyes and her head bowed. "So be it," she said, in her normal voice.

Hylcarian echoed her words, sealing the prophecy: *"So be it, in this hour and in the time to come."*

When Yorindesarinen looked up again the familiar, wry humor was back in her face. "So now you know as much as I do, seer or no. They always had a will of their own in any case, shield, sword, and helm. But you will know that better than I, having known them longer."

"Long enough to know that like all objects of power, they are capable of finding their own path. As it would seem, from your prophecy, they have been doing for some time now."

"Since the hour of my death," said Yorindesarinen, dryly, then she shrugged. "Well, I cannot complain. They served me well and did not fail me, even at the end."

"Some might say," Hylcarian observed, matching her tone, *"that they held by you in death, as in life. The proph-*

ecy I just heard clearly suggested that the weapons abandoned the Derai, with attendant consequences, because the Alliance abandoned you. They could, after all, have awaited the next Chosen quite easily amongst the keeps."

The hero's dark brows rose. "I had not considered that," she said. "I suppose I still tend to see them as inanimate objects, despite their power." Her expression became somber. "But if you are right, then they have punished the Derai far more harshly than I would have done. And despite what legend says, not all fell away. Rithor would have stood with me until the end, except that I commanded him to go—and Tavaral." Her voice and expression softened suddenly. "I know now that he brought his wing forward, defying his own Earl, but came too late."

"Ay, that surprised me, even at the time," murmured Hylcarian. *"He was well named, since Tavaral means faith keeper in the tongue of the ancients. But he paid for that faith keeping. He was stripped of his command and all his honors, and from that time to this his line have been barred from regaining them."*

"Thus the Derai mind!" exclaimed Yorindesarinen. "I could despair—except that there is too much to be done, counteracting it! But what of more recent events? What you have been doing, old friend?"

"Not nearly enough," the Golden Fire replied, *"but I have uncovered some secrets that you should know."* Reluctance, distaste, and even fear mingled in the summer voice.

"Let me see what you saw," Yorindesarinen replied, "hear what you heard." She dipped one scarred hand into the fire and scooped out flame, then touched the edge of the golden cloud. The two fires blazed and Yorindesarinen's dark brows drew together, her expression grim. "I see," she said at last. "Well, that explains how our enemy came to learn of her existence. You have done well, both to discover this and to guard the child as you have."

"She is mine to guard, Child of Stars, as is this keep, and there is little that can be hidden from me in my own halls,"

now that I am fully awake. But I cannot act effectively in the New Keep, for in their anxiety to wall off the past, Night shut me out as well. Those wards are down, for now, but I am not grounded in that place as I am in the Old Keep. And until I am stronger, I must stay connected to the heart of my power."

"Agreed," Yorindesarinen said briskly. "But you can certainly act now, in the Old Keep, to ensure that the child and her friends return safely to the New. I, too, will bend all my power to that end—but for now, my moon has nearly set. We must both go."

"Farewell, Child of Stars." The fiery voice was full of regret. *"It was good to see you again, if only for a brief time."*

"And you," Yorindesarinen replied. She let the handful of flame slip back onto the fire in a shower of sparks that flared briefly, then extinguished. Slowly, the moon disappeared from view—and the fire went out altogether as the hero vanished. The golden cloud began to contract, dwindling again into a ball of light before it, too, disappeared; only the trees, and the distant stars, and a circle of charred earth remained. In a while the white mist came flowing in over everything, damp and cold, as though the glade and the fire had never been.

13

Path Through the Mist

The fog pressed in, blotting out both moon and trees, so that the four on Yorindesarinen's path walked in a blank, cold world with no reference point except the glimmer of silver ahead. When Kalan looked back he could see no sign of the way they had come; the pathway behind them had disappeared.

"There is no going back, not through these mists," said Jehane Mor, whose presence had grown more substantial as the glade disappeared. "Don't be afraid," she added, as Kalan shuddered. "Even without this path I would still trust Tarathan to find his way."

"I'm not afraid," Kalan said quickly, although he was. He could imagine wandering along this track forever, caught in some endless whorl of time. Frowning, he rubbed at the ring on his finger; it was real, tangible—reassuring, Kalan thought. He might not know the herald Tarathan, but he knew every hero tale that Brother Belan had ever recounted of Yorindesarinen the Bright: the most powerful enchanter ever born to the House of Stars; the Chosen of Mhaelanar, foretold by prophecy; the brightest star in the long darkness of the Derai struggle against the Swarm. And she had slain the Worm of Chaos, which everyone had said could not be done.

Even beyond death, Kalan thought, Yorindesarinen would be a force to be reckoned with. He looked back again and met Jehane Mor's calm, gray-green gaze. "Are you not?" she asked. "I am. This is a very dangerous place and more dangerous still when the mists roll in. The Great One's path is like a ropewalk above vast deeps, with no knowing where a misstep might lead."

Kalan shivered and looked at Tarathan walking ahead. The herald seemed certain of where he was leading them, but it felt strange having to trust in someone who was not Derai. Kalan studied the ring on his finger again and wondered if this was not all some fantastic dream, and whether both ring and mists might vanish when he woke, back in his narrow bed in the novice dormitory.

"It is a hero's gift," Jehane Mor said quietly from behind him, "and should not be underestimated, particularly considering the place where you received it."

But who in the Temple quarter would believe me, Kalan wondered, if I told them the story? He wished he had summoned the courage to ask Yorindesarinen who had given the ring to her, and why—what its story was, since the hero had implied that the ring was already old when it came to her. The history might be hidden in a musty scroll somewhere, but if they were to leave the Wall, he would never get the chance to search for it.

If we leave the Wall . . . Kalan shook his head, remembering what had happened to other priests who had tried to flee the Wall of Night.

Malian said something to Tarathan, her voice very low, as though she feared there might be hidden listeners in the mist. Kalan reminded himself to concentrate, stretching his keen hearing to detect anything other than their own breathing and occasional murmured word. For a long time he heard nothing, but eventually detected a whisper beneath the white silence. The whisperer was chanting something, a cantrip or a curse, and Kalan sucked in his breath as he recognized that cold, sibilant tone.

Tarathan turned, his eyebrows raised in question. "There's a voice," Kalan said, whispering, too. "I've heard it before, when the Darkswarm invaded the New Keep."

"They are searching everywhere, questing blindly through the whiteness for their quarry." Jehane Mor's reply was even softer than the whisper, and Kalan realized, with a sharp little jolt, that she was speaking directly into his mind. He saw the sudden flare in Malian's eyes as she turned toward the herald and knew that she, too, could hear the mindvoice.

"But they have not found us yet?" Tarathan's mindvoice answered Jehane Mor's. *"Your shield still holds?"*

She nodded, but Kalan felt the touch of her mind on his, light as a hand resting on his shoulder. *"These Darkswarm are strong and determined, but you can help me thwart them. You, too, have the shielding power."*

"He hid us from them before." Malian's whisper rang in the silence and Tarathan shook his head.

"Do not speak it. Show us."

So Kalan showed them his memory of the Darkswarm warriors entering the Temple quarter, when he first heard that cold, sibilant voice. He also relived the memory of building a wall of stone and not-seeing between the Darkswarm and his hidden presence, both then and again when he and Malian hid from the were-hunt in the Old Keep.

"Exactly," said Jehane Mor, intent on his image of the wall. She showed him how to join his power to hers and support the psychic shield. Kalan, frowning in concentration, followed her step by step. The herald's power was like water, cool and deep with sunlight sifting through its layers; his own strength, sliding beneath hers, was rock, gray and strong. As soon as it settled into place, the sibilant whisper vanished.

"We have shut it out," thought Kalan, full of wonder.

"We have," said Jehane Mor, and smiled at him. *"It was well done."*

"But now," said Tarathan, *"we must hurry, before they strengthen their search again."*

They pressed on, Kalan very conscious that part of his mind was still tied to the shield. Holding it in place required energy and constant focus and he looked at Jehane Mor with new respect. Like the herald, he remained alert to any threat from beyond the shield's protective barrier, but detected nothing more. Soon the mists began to thin and then disintegrate, revealing a silver arch above the path ahead. It reminded Kalan of the twelve doors in the heart of the Old Keep, except that the mist within the silver frame was stretched gossamer thin and they could see dark shapes on the other side.

Tarathan stopped, nodding to the arch. "This is your way," he told Kalan and Malian. "You must step through this gate physically, while Jehane Mor and I take the spirit path."

Kalan peered through the veil, but the forms on the other side remained indistinct. Malian, too, seemed doubtful. "Will you join us there?" she asked the heralds.

"We will," Jehane Mor reassured her. "You need not be afraid," she added, when Malian still looked uncertain. "This portal is an extension of your Great One's power, formed from her path, and it is your own people on the far side."

Malian tossed her dark head and stuck out her chin. "I am the Heir of Night," she declared firmly, then added, much as Kalan had done a little earlier: "I am not afraid!"

"Nor I," Kalan said at once, not to be outdone.

Both the heralds smiled slightly, mirroring each other, then winked out before his startled eyes. "Perhaps I am a little nervous," Kalan admitted to Malian.

She grinned in answer. "I am, too! Still, a door into air worked for us last time."

"I suppose," said Kalan, reflecting that it had taken them somewhere quite other than their intended destination. But once again, they could not remain where they were. "Ready?" he asked, and stepped forward, Malian keeping pace so that they crossed the threshold at the same time.

For a brief moment they hung suspended, caught between the silver path and a rough, dimly lit chamber. Kalan could make out Derai warriors standing guard at the two door-ways, but for all their watchfulness no one seemed aware of the portal in the air above them. Then one of the warriors turned, eyes narrowing in a keen dark face—and both Kalan and Malian were through the veil of mist and stumbling to their hands and knees on the chamber floor.

There was a startled hush, followed by a sharp outcry from the guards. On the other side of the room, the heralds were slowly sitting up and the young priests keeping vigil around them began to stir at the same time. "Nine forfend!" someone exclaimed, in a shaken voice.

Beside Kalan, Malian was lifted to her feet and swept into a fierce embrace. "Asantir!" she cried, and Kalan stepped aside, feeling awkward and shy at the same time.

"So they did find you!" Asantir exclaimed. She held Malian back a little as though to see her better, then her keen gaze shifted to Kalan. "And who," she asked, "are you?"

"This is Kalan, who is my friend," Malian replied simply, before he could answer. "He saved my life when I fled from Swarm assassins."

"Then you have my deepest gratitude," Asantir said. Kalan scuffed one foot and mumbled something indistinct in response, because this was the Earl's Honor Captain and she was talking to him, *thanking* him. She smiled at his mumble, before her eyes went back to Malian. "But how did you get here? One instant I thought I saw a door opening in the air, the next it vanished and you were both here!" The captain shook her head. "I suppose it must have been some power of the heralds." But her look was searching, at odds with her words.

Before Malian could speak, Kalan swayed into her, as though from weariness, and trod heavily on her foot. Malian stared at him, but must have understood the unspoken warning, for she shoved him upright again and replied gravely: "The heralds did find us and lead us back safely, for which I am truly grateful."

It was not a lie, thought Kalan, but he found the glint in

the captain's eye disconcerting. He shifted uneasily, wondering how much she knew, or suspected, but all Asantir said was: "Ay, and at some risk to themselves, so they have my thanks also." Her expression became grim. "Though you are not safe yet, Heir of Night."

Kalan looked around properly for the first time, taking in the wounded guards and the cloak-covered bodies of the dead—and the astonishing presence of Temple initiates, with blackened faces and warrior's garb, surrounding the heralds. Disconcerted, he looked back at the bodies of the dead and found Malian staring at them, too, her expression set. "Is this all . . . because of me?" she asked slowly, turning to Asantir.

" 'If Night falls, all fall,' " the Honor Captain quoted softly. "You know the old prophecy. Do not doubt it, just because it applies to you." She sounded, thought Kalan, like an uncanny echo of Yorindesarinen, even to the wry reassuring tone. "Each and every one of us volunteered and we all knew the risks involved: *'Our blood for the House of Night, Earl and Heir, our blood for their blood, our lives for their lives, our hearts only for this House and for the Derai cause.'* Everyone present is bound to that service, my Malian, so we ventured this place to keep faith with ourselves, as well as with you."

Malian sighed and looked around the small, weary company again. "So what happens now?"

"We go back," Asantir replied. She turned her head, raising her voice just enough to gather the company together. "We have found the Heir, but now we must get her safely back to the New Keep before our enemies return. So let's get moving!"

There was a subdued murmur as the party retrieved packs and completed the binding up of wounds and injuries. Asantir walked over to the heralds and formally embraced them, first Tarathan and then Jehane Mor. "This expedition may not be over," she said, "but you have my thanks anyway, for all that you have done. I stand in your debt, if such a debt can ever be repaid."

Tarathan shook his head, smiling a little. "We are not back yet, as you say." His expression sobered as he looked at the wounded and the dead. "It was bad here, I see."

"It could have been much worse," Asantir said grimly. "But how are the two of you? Are you able to start back at once?"

"We are both tired, but not exhausted yet." Jehane Mor's reply was soft. "And cannot afford to be. The danger here is still great, Captain."

Kalan glanced at Malian, wondering whether she had heard that quiet comment. Malian, however, was watching the priests, who had come out of their shield pattern to realize that two of their number were dead. Eria had lifted the cloaks from Ilor and Serin's faces, then put her hands over her mouth to hold back an exclamation of horror. Armar was kneeling beside her, his hands covering his face, and Tisanthe was crying openly; the others seemed numb with shock. After a moment Armar began rocking back and forward, shaking his head from side to side and muttering through his hands. Malian turned a look of mute inquiry on Kalan, who shook his head. He could make out what Armar was saying, but would not repeat the words aloud.

"I felt them go," Armar muttered, "felt them being torn away, blotted out, but I couldn't do anything. I wasn't strong enough to hold on to them—the Nine Gods forgive me! I tried, but I couldn't do it."

"We all tried," Torin said dully. "None of us were strong enough."

His words were clear enough and Malian took a step forward, but Kalan reached out and stopped her. "The captain and the heralds are closest," he whispered. "I think we should leave it to them."

Asantir had indeed got there first, with the heralds only half a pace behind. She knelt down and lifted Armar's hands off his face, holding them between her own and making him meet her eyes. "Do not forget," she told him, "that when your comrades fell the rest of you still held your shield together and called forth the fire that drove off our enemies. Even after that, you didn't let the shield go but held to your appointed task until the heralds returned safely. I see no cause for shame in any of this."

Armar said nothing, but his shoulders slumped and he stopped straining against her hands. "But," Torin said uncertainly, "I don't think we did call the fire. It just came."

"Perhaps," said Tarathan, from behind Asantir's shoulder. "But it came through you. And if you had failed, our bodies would have been slain and our spirits extinguished where they walked, far from here."

"We set you a hard task," Jehane Mor added, "but you did not fail us. It is as the captain said: You have no need to be ashamed or to blame yourselves."

"In fact," Asantir said, "you should be proud. Without you, we may all have fallen and the Heir might not have been found. You have fought your first battle and in battle comrades fall. We mourn that fall, but to survive we must carry on—which is what you must all do now, for we are not out of danger yet. You, too, must ready yourselves to leave."

The priests nodded silently, turning away from their dead, but Kalan had seen the change in their faces as Asantir and the heralds spoke, the mix of wonder and dawning self-respect. He could not help envying them, just a little, despite their grief, for they had been part of the battle, comrades in arms with Asantir and her guards. He pushed away darker thoughts, the memory of what his father had said when he found that his youngest son had priestly powers, hard contemptuous words about cowardice and pollution.

Best to forget, Kalan told himself.

All the same, he could not help staring at Asantir and wondering if she really believed that the young priests had acquitted themselves honorably, or was simply saying what they needed to hear because the situation demanded it. The Honor Captain looked up, as if feeling his scrutiny, and quirked one dark, questioning brow at him. Hurriedly, Kalan looked away and saw that Eria was watching him in her turn.

"Why," she said, "you're Kalan, aren't you? I thought that was a novice's robe under all the grime."

He nodded and went over half unwillingly, for novices generally kept clear of the initiates and sworn priests—with the exception of their teachers—and he did not know her well. Eria, however, seemed pleased to see him. "We all thought you were dead," she said, "even though we couldn't find your body. But there was so much killing and so many bodies . . ." Her voice trailed away.

"But how in Haarth," said Var, who had been eyeing Kalan sharply out of his narrow eyes, "did you end up with the Heir?"

"It's a long story." Kalan shifted uncomfortably. "But what about your battle? Did you really call down the Golden Fire?"

"Apparently so," began Var, but Eria stopped him with a small, weary gesture.

"We don't know that. It may just have been a residual power in these lamps, which were made in the days when we still had the Fire. It did come out of nowhere, though, just like in all the stories."

"Actually," said Torin dryly, "it was more like it took hold of us, rather than the other way around. It was like being in the middle of a wildfire—we felt the heat and the power, only without getting burned."

The other initiates murmured their agreement and one of the guards, who was lashing closed a pack nearby, turned his head. "Well, it burned a few others, and in the nick of time, because a lot more of us would be dog's meat now if it hadn't." He spoke gruffly and didn't wait for an answer before hefting the pack and joining the guards around Sarus.

Eria ran a hand over her untidy hair. "That's Garan," she murmured. "He has been . . . almost friendly . . . on this journey."

"Journeys like this change things. And people," Kalan said, deciding that it could, perhaps, be possible. "I'm sorry, though, about Serin and Ilor."

Eria frowned up at the roof, and it was a moment before

Kalan realized that she was trying not to cry. "At least they died doing something worthwhile, which is more than most of the Temple dead last night, who had their souls sucked out of them while they slept." She looked down again, meeting his eyes. "We thought you had died that way, too, and that we'd find your body eventually, or what was left of it, in one of your many hiding places."

Kalan blushed to think that his hideaways were common knowledge, but felt increasingly uncomfortable as they told him more about the devastation wrought by the Raptor of Darkness. He couldn't help feeling that he should have done more, tried harder to warn the Temple of the imminent attack. Wanting to get away, he looked around and saw Malian talking with the heralds. He caught her eye and when she smiled he drifted over to stand beside her, feeling a little less miserable as he reflected that he had helped her escape the were-hunt and played his part in rousing the keep at last.

Malian had turned to frown at the cloak-covered bodies. "Will we take them with us?" she asked Sarus.

He shook his head. "There are too many of them and too few of us, Lady Malian. We all hate the necessity, but we must leave them behind."

Malian said nothing, but Kalan saw her bite her lip and stare fiercely at the ceiling, much as Eria had done a few moments before. Looking round, he saw the same bitter set in all the surrounding faces, warrior and priest. He hoped they would start moving soon, get it over with. One of the nearby guards, an older man with a dour expression and gray in his short beard, seemed to feel the same. "Let's get on with it," he said.

"Peace, Kyr," growled Sarus, who was older by far, gnarled and weatherbeaten as a Wall tree. He was interrupted, however, by the guard keeping watch by the main door. She was looking toward the Swarm dead, piled outside in the corridor.

"Captain!" she called, her voice high and hard. "Come and look at this. I'd swear I saw one of those corpses twitch!"

14

The Black Spear

*A*santir and half the party crowded to look and Malian ducked under elbows to stand at the captain's side, Kalan close behind her. "Ugh!" the guard exclaimed. "It did it again! There! That finger definitely twitched!"

Malian stared hard but saw nothing, until Kalan said quietly, "Yes, there. The hand moved, too." She followed the line of his pointing finger and this time she saw the corpse's hand quiver—then give a slight but very definite jerk.

"Is it possible that it's not dead?" Eria asked uneasily.

Garan's answering headshake was decisive. "No. They were all quite dead when we dragged 'em out there."

"Well," said the guard, equally firmly, "they're definitely moving now!" Her name, Malian recalled, was Lira and the high note in her voice was almost, but not quite, panic.

Instinctively, Malian's eyes moved from Asantir to Tarathan, who looked singularly grim. "What's that light?" he asked. "Playing over those corpses there?"

Malian looked again and saw a pale glow around some of the bodies. Her mind flew back to the eldritch fire that had nearly snared her when she floated in the darkness, and she was certain this was the same light. For a moment she almost panicked, remembering her inability to fight against it, before she recalled how Yorindesarinen's voice had saved her. Involuntarily, her hand moved to touch the smooth, cold silver of the hero's armring, which burned beneath her fingers like dry ice. Yorindesarinen's voice spoke, fire in her mind.

"You must burn them all, both the Swarm dead and your own. A Darkswarm sorcerer generated the witchlight when the attackers assailed your comrades. It is a foul, necrotic substance and the residue will stay in their corpses, allowing the sorcerer to reanimate them. Such reanimations will hunt and kill even more remorselessly in death than they did in life. No blade, however sharp, will stop them. And once started, the reanimation process is frighteningly swift. They must be burned, child, and soon."

"But how can we do that?" Malian protested silently. *"We don't have enough fuel for a pyre."*

"You *must do it*," Yorindesarinen told her calmly. *"You must call the Golden Fire with your mind and immolate the corpses."*

Malian hesitated, knowing that calling the Golden Fire would banish any hope of keeping her power secret. *"Couldn't you just send down your own fire?"* she asked. *"Then no one would have to know about me—what I can do."*

"Malian," Yorindesarinen's mindvoice was both patient and stern, *"I am not present on the physical plane, so I cannot act there. You are both present and of the Blood of Night; the Golden Fire will answer to your need. There is no time and no other option. You must do your duty. The Fire,"* she added, *"is called Hylcarian. He is Night's oldest ally, bound to your House from the beginning."*

"Didn't he come here before," Malian said doubtfully, *"to aid the priests in the battle?"*

"That was not Hylcarian," Yorindesarinen explained, still patient, *"but a remnant fire that was bound into their cone lights long ago, against exactly the situation they encountered. The residual fire was sufficient to combat the*

eldritch light but not to slay the Darkswarm outright, since only the Blood may call on the Golden Fire to kill or consume. Now call Hylcarian, while there is still time!"

The entire pile of bodies was twitching now, wriggling like maggots and as loathsome to the horrified watchers. "Nine forfend!" muttered Sarus. "How in the name of all the Nine do we kill something that is already dead?"

Malian stepped forward, shaking Asantir's hand from her shoulder. "You don't," she said quietly. "I do."

She smoothed back her tangled hair and pushed up her sleeves. On her arm, the silver armring burned with cold fire. Now the first step had been taken, it was as though she knew what to do by instinct. She opened her mind to the vastness of the Old Keep, layer on stone-built layer, from its secret heart to its abandoned crown amidst the windswept peaks of the Wall. She felt the touch of Kalan's mind like an anchor at her back, solid as the rock of the keep, as she sent her mindcall spiraling out, summoning the Golden Fire. *"Hylcarian! I, Malian of the Blood of Night, call on you by right of the ancient bond between your kind and the Derai! Hear me, Hylcarian, and answer!"*

She closed her eyes, shutting out the faces around her, some puzzled, some disbelieving, and prayed that Hylcarian would not take long to respond. The Fire, after all, was not the only power that might hear so compelling a call. *"Hylcarian!"* she cried again and could not repress a flare of excitement, knowing it was the first time that name had been called by anyone in Night for half a thousand years.

"Summoned, I come; called, I answer!" The light-filled voice was a thunder in the room as well as in Malian's mind and she opened her eyes to see amazement replacing disbelief on the surrounding faces. Light flowed into her like a golden river, a torrent of molten fire that seared down every artery. She was alive with it, blazing like a torch and in danger of being immolated herself unless she could redirect the energy and power. Malian raised her arms and the Fire crackled around them like lightning, golden white and

blinding as it streamed out from her fingertips. She sensed rather than saw those around her turn away, throwing their arms over their eyes as she extended her fiery hands toward the twitching bodies of the Darkswarm dead. She alone was able to watch, steady-eyed, as fire engulfed the corpses, incinerating them to fine ash.

She saw something else as well, a pale thread of light that spun away from the place where the ashes lay and fled back into the darkness. Pursuing it with her mind, she saw a tall figure standing at its other end, surrounded by a swirl of power. The figure was eldritch as the light, but unmistakably a man. His face was more skull than flesh, all sharp planes and hollowed eyes with one long elflock of pale hair curving down beside it—although he still, Malian thought uneasily, bore a resemblance to the Derai. In his hands, he held a long, pale rod carved with hieroglyphs and runes; even looking at it made Malian feel nauseous.

"Come away, Child of Night," Hylcarian's mindvoice was inexorable. *"Do not let him perceive you, for he is both powerful and vicious. Destroying his works here will give him enough of a setback, until you grow into your full power."*

Reluctantly, Malian turned away and Hylcarian sent a final tongue of fire crackling along the pale thread, so that it snapped and recoiled back toward its source. *"More than enough of a setback,"* the Fire said with satisfaction. *"Nirn always did bind too much of himself into his spellcraft. But now for our own dead."*

The golden wildfire surged as Malian turned, raging so hot and fierce that her body stumbled. Hard hands came down on her shoulders, steadying her. Kalan was still there, too, Malian realized, an anchor in her mind; she could feel Jehane Mor's strength supporting his, deep and cool as water. Malian sheered away from the coolness and depth, raising her hands again. The golden fire poured out of them, onto the bodies of their own dead, and consumed them utterly.

"Done," said Hylcarian, a long hiss of satisfaction. *"And well done, Child of Night!"*

"Not quite done," Malian said aloud. Maintaining her link to the Fire was like riding a wild horse, but she held on. "That sorcerer was not the last of them. His was only one of the voices that I heard in the darkness. If we take the long, slow way back they will snap at our heels and bring more of the company down—unless you can hold them off on your own?"

"If I could hurl them from this place by main force," Hylcarian replied, his thunder filling the room, *"I would have done so long before now. I lost too much, alas, on that dire night when Xeriatherien ripped our fire from all the keeps—and afterward the Blood of Night abandoned the defences that might have kept this evil out."*

Malian reeled from the sense of loss and the sorrow that accompanied the Golden Fire's words. What had Haimyr called this story when he first learned the Derai sagas? "A tragic history," that was it—but she did not want to add another footnote now. "Why throw lives away unnecessarily if together we can open another portal, directly into the New Keep?"

She felt Hylcarian's reluctance before the golden voice spoke. *"It is a grave risk for you, Child. Opening and holding a portal for such numbers takes enormous strength and will light a beacon for your enemies."*

Malian shook her head. "I suspect we've done that already. But look at the company. There are too many wounded and everyone is tired. Add our enemies into the mix and the road back may kill us all."

The hiss and crackle of fire filled the air. *"You are right,"* Hylcarian said at last. *"The risk must be taken. But even with the barriers down, I will not open a portal from the Old Keep into the New, not while the House is still reeling from last night's attack."* The fiery voice paused again. *"I could take you close, though, somewhere in this Old Keep."*

"The old High Hall!" Malian cried eagerly. She could

still see the faces of the dead disintegrating in the searing blaze of golden flame, and feel the creeping chill of the eldritch light. Turning her head, she saw black gauntlets, steady on her shoulders, then looked up to meet Asantir's eyes. The heavy leather of the gauntlets had begun to smoke, but the Honor Captain's gaze was unflinching.

"We heard, my Malian," she said. "And we stand ready. Command us!"

Malian strove to keep her voice steady, although she still felt half on fire. "As soon as the gate opens, everyone must go through. It might feel like stepping into air, but you will be quite safe." She did not wait to hear Asantir's reply, but focused on the Golden Fire again. Kalan and Jehane Mor were still with her, supporting her strength with theirs; now she reached for Tarathan's power as well, letting it tap into her own like a thread of fire from the earth's heart. The Golden Fire flowed through her and into them all, a connecting web of molten gold.

"Ready, Child of Night?" asked Hylcarian, a rumble of distant thunder.

"Ready!" cried Malian, the lightning's snap after a thunderclap has died away. She pictured the old High Hall in her mind: the wooden minstrel's gallery, the pillars of stone, and the ancient doors. "There!" she said and felt Hylcarian's quick, wordless agreement. She shuddered as the Golden Fire blazed up in her again, and felt Asantir's hands tighten, holding her up. Malian straightened and extended her arms once more as the golden light flowed down them, not to destroy this time but to save. She watched it flicker and twist along her fingers before curling outward like a fiery vine, creeping and growing until it formed a door in the air. The burnished threshold hovered just above the floor and the flaming apex pressed into the roof; within the frame, the air shimmered like a golden veil.

Malian looked around and saw mingled hope, wariness, and wonder as the veil thinned and they all saw the old High Hall, close on the other side. She wondered if she had enough strength left for speech, then relaxed as Jehane Mor spoke for her. "We must be swift," the herald said.

"The Heir must go first," said Asantir, iron in her voice, but Malian shook her head. The door would close once she passed through, so she would have to go last. She closed her eyes, feeling the effort of holding the door open—but soon, soon it would all be over with, and done. They would all be safe.

"'Ware!" said Kalan, in a queer, strained voice. "We've got company."

Malian opened her eyes and turned her head slowly to where another portal was forming in the air behind them. This one was all smoke and darkness and the substance within it bubbled and heaved like boiling pitch, only without heat. A bone-chilling cold emanated from its center, accompanied by a wave of relentless hunger and dark, driven malice.

"The Raptor of Darkness comes," said Hylcarian, *"diminished though it must be from last night's battle. The Darkswarm insurgents wager all on a last, dire throw."*

"The hunter-in-darkness," said Tarathan calmly, as though calculating odds, but Malian saw sick fear in all the young priests' faces.

Asantir's touch on her shoulders lightened. "Then we had better stop it before it gets through."

"She is right," said Hylcarian. *"Even wounded it is still a dire foe—and we cannot fight for long and still hold our own gate."*

"Can't we just flee now and close our gate behind us?" Kalan asked.

Everyone looked at Malian, forcing their eyes away from that deadly portal, but she shook her head. "It would only— follow us." She had to force the words out. "We must—deal with it—here."

If we can, she added silently, although her thoughts were racing. Yorindesarinen had said that only the Blood might call on the Golden Fire to kill or consume—and the last

time they fought the Raptor she had been the only member
of the Blood present, but had fallen away before the end.
Malian bit her lip, knowing that this time she *had* to hold
on. Whatever had happened before, or the reasons for it, the
Raptor was still hideously strong.

Beside her, the guard called Korin was shaking his head.
"It will deal with us, more like," he muttered.

"Enough!" Asantir's eyes were narrowed on the bubbling
center of the Raptor's gate, where a form was starting to take
shape: an impression of vast but still partly folded wings with
a sharp, avian head emerging between them. Power, too, was
spiraling out through the half-open portal. It plucked at the
edges of their minds, famished and searching, seeking for
weakness: a chink, Malian realized, through which to suck
out their souls. "We must attack now," said Asantir.

"*Yes!*" said Hylcarian. A line of golden flames ran across
the floor between the Derai and the dark gate, checking—
but not stopping—the Raptor's gyre of power. The dark
portal nearly filled the chamber now and the Raptor's avian
form was clearer. Through the Golden Fire, Malian sensed
that it hung on the lip of a vast abyss into which all life and
matter flowed.

Behind her, someone sobbed. Tarathan was beside her
now, fully joined in the Golden Fire, and Malian recognized
the lightning that coruscated around him from the previous
battle with the Raptor. His voice wove in and out of the Fire,
part of the hiss and whisper of the flames. "We must hit it
now: through you, but with all our strength, or it will be too
late."

Slowly, Malian raised her arms and touched the fingertips together, directing their apex toward the center of the
dark gate. A long tongue of flame licked along her arms and
hovered there, coiling around them like a serpent.

Darkness seeped from the Raptor's portal as the avian
head stooped down, turning sidelong to fix them with a baleful eye. "*Do not meet its stare,*" Hylcarian warned, "*or it will
consume you utterly, mind and soul.*"

Beneath the hiss and crackle of the Golden Fire, a new voice sang. Its note was dark and grew swiftly into a glittering, menacing hum, as though a nest of hornets had woken in their midst, angry and prepared for battle. The voice fueled Malian's will to resist the Raptor, but she had to exert all her self-discipline not to release her concentration on building power and trace the song's source.

"Nine!" exclaimed Korin, sounding shaken. "What is that?"

"An edge," said Asantir, cool as steel, and stepped forward, a tall, black-shafted war spear in her hand. She was smiling, a smile so terrible that even Malian wanted to avert her eyes, while the spear itself made her shiver. The blade was black as night and shaped like flame; its voice was the hornet's song, that fierce, fiery battle hum.

Afterward, no one could say exactly what happened next except that everything happened at once. The Raptor filled the dark portal completely, thrusting both its beaked head and half-open wings forward for the final push into the chamber—and the Golden Fire exploded. Flame lanced from Malian's outstretched arms in the same moment that Asantir cast the black spear, a smooth, powerful throw. Spear and fire blazed through the air together on a deadly trajectory that tore apart smoke and shadow and pierced the heart of the Raptor's darkness.

The Raptor screamed, a furious cry that echoed on and on and made everyone clap their hands over their ears. Cracks ran across the roof and mortar began to fall as the avian shape reared toward the ceiling, its vast wings fanning wide as the Golden Fire lanced into it again. A conflagration ignited, deep within the Raptor's mass, and the scream became a shriek as the demon was sucked backward, teetering on the edge of its own abyss. The portal shook—then the fiery darkness at its core exploded and the Raptor's gate collapsed, vanishing completely.

"*Well!*" said Hylcarian to Malian alone, and she could feel his sudden focus on the Honor Captain, who was kneel-

ing on the stone floor, her head bowed. *"Ay, casting that
spear might well drain her."*

Asantir lifted her head. "Look!" she gasped out. "See—
what is happening!"

Everyone followed her upward gaze and saw that the
cracks from the collapsed portal were spreading across
walls and roof. *"Flee!"* Hylcarian cried. *"Through the
gate—swiftly! I will stay and hold back the collapse lest
it bring the whole keep down, Old and New alike."* A cop-
ingstone fell out of the ceiling and shattered on the floor.
"Run!" Hylcarian urged again. *"I cannot help you hold the
gate open and bind this place together at the same time, not
for long."*

They ran. The sound and the strong snatched up their
gear and the wounded at the same time; even those who
had looked askance at the golden portal before did not hesitate, but plunged through. Soon only Malian and Tarathan
remained, still locked into the Golden Fire, while Asantir
leaned heavily on Garan's arm. Another stone fell, smashing
into shards beside them.

"Why do you wait?" demanded Hylcarian. *"Go!"*

Tarathan spoke for Malian, who was beyond words. "You
must go through," he told Asantir. "Malian has to wait until
the last, for she links our gate to the Fire."

Asantir frowned, then nodded and stepped through, still
supported by Garan. Tarathan looked down at Malian. "Can
you hold?" he asked. She managed a minimal nod, knowing she would be all right so long as she remained locked
into the Golden Fire. But the pressure on Hylcarian was immense. She could feel his power and strength pouring into
the fabric of the Old Keep, trying to halt the process of dis-
integration—yet he needed more. He needed the power he
had lent to her, but she was not sure that she had sufficient
strength left to release that power and her connection to the
Fire at the same time, without collapsing the portal. She was
not even confident of being able to move on her own.

Tarathan, still linked to both her and the Golden Fire,

seemed to understand. He scooped her up and in two swift strides they were in the gate, momentarily suspended there. A split second and another long stride later and they, too, were through. Willing hands reached out to take Malian, setting her gently on her feet. She swayed, but Tarathan kept a steadying hand on her arm. "Not yet," he said, commanding her. "You must close the gate."

"That's . . . easy," whispered Malian, and released the link to Hylcarian. The Golden Fire fled away like a tide and the last of the flames around the doorway flickered, then snuffed out with a soft huff of disturbed air. Dark flecks danced before Malian's eyes and she thought she might have fainted, except for Tarathan's hand on her arm. Another hand touched her hair, very gently, and she reached out blindly, clinging to the physical reassurance of hardened leather and cold mail. "Are we safe?" she whispered.

"Very safe," Asantir's voice said. "It was well done indeed, my Malian."

"It was your spear that slew the demon, Captain," said Tarathan, his low tone matching hers, "as much as the Fire did." Malian lifted her head blearily, trying to focus on their faces, unsure whether Tarathan meant anyone else to hear him. She should have guessed, though, that Kalan, hovering close by, would overhear.

"If that spear was what I think," he said, a thread of excitement burning through the weariness in his voice, "then it would kill anything, even a Raptor of Darkness."

Asantir was standing without support now, although she still looked drained. "And what do you think it was?" she asked, with the slightest rise of her brows. Everyone was listening now and Kalan looked suddenly nervous. His reply, though, was steady.

"*'Of death my song and black my blade, for Kerem's hand by Alkiranth made.'* Even to touch the edge of such a weapon, the slightest nick or scratch, is to die."

"But that can't be right," protested Var. "The black blades of Kerem were swords."

Kalan nodded. "It's true that Kerem's swords were black blades, but he also had other weapons. And Brother Belan said that because the legend of Kerem is one of our oldest, some variants confuse or intertwine the hero with even older stories, myths even, of the god Tawr, the Spearbearer. In those stories, Kerem had the use of Tawr's own weapons, including the spear." He had lost his nervousness, Malian noted, when it became a question of what the histories did or did not say. "But every variant agrees that Kerem's arms were *all* black blades."

"Surely," said Tisanthe, looking confused, "you are not suggesting that the captain's spear was one of Kerem's weapons?"

"Even if it was," growled Sarus, "what does it matter so long as it slew the demon? The Kerem of the stories would say it had been put to good use!"

There was a murmur of agreement, but Asantir and Kalan remained intent on each other. Kalan's jaw jutted stubbornly, but Malian could see that he was nervous again. She blinked at them, puzzled, and then Asantir smiled, a wry expression that reminded Malian of Yorindesarinen.

"What Kalan is wondering," Asantir said, "is how I could possibly possess a black blade without anyone knowing, when such a weapon should be an heirloom of the House of Night. Am I right, Kalan?"

Kalan nodded, but his eyes remained fixed on hers.

"The answer," she continued, "is simple enough. I was never told what it was and nor, I suspect, was any other Honor Captain of Night for many centuries. It has hung on the wall of the Captain's room and been handed down from one to the other, along with the command—and the counsel that it has potency against the power of the Swarm, but is only to be used in dire need. So when the heralds warned of the dangers that might wait in here, it seemed prudent to bring it with me."

There was another murmur, this time of approval, and Kalan's eyes fell. Asantir watched him for a moment longer, then turned to study the faces gathered around her. Warriors and priests looked back at her wearily, but Malian saw something else in their expressions—the stamp of those who have been into a dark and dangerous place together and come out alive. There was sadness, too, for they had left comrades behind and seen the Derai's ancient enemy made manifest for the first time. Malian caught more than one quick, covert glance toward herself and Kalan, although Kalan seemed unaware of it. He was still looking down, studying his feet with every evidence of interest. The heralds, as though feeling that their part was done, had moved aside from the Derai.

Asantir rested a hand on Malian's shoulder, while her eyes circled the others again, warrior and priest alike, pulling them close. "We all know," she said quietly, "what we have been through together and what we have done, but soon we will return to the New Keep and our comrades there, who will not share that understanding. There is much that we could say to shock them and still more that they will find easier to disbelieve. For these reasons, I believe that we must hold what we know to ourselves, telling only the Earl and those he deems wise. That way, we will fulfill our duty to House and keep while ensuring that rumor, doubt, and fear are not spread through our agency." Her fleeting grin was twisted. "Rumor will spread abroad quickly enough in any case, without our help."

Kyr shot a quick, frowning look toward Malian. "Do you mean the Heir, Captain, and her powers? Is that what we should keep silent about?"

"That is part of it," Asantir agreed, "but only part. The rest you saw as clearly as any of us—the Golden Fire, the power of the heralds, and the powers that the Swarm brought against us."

She did not mention the black spear, but Malian caught the flicker of Kalan's upward glance and knew that it was still in his mind. She repressed a shiver, remembering the spear's glittering hornet song.

Sarus scratched his chin with his thumb. "As you said, it'll all be out quick enough anyway, especially if the Earl tells those councilors of his."

"Maybe so," replied Asantir, when the general chuckle had died away. "Just as long as it does not get about through our indiscretion."

There was a small silence as they mulled this over, but Malian thought they would follow Asantir's lead in the end. She could see it in the way the Honor Captain held them in their circle around her. She thought, too, about everything that had happened since she fled the New Keep, strange and frightening and wonderful things, and knew that her life would never be the same again, either in her own eyes or in the eyes of others.

As if in answer to this thought, Garan stepped forward and stood directly in front of her. Probably only Malian, standing so close, caught the infinitesimal tightening of Asantir's body as the guard drew his dagger. Slowly, his eyes never leaving Malian's face, Garan drew the tip of the dagger across the palm of his left hand, leaving a fine line of blood. "Chosen," he said. "Shield of Mhaelanar, Beloved of the Nine. My blood for your Blood, my life for your life, my heart only for you and the Derai cause, now and until my life's end. If I fail you in this, or if harm comes to you through any deed or word of mine, then may the blood be drained from my body, even to the last drop, and my soul walk naked before the Nine, without succor or respite, forever."

Malian felt the color blanch from her face as she stretched out a restraining hand. "That is a blood oath, Garan," she said, her voice harsh in the silence, "binding beyond death. Are you sure you know what you are doing?"

Slowly and deliberately, the guard sheathed the dagger. "I have seen what I have seen, Lady Malian. To my mind, there can be no doubt. You are the Chosen of Mhaelanar, the champion foretold in the old prophecies, the Shield of the Nine sent among us. I have sworn my oath."

He stepped back and Nerys—Nerys the silent, Nerys the reserved—stepped forward to take his place. One by one the other warriors followed, drawing their daggers and swearing the same oath, even dour Kyr and the sergeant, Sarus. When they were done, Eria held her hand out silently for Garan's dagger. Just as silently, the guard gave it to her and so the thing was done: All the initiates followed Eria, just as the warriors had followed Garan. In the end, of the Derai present, only Kalan and Asantir had not sworn. But when Kalan made a move as though to step forward, Malian shook her head with passionate intensity. "Don't you dare!" she said. "Not you, Kalan."

Kalan stopped, his expression so comical that Garan guffawed, breaking the tense, solemn atmosphere. For a moment his laugh rang out alone—and then everyone was laughing and hugging each other, at first just warrior and warrior, priest and priest, but then Asantir extended her free arm to catch Kalan close. "Well done!" she said, looking from his face to Malian's. Kalan still held back a little, but Malian hugged the captain unreservedly until she winced at the pressure on her wounded shoulder and cried for quarter. Garan, seeming to think this an excellent example, caught the astonished Eria up in a bear hug.

"Garan just doesn't like to miss an opportunity to kiss a pretty face," said the guard Lira, who had a darkly pretty face of her own. "And I am much the same!" she added, stepping up to Tarathan and kissing him on the mouth. The herald looked startled for a moment, but then he laughed and kissed her back. She laughed, too, and shot a half-defiant, half-triumphant glance at Nerys, as she stepped back—and suddenly the hugging and the congratulations and slapping on the back had widened to include everyone.

Malian shook her head in disbelief. "I can't believe they did that!" she said to Kalan. "Swore the oath, I mean, not the kissing—but now look at them! You wouldn't think they had just sworn the gravest of oaths, binding beyond death!"

Kalan looked round at the jubilation and back slapping

that was slowly dying away. "I think they do know," he said slowly.

"Kalan is right," said Asantir. "And it is right, too, that they should have this moment, before we walk the last few steps to the New Keep and their oath binds them."

Malian studied her. "You didn't swear," she pointed out.

Asantir nodded. "I am Honor Captain, Malian. I swore my oaths long ago. Did you wish me to swear to you also?"

"No!" Malian said passionately. "I'm glad that you didn't, and Kalan, too! I don't want people going around swearing blood oaths, and cutting their hands and other such nonsense, even if I am Heir of Night or the Chosen of Mhaelanar! I was just surprised," she said more calmly, "that you didn't stop them."

The Honor Captain regarded her gravely. "I would not think it right to stop anyone, warrior or priest, who chooses to swear such an oath to the Heir of Night."

Malian hesitated, wondering if the oath-taking was the outcome that Asantir had intended all along, when she pulled the circle close. She was still considering that possibility when Kalan said slyly, "Well, I hope you realize that you've had your last chance with me, Heir of Night. I won't offer to swear again."

Malian laughed. "I'm glad that you and Asantir had more sense! Besides, you're my friend," she added more soberly. "People can't be your friends if they swear blood oaths to you."

Kalan shrugged and grinned at the same time, but Malian could tell that he was pleased. She turned back to Asantir. "Right now," she said, "I've had enough of the Old Keep. Can we go home?"

The Honor Captain smiled, not the terrible smile of the black spear but the one that was wryly kind, and saluted her. "Of course. The way is clear and the place of honor belongs to you and those who brought you back to us: Kalan and the heralds of the Guild. So lead us home, Heir of Night!"

* * *

It was very quiet in the old High Hall after they had gone. The dust settled slowly and the golden motes began to disappear. Some time later, a disturbance rippled through the air. The tremor faded and the air grew still again, only to be redisturbed, first by another ripple and then by a slow rent opening in the center of the hall—just wide enough to let a shadow ooze through onto the floor. The shadow paused, swaying, while the rent closed behind it.

Slowly, the shadow undulated across the floor and up one of the frayed tapestries, blending into the fabric of decay and age. It was weary, both from its journey through the Place Between, moving cautiously so that its enemies remained unaware, and from expending the vast energy necessary to open a door into this place. Now it must rest and restore its strength, and this dim, derelict hall would serve that purpose well. It was not a place where people seemed likely to come. The shadow hissed softly at that thought, the sound unexpectedly loud in the silence.

The creature hissed again and drew back further into the shadows, merging with the stone of the walls, for becoming one with its surroundings was part of its strength. For the moment, it would lie low, so that when it did make its move there would be no mistakes. Not like Nirn and the Raptor, both of whom had underestimated their opponents. Still, they had served their purpose, distracting the enemy from its own secret presence and doing sufficient damage to tie up the Golden Fire for some time.

The shadow reflected on that last point with satisfaction as it settled down to wait. After all, it could afford to be patient. Even if someone came and looked there would be nothing to see, just a darker patch of shadow that was part of the wall with its tattered hangings. But as it turned out, concealed or not, the shadow was completely safe. No one came.

PART II

Storm Shadows

15

The Darkness of the Derai

*I*t was well past midnight and the Keep of Winds was quiet, although the Earl of Night did not think that it would sleep easily again for a long time. He was sprawled in a chair before the fire in his chambers, bone weary and still in the armor he had worn since the attack. So much had happened in so short a time, a potent reminder that their long vigil on the Wall had some meaning, after all.

As if, he thought, anyone with eyes could doubt that, given the withered lands that surround us and the foul creatures haunting every pass and dark ravine!

The Earl sighed, shifting in his seat. He was fortunate, he supposed, to have seen some of the other lands and creatures of this world and to know how twisted and tainted the Wall was by comparison. For most Derai, the Wall and its strongholds were all they ever knew: a bleak and narrow world—and one ill equipped, now, to withstand its enemy. The attack on the keep had proven that.

The frown between the Earl's brows bit more deeply as he considered the consequences of the attack, some immediate, others more long-lasting. The death and destruction was bad, but could be borne; the sweeping away of the Derai belief in the inviolability of their keeps could prove harder to overcome. But the news that Korriya had brought him—that was far worse than any physical attack. The Earl's hand closed into a fist. If only Korriya had not been so compelling and he could have dismissed her words. But he remembered the priestess well from their childhood together. Level headed and pragmatic, that was Korriya, with both feet firmly on the ground. She was not a person whose arguments should be dismissed lightly, if at all.

I should have known, the Earl thought. Maybe he *had* known. Malian was so like Nerion had been at the same age, but he had closed his eyes to the likeness, denying its potential implications. He had even dared to hope that Korriya might be mistaken, when he should have learned the futility of hope long ago. But Asantir's account of events in the Old Keep had swept away any vestige of doubt, and the news would not stay quiet for long. Someone would talk; sooner or later, someone always did.

He shook his head, wondering how many Earls of Night before him had experienced such a succession of disasters. The aftermath of battle he could deal with: the endless discussions of how best to secure the keep and the daunting logistics of maintaining everyday life, despite the destruction everywhere. He could also understand and manage both those who seemed frozen in bewilderment and shock, unable to act, and the others who raged and called on him to exact swift retribution. That was all part of his duty as Earl, as fighting in defense of the keep had been. But these other matters, the stories of demons and old powers, the part his own daughter had played—the Earl shook his head again, staring blindly into the fire.

He had been stunned when Asantir came to him with Haimyr's story that one of the heralds was a seeker. He had inherited his father's aversion to those with the old powers, but he was still shocked to think that those despised powers might not, after all, be unique to the Derai. The Earl could not recall any instance in the long history of the Alliance where the Derai had encountered any other race with powers comparable to theirs—aside from the Swarm, of course. It was part of what set them apart, even if they now feared and mistrusted that particular aspect of their heritage.

The fingers of the Earl's right hand drummed on his chair arm. "Ay, we fear it. But we've relied on it, too, just as we've relied on the long tradition of the inviolability of the power bound into the Old Keep." *The more fools we,* he added to himself, thinking *we could abandon the place so completely and still rely on its wards to defend us.*

Now he was faced with the unpalatable probability that neglect of the old powers might prove to be the Derai's undoing. And he was still his father's son. It galled him that the priesthood might be essential to Derai survival, but he could not deny the evidence of recent events. Even so, he had been deeply reluctant when the heralds asked for the aid of Korriya's priests. He had only agreed, unhappily, at Asantir's urging.

The first time in five hundred years that the warrior kind had sought aid from the Temple quarter—and he was the Earl who had allowed it. His father, the Old Earl, would not have done it; he would have let Malian die first.

If he were here now, he would call me weak, the Earl thought, his expression weary. *And perhaps he would be right, since I found that I could not bear to lose my child, as I lost my wife. Yet now I will lose Malian anyway, for exactly the same reason that I lost Nerion.*

He could feel the weight of his duty—to his House, to the Derai Alliance, and to the Blood Oath that bound him, as it had bound every Earl for five hundred years—settling on him now, heavier by far than the weight of his armor.

Heavy, yes, but not in the same way as the message delivered to him by the heralds of the Guild, which sat in his belly like a stone. He could not speak of it to anyone, dared not, and that circumstance, together with their priestlike powers, made him reflect dourly on the breed called heralds. Their very presence was like a rock dropped into a pool and he had seen the dark looks and heard the mutterings that followed them.

"They have witnessed Derai weakness and seen too much for outsiders," the mutterers said, giving *outsiders* its old, dangerous twist, which meant both stranger and enemy.

The Earl grimaced as he remembered the uncanny power of the heralds' sigil of silence. Once invoked, it was as though an invisible wall had sprung up around themselves and the Earl. Asantir—watching to make sure that he came to no harm—could see, but not hear a word that was spoken. And the heralds had spoken sometimes in unison, sometimes alternately, as though neither of them knew the message in its entirety.

They had been sent, they told him, by an old friend of his youth, from the time when he traveled in the River lands. The friend was a River merchant called Vhirinal, who had risen to be an Ephor, or ruler, in the city of Terebanth. It appeared that information flowed as freely as gold along the trading routes between the River cities, and that in recent years these flows had widened to include some of the Derai Houses along the Wall. Eventually, all the information, like much of the gold, came to the Ephors of Terebanth and so it was that Vhirinal had learned something that concerned his old friend, Tasarion, who was now the Earl of Night.

"There is a traitor in your household," the herald Jehane had said, speaking the Ephor's warning aloud.

"One who is close to you but whom you suspect not," the herald Tarathan had continued. *"Beware!"* the heralds had then chanted in unison. *"Beware, Earl of Night, for the hounds of your enemies hunt!"*

One who is close to you but whom you suspect not. It could be anyone—anyone whom he saw every day and trusted, as a retainer or a friend, even a lover. The Earl flinched away from that last thought, but it could not be ignored.

"Someone close to me, whom I suspect not." He spoke slowly to the quiet night. "Rowan is the obvious choice, the stranger out of the Winter Country. There are already plenty who say that she has bewitched me, and why else but to betray me in the end? Or Haimyr, the outsider who has dwelt so long amongst us. Yet if they are traitors, whom do they serve? Are the people of Winter or far-off Ij *my* enemies? There is no sense in that." The Earl's fingers drummed again: *Beware Earl of Night for the hounds of your enemies hunt.* He frowned at the fire. "I know that our Derai enemies were not responsible for last night's attack, but they could have suborned someone close to me, all the same. But if so, who? And to what specific end, beyond the obvious betrayal?"

There were so many possible candidates. Gerenth was dead, but he had served the Old Earl faithfully all his life; it seemed unlikely that he would have turned traitor. Asantir? The Earl hesitated, but only briefly. She had been so close to him for so long, and he would sooner mistrust his own right arm. It was much the same with Nhairin, for if Asantir was his right arm then the High Steward of the keep was certainly his left. And Teron came from the family that had always commanded Cloud Hold for the House of Night; a family as famous for their unswerving loyalty and courage as they were for their dogmatism and lack of imagination.

It was unthinkable, the Earl reflected wryly, that one of that family would have the initiative to be a traitor, let alone the inclination.

The other unpleasant possibility was that the message itself was a ploy, a poisoned barb planted by his enemies to sow suspicion and distrust. It need not even mean that Vhirinal, once his friend, had become his enemy, or the friend of his enemies. Those same adversaries need only have ensured that the rumor of a traitor came creeping to the Ephor's ears. Still, the Earl told himself, the Vhirinal he remembered would know to be wary of such ploys. He must have given the tale considerable credence to go to the expense of employing heralds and sending them on the long journey to the Wall of Night.

"A very great friend then," the Earl mused, "or a great enemy." But he had no way of judging which was true, any more than he could determine the identity of the traitor—if he or she truly existed. He had to suspect everyone while continuing to act as though he trusted all, and hope that sooner or later the traitor's mask would slip.

The door opened softly onto the darkness of his thoughts and a tall, white-clad figure was outlined briefly against the corridor before stepping inside and closing the door. The firelight fell short of her face, leaving it in shadow as she crossed to his chair. "You are awake late, Earl of Night," Rowan Birchmoon said gently. "It would be better if you took off that armor and got some rest."

He gazed back at her. "I am well enough, my Lady of Winter. The armor helps remind me of my responsibilities."

She stroked his dark, gray-flecked hair with one white, slender hand. "It does no good to spend the night gnawing over your troubles like an old hound. You need sleep."

"Sorcery, attacks in the night, and attempts on the life of my Heir," he said, matching her tone. "These are troubles enough for any Derai hound to gnaw on, don't you think?"

Her gray eyes, cool as silver, looked down into his. "Perhaps," she said, "but I do not think it is those bones that keep you awake now. There are other things, are there not, that trouble you more?" She studied his closed expression and nodded, as though her question was answered. "But if these are deep Derai matters, then maybe it is best that you keep silence." She spoke without rancor and settled onto the floor before the fire, gazing into it in her turn.

The Earl's expression softened. "You know it is not that, my heart. Some matters are too heavy for words, that is all."

She looked gravely back at him. "Is your daughter part of this heaviness, Earl of Night?"

He nodded, his mouth tightening, but said nothing. She shook her head. "I have never understood this schism between warrior and priest. It seems to cause nothing but pain and grief and does your Alliance great harm. I can see no good in it."

The Earl gave a short laugh. "Haimyr would say that the

pain and grief of it, without the good, is all Derai—the very heart of our songs and stories."

Rowan Birchmoon smiled. "That is exactly what he says," she agreed, "but I am sure I could recall a saga with a happy ending, if I thought for long enough." The smile faded. "It seems to me that it is one history alone, this Great Betrayal, that has been twisting your lives for half a millennium. Yet no one ever tells the full tale, or at least, not within my hearing."

"Because we suck it in with our mother's milk," he agreed somberly, "and breathe it through the very air, an intrinsic part of who and what we are. I think that this is the first time I have ever questioned whether the bitter division to which we cling has not been our greatest folly."

"And you," she said, "are a thinking man." She hesitated, and then continued: "Yet I, who am not Derai, did not think that the priestess Korriya was so very much your enemy."

He yawned, stretching. "I didn't think so either; that is partly what bothers me. Although Korriya is my kinswoman and we knew each other as children. But I cannot forget the faces of the initiates who went into the Old Keep with Asantir. None of them would look at me directly when I farewelled the search party. But I could see every single one watching me out of the sides of their eyes, exactly like the raw recruits we get in the barracks, desperate to prove their worth and serve Night. And now," he finished softly, "I see the faces of the dead, those who did not return."

Rowan Birchmoon stretched out a hand to his. "So many died in the attack, especially in the Temple quarter where the demon hunted. At least Serin and Ilor knew what they were dying for."

The Earl's brows rose. "Serin and Ilor," he repeated. "Yes, that was what Asantir called them. But their death is my point. They died for House and keep, just as much as the warriors did; I would be blind not to see it. Yet at the same time I hear the echo of my father's voice, cursing the priest kind as our enemy within, a foe as bitter as the Swarm."

"Although even before today, you did not believe that." It was a statement, not a question, and he nodded.

"No," he said, and stared straight ahead with a harsh set to his mouth, remembering the Hall of the Dead and the bodies of the fallen laid out in their rows. He had walked every row and looked into every face. There had been so many of them, line on line of warriors with their death wounds, and priests who had died screaming, their souls sucked out of them by the Raptor of Darkness. He had paused longest by the bodies of the Heir's household, who had all died in the first onslaught, betrayed by the New Keep alarms that had remained blind and deaf to the attack.

Swarm magic used against us, the Earl thought now. But his bitterness could not bring back Nesta and Doria, or the pages, their bodies pathetic in death, or any of the other servants who had fallen in the Heir's quarter.

Faithful, he had thought then, as he thought it now, for they had tried to keep the attackers out although they had no weapons, possessed no old powers to defend themselves. Honorable, too—like Serin and Ilor, dying for him and for Night, far down in the darkness of the Old Keep.

He heard the echo of his father's voice again, ranting at him for being a weakling and a fool. But he could not find it in himself to deny any one of the dead their share of honor, even if they had worn a servant's clothes or priest's robes, rather than a mail shirt.

"You need to put these troubles aside and let yourself sleep." Rowan Birchmoon rose and bent over him, framing his face between her hands and kissing him gently on the mouth. "Your difficulties will not change their fate, even if you worry them to death."

He touched the pale brown silk of her hair, wondering how he could even think of not trusting her, when she had never given him anything but kindness and truth. Yet he knew that he must retain that small inner question, a hint of doubt.

Rowan Birchmoon took his hand and kissed the palm.

"You may be right to be troubled, my Tasarion," she whispered, "but we have a saying in the Winter Country: Do not be afraid to wear your sorrows, but beware if they wear you."

He turned his hand around to clasp hers. "You need not be afraid of that," he replied, a little grimly. "I have given tonight to my grief, but tomorrow I will do what I must to secure the House of Night."

"I believe you will," she said, a hint of sadness in her expression. As quickly as it had come, however, the sadness vanished and she murmured with her faint, delicate smile: "For are you not Derai, stern and dark and duty bound?"

The Earl, too, smiled and drew her down into his mail-clad arms. "How dear you are to me," he murmured, "my woman of the Winter Country." The dearer perhaps, he added to himself, because you are neither stern, nor dark, nor any part of my duty.

He remembered when he had first seen her, tall and fair as one of the white-stemmed birches of her own Winter land, with eyes as gray as its skies. It had never been his intention to marry again. He had turned a deaf ear to all the persuasions brought to bear, particularly from those who argued that it was his duty, first as Heir and then as Earl. He had not expected to journey to the Winter Country either, not after he had been called back to the Wall to take up the heirdom, and certainly not after he became Earl in his turn. The Earl of Night's place was in the Keep of Winds, foremost of all the Derai strongholds on the Wall of Night.

"First and oldest." He repeated the saying to himself, thinking how little, beyond duty, he had expected—least of all love.

Winter itself had intervened, coming early when he rode the boundaries three years before, and had caught his company in a severe storm. He still shivered, remembering how the wind had raged, hurling snow and ice across the land and driving his party before it, further and further from the Wall until they came to the boundaries of the Winter

Country. Many perished before they got there and the Earl knew that all would have died if the Winter people had not taken them in. He recalled stumbling, gaunt and exhausted, into the dim, smoky warmth of a hide-and-felt tent and seeing Rowan's face for the first time, pale and lovely between the weathered, deeply lined faces of hunt leader and shaman. The snows of winter lay deep but the light of her eyes was like spring, cracking and melting the ice that had encased his heart for the nine long years since Nerion had been sent away.

He remembered his followers' dismay when they realized that Rowan Birchmoon would be riding back to the Keep of Winds at his side—and how Rowan had laughed when he explained that the laws of the Derai would not allow him to marry her. She had been standing straight and tall amidst the white and blue of a sparkling winter's day, her breath clouding the freezing air. "Marriage," she had said, and shrugged. "Among the Winter people it is love and the commitment to each other that binds two people together, not a ceremony. I love you, my dark-visaged lord of the Derai. Being with you is what matters to me, not the outward forms of your people or mine."

He had loved her fiercely in that moment and he loved her still, even more—if that were possible—for enduring three long years in the Keep of Winds, amidst the scandalized and often hostile Derai, to be with him.

Yet now he could see his duty again, plain and cold before him. If he lost his Heir to the Temple quarter he would have to marry again, a formal and binding alliance with a woman of the Derai Blood, and get another heir for the House of Night. He could not insult a wife by having his lover in the same keep, or expect her to tolerate such a situation. Nor would he ask Rowan to dwell in one of the holds, a stranger amongst strangers, unwelcome and despised—but he could not bear to let her go, either.

The Earl's arms tightened around his lover, breathing in the scent of her long hair as he looked into a future that was colder and more bleak than any winter. I have had three years, he thought wearily, perhaps I should count myself lucky. But she, the heart of my heart, how will she count the cost?

He looked into her eyes and the faint smile was still there, lingering in their depths. "Too tired even to take off his mail," she said, "although he does not need it now, with the guard doubled throughout the keep and a small army camped outside his door."

"Do you mock me, Winter woman?" he demanded.

"I?" she said. "Mock? Who could mock the Earl of Night, leader of the first and greatest House of the Derai Alliance, even if he seems determined to sleep in his armor? Nay, do not call your squires. They were all snoring soundly when I passed the antechamber. I will be squire for you instead."

"You do not have armor in the Winter Country," he observed, but he let her help him anyway. It was a relief when the weight of the cuirass was lifted off, and the mail shirt, the greaves, and the vambraces, were laid aside.

"Sleep now," she said, pushing him toward the great bed with its black canopy and curtains, shot through with gold and silver thread. Yet for all his weariness, sleep eluded him, and finally Rowan Birchmoon said, "Well, if you cannot sleep, why not explain one of your Derai mysteries? Tell me this story of the Great Betrayal, your civil war."

"It is a dark history," he replied slowly, and listened to the wind gust along the eaves and pry at the tightly closed shutters, noting the rising tone that meant a storm was coming. Yet what better time to tell the old, bitter story, with a Wall storm brewing and darkness stalking all around? "But I will tell it as I first heard it, as a storyteller's tale, rather than trying to give a true and accurate account." He shifted in the bed, drawing Rowan Birchmoon's head to rest on his shoulder.

"Be still," he began, using the traditional opening. *"Be silent, and let me speak to you of the Darkness of the Derai.*

It arose, as such things often do, seemingly out of nowhere, with a quarrel between two close friends. And what friends they were, for one was Aikanor, the Heir of Night, the other Tasianaran—Tasian—the Heir of Stars. Both were young and valiant and fair, the flower of Derai chivalry and the most beloved.

"Now Tasian, the Heir of Stars, also had a twin sister and powerful indeed was she, as well as fair, one of the greatest priestesses in the Alliance. Her name was Xeri-atherien—Xeria—but all called her the Star of the Derai. Who knows when Aikanor, the Heir of Night, first looked on Xeria and loved her? Perhaps the love had been a long, slow time growing, or perhaps it dawned in the turning of her dark head, a glance from her starlit eyes—but love her he did. Yet Xeria did not return his love, for she was wedded to her training as a priestess, to the powers and arts sacred to the Nine Gods of the Derai. And gradually, when he saw that his love was not reciprocated, the light in Aikanor's heart turned to darkness and a slow burning anger grew in its place.

"No one knows what truly happened or how the quarrel arose, only that Aikanor invited Tasian and Xeria to the Keep of Winds as his guests, at a time when the Earl of Night, his father, was away visiting the lesser holds. What is suspected is that Aikanor then tried to take Xeria by force. The details are lost but the inevitable happened. Weapons were drawn and the matter ended with Tasian and all his Honor Guard, who of course were greatly outnumbered, being slain. Only Xeria and one page escaped, fleeing to the Temple quarter and claiming sanctuary from the priests of Night.

"Cursed is the name of Aikanor now, in all the annals of the Derai, for he broke the sacred laws of hospitality and the bonds of friendship, betraying the honor of the House of Night. Mourn the murder of Tasian, the Heir of Stars, with his friends and retainers slain around him. Weep for Xeria, the Star of the Derai, trapped in the keep of her enemies.

Most of all, grieve for the Derai Alliance, which was nearly destroyed by this deed.

"Perhaps the situation could have been salvaged if the Earl of Night had returned and been able to control his Heir. But he was far away and Aikanor's madness raged unchecked. He flung Tasian and the other House of Stars dead outside the Gate of Winds for the carrion eaters, then marched to the gates of the Temple quarter and demanded that Xeria be yielded to him. But the priests refused his demand and the Temple gates remained closed against the Heir of Night, for the first time ever recorded in all the long history of the Derai.

"Cursed be the High Priest and his followers for this deed, for they broke the sacred vows sworn by all Derai, to obey Earl and Heir first, before all other duties. Through their defiance they brought civil strife into the keep itself, siding with another House against their own so that Night was at war both within and without. And war it was, for the priests had their own temple warriors in those days and they were strong in powers and arts that allowed them to turn back the attacks of the Heir and his followers. The flames of their conflict leapt the walls of the Keep of Winds and ran the full length of the Wall, engulfing the entire Derai Alliance in the conflagration. The House of Stars marched in open war against the House of Night and all along the Derai Wall the other Houses took up arms, some declaring for one side, some for the other.

"In the end, most of the Houses fought against Night because of their horror at the slaying of Tasian and his retinue, and the wrong done to Xeria, whom many still held in their hearts as the Star of the Derai. For are not the children of Stars the most beloved of all the Houses, the getter of heroes and enchanters whose light has shone on the whole of the Derai Alliance, time after time? Only the House of Blood stood with Night at the last, and only the House of the Rose stood aside from the conflict, striving to heal the rift within the Alliance.

"The war was grim and bloody and the Keep of Winds endured a long and grievous siege but it did not fall, for who can take any keep that is filled with the Golden Fire of the Derai? Not even other Derai, it seemed—and at length both sides realized the futility of their strife and the House of the Rose was at last able to negotiate a peace. The final terms were signed in a great pavilion set amidst the killing grounds before the Gate of Winds, which remained closed until the signing was complete.

"Now in all that time there had been another gate that never opened, and that was the gate of the Temple quarter inside the Keep of Winds. Through all that long and bloody war the priestess Xeria and the priests of the House of Night had been besieged in their turn. Yet the treaty stipulated that there was to be peace between the Earl of Night and his priests, and that Xeria and her page were to go free at last. So the Temple gates swung open and they came out together, the High Priest with his people around him and the priestess Xeria, powerful still and fair, even in her sorrow. They all sat down together in the High Hall, the House of Night with the House of Stars, and priest beside warrior, to break the bread and drink the wine of peace, honoring the terms that had been sworn to and agreed.

"Yet the bitterness is not yet done, my hearers, for the direst chapter in this whole grim tale must now be told. Darkness still bloomed in the heart and mind of Aikanor and there were many in the House of Night who remained apt to his will. So he sat in the Heir's Seat and when the rituals were completed, he and his followers turned upon their recent enemies, betraying their pledged word.

"All accounts say that what followed was utter carnage, for at first few could believe what was happening and then, when they saw the blood blossoming and the bodies falling and did believe, confusion reigned. Some of the warriors of Night rallied to their Earl, who tried to stop the slaughter, but others joined the Heir in his killing, turning especially on the priests of their own House. Weapons were seized from the walls and the hall became a battlefield. The flagstones were awash with blood and every wall hanging was splashed and daubed with red. Even the peacemakers from the House of the Rose, who never bear arms, were cut down along with the rest.

"In the midst of all this horror was the Heir of Night, his face a fiend's mask of hatred as he and his closest followers sought to cut their way to Xeria. No one will ever know his purpose at the end, whether it was to slay her as he had slain her brother, or to seize her and drag her away. Warriors from the House of Stars battled to reach and defend her and many priests of the House of Night, who stood with her still, fell protecting the daughter of another House from the swords of their own clan and kin.

"All agree that Aikanor must have been mad and the certain proof of this is that he appears to have forgotten the power of the priestess he attacked. As for Xeria, it is said that she was half mad also, both from the long siege and grief for her murdered twin. The sight of so many being slain around her, and her brother's killer before her, proved too much. The priestess's last hold on sanity was swept away on a tide of fear and rage and she used her tremendous power to wreak the greatest betrayal of all, calling down the Golden Fire of the keeps to kill her own people.

"Perhaps Xeria only meant to strike at Aikanor, but the cataclysm of destruction that followed fell equally upon the heads of friend and foe alike. Half the valor of the Derai died that night, by the sword and by the fire that struck like bolts of golden lightning and in curtains of coruscating flame. It is said that the entire keep resounded to the screams of the dying and the fire consumed everything it touched. Xeria, too, was immolated, but her death was as nothing to the destruction she wrought upon the Derai. Both the Earl of Night and his Heir were slain, as were the Earl of Blood, the Sword Earl, and the Count of the Rose. Most of the priests of the House of Night lay dead and the Golden Fire that had lived in the heart of every keep was extin-

guished. It could not be roused again, not even by what was left of the Blood. Every keep of the Derai Alliance was left gray and cold and has remained so to this day.

"After the full reckoning of the dead had been made, each House withdrew to mourn their own. The House of Night forsook the old Keep of Winds, for the priest kind were not the only ones to dream of slaughter and have nightmares filled with the screams and pleadings of the dead. And so the New Keep was built—but on the day that the Old Keep was finally abandoned the Earl of Night's successor swore a great oath. He was a grim, cold man with no forgiveness in him and he named all priests as faith breakers and traitors, banishing them from his newly built halls. The oath he took to uphold this deed was a blood oath above and beyond any sworn before or since—grounded in lifeblood drawn from every scion of the Blood of Night, in the shades of the dead, and in the secret names of the Nine Gods. The Blood Oath, the new Earl called it, enduring beyond death. And so it has proven, for the Oath has remained unshaken, binding Earl and Heir and House from that day to this.

"The Earl of Blood was swift to adopt the Blood Oath and although it may not have been sworn to formally by all the Derai, its practice quickly became tradition throughout the Alliance. If alliance you could call it still, when no new peace was sworn between the Houses and vendetta and blood feud took the place of outright war. There has been no friendship between the Houses of Night and Stars from that day to this, and one by one the remaining Houses have realigned to one side or the other: The warrior and Sea keeps with Night; the priestly Houses with Stars—and the House of the Rose withdrawn into itself.

"House against House, warrior against priest, therein you have the heart of the darkness that has fallen over the Derai."

The Earl's voice fell silent and the wind was suddenly very loud, an alien presence that sobbed and moaned, straining to find entry. Rowan Birchmoon, too, was silent, as though listening to the wild voice off the Wall. "That is a dark tale indeed," she said finally. "Until now I have always understood that it was your priest kind who betrayed the Derai. Yet in your tale it was Aikanor who committed the first betrayal, just as at the end he was the first to break his sworn oaths of peace."

The Earl's lips tightened. "Apparently," he said grudgingly, "Aikanor himself had priestly powers. In those days, many warriors had the old powers, while priests learned warrior skills. Aikanor had trained with the warrior priests before he became Heir and it is said that there were several like him amongst his own guard. That is why the Oath specifically precludes those of the Blood with priestly powers from ever again leading the Derai. It is to protect us from the likes of Aikanor."

"So according to the tale, there were really three betrayals." Rowan Birchmoon spoke slowly. "The crimes of Aikanor, which started it all; the subsequent defiance of the priests; and the final, calamitous act by Xeria. The betrayal by the priests in giving succor to Xeria, if betrayal it was, seems the least of these dark deeds, yet they are the ones punished by the Oath."

The Earl frowned. "You still don't understand," he said. "They were all priest kind, every one of them: Aikanor, Xeria, and those who gave her shelter."

"But surely," she protested, "the Temple was right to give Xeria sanctuary?"

The Earl shook his head. "The Derai are a people under arms and the Earls and their Heirs are war leaders first and foremost, whose commands must be obeyed by House and keep. Any other consideration must come second to that. There can be no exemptions or special cases."

"But how could it be right," asked Rowan Birchmoon, "to obey an order that was so plainly wrong, morally, and in terms of every Derai value of honorable conduct and hospitality? Can an Earl command his captains to commit evil deeds, deeds that are not even part of the war you say you are fighting, simply because the Derai are an army first and a people second?" She paused, then added softly, "Is this truly what you believe, Tasarion of Night?"

He looked away from her, his mouth thinned into a hard line. He loved her—but who was she to question the Derai? The Winter people were little more than nomads, wandering hunters who dwelt far from the Wall of Night and had never encountered the terror of the Swarm, or experienced the bitter sacrifices required of those who opposed it. Yet it was the Derai Wall alone, although they knew it not, that protected all the safe, complacent peoples of Haarth from being overrun by the Swarm.

The Earl checked himself, hearing the echo of his father's contempt when he spoke of outsiders, calling them leeches who fed off Derai blood. It had always been moot, Tasarion reflected now, whether the Old Earl had despised priests or outsiders more. A quick stab of shame accompanied that thought, for those same nomads and hunters had saved him and his followers from death in the snow, three years before. And afterward, for love and love alone, Rowan had returned with him to the Wall of Night.

She was entitled, he reminded himself, his anger dissipating, to see the world differently from the Derai. "No," he said quietly, "I do not think it right for me to order evil done in the name of the Derai cause, any more than it was right for Aikanor to do so. Nonetheless, the Derai Alliance could not function if every time an Earl gave an order it was debated and endlessly questioned by the rest of the House."

Rowan Birchmoon remained silent some time, although he guessed that she was still pondering what he had said. "But surely," she said at last, "the Betrayal could not be seen as normal circumstances, especially since Aikanor had already broken several sacred laws? Given that his breaches had such far-reaching consequences, should he not have forfeited any right to exact obedience from the House of Night? Perhaps the priests believed that by denying the Heir they were holding true to the Earl, maintaining Night's honor by refusing to countenance his son's misdeeds?"

"You argue like an envoy from the House of the Rose," the Earl observed dryly, "but in the end, it does not matter what I believe. I am bound by the Blood Oath and must observe its terms. And how can I hope to hold this House together if I do not uphold its laws?" His voice, in the fire-shadowed darkness, was deeply weary. "I am tired and grieved, and I do not wish to wrangle over our old darkness and all its ills, which I can do little or nothing to mend."

She slid her arms around him, by way of answer, holding him close within their circle. Outside, the wind hurled itself against the keep and the Earl closed a hand over one of hers, holding it against his heart. "I have always thought," he said at last, almost reluctantly, "that the Oath reflects the depth of the shock and betrayal felt at the time. No simple retelling can adequately express the horror of Xeria's deed. Aikanor's madness was bad enough, but Xeria's . . ." His voice trailed away as even now, five hundred years later, he struggled to come to terms with the enormity of what Xeria had done and its implications for the Derai.

"The Golden Fire of the keeps," he murmured eventually. "The very name is magic still, but then it was the heart of the Alliance, our most powerful bulwark against the enemy. Xeria did the unthinkable when she used it against the Derai, immolating friend and foe alike. The extremity of that act nearly shattered the Alliance completely—and generated an equally extreme response in the Blood Oath. The new Earl of Night was not alone in resolving that such a catastrophe must never, ever, happen again. The histories suggest that many of the priest kind felt the same way. Some may even have supported the Oath initially, for that reason. Perhaps it was easier, as well, to see the betrayal by our own as the greater threat, since we had been here for nearly a thousand years by that time without any major attack by the Swarm. Who knows? Certainly I do not, five hundred years later. All I know is that the Oath continues to bind us, generation after generation, and there is neither peace nor reconciliation between our divided Houses. Blood feud and vendetta, conflict and war: It goes on and on, and I for one cannot see an end to it."

"And now," she observed, "some of your councilors will put this attack down to the old schism and demand revenge."

He moved restlessly beside her. "Oh, they are already baying for the blood of some nice, safe enemy to appease their shame and fear. We must prove that we are still strong, they say, by sweeping down on some House that is both unprepared and weaker than ourselves—not that they put it in those terms!" His laugh was short and mirthless. "The House of Peace perhaps, that should be safe enough since they follow Meraun and eschew the sword. Except that the Sword Earl would not allow it, since Peace is in some wise under his protection. So that will not do, we had best choose some outlying hold of the House of Morning instead."

Her arms tightened around him. "You are bitter, my heart."

"I am," he said. "All know it was the Swarm that attacked us, yet still they persist in this old clamor of the Betrayal. It is as though they are willfully blind and deaf!"

"They are afraid, beloved." Her voice was soft. "You said it yourself. They are looking for an easy victory, to make themselves feel safe again."

He stroked her hair with a gentle hand. "How is it," he asked, "that you were born so wise?" She made no reply and after a while he spoke again, into the darkness above her head. "What are you thinking now, woman of the Winter Country?"

Her voice, when she answered him, was grave. "I am thinking, man of the Derai, that you come of an implacable and inflexible people, to nurture your enmity down so many generations."

"I suppose," he said, with a flash of grim humor, "that you are seeing the dark side of the qualities that have enabled us to oppose the Swarm for a far, far longer time than five hundred years. It may be that we Derai have become a double-edged sword, cutting against ourselves as well as our enemy."

"Perhaps you have," she agreed quietly, "for even you, the Earl of Night, have lost a wife and now you will sacrifice your daughter and your Heir to this same Blood Oath."

The Earl shook his head, for the thought of Malian was still a sliver of pain, sliding into his armored heart. My daughter, he thought, the child of my youth and love. How can I bear to let you go—except that I must.

"The Oath binds us all," he said finally, speaking as much to himself as to the woman at his side. "In the end I must be the Earl of Night first, before I am either a husband or a father." *Or a lover.* The words hung in the air between them. "The House of Night looks to its Earl to see justice done, no matter the cost to the man."

Ay, he thought, folding his arms behind his head and staring into the darkness as though it held answers: I am the Earl of Night and will do what I must. I am not yet ready to let the House of Night fall and the Derai Alliance with it. Nor will I sit and wait for my enemies to show themselves in their own good time. I will hunt them out, every one, without respite.

"I will do whatever I must." He repeated the words aloud and hoped that it was true—that he would have the strength to hold his House and the Derai Alliance together, however bitter the road. Beside him, Rowan Birchmoon stirred.

"You always have, have you not?" she said, and the Wall wind shrilled, rising to a berserker shriek as the storm broke.

16

Woman of Winter

The fire died down in the grate and the Earl's breathing shifted into the rhythm of sleep. Rowan Birchmoon continued to hold him close, listening to the storm rage. "So much blood," she whispered, "so much grief and pain. And you at the very heart of it—my man of peace, caught in the maw of war."

She was filled with grief for him, but was not sure which shocked her more, the harsh reality of the Swarm attack and its aftermath, or the terrible tale of the Great Betrayal. She had seen the reflection of its bitterness in so many faces since the attack, and in some cases open hostility toward herself. *Outsider*, those hard looks had said: *enemy.* The hostility might not be there in every eye, but she had seen it in enough. Even Nhairin had taken to looking away rather than meeting her gaze. And Rowan had not missed the covert glances between the councilors summoned to hear Asantir's report on events in the Old Keep, the quick calculation that if the Earl lost his Heir to the Temple quarter then he must beget another one, and quickly.

"And rid himself," Rowan murmured, "of the unwanted outsider consort." As if she had wanted to come here, to their blighted, forbidding Wall. She remembered the Derai survivors stumbling into their camp on the borders of the Winter Country, how grim and dark and formidable she had thought them, even when they were half dead from exposure to the cold. It had been a miracle that any of them were alive at all, or so the experienced hunters claimed. They had shaken their heads over it around the fire, recalling all the old tales of the Derai for the occasion.

"They are warlike and fierce," one storyteller had said solemnly, while another recounted an even older story that claimed the Derai were not from Haarth at all, but had come from the stars long ago. They had, the teller said in hushed tones, built their great strongholds in a night and a day while the world still reeled from their coming. The plains had been riven with earthquake and fire, every river and lake had boiled—and when the cataclysm was over the vast and terrible Wall of Night marched along the northern boundary of the world.

Rowan had heard these tales before, but the presence of Derai amongst them made the stories seem more real. Her great-uncle, the shaman, had listened to the stories and the speculation but said nothing, just nodded and smiled while the smoke from the fire wreathed his seamed face. Later, when everyone else was asleep, he had looked at her with bright, shrewd eyes. "It is no accident," he said, "that they have come here. Winter brought them." Rowan had felt compelled to point out that it had not brought all of them, that over half the Derai company had perished. He had not answered; they were both of the Winter Country and knew that the weak and unwary must pay Winter its toll.

Life and death, Rowan thought now as the Wall wind shrieked again. Death and life, but not as the Derai understand these things. They have no conception of the infinite circle of the Winter world.

The last thought in her mind, in those first days, had been that she might fall in love with one of these dour, dark-visaged strangers. She had only been surprised that she did not despise them for being caught out by Winter, and that even the most hardened of the hunters seemed to grant them a grudging respect. "You cannot call those who died weak," her great-uncle had said when she remarked on this to him. "Few of our own would have survived a storm like that, so we must call those who survived extraordinarily strong. Their Earl is the heart of them, the magnet. The other survivors are the filings that have held to him most strongly, the ones with the most iron in their souls."

She had looked at the Derai with new eyes then, and at this Tasarion, the Earl of Night, in particular, and seen the truth of her uncle's words. She watched him hold the Derai to their discipline as the weeks dragged by and blasting storm followed blasting storm in quick succession. In the few clear days between each onslaught there was just enough time to hunt and breathe deeply of the crisp, impossibly dry air—but not for the Derai to return to their own lands. "Spring," they were told, gently but firmly. "You must wait for spring and the thaw and the traveling weather."

They had not liked it, but they had tried to fit in with life in the storm-bound lodges. Slowly, Rowan had come to like them, but she remained wary of both the Earl and his Honor Captain, Asantir, with her keen, dark face. They were the most courteous of the Derai, the most patient with the restricted life when the storms blew, but also the hardest to get to know. As though, Rowan had thought, they used courtesy like a shield, a polished convex barrier that reflected only what they wanted you to see. And she had not needed her great-uncle to look into his shaman's smoke to know that of all their strange guests, the Earl and Asantir were the most dangerous.

The shaman had nodded when she confided this thought to him. "Of course. And like all good weapons they will cut deep, even if you are only careless around them, or unwary."

Rowan had not told him that she also found their dark, alien allure fascinating. The Earl of Night himself was beautiful, like an icon of the Old Empire etched into narwhal ivory, although she did not think he knew that. She still remembered the first time she had realized that she loved him. It had been one of those bright-as-diamond days between blizzards, with the sky pale blue crystal and the snow stretching away forever, white and gleaming. She had been out hunting and come upon him some distance from the camp, a solitary figure in the circling world of white and blue, staring at something far up in the sky. Rowan had stopped, following his gaze, and seen the hovering speck that was a snow falcon, riding the currents of the air.

The Earl had watched it for a long time and when at last he turned his head, he had looked straight into her eyes and smiled, an expression as rare as winter sunshine in the grimness of his face. "It is Winter itself that hawk," he had said, "the brightness and the wildness and the freedom of it. I could watch it forever."

It had happened that quickly. Between one moment and the next, between the silence and the spoken word, she was in love and recognized that he loved her in return. Yet for all its strength and intensity, the wonder and the joy, Rowan had assumed in her heart that theirs was a winter love: light and warmth for the months of snow and dark that would dissipate with the returning spring. But when spring finally came and the Derai prepared to depart, the Earl had asked her to go with him.

They had walked together in woods that were faintly misted with green, the first shy flowers peeping above the snowdrifts. He had stood, bare headed beneath the birch buds, dragging his leather gloves through his hands, and asked her to leave her home and her kin and her beloved Winter Country. He had not spared her the truth of what a Derai keep was, or the Wall and the surrounding Gray Lands in all their grimness, but he had still asked that she come and live with him there.

And she—she had stood in the midst of her own world and looked up into the infinite layers of the sky and wondered if she could bear to leave, or bear to forgo his love, one or the other.

Her great-uncle had summoned her to his shaman's lodge with its smoky, herb-scented interior. "Winter brought them, daughter of the Birch Moon," he had told her, "and that is a matter of destiny, both theirs and yours. We have left it late, but it is time that we knew these Derai rather better than we do. So you must ride with them now and cleave to their stranger lord and learn their ways." He had paused, throwing a bunch of herbs on the fire so that their pungency filled the lodge and stung the back of Rowan's nose, before speaking again. "Your Tasarion, this Earl of Night—the smoke tells me that he is the key to the unlocking of doors that have long remained closed to us. It is a great matter, although I cannot see what the end of it will be, for good or ill."

The shaman's eyes had glazed as he stared into the curling smoke, his voice taking on a singsong quality. *"He is not the one foretold, long sought through both smoke and stars, but he will bring you to that one. And when you walk amongst the Derai, Winter will walk with you; when the time comes, Winter will answer your call."*

"But how," she had asked him, "will I know when Winter should be called?"

"When the time comes," he had replied, *"you will know."*

"When the time comes, you will know," Rowan Birchmoon repeated now, wakeful in the darkness. The world turned, the circle revolved—and she, who had come only reluctantly to the Derai Wall, despite her love, would now leave with equal reluctance. Given everything that had happened, she could never ride lightly away, leaving Tasarion alone in this deadly place. "He will have to bid me go," she said to the night and the storm, "and I can see, as clearly as anyone, that the time when that happens may be coming soon. Yet despite everything, I will stay if I can."

Despite everything. The words had a curious finality to them and she shivered a little beneath the warm covers. She had met the heralds before their expedition into the Old Keep, on her way to the kennels that adjoined the stable yard. The heralds must have been to check on their horses, for Rowan had met them walking up the yard stair as she was walking down. She had paused to let them pass and the heralds had stopped as well; the man's dark gaze had bored into hers and his voice, too, was dark, like wild honey. "What are you doing here, Woman of Winter? The Derai Wall is no place for you."

She had looked back at him, cool as her own Winter skies. "What is that to you, Herald? The affairs of Winter are no business of the Guild."

"I speak what I see," he replied simply. His dark gaze had fixed on the middle distance and his voice, even if it lacked the singsong note, had reminded her of a shaman's, looking into the smoke. "*I do not see clearly, except that this place will bring no good to you, a woman of Winter. You had best return to your own country, while you still can.*"

Rowan had shivered then and she shivered again now, for only a fool argued when a shaman spoke in that voice. But what, after all, had the herald said that she had not known since first seeing the gray, stunted lands that surrounded the Wall? She stayed because she loved Tasarion, the Earl of Night, and because of the purpose her great-uncle had laid on her: that was all.

Rowan Birchmoon sighed and touched Tasarion's face gently, but he did not stir. He will do what he must, as he always has, she thought, tracing the outline of his mouth with her fingertip. Or will try to. And I, what will I do?

She turned away, aware of her own weariness. "Sleep," she murmured. "If the storm allows. Then see what tomorrow brings."

But it was not until the dawn trumpet, faint with distance, rang out from the main gate, that her eyelids closed.

17

Eye of the Storm

Malian rested one forefinger on the table that was one of the greatest treasures of the Red and White Suite, in the Earl's quarter of the New Keep. A map of the Wall and all the known lands of Haarth had been etched into the wood and inlaid with precious metals to show the salient details of each country. A sinuous vein of gold marked the River, the mighty Ijir with its two great tributaries and multitude of prosperous city states, all built on the back of the river trade. Each city was picked out in a minute precision of turrets or minarets or spires, depending on its character, and in whatever heraldic colors had belonged to it when the table was made.

Malian's dark, slender brows were drawn together, the set of her young mouth thoughtful as she spun the table surface slowly round, so that the Wall and surrounding Gray Lands gave way to the Barren Hills, then to the River and all the countries to the south. A line of pewter marked the thousand leagues of road that ran from Ij to fabled Ishnapur and beyond that again was the vast and unknown desert, a sea of dunes wrought in jasper, topaz, and bronze.

It was all so vast. Even the Winter Country, which was considered close, was a very long way from the Keep of

Winds, with both the Wall mountains and league on league of Gray Lands in between.

Malian sighed deeply and let the tabletop grow still under her hand. The Red and White Suite was richly furnished and strewn with entertainments for her amusement but—however well gilded—she was aware that it was a cage. "Confined," she muttered, "until my father decides what to do with me."

It was hard, now, to believe in the events of the Old Keep, even though her flight into darkness had occurred only a week before. Kalan had been sent back to the Temple quarter, of course, and the heralds, too, were gone. There had been a formal farewell for them in the antechamber of this very suite, just three days ago. The Earl and most of his council had been present and her father had named the heralds as guest friends of Night once again, giving them the kiss of peace. But Malian had seen the councilors' stiffness and how most of them avoided looking directly at the heralds—or at her. Asantir and Sarus had been right, it seemed; word of events in the Old Keep had gotten out quickly enough.

At the time, she had been gray with fatigue still, unable to care enough to react to the councilors' aversion. The whole ceremony of farewell had seemed more than a little unreal and the heralds' good-bye to her had been a reflection of her father's words: formal, graceful, and meaningless. She had stared into their impassive faces and wondered if Tarathan of Ar had really come walking to meet her through Yorindesarinen's fire, or whether she had imagined it all.

The first few days after the return from the Old Keep she had slept the dreamless sleep of exhaustion, waking at rare intervals to the howling shriek of a Wall storm and a succession of watchers by her fireside. They had tried to keep the slaughter of her household from her, but she had fretted and tossed every time she woke, calling repeatedly for Doria. In the end, it was Haimyr who had told her of the deaths and held her while she wept. Afterward, he had played the plaintive lullabies of his own land until she sank back into sleep, but Malian had not seen him since then and even Nhairin only paid fleeting visits.

Perhaps, Malian thought now, the tales told about me have grown so wild that even my friends are afraid that I'll turn into some kind of darkspawn before their eyes. "Or perhaps," she added out loud, "the simple truth is enough to keep everyone away." She stared at the red and white doors of the suite. "Or my father's guards are turning them back."

Left to her own devices, there was little to do except mull over the current situation. Even her father had only been to see her twice; he was always stern and remote, but he, too, had seemed reluctant to meet her gaze directly. For the moment, Malian guessed, she was less his daughter, more an awkward problem that the Earl of Night needed to resolve.

She sighed again and turned away from the table to pace up and down the luxurious room, knowing that in the end he would send her away. Since the Betrayal, only one member of the Blood had been permitted to reside in a keep's Temple quarter at any one time. The Oath did not require it, but the custom had evolved as successive generations of Derai Earls had brooded over the rights and powers that might still accrue to priests of the Blood. From brooding, they had grown to fear any concentration of the Blood in their home temples and the custom of exile had become an unwritten law.

Malian knew that her father could order Sister Korriya away instead, but she did not think he would. He would be reluctant to banish a senior and established priestess at the current time—and even more reluctant, she suspected, to have the former Heir residing in the home Temple. The old powers had not manifested in the Earl's direct line since Aikanor's day, but Malian knew that her father would be thinking of Aikanor's legacy now. Inevitably, his reflections would convince him she was the one who must be exiled. Her power, after all, far outstripped Sister Korriya's, and presented a greater threat to the established order.

The latter thought was barely more than a riffle across

the surface of her mind, yet once registered it could not be dismissed. But could she really be likened to the cursed Ai-kanor? Once again, Malian recalled the absence of those she had thought her friends, even Asantir—then checked both her thoughts and her pacing as she remembered the Old Keep. No, she could not believe that Asantir feared her, would not believe it.

Malian took another step then paused again, facing the red and white tapestry that covered one wall of the room. A white deer fled across a red field, a pack of milk-white hounds and a band of hunters in pursuit. The expression in the deer's eyes was haunted, desperate; the hounds were fierce and intent on their prey. The hunters, by contrast, were laughing, their hair lifting in an unseen breeze, their eyes bright with joy.

So much detail in one tapestry, thought Malian, really noticing it for the first time, although she must have walked past it a hundred times, at least, this past half week. She looked at the horned deer again and pulled a face, because she, too, felt trapped, beset, with nowhere to run and no friend to turn to.

Despite the oaths sworn to me in the old High Hall, she thought a little sourly. But perhaps everything that happened in the Old Keep meant nothing—or I dreamed it all.

If Night falls, all fall. The old saying whispered in Malian's head as she turned back to the table, because Night was vulnerable, shockingly so, with only three of the Blood left and one of that three already bound into the Temple quarter. She stared down at the path of the Ijir, gleaming in gold, but did not see it. *If Night falls, all fall.* "Is that why the Swarm struck at me?" she whispered. "What if it wasn't because I'm the Chosen of Mhaelanar at all, or not *just* because of that? What if the Darkswarm saw the opportunity to trigger the ancient doom by striking at the remaining Blood, leaving Night and the whole Derai Alliance exposed?" A strata-gem that must count as partially successful, she supposed, if she were to be exiled and shut away for the rest of her life.

Slowly, Malian's head came up. She would not let that happen, *could* not, if everything that Yorindesarinen had told her was true. And even if it wasn't, if she really had dreamed it all— Here Malian shook her head. She hadn't dreamed it, but she had let this suite cage her mind as well as her body, so that she thought only as her father did, in terms of Oath and law and duty.

"And look at where that's got us." Malian frowned. "There must be another way, a way around the Oath that will save Night without sacrificing my honor."

Yorindesarinen herself had said that she must leave the Wall and surely the greatest hero of the Derai would not counsel a path that led to dishonor? Automatically, Malian's hand circled the silver ring on her upper arm, hidden beneath her sleeve. What if she escaped, rather than passively waiting to be sent away? But where could she possibly go?

She wondered what Kalan would say if he were here. She had tried several times to reach him with her mind, but without success. Now she wondered whether the distance from the Earl's quarter to the Temple precinct was just too great, or if they needed an intermediary, the heralds or Hylcarian, to make the mindspeech work?

Malian paced slowly back to the fire and sank into a wide armchair, her chin propped on her hands. She needed someone to talk to that she could trust, not just with her thoughts about the future but also with everything that she had discovered in the Old Keep: the Golden Fire; Yorindesarinen; and not least, Kalan's suggestion that there were Derai renegades amongst the Swarm—that there had been since the beginning. Even the eldritch sorcerer, she reflected uncomfortably, had looked Derai, despite his emaciation. Malian wondered what she would have seen if she had looked beneath the closed visors of the dead. Would the faces have been recognizable as Derai, or deformed by their long association with Darkswarm evil? Would there have been faces there at all?

Malian thrust out of the chair to pace again, tense and uneasy. She had hoped to discuss some of her Old Keep experiences with Nhairin, but the steward had been terse and distracted, almost distant, on her brief visits. And *why* were Haimyr and Asantir keeping away? Malian stopped, chewing at her lip and staring into the heart of the fire—and realized that for the first time in the three days she had been fully awake, she could hear the crackle of the flames. The storm's roar had died away.

"It must be the eye," Malian murmured, knowing that three days was too soon for a Wall storm to blow itself out; the calm could not last. The raging winds would be on them again before the swirling mass of Wall debris that surrounded the keep could settle. Malian shuddered, thinking of Doria's tales of Darkswarm demons that rode shrieking on those winds. She still didn't entirely believe her nurse's stories, but after everything that had happened since the attack she was no longer prepared to dismiss any possibility out of hand.

There was a bustle beyond the doors, loud in the unexpected quiet. Malian listened intently, then let her breath out on a half laugh as she heard the tinkle of golden bells. The door was flung wide and Haimyr stood on the threshold, his hands on his hips and his head held high, a glint in his golden eyes.

Making his entrance, Malian thought, amused—and her heart rose.

Haimyr waited, simply looking at her, while a guard leaned in and closed the door behind him. Then the minstrel took a step forward and opened his arms wide, and slowly, wearily, Malian walked into their golden circle. "Oh, Haimyr," she said, and that was all.

"Did you think I had forsaken you, my Malian?" She could hear the steady rhythm of his heart, the familiar lilt in his voice. "Alas, your father in his infinite wisdom ordered a full honor escort to accompany the heralds to the border—in recognition of their service to Night, he said. I was one of those he asked to ride with them, and Asantir herself commanded the guard."

Malian stepped back. "That was honor indeed," she said, puzzled, "even for those who have done great service to the House of Night. And out of character for my father."

Haimyr looked down at her with a crooked smile. "Do you think so? I would say that he mistrusts the heralds' power, which is so like those of your own priests—and he distrusts the opportunity they have had to influence you even more. At the same time, his honor as Earl will not allow him to overlook what they have done for your House, at considerable risk to their lives. So we must all ride forth, in the narrow chasms and paths that run through the mountain wall, with the howl of the storm far above us, to bring the heralds of the Guild safely to the Derai border—and very far from this keep and from you."

"I see," said Malian slowly. Put like that, it did fit. She shivered at the thought of riding those narrow, twisting ways in the claustrophobic dark of the storm. "Well, I am very glad that you're here now."

"Yes," the minstrel replied. For once, the sheen of mockery was absent from his face. "I can see that you are. Has it been very bad, my Malian?"

Malian's eyes met his. "Yes," she said simply, "very bad. I thought," she added after a moment, "that both you and Asantir had deserted me."

He drew her to sit on a couch opposite the armchair, as they had sat together so often since she was a very small child. "I was afraid of that," he said. "I believe Asantir may have been, too, given the grimness of her silence. But even Honor Captains and minstrels must obey an Earl's command, at least some of the time."

Malian smiled, a little stiffly. "Tasarion the Terrible. That is what Nhairin would say."

"Would she?" queried Haimyr. "She is brave, our Nhairin. But then she and your father have known each other since they were children. Outsiders such as myself, and gleemen desperate for a lord's golden coin, must be more circumspect."

"You?" demanded Malian. "Circumspect? I do not think so, Haimyr the Golden."

"Do you not?" he said. "I assure you, it is a chancy thing being a minstrel in the court of a great and stern lord, an Earl of the terrible and warlike Derai. There are days when I am almost too frightened to sing another note lest I give offence and be turned out to beg along the Wall."

Malian looked at him. "I do believe," she said carefully, "that you are trying to cheer me up, Haimyr."

"I believe," he replied, profoundly grave, "that you are right."

"Well, I do feel more cheerful," Malian admitted. "But I think that is because you are here, not because of all the nonsense you talk."

A lean hand stroked her hair, gentler than his mocking face or satirical eye. Malian sighed deeply, relaxing for the first time since she had sat beside Yorindesarinen's fire. "You know," she said conversationally, "that my father will send me away."

"I fear so," he answered. Haimyr never wasted breath denying the obvious.

"It is the Oath," Malian continued sadly. "It rules us all and cannot be gainsaid. But I do not want to be sent away to a keep that is not my own and locked up in a temple there for the rest of my life."

Haimyr laid one finger against his lips in warning before rising and picking up a lute that lay on a chest against the wall. He turned it one way, then another, smiling a little at the red and white ribbons that trailed from its neck. "A pretty toy," he murmured, "but it will serve." He shook his head at Malian when she started to speak and began to tune the instrument, all his attention bent on the strings and pegs beneath his fingers. Eventually he gave a small nod and began to play.

It was an odd tune, almost dissonant in its stops and starts followed by a sudden rush of notes that buzzed and hummed before spiraling sharply up, then falling back into another vibrant, murmurous rhythm. Malian thought it curiously like the sharp humming song of the black spear, although without the spear's ferocity. She shook her head to clear it of the buzzing sound and stared at the minstrel, puzzled. His eyes smiled into hers, a long, slow, lazy smile with a good deal of mockery in it. A gesture of his head invited her to step closer, but his hands never stopped playing and the strange tune spiraled around them both.

"What is this, Haimyr?" Malian whispered. "Is it some sorcery the heralds taught you?"

His eyes gleamed. "Not they, my Malian. We have our own charms in Ij; tricks for those who do not trust in walls or doors to thwart prying ears."

Malian thought of the secret ways and listening posts that riddled the New Keep, and nodded. But the minstrel's eyes still held hers, searching and intent.

"You have told me," he said, "what you don't want. But what fate, Malian of Night, would you choose instead?" He held up one forefinger, warning her not to speak too soon. "Not as a Derai or as one of the Blood of this House, nor as daughter to your father, or in fulfillment of any other obligation that has been drummed into your short life. What is that you desire for yourself?"

Malian stared at him, transfixed, and was seized with a sudden wild longing to run away, to leave the Wall and all it stood for, bidding farewell to the Swarm and the bitter legacy of the Great Betrayal. Most of all, she longed to be free of whatever destiny Yorindesarinen had seen for her in the fire, which felt too dark, too heavy for her slight shoulders.

Yet even as she felt this, another thought came winging in: But what would happen if every Derai forsook the Wall for a life that seemed easier, more pleasant? What would have happened if Yorindesarinen had not shouldered her duty and stood forth against the Worm of Chaos? And if she,

Malian of Night, really was the prophesied One but abandoned the House of Night and left the Derai Wall to stand or fall without her, then it would not matter where on Haarth she dwelt. Night would fall everywhere.

Malian closed her eyes, shutting the minstrel out. "It's no good," she said. "I suppose that is my father's lesson: If we believe in the Darkswarm and the Wall, then we must remain committed to our vigil here. But if I accept that—" She opened her eyes again. "If I accept that," she repeated slowly, "then it follows that I must learn to use the power within me effectively, even if it means leaving this keep and everyone I love."

"A paradox," Haimyr murmured, and Malian nodded, her eyes falling away from his to frown at the honeyed grain of the lute. When she lifted them again, her look was challenging.

"As you say, a paradox. But that does not mean I must meekly accept exile to a place my father has selected, where I will be little better than a prisoner for the rest of my life." She shrugged. "I cannot see how that will help me or the Derai Alliance. If I go, it must be to a place of my own choosing."

"Ah," said Haimyr the Golden. He spoke softly, but Malian thought that he looked satisfied.

"Will you help me?" she asked quietly.

He inclined his head. "Of course. But it will not be easy. The Wall is a harsh environment at the best of times, and it will be harder still if the Derai are on the hunt for you."

"And they are bringing wyr hounds here," said Malian, "which will make escape far harder, if not impossible." She thought about what Yorindesarinen had said to her. "I suppose it doesn't really matter where I go, so long as I can find someone to teach me. Once I would have thought that meant I had to stay on the Wall, but having seen what the heralds can do, and now you . . ." Malian leaned toward him, keeping her voice low. "I could go south and lose myself in the cities of the River, or in any of the lands between Ij and Ishnapur."

Haimyr nodded. "You could," he said. "And it seems that the heralds of the Guild share your way of thinking. They gave me this message, before our ways parted: *'Tell Malian of Night that we will wait for her by the stone pillar that marks the border between the Gray Lands and the world beyond. For the turning of one moon we will wait, so that we may bring her safely to the River—if that is what she wishes. But even if she misses us, tell her that she has only to ask at any Guild house to find succor. We will pass the word.'* Then Jehane Mor added, *'Tell her not to come alone, but to bring the boy.'* Now why," Haimyr finished, "would that be, do you think?"

Malian shrugged. "They work in pairs themselves and they know I would not have survived the Old Keep without Kalan." She frowned again. "But bringing him with me is easier said than done when I am locked up here and he is in the Temple quarter. In fact, it's hard to see how we're going to get out of the keep at all, let alone reach the Border Mark or the River!"

"Difficult," murmured Haimyr, "need not mean impossible, my Malian. There is usually a way if one has the will to find it."

Malian frowned and bit back a tart reply, wondering whether any of the spyruns extended into the Temple quarter. But even if they did, she still did not know of any route out of the keep—and it would take time to explore the spyruns exhaustively, time she did not have. "It might," she said, thinking aloud, "be easier to escape my escort once I am sent away. I just need to find a way of getting Kalan exiled with me."

"Just," Haimyr said, with a glint behind his gravity. "But you may be right about it being easier to escape on the road, especially if you wait until well clear of the keep. Your escort would then have to return here to fetch the hounds, giving you a chance to reach the Border Mark. And once there—" He shrugged. "I believe the heralds will be able to deal with any pursuit, even wyr hounds."

Malian's frown eased, then deepened again. "What if I am so closely watched, even on the road, that escape is impossible?"

"I think it more likely," the minstrel replied, "that the escort will see you as the child they have always known, your powers just a rumor. And from their point of view, where would you go? No, all their attention will be focused outward, toward the usual dangers that infest the Wall, providing your best opportunity for flight. As for the boy," he smiled his lazy smile, "there is already talk that he, too, should be sent away."

Malian struck one fist against the other. "If only I could be certain they would send him with me! Although," she added, suddenly thoughtful, "I could ask it of my father as a boon. It's not unprecedented for the Blood to take retainers into exile, and he knows that Kalan saved my life in the Old Keep."

"That could work," agreed Haimyr. "I will have to make sure that I am part of your escort as well, so I can assist in your escape and delay or confuse any pursuit."

Malian threw him a doubtful look. "It will be dangerous for you to return to the Keep of Winds if you are implicated in my escape."

The minstrel shrugged. "I will have to take good care, then, not to be implicated, for where else would I be paid such good coin to sing my songs? You should be safe enough with the heralds, my Malian, if I can get you to them." He turned his head, as though listening to something at a distance—and the tune beneath his fingers became light and merry, filled with a rippling note, like laughter. "But it appears we have been secret too long and now company comes."

"So I am indeed spied upon as well as confined," Malian said, with a snap. She returned to the sofa and sat very straight, her hands folded in her lap. The merry tune jigged on, and Haimyr's smile deepened as the doors swung open and Lannorth strode in with the two door guards at his heels. The Honor Lieutenant looked around keenly, then flushed as he met Malian's inquiring gaze and the surprised lift of her brows. "My apologies, Lady Malian," he said stiffly, and gave her a belated salute. "The guards were concerned for your safety, it had grown so quiet in here."

Malian's brows climbed higher. "So they came to you? How zealous, when they only had to knock and open the door to see that all was well. Could they not hear Haimyr's playing?" She turned back to the minstrel, who had laid the lute aside. "You are right, that is probably enough music for now. But I would be glad if you returned tomorrow and played for me again."

Haimyr bowed. "It shall be as you wish, my lady," he murmured. Lannorth shot a quick, frowning glance between them, but Malian returned his gaze blandly. The two guards remained stolidly at attention, their eyes fixed on a point somewhere above Malian's head. No one tried to stop the minstrel when he strolled to the door, although Lannorth continued to frown.

"Lieutenant?" Malian inquired, and his gaze swung back to her.

"In any case," he said, as though this was a perfectly reasonable errand for the Second of the Honor Guard, "the Earl, your father, advises that he will dine here with you this evening. If it pleases you," he added, the last clearly an afterthought.

Malian inclined her head. "I will be here, of course," she replied, but suspected that he missed the irony. "You may tell him so for me."

This was plainly a dismissal, but Lannorth hesitated. Malian observed him dispassionately, but said nothing. He opened his mouth as if to say something more, then plainly thought better of it, saluted and withdrew. The guards trailed out in his wake and Haimyr gave her a last smile before the door closed behind him. Malian allowed herself a small smile in return, but not the luxury of hope, since a half-conceived escape and a secret conversation were a very long way from escaping the Keep of Winds and her father's plans for her future.

"Also ill conceived," she murmured, but low enough that no hidden listener would hear. And even a half-conceived plan for escape was a beginning.

18

Parts of the Truth

The day wore on, as long and slow as the three that had preceded it, except that the eerie calm of the storm's eye still prevailed. There had been many times, especially when Malian was very young, when she had wondered whether a storm could last forever, particularly with the full malice of the Darkswarm behind it. Those had always been the worst fears of the Derai vigil: The storm that never passed, the dawn that never came.

But this storm, too, will pass, Malian told herself, as the day darkened and Nhairin's stewards came in, soft footed, to turn up the lamps and build the fire so that both light and warmth spilled out, banishing gloom. The stewards did not meet her eyes and nor would they speak; they simply completed their tasks and left as quietly as they had come. They, too, it seemed, had their orders—or were afraid to speak with the Heir in case the old powers proved catching. Even lamp and firelight could not dispel such gloomy reflection, and Malian was curled up in the armchair again, brooding, when her father arrived.

He came alone, but although she heard the thump of the guards' spears as they sprang to attention, and the soft creak of the opening door, she did not look around or stand up when he walked over to the fire. That was a breach of etiquette from Heir to Earl, but they were alone and he, too, seemed abstracted, gazing down at the fiery coals. The winged horse of Night glittered on the breast of his long, blue-black tunic, and firelight played across the hilt of his sword and the dagger thrust into his belt. His expression was grim, his face a mask of hollows and angles despite the mellow light.

"You are sending me away, are you not?" Malian asked, before he could speak, and was pleased with the steadiness of her voice, despite the ache in her throat.

The Earl sighed and his stern eyes met hers squarely. "Yes," he replied, "I am."

He went on, as she had known he would, to lay out all the reasons for his decision. Malian had gone over them so many times in her own mind that she hardly had to listen at all, so she fixed her eyes on the red and white tapestry behind his head and let the words roll over her. When he had finished, she did not protest and was careful to keep her expression neutral. "So where am I to go?" she asked. "And when?"

"I am sending you to the Sea Keep," the Earl replied, "for the Blood of that House are your mother's kin, as well as our allies; they will receive you kindly there. As for when, as soon as possible now that you have recovered from your experience in the Old Keep. Prolonging your departure will only make the situation unnecessarily hard for both of us." He paused, searching her face; and however unlikely it might seem, she thought he was ill at ease. "Is there nothing that you wish to say?"

Malian allowed herself a slight lift of one shoulder. "What is there to say? I have been expecting this since my return from the Old Keep." She thrust her hands into the folds of her skirt to still them and kept her manner calm. "But there is one boon I would ask of you, both as my father and my Earl. All my household were slain in the attack, but I am still of the Blood of Night. I should have someone to accompany me on this journey and into my . . ." she paused on the word *exile* and said instead, "new life. The novice, Kalan, saved my life in the Old Keep. Given the attack and everything else that happened, I would feel safer if he went with me to the Sea Keep Temple."

The Earl frowned, clearly turning the matter over in his mind, and Malian tried to appear unconcerned. She studied the detail in the red and white tapestry behind him and thought of Ornorith, that deviser of ways and means, and wondered which of the goddess's two faces would turn her way.

"Nhairin has already asked that I let her make the journey with you," the Earl said at last, "but she cannot remain with you in the Sea Keep Temple." His eyes searched her face again and she met his gaze with an assumption of ease. "It will be the Temple's decision whether or not they let the boy go," he said finally. "I will not command them in a matter that does not affect the well-being of either House or keep. But I will ask on your behalf and I think it likely they'll agree." He shrugged. "I understand there is talk of sending him to another Temple anyway, since he may be a disturbing influence if he remains here."

Like me, Malian thought. She wondered, briefly, how the Sea Keep would react to being sent two "disturbing influences"—but perhaps the matter would not be put to them in that way. She blinked and realized that her father was studying her closely, as though sensing he had missed some nuance. "Will it please you," he asked, "if Nhairin and this boy go with you?"

Would it make any difference, Malian wondered, not without bitterness, if I were not pleased?

But she only said, "It will please me if I do not have to go alone." Which was true enough, although she would have greatly preferred *not* to have Nhairin as part of the escort. The High Steward knew her too well and was hard to fool; her presence would make it harder to escape.

"Such journeys are never easy," the Earl agreed. "And

more difficult still if one must make them alone." His expression grew brooding, dark. Malian watched the play of firelight over his face and wondered if anyone truly knew his mind or heart; certainly she did not, even if she was his daughter. It seemed unlikely now that she ever would.

Her father met her eyes again. "There is something more that you should know," he said and Malian straightened, caught by the gravity of his tone. "It concerns your mother. Up until now you have always been told that she died when you were young. But although that is true, or we believed it to be so, it is only part of the truth."

Malian's heart began to pound and she realized that she was waiting for some blow, long suspected but never acknowledged, to fall. "It began when you were less than a year old," the Earl said. "Your mother had not been well and it was discovered that the cause of her illness was the abrupt manifestation of the old powers, which had only emerged following your birth. Apparently it can happen that way: The power lies dormant until shaken into life by some major physical or emotional event."

He paused, as though ordering his thoughts. "I was Heir at the time and your grandfather, my father, was Earl. As long as I can remember, he was consumed by a great hatred for those with priestly powers. It was intolerable to him that Nerion should have brought the taint into our line and he insisted that she be exiled from this House, even though she was not herself of the Blood of Night. The exile he named was to the stronghold of the House of Adamant, which is perhaps the oldest and certainly the most implacable opponent of Night."

The Earl paused again, a deep line between his brows as his right hand clenched into a fist. When he resumed speaking, his voice was harsh. "Your mother was sent to the Keep of Stone and no word came back to tell us how she fared until two years later. Even then, we simply received a bald message telling us that she had died. There was no detail, no explanation. I was Earl by that time, but it still took considerable effort to find out that she had, in fact, committed suicide. Apparently she just walked out into the heart of a Wall storm, the kind that shreds flesh from bone. We found out later still that she had been very badly treated in the Keep of Stone, to the extent that death was preferable to continuing to live and breathe within its walls."

Malian stared at him, her mind reeling.. She remembered all the stories that Nesta and Doria had told her, of her mother's kindness and laughter, her wit and spirit—and of how much she and her father had loved each other. Doria had always said that was why there were no portraits of her mother in the keep: "Because your poor father could never bear to look at her dear face, not after she was gone, my poppet." *Truth*, Malian thought now, Doria's voice resonating in her memory: Every word true—but not as she had understood them.

Sick and dizzy, she shook her head. "And you let her go," she said, "alone amongst enemies." The tapestry behind his head swam and glittered through the tears standing in her eyes; momentarily, it appeared to move, coming alive. Malian blinked the tears away as her father made a sharp gesture, as though warding off a blow.

"I live with the regret and the pain of that every day," he replied, his voice hard. "But be sure of this, I will not let the same thing happen to you."

"Won't you?" Malian asked. She sat even straighter, challenging him. "Yet you are still sending me away, just as you let my mother, your wife, be sent away. And what can you do to help me, any more than you helped her, once I am in the Sea Keep Temple, far beyond your reach and that of Night?"

The Earl's face darkened. "I do what I must, Malian," he said harshly, "for the Alliance and for our Derai vigil. You are of the Blood of the Sea House, through Nerion, and unlike the House of Adamant they are our friends, not our enemies. It is also said that they hold the Oath more lightly than we do, perhaps because Sea is not a warrior House." His face and voice softened. "I am doing the best that I can for you. And you know as well as I what it means to be Earl and leader of this House, the first and oldest of the Derai Alliance. You know the Oath that binds us."

Malian refused to soften. "It does not bind you to send me away," she replied, quick and cold as steel. "That is tradition only. And why *should* the Oath overwhelm every other tie that has ever bound the Alliance together, including the obligations of love and honor that make both House and family strong?"

The Earl's headshake was weary. "It is the Blood Oath, Malian, binding beyond death. It cannot be broken or set aside. You know that. But there is another reason why I believe it best to send you away."

"What is this other reason?" Malian asked carefully. She was surprised when her father began to pace much as she had done earlier in the day, restless and almost angry, up and down the room.

"Korriya," he flung at her over his shoulder, "thinks that your mother is not dead, after all." He turned on his heel. "She believes that she is alive and gone over to the Swarm— that it was Nerion who spearheaded the attack on Night, silencing our protective wards and leading the raiders through the Old Keep." He ran a hand through his hair and turned again. "Korriya is concerned, given this, that the invaders' main target, whether to slay or to capture, appears to have been you."

"Kill," Malian whispered, "they were trying to kill me." Her eyes flicked to the tapestry as she remembered the ululating cries that had hunted her through the Old Keep. Suddenly the milk-white hounds seemed crueler and more menacing, the deer smaller and more desperate. "Is it possible?" she whispered again. "Can it possibly be true?"

The Earl sighed and came back to her. "I don't know," he said quietly. "I hope that it is not, that Korriya is just another priest gibbering at shadows. Unfortunately, she was never much of a gibberer when we were young together, quite the contrary in fact. And if she is right, then you remain vulnerable. Nerion was of this keep before she turned, she knows our secrets well. And like you, she ran wild in the Old Keep as a child." He grimaced slightly at her expression. "I find out what goes on in my own keep eventually, and even if I do not, there is no secret that you can hide from Asantir. She ferrets them all out, in the end." He shook his head. "But you will be safe in the Sea Keep. Nerion never went there, even though she came of their Blood. She will have no knowledge of its ways."

"I see," said Malian. Her throat ached with the effort not to cry in front of him, so she stared fiercely into the fire instead, willing the tears away. His words echoed in her mind: *She knows our secrets well.* She remembered Yorindesarinen's words, too, from beyond the Gate of Dreams: *As for the secret of your heritage, it seemed well kept, but this attack can only mean that the enemy has learned of it at last.* The priestess Korriya's suspicions would certainly explain how the Swarm had come by that knowledge, although not why it had taken so long for the Darkswarm to act.

Malian tipped her face forward so that it was hidden against her drawn-up knees. After a moment she felt her father's hand rest on her shoulder; his tone, when he spoke, was heavy. "If Nerion is with the Darkswarm, she will not be the childhood friend or lover I once knew. Nor will she be the mother that you lost. The gods only know what twisted sort of creature the Swarm will have made of her."

Did the Swarm do that, Malian cried silently, or was it the betrayal by husband, friends, House?

Because of her father's brief gesture of tenderness, and the pain she heard in his voice, she did not speak the words aloud—but nor could she fling her arms around him and blot her tears in the folds of his tunic, as she had done so often with Haimyr. Malian took a deep breath and lifted her head.

"Thank you," she said, as steadily as she could. "I needed to know this. But it is a great deal to have to think about—" She paused. "And I would prefer to do so alone."

"Yes," the Earl said bleakly. He hesitated, and Malian thought he might remind her that he had intended to eat with her. But in the end he just sighed. "I will let you know what the Temple says about the boy. And tell you myself when your departure has been arranged."

After he left Malian wept, flinging herself down on the bed and crying in low, shuddering sobs. She felt as though she were weeping for everything that had happened: the fear, loneliness, and terror of her time in the Old Keep, and the grief and isolation of her return, all flooding out on a tide of tears. She cried, too, at the cruelty of her mother's fate—as well as for the possibility that Nerion might have led the Darkswarm invaders who had tried to kill her. But most of all Malian grieved for Doria and Nesta, who had been the comfort, stability, and warmth of her solitary childhood.

The great storm of tears left her limp and wrung out. Yet slowly, other memories of the past days began to creep in: Yorindesarinen in the glade between worlds, with stars in her hair; the warmth of Kalan's hand holding hers, far down in the dark; the unexpected friendship of the heralds; and the wonder of the Golden Fire that had saved them all and enabled her to bring everyone safely home. Malian's fingers sought the cold silver of Yorindesarinen's armring and just for a moment she saw the warmth of the hero's smile again, and heard her musing voice: *"I was promised, even as I lay dying, that another would come to unite the Derai, and that one would not have to stand alone—would not be alone."*

"And I'm not alone," Malian said, sitting up and wiping her eyes. There was Kalan—and Haimyr and the heralds and even Hylcarian, somewhere in the depths of the Old Keep. She sighed and looked around, then blinked at the tapestry on the wall. Surely it wasn't quite the same as when she had last looked, surely, it had—"Changed," said Malian and slid to her feet. She walked closer, staring.

The tapestry still depicted a hunt, but now the prey looked less like a deer and more like a unicorn: a small unicorn with a slender horn. The hounds had narrowed the gap on their quarry and they seemed larger and whiter, their fierce eyes a deeper red. Malian could almost hear them baying. The hunters, too, had crowded closer together, their faces turned away; what little she could see of their expressions seemed veiled, secretive.

Malian shivered, deeply uneasy and reluctant to turn her back on the tapestry's strangeness. She felt that at any moment the figures in it might speak and move, but although she stared hard they all remained frozen in place. Yet she was sure that they *had* moved—the pattern had definitely changed. She forced herself to look away and then swung quickly back, trying to catch the hunt out in some shift or trick, but there was no further alteration.

Malian scowled at the tapestry, wondering whether to tell herself that it had all been an effect of the light, or to appear a nervous fool by requesting that the guards keep watch inside the chamber as well as outside the door. "Gibbering at shadows," she muttered, repeating her father's phrase, but after the Old Keep she could not help feeling wary. Still watching the tapestry, she backed toward the double doors, but before she could reach for the handle, someone knocked. "Come in," she called, and one of the doors opened to admit Nhairin with a covered tray.

"I thought I would bring your meal myself," the High Steward said, "and see how you were feeling."

Malian stood aside to let her enter, then closed the door on the guards outside. Nhairin set the tray down on the table and went to stoke the fire, building it up again while Malian nibbled at the tray's contents. "There," the High Steward said at last, sitting back on her heels, "that should see the night through." She held out her hands to the warmth and slanted a look at Malian, the old scar cast into lurid relief by the flames. "So," she said, "I take it that your father has told you his plans?"

Malian nodded. "But I was expecting exile anyway."

"Well," the steward answered, "I spoke against the idea, for whatever that's worth, both privately and in the council."

She shrugged. "Not that it did any good. Your father is resolved on his course."

"Thank you anyway," Malian said slowly. "He says," she added, "that you are to lead my escort to the Sea Keep?"

Nhairin gave a little snort. "With this leg? It will be Lannorth or one of the other honor guards who leads the escort. But I am to ride with you, in lieu of a governess or other suitable duenna."

"Why, Nhairin," said Malian, "you sound bitter. That's not like you."

The steward sighed. "The last few days have brought reality home to me. I may have been a guard once, but because of my lame leg I couldn't fight off the invaders, or form one of the Old Keep rescue party. And I'm certainly not fit to lead a party into the wild country of the Wall. I am like an old hound, snapping over its scars and of little use to anyone."

Malian considered this. "You could help me now," she said gravely. "I had much rather ask you than one of Lannorth's guards."

The scarred face turned fully toward her. "Help you? How, my Malian?"

"I know this will seem silly," Malian answered, wishing she did not sound so defensive, "but I'm *sure* that tapestry has changed its pattern." Before she could say anything more, Nhairin had risen to her feet and was limping over to the wall hanging.

"Are you sure its changed?" the steward asked, studying the hunt scene closely.

"Yes!" said Malian. "Until this evening it was a deer the hounds were chasing, but now it looks more like a unicorn. The hunters are different, too. You used to be able to see their faces and they were all happy, laughing. Now every head is turned away, their expressions mostly concealed, but I doubt anyone is laughing!"

"They're a grim lot," Nhairin agreed, then shook her head. "Although I have to say that everything here looks very much as I remember." She turned back to Malian. "It's too late now, but in the morning I'll have the hanging removed. And if you wish, I can stay with you until you get to sleep."

Malian hesitated, feeling rather foolish—but given everything else that had happened recently, what could it hurt to be careful? "I do wish," she said finally, and Nhairin nodded.

"These have been hard days," she said, as though following Malian's train of thought. "You get into bed, then, and I'll take this chair by the fire so I can keep my eyes on your tapestry!"

"Thank you," said Malian, with real gratitude. "I am not afraid," she added, as she hurried to get beneath the red cover on the bed. "I'm just being cautious, that's all."

"Very prudent," the steward agreed, settling into the armchair.

Silence fell, but after a while Malian turned to face the fire again. "Did you know my mother, Nhairin?" she asked.

She watched the steward's head turn. "Now what," said Nhairin, "brought that up? Yes, I knew her. We played together as children, here in the keep."

"Were you friends?"

"Yes," Nhairin said again, "we were friends." She picked up the poker and leaned forward, stirring the fire so that a shower of sparks flew up, orange and golden above the hearth.

Malian persisted. "But you didn't go with her when she was sent away?"

The poker froze above the fire. "No," said Nhairin. "I did not. Now who has been telling you that story, my Malian?"

Malian pushed up onto one elbow. "My father," she said slowly. "He told me tonight. He thought I should know, since I, too, am being sent away." She hesitated, not knowing how much Nhairin knew of the Earl's other suspicions and reluctant to say more.

"Did he now?" said Nhairin, half under her breath.

"Well, I suppose you had to know sometime. What else did he tell you?"

"That she was sent away alone, to a fastness of our enemies. That they did not treat her well, and that she killed herself."

Nhairin nodded. "Those are the bald facts."

"But why," asked Malian, "was she treated so cruelly? Why did she not simply go to a Temple in one of our holds, or at least to one of our allies?"

The poker was set back, very carefully, onto the hearth. "The Old Earl, your grandfather, was a harsh man, and those with the old power were anathema to him. It was a point of pride with him that the priestly powers had never appeared in his direct family line since Aikanor's day. And he had never liked the Lady Nerith, Nerion's mother, because of what he called her 'lax, Sea House ways.' So when the power emerged in Nerion, it was as though all his hatred for the priest kind was unleashed against her."

"But what about Sister Korriya?" Malian protested. "Isn't she of the Blood as well?"

"She is of the First Kin, but not of the greater line that has endured since the beginning," said Nhairin. "That is how the Old Earl saw it anyway."

"My father should have stood against him," Malian said vehemently. "He should have opposed my grandfather's extremity."

Nhairin hunched one shoulder. "The Earl is always the Earl," she said, "and your father had only recently become Heir. Do not judge him too harshly, Malian, for if he could not protect Nerion he at least saved you. Ah," she said, seeing the expression on Malian's face. "Didn't he tell you that? Well, I suppose he wouldn't. Initially, the Old Earl wanted you killed, to remove the threat to the line. But your father would not allow it."

Malian was silent, digesting this. "Why have I never been told any of this before?" she asked at last.

"Would it have changed anything?" Nhairin asked. "Or

helped you, to have knowledge of your mother's fate hanging over your head like a sword?"

Malian frowned at the ceiling. She knew what Nhairin meant, but she was the Heir, as well as the person most directly affected by this history. And now not knowing had ambushed her . . . Malian bit her lip, unsure what she could or should say and so reluctant to reply. In the end, it seemed easier to say nothing at all—and Nhairin must have considered her silence an answer in itself, for she, too, said nothing more.

The fire crackled on the hearth, and the tapestry on the wall stirred. Outside the wind's voice rose on a knife-sharp edge: The eye had passed and now the tempest would rage around the keep again. The figures in the hanging rippled and shifted as though answering the rising wind, but Malian was already asleep and Nhairin gave no sign of noticing.

A blot of darkness, deeper than the shadows cast into relief by the fire, uncurled from the hanging's depths. A flat, narrow head swayed forward and a sinuous body followed, disengaging from the fabric. The head swung slowly from side to side, surveying the room, before dropping silently to the floor. Still Nhairin did not move or turn her head, and the red glow of the fire sank back onto its bed of coals. The creature waited for a long moment more, watching the steward, before turning toward the bed and the girl who slept there.

19

The Huntmaster

The storm assaulted the Keep of Winds with renewed fury, battering the watchtowers and shrieking along the ramparts of spear-deep stone. Even in the inner fastness of the Temple quarter, its voice formed an uneasy backdrop to the tumbled darkness of Kalan's dreams. He had dreamed every night since returning to the New Keep, a jumble of faces and voices and scenes that were as random and disconnected as the debris caught in the storm's vortex.

On the first night back, Kalan had seen his father's face, cold and closed, just as it had been on the day he disowned Kalan and threw him out. Although not the formal rite of renunciation and expulsion, his father's words had been sharp and cold as stone. "What are you, boy? Who? You must be a changeling, an incubus, for none of our family ever had such powers!" In the dream Kalan had stretched out his hands, trying to protest, but his father had turned away. Only his voice came floating back: "Nay, do not cry out to me for I invoked the rite long ago. You are no more son of mine!"

You are no more son of mine. Kalan had woken in a panic to the pressing darkness of his sleeping cell. The storm had still been building then, but he had felt its power closing in on him like the walls of the narrow chamber.

The dreams, like the storm, had grown in strength as the days passed and although none were as clear as that of Kalan's father, they were all shot through with a sense of threat, snatches of conversation, and the keep seen from odd angles. Other images intruded as well: Malian pacing in a red and white room; a glimpse of the heralds standing by a great pillar of stone, the wind whipping their hair beneath a sullen sky—and a great war spear with a blade like black flame and a collar of feathers, darkly iridescent as a crow's wing. It sang to him, a low, fierce song of *danger* that reverberated in the core of his being.

"But you are lost," Kalan said, coming on it unexpectedly through a wreathing of mist. "You pierced the Raptor of Darkness and fell with it, into the void."

But the spear sang on, pursuing Kalan through his dreams, and sometimes the sense of menace grew so oppressive that he would fight to wake up, only to spend long hours afterward counting the stones in the walls of his room. The days were little better, for he was no longer free to come and go as he pleased. Sister Korriya wanted an eye kept on him, and so there was no more slipping away on his own: Library or Temple, every minute of his time was closely watched. He even slept alone, in the narrow cell rather than the novice dormitory.

Sister Korriya had said that it was for his own good. There were still dark forces at work, she explained, and grave fears for both his safety and that of the Heir. He would have to be patient and put up with their watch over him until things settled down.

The priestess's face had been drawn with exhaustion, for the High Priest, already old, was now seriously ill and the burden of setting the Temple quarter to rights had fallen heavily on her. And she, like many others in the quarter, still wore the haunted look of those who had survived the Raptor's attack. So although Kalan found it hard to believe that so close a watch was really for his protection, given that they had beaten back the Darkswarm attack and slain the Raptor of Darkness in the end, he said nothing. Sister Korriya did not need the burden of his rebellion on her already weary shoulders, and besides, he still felt guilt for that haunted look.

Again and again, Kalan went over what had happened on the night of the attack, asking himself whether the real reason he had gone into the Old Keep might not have been because it was safer than turning back to face danger and death? Maybe he could have done more to foil the Raptor's attack, *should* have done more. Was that, he wondered, why Ornorith had turned her face away and let the walls of the Temple quarter close in on him again?

"I can't go meekly back to the old life," Kalan vowed to his silent room. "I won't!" But as the days dragged on and the dreams worsened, so that he always woke feeling exhausted, he could not help wondering if the Old Keep had just been another dark dream, the ring on his hand part of some greater confusion.

The dream he tossed in now was the wildest yet, but clearer than any except the first. He felt as though he were hurtling forward on the back of the storm itself, and the darkness was filled with voices that shrieked of despair and death. Kalan could not unravel exact words, but he caught the note of rising panic and a sense of danger so pressing that he could almost taste it. He knew that he was searching for someone that he needed to find, but could not; and now even he, the keen sighted, was lost—until the blindness of the dream shredded and he found himself looking into a room that was richly hung in red and white, but full of shadows.

A woman with a scarred face sat in a chair by the fire, lost in contemplation of its depths, while on the wall a tapestry stirred. Slowly, a clot of darkness began to emerge from the surface of the hanging cloth. The figures in the hanging rippled and shifted as the darkness took shape, a flat head swinging to survey the room. The woman continued to stare into the flames, oblivious to the movement on the wall.

The swinging head moved with the draughts that crept through tightly closed shutters, and the current of the creature's excitement sifted into Kalan's dream: *It was close now, so close to its prey—and no one had even suspected it was there as it worked its way from shadow to shadow, slipping from the Old Keep into the New beneath the noses of the watching guards. Blind they were, blind and deaf to their danger in these perilous times, even when it ghosted past. Fools! It would deal with their kind later.*

The creature's only concern was the corrosive taint of silver in the air, a taint that had strengthened as it drew closer to its quarry. The silver burned in its nostrils and throat like acid, making it hard to think clearly, although it could see now that the girl herself was the source. A faint silver glow hovered around her, like corruption around a corpse.

The flat head drew back, the sensitive nostrils flaring, for the taint was elusively familiar: The creature felt it should recognize it from some other place or time. And the tapestry itself, which had seemed the obvious hiding place with its thick folds and detailed hunting scene, was now stirring with an uneasy life of its own. In the end, however, what could it signify? The girl was safely asleep, alone except for the one lame retainer who might as well have been asleep herself.

Deliberately, the long sinuous body disengaged itself from the concealing tapestry and dropped to the floor. There it paused, gathering itself, before flowing toward the bed and the girl who slept there.

Kalan tried desperately to shout or intervene in some way, if only to rouse the woman by the fire into action, but the darkness closed around him again, pulling him back into the storm. He fought against it, but the dream swept him on. When it finally released him, battered and breathless, it was into the gray and black of a fogbound night—and Kalan could not quite remember what had happened immediately before.

He stood on a path surrounded by banks of fog that stretched between the stark trunks and branching black of a great forest. The Gate of Dreams, Kalan thought—except that this forest seemed vaster, wilder, and infinitely older than the wood that surrounded Yorindesarinen's fire. He shivered, for the space between the trees was dense with impenetrable undergrowth and the voice of the storm had gone, replaced by the creak and rustle of branches rubbing together. It sounded, he thought uneasily, like some dark, secret, and not altogether friendly conversation.

The fog in front of him lifted slowly and drifted apart, revealing the tall figure of a man. His back was turned to Kalan and a long black cloak fell almost to his booted heels; his right hand grasped a tall, hooded spear and a crow perched on his left shoulder. The bird's head turned, snaring Kalan's gaze with one bright eye, then it lifted its wings and cawed, the harsh cry echoing through trees and mist. The man looked around and Kalan gasped, for the stranger's face was concealed beneath a mask of black leather and his left hand had been severed at the wrist.

Kalan forced himself to speak boldly. "Who are you?" he asked. The mask's blank eyeholes were fixed on him but the man did not speak, just stood there, leaning on the hooded spear. "What is your name?" Kalan said, trying again.

The crow cawed a warning; the masked man's voice, in the quiet of the wood, was as harsh as the bird's. "Welcome, Token-bearer," he said. "It has been a long time since the Huntmaster was summoned to the Hunt."

Kalan hesitated, uncertain what he meant and whether it would be safe to ask. "The Huntmaster?" he echoed uneasily. "What hunt?"

The black mask continued to watch him. "It is a wise person," the harsh voice said, "who knows the face of his friends—and of his enemies."

"What?" said Kalan, but the man was already walking away, the black cloak billowing at his heels. Kalan stood rooted to the spot, staring after him, but just as the stranger seemed about to disappear completely into the grayness, the black mask looked back.

"Well?" the harsh voice said. "Yours is the choice, to walk with me or to turn back. But the Hunt calls, so choose swiftly!" He did not wait for an answer but strode on, into the thick fog between the trees.

Kalan hesitated, more than a little unsure of this stranger but equally reluctant to be left behind. He took a deep breath and followed, plunging deeper into the dream—if dream it was—until the fog rolled in around him and he could not see even the trunks of the forest trees. Remembering what Jehane Mor had said about the dangers of the Gate of Dreams, Kalan stopped.

"Do not give in to fear," said the harsh voice, from directly ahead. "There are too many powers in this place that feed off it and will be drawn to you."

The fog lifted again with the voice and Kalan saw the masked figure waiting for him. "You did well to follow this far," the Huntmaster said, "but we still have a long way to go."

Through mists and time, thought Kalan with an inward shiver, and wondered exactly where his dream had led him.

The mouth beneath the mask was set in a hard line, but now it twisted slightly. "A very long way from anywhere you know, boy."

Kalan was not even surprised. It seemed inevitable, so far beyond the Gate of Dreams, that this chance-met stranger should be able to read his mind. The twist to the mouth beneath the mask grew even more pronounced. "I assure you, boy, there is no chance to this meeting."

Kalan stared hard at the black mask and the hooded spear, the severed hand, and the crow on the black-cloaked shoulder. Motionless, silent, the crow stared back. This close, he could sense the link between man and bird, like the current that flows cold between moon and tide. He wondered who they were and why—since this meeting was not chance—they had sought him out?

"Who are you?" Kalan asked for the second time. "What does it mean, to be the Huntmaster?"

The black mask looked down at him, expressionless. Then the harsh voice said: "Every question must find its own answer, every questioner his or her own."

"What kind of answer is that?" demanded Kalan, exasperated, but only the echoes of his own voice answered him and even they dissipated into the fog. In the distance a hound bayed, and the black mask turned toward the sound.

"Ah," the Huntmaster said, as though hearing something he had been expecting. He strode away without another word, and the crow rose from his shoulder and flew ahead on silent wings. The ground was rising and the trees drew in close, their roots twisting across the path, and Kalan had to hurry to catch up. Mist trailed between the branches like moss and every now and then, when Kalan glanced up from watching his feet, he could have sworn he glimpsed movement in its depths. Slowly, a fierce humming song rose above the rustle of the trees.

"So it can follow me even here," Kalan muttered, his footsteps lagging. Soon he detected something swimming toward him through the mist and stopped altogether, even though he had already guessed the shape of what hung there, just beyond the limit of his keen vision. The song was darkly exultant and grew stronger when he halted, filling the world of mist and forest. The crow circled back, hovering silently overhead.

The mist grew transparent as a veil and now Kalan could see the spear, floating in midair: There was the leaf-shaped blade of black steel and there, the collar of dark, shining feathers. The fierce, compelling song poured out of it and Kalan wondered whether the spear sang for him or for the masked, enigmatic figure who had turned and walked back to join him.

"I thought this spear was destroyed," Kalan said, without taking his eyes off the black blade, "when Captain Asantir used it against the Raptor of Darkness." Out of the corner of his eye, he could see the dark mask watching him.

"It is not the same spear," the hard voice replied at last, as though grudging the answer, "although it is like enough to be its twin." He paused, as though weighing some other thought, then added, "This is a Great Spear. Such weapons are not to be used lightly."

Kalan frowned, thinking about what had happened in the Old Keep. "Was it wrong, then, for the captain to wield the other spear against the Raptor of Darkness? Was that using it lightly?"

The mouth beneath the mask twisted again, in what Kalan suspected was meant to be humor. "Boy, anything that slays a Raptor of Darkness is never used lightly. Do you have any idea how powerful an enemy that demon was? Hylcarian himself, given his current strength, would have struggled to destroy it outright, even with all the smaller powers from your keep gathered in. Make no mistake, it was the cast with the Great Spear that made the end certain, for even the slightest touch from such a blade is death."

Kalan continued to frown, while his eyes drank in the terrible beauty of the spear. "The Darkswarm must have placed great importance on that raid," he said eventually, looking around, "to have brought such an ally with them."

The eyeholes studied him, wells of darkness in the surface of the mask. "Ah, so you are thinking now, are you? I was beginning to wonder if that was something the Derai had forgotten how to do. But you are right. I would call that raid a great cast of the dice, one made for very high stakes."

Kalan's thoughts raced back to what Yorindesarinen had said in the glade between worlds; he did not even try to conceal the memory from his companion. "*She* said that Malian is the Chosen of Mhaelanar, the One who will finally defeat the Swarm, once and for all—but that the Swarm knows her identity now. They must have thought a Raptor would make certain of her death."

The lip beneath the black mask curled. "*If Night falls, all fall.* Did you think it was just an old saying, boy?"

Kalan's chin jutted. "No," he said. "But even if they had killed Malian, there is still the Earl and Sister Korriya after him. Malian alone is not Night."

The mouth's hard curl became sardonic. "She is the Child of Night, the single thread on which prophecy suggests that the fate of both the Derai and the Swarm is balanced. Without her, at best the stalemate continues; at worst, the balance tips toward the Swarm. High stakes, indeed, and worth more than a little risk, especially if one can weight the dice in one's favor with a Raptor of Darkness. And if the Golden Fire had not pushed the Raptor back, that night in the Temple quarter, then there would have been no Sister Korriya. Night and the Derai would have hung by a single thread—and I think your enemies had plans and to spare for him."

A chill crept along Kalan's spine. "For the Earl of Night?" Annoyed when his voice came out between a whisper and a croak, he tried again. "What plans?"

"Vengeance served very cold, boy, out of the darkness of the soul, what else?" There were echoes in the harsh voice that had not been there before, like the distant grumble of thunder when a storm was brewing along the highest ramparts of the Wall. Echoes of power, Kalan thought with a shiver, and had a swift flash of long years spent gazing into the void between worlds. But the spear's fierce song twined into his mind, pulling him back from that edge to concentrate on what his companion was saying.

"Oh, yes, they had their plans for your beleaguered Earl and none of them a quick death upon the blade. The gradual destruction of his House and keep around him, that would have begun it; then the inexorable erosion of trust and the attrition, one by one, of all those whom he loves. Perhaps then his enemies would have been content with the smaller pleasures of capture and torture and finally, in absolute and utter despair, death. But then again, perhaps not."

Kalan shuddered, feeling the bitter chill of the void tearing at the edges of his soul, but he kept his voice steady. "How do you know all this?"

"I?" the other answered. "I know many things, as do all who dwell within the folds and mists of time. You have spoken with the star-bright hero already, yet I have dwelt here longer, and deeper, too, in the twists and turnings of the mist—perhaps the deepest of all. There is little that is hidden from me, especially of the darkness that eats at the soul, brooding and festering in on itself. And there are too many who walk here heedlessly, sure of their own power: They never think to ask who may ghost through the mist beside them, or overhear when their words or thoughts plummet like stones into the deep places."

The hard voice was dispassionate, yet Kalan shivered, mesmerized by the black mask. In above my head, he thought, and shivered again. He cleared his throat. "Does that mean you're stronger than Yorindesarinen, then?" he asked.

There was a moment's complete silence and then the Huntmaster gave a short, rasping bark of laughter. "What a boy's question! Even I would hesitate to put it to the trial, never having gone up against a Chaos Worm." The voice grew sober again. "I am older, boy, that is all, and much, much darker."

Kalan struggled to comprehend how old that would be, and the crow uttered a small, derisive squawk. Even the spear song thrummed with dark amusement as the questions swarmed through Kalan's brain. But the hound bayed again, much closer now, and his companion turned. "There is no more time," he said. "The Hunt wakes and must be mastered. Even a Great Spear may not argue with that!" He paused. "Such weapons choose their bearers and it has shown itself to you, but the time is not yet, boy. It would kill you, if you grasped it now."

The spear, Kalan saw, was drawing back into the surrounding mist, its song fading. He felt a wild impulse to reach out and seize it before it vanished altogether.

"Nay, young one. The Huntmaster is right; the spear will choose its own time and place. Presume not lest it turn against you." The voice was scarcely more than a whisper, a faint rasp speaking directly into his mind. Kalan started, staring at the tall figure beside him, but the black mask was intent on the fading spear. Only the crow moved, ruffling out its feathers and cawing again. Perplexed, Kalan turned Yorindesarinen's ring on his finger. He could not help hoping that one day the same hand *would* hold the black spear.

"Perhaps." The mind voice was still faint. *"But anyone who grasps a Great Spear must be strong, lest the weapon master the bearer. You are not yet ready for that trial."*

Kalan remembered both the terrible, compelling lure of the song and how drained Asantir had been after she cast her black spear into the Raptor of Darkness. But his feet dragged anyway as he turned to follow the Huntmaster, who was already striding away from him through the trees. Now that the black spear had gone, Kalan could hear the distant belling of hounds, rising to a clamor that was as dark and terrible as the spear's song. There were voices, too, hallooing and urging them on, and the sudden clear winding of a horn.

The mask looked back over the black-cloaked shoulder. "Hark at the sound, boy!" the harsh voice said. "The milk-white hounds with their blood red eyes give voice, for the first time in many a long year. The Huntmaster may not tarry once the Hunt is awake—and they are well awake now!"

The ground grew steeper, and Kalan felt the strain in his legs and heard the quick gasp of his breath as he struggled to keep the black cloak in sight. The fog cleared and the wood became more open as the hill rose; the moon shone through and turned the world to silver. The pearl in Yorindesarinen's ring glowed in answer as the ground leveled and Kalan put on a burst of speed—then came to an abrupt halt.

He was standing on the edge of a wide, open hilltop that was filled by a pack of milling hounds, a band of hunters behind them. The beasts were white as milk, and huge, with eyes the red of rubies and deep, belling voices.

"Blood!" the deep voices bayed, a clamor in Kalan's mind. *"Blood and death!"*

20

The Web of Mayanne

Kalan stood very still. He noticed that the crow had come back to rest on the Huntmaster's shoulder, where it did not twitch so much as a feather.

"Are they wyr hounds?" Kalan whispered, not daring to speak any louder. He had never seen a wyr hound, for the Earl of Night would not have them in his keep, but knew that they were both a power and a terror of the Derai.

The Huntmaster snorted. "Wyr hounds would turn and run with their tails beneath their legs if they met this pack!" The dark eyeholes bored into Kalan. "Will *you* dare the Hunt, boy?"

Kalan scowled, because it was impossible not to be afraid of the savage, restless hounds, but he was tired of being challenged and told what to do without having any of his questions answered. He folded his arms. "Aren't both you and they simply a figment of my dream?"

"A figment of my dream," the Huntmaster mimicked. "So that's what you think this is." The harsh voice turned savage as the hounds. "Is that what the Derai have come to, the elder Token on the hand of an ignorant boy? Think! You are a dreamer. You can pass the Gate of Dreams in your spirit and in your waking flesh. There is no such thing as *just* a

dream for you, not ever—and most particularly not when you bear the Token on your hand. See how it glows, boy! Did you truly think it was chance that brought you here to me and roused the Hunt?"

Involuntarily, Kalan glanced down at his hand, then swallowed, for like the moon overhead, the ring was getting brighter. But, a token? He tried to remember what Yorinde-sarinen had said when she gave it to him, about it belonging to a friend and that people would not remember it anymore. Some other thought niggled as he looked at the ring, something that he was missing or forgetting, but he could not place it.

Slowly, his head came up. "My name's Kalan," he said, "not boy. You needn't tell me your real name if you don't wish to, but I at least have one." There was a pause while he held his ground and his stare. "I don't understand any of this," he continued more quietly: "the Hunt, you, this ring, although I know I need to."

The Huntmaster shrugged. "Why waste time with names? It is deeds alone that matter when you follow the Hunt."

"So you say," the faint, slightly hoarse voice said, although this time Kalan was not sure that he was meant to hear it. The Huntmaster's head turned slightly, as though listening. *"But then, you have forgotten what it is to be young—and perhaps even your own name, since you speak it so seldom. The boy is right. He needs to know what part he must play here."*

A part? Me? Kalan wondered, alarmed. The Huntmaster was studying him, the mask and its eyeholes equally blank.

"Our time grows short and you have much to do, so listen well, boy—Kalan. These are no Derai beasts. They are wild hounds, untamed and untameable, that used to hunt across the void between the stars, baying for vengeance and blood, feud and war. Fierce they were, and terrible, the milk-white hounds and the wild, merry hunters. All were afraid of them, even the gods, or so the legends say. Who knows, it may even have been true. But in the end, the Nine mastered them to save all worlds, binding them into the web that Mayanne wove. Yet even the Nine dared not bind the Hunt completely, for Mayanne warned that everything in the worlds and between them has a purpose that must be fulfilled."

"There must be an out, she said, one loose end that is not tied off lest the whole snap and tear—and the very fabric of reality with it. So Terennin, the great Artisan, the Artificer of the Nine, made the ring—the Token as it is called—so that the power of the Hunt might be loosed at need. Both the Hunt and the Huntmaster are bound to that Token and will rouse to its call, within the bounds set by Mayanne's web." The Huntmaster's voice grew somber. "Terennin also foretold that it would not be forever, this binding, and that the old weaving would be replaced by a new that would allow the Hunt back into the circle of worlds and time. That, too, Mayanne wove into her design—although it has not happened yet."

"No," said Kalan. He looked sidelong at the milling hounds and was inclined to hope that it would not happen for a long time. His mind was reeling, trying to take in the significance of the ring upon his finger and wondering whether Yorindesarinen had known all this when she gave it to him. Surely she must have. And since the Nine had mastered the Hunt and the Derai served the Nine, that must make the Hunt a potential ally, not an enemy . . .

"Make no mistake," the Huntmaster said, cutting across this reasoning, "they hunt for themselves, lest a strong will bind them. The chase itself is all they care for, the wildness and the joy of it, the warm blood and the kill at the end."

"So why," Kalan asked, puzzled, "have they woken now when I didn't even know that I bore the Token? And I certainly didn't call either them or you!"

The Huntmaster's tone was dry. "Maybe we should look to your star-bright hero for the answers. But the Nine wrought both web and ring, after all. Perhaps it is not surprising that if something disturbs the web, it will rouse both the Token and the Hunt."

Kalan remembered his dark, restless dreams and the sense of imminent danger stalking through them. The feeling that he had forgotten something important stirred again. "What did disturb it?" he whispered.

"You wear the ring," the Huntmaster said. "See what the hounds see. Then you will have your answer."

Reluctantly, Kalan focused his attention on the Hunt. He could feel the hounds' wild power, straining as though at some invisible leash, in stark contrast with the band of hunters who had neither moved nor spoken since he and the Huntmaster arrived. It was as though, despite the hounds that surged and bayed around them, they were frozen in place. Kalan's eyes narrowed, for although the hounds' movements were restless, all their attention was focused in the one direction. He turned, following their avid gaze, and saw that the hillside beyond the pack was bounded, not by more forest but by a shimmering curtain of air. At first glance, Kalan thought that the curtain was just a skein of fine mist, but as objects beyond the shimmer came into focus he recognized the red and white room—and memory and horror came flooding back together.

A fire burned brightly on the hearth and a woman sat motionless beside it, her gaze fixed on the flames. The firelight flickered across her scarred face and over the red-and-white canopy of the bed that stood against the opposite wall. A black-haired girl lay beneath the canopy's shadow, deeply asleep, but a silver light, brighter than the fire, shone around her and had spread out to form a circle of clear, cold flames around the bed.

The girl, Kalan realized, with a queer sinking feeling at the pit of his stomach, was Malian; the silver fire, he surmised, must be coming from Yorindesarinen's armring. It was holding back a dark, sinuous form that probed at the margin of the flames, trying to find a way through. Seeing it, the hounds bayed as one and crowded close to the edge of the veil, their crimson eyes aflame.

Now, finally, the hunters began to move; but in the slow

manner of sleepwalkers, or like people wading through sand, coalescing around a man with a stern, resolute mouth. They all wore half-masks, Kalan saw, and one hunter stood aside from the main group—a figure swathed in a great hooded cloak with neither face nor mask visible beneath the cowl. The other hunters seemed unaware of their lone companion, except for one who lingered at the rear of the group and had half turned back, holding out a hand as though in supplication. Kalan stared at them, bewildered, then switched his attention back to what was happening in the red and white room.

"What is that thing?" he whispered fiercely. "Why does the woman by the fire do nothing? Can't she see that it's after Malian?"

"It is a siren worm," the Huntmaster replied, "a creature of the Swarm. Although it cannot be compared to a Raptor of Darkness, it is still a master of stealth and sly but powerful magics. Siren worms change form at will, and few can withstand their venom if bitten, falling first under the worm's power and then dying when it has no further use for them. In this case, it may simply have cast its siren spell over the woman so that she remains blind and deaf to its presence, saving its venom for the girl."

Kalan's fists clenched. "First it must overcome the fire that protects her!"

"True," the Huntmaster replied, "but it will do so eventually. The silver fire is only generated by a device, however powerful, while the siren worm is a power wielder, able to call on spell and counterspell until it prevails. It must have hidden in the tapestry," he added, "blending itself into its surroundings after the manner of its kind, without realizing what the web was. Once there, its presence will have woken the Hunt, which hates the Swarm and all its minions."

"Then let the hounds have it!" said Kalan fiercely. "Isn't that why you're here? What are you waiting for?"

"Gently, boy." The Huntmaster's voice was stern. "The hounds must not pass the Gate, for the blood of the worm alone will not sate their thirst. Everything in your world will die if the Hunt breaks through Mayanne's weaving. It must remain bound to this place."

"So we cannot pass through and save Malian either!" Kalan wanted to pummel the veil-thin barrier, forcing it to let him through. "What is the point of the Token and being a dreamer if all I can do is stand here and watch her die?" He groaned aloud as the siren worm reared into the air and began to sway from side to side in a slow mesmeric sweep. Its shadow lengthened with every pass, coiling around the silver fire like a wreath of oily smoke—and very slowly, the flames wavered and began to contract. The hounds threw themselves against the veil, howling and trying to push their way through, but the worm appeared oblivious to their presence.

Kalan swung round on the Huntmaster. "There must be something we can do!"

"It is not we," the Huntmaster replied quietly. "It is you, boy—Kalan. You bear the Token and you must rouse the hunters to act. My part is to bind the hounds so that you may do your work without being torn apart."

Kalan swallowed, looking at the straining, slavering hounds, then his eyes darted back to the red and white room and the dwindling silver fire. "What am I supposed to do?" he asked. "What can the hunters do? Aren't they bound, as well, being part of the Hunt?"

"As I told you," the Huntmaster said, "the ring you bear is an outlet for the Hunt's power. The hounds are too powerful and dangerous to ever be let loose, but the Token allows the power of the hunters to work on more than one plane. No one knows who the Merry Hunters were originally, or what, but now they serve as a reflection, an image of the forces playing out in the world on the other side of the web. Right now, those forces are focused inside your Keep of Winds, on the Derai Wall."

Kalan frowned, concentrating on the hunters in their strange tableau. "They are all masked," he said. "Like you."

The Huntmaster shook his head. "Not like me. When the hunters wear masks it means that the forces at work on the other side, the purposes and motivations of those they represent, are concealed. But every one of those masked hunters represents someone who is close to the Child of Night in the world beyond the Gate. What we do not know is whether they are they friend or foe."

"And I," said Kalan wretchedly, "don't know any of those close to Malian well enough to tell the difference."

"Nonetheless," said the Huntmaster, and his voice was stern, "you are the Token-bearer and you alone have the power to walk amongst the Merry Hunters. Those you touch with the ring will rouse to action beyond the Gate, but whether to save the Heir of Night or to harm her will depend on your wisdom. Only you can discern who will act as a friend to the Child and who would destroy her."

"How can I possibly tell between them?" Kalan asked, despairing. "I don't even know who they're meant to be!"

"If you wish to save your friend, you will find a way." The Huntmaster was dispassionate. "The wise person knows the face of an enemy—and of a friend, even when hidden behind a mask. The Child of Stars gave you the Token, Kalan. Now you must prove worthy of it."

It would be useless, Kalan supposed, to say that he had not asked for the ring; in any case, that would not save Malian. "All right," he said, more desperate than determined, and took a step toward the hunters. He did not look at the hounds, but he sensed the sudden switch in their attention. The Huntmaster stepped forward at the same time, his black cloak swirling, and spoke to the hounds in a language that Kalan had never heard before. He tried not to listen to it, or to the fierce, bloodcurdling answer from the hounds, but continued walking until he stood on the fringe of the group of hunters.

The harsh voice came floating after him. "Choose well, boy, or the Child of Night will surely die."

Kalan scowled, shutting out everything but the hunters.

The light from the black pearl began to intensify, like a full moon shrouded by clouds, rising on his hand.

Terennin's ring, he thought. That information was hard to take in, let alone accept. Yet Yorindesarinen herself, the Child of Stars, had given the jewel to him, and all knew that the House of Stars served Terennin first amongst the Nine. Yorindesarinen was a seer as well, so perhaps she had foreseen this attack on Malian and sought to thwart it through her gift.

Don't think about that now, Kalan told himself sharply. It's not helping. Just get on with what you're supposed to be doing here.

He stared at the faces around him, but only the mouths and chins beneath the half-masks revealed any expression. Kalan studied each one closely, seeking some clue to the nature and purpose of the mask wearer. Sternness, bitterness, resolution, sorrow—these were all plain enough to read. But there were other faces that he could not make out, like the one concealed by many masks that were constantly shifting, metamorphosing every time Kalan tried to focus on one or all of them. Another figure stood close behind this hunter, its face concealed by the other's head and shoulder. Every time Kalan tried to move in order to see the hidden mask, the hunter in front would also move and the many masks would change again: now black, now gilded; now of leather, now of feathers; now feline in cast, now reptilian.

Kalan became disorientated by the constant transformations and turned away, giving up on the hunter in the concealed mask as well. This brought him face-to-face with the hunter who stood alone, so deeply cloaked and hooded that Kalan could make out nothing of the person beneath. Cold fingers walked along his spine and he turned quickly toward the hunter with the bitter mouth, the one who always had one hand extended, either in invitation or entreaty—or perhaps in both—toward the one who had just made him shiver.

Kalan paused and looked around the masked faces again,

thrusting aside his awareness of time passing. For Malian's sake, he could not afford to panic and choose wrongly. But it was an impossible task.

The stern mouth, he supposed, did not make him shiver, but the hunter seemed cold and untouchable, remote as the moon. The one with the sorrowful mouth seemed more approachable, but Kalan sensed a deep-seated caution in that figure, and weariness as well, which made him hesitate. He definitely hesitated over the hunter with the many masks that kept shifting from one thing into the other. Shifting, after all, could well mean shifty—and *could* one be shifty and yet be a friend?

Kalan did not know, so he walked around the hunter with the shifting masks again, trying to obtain a better look at that other hunter, hidden behind. Yet still the many masks melted from one shape into the next, always moving so that the second hunter remained concealed. Kalan cursed, turning away for the second time.

As he turned, a small movement caught in his peripheral vision and he saw the hidden figure clearly for the first time. Kalan stood rock-still, and although he could not make out the mask's details he gained an impression of something very plain: worn and dark with age. He sensed clarity, too, coupled with firmness of purpose in the wearer. He moved slightly so that he could see the other hunter as well, the one with the multitude of masks. For an instant a great cat seemed to look back at him, lambent eyed and amused; slowly, and quite deliberately, the beast winked. Kalan whipped around, determined to catch it out, but the cat had already vanished in another flurry of shifting masks.

"Nine!" Kalan exclaimed, then took a deep breath and forced himself to assess what he had seen. "Strength of purpose and humor. What else?" he wondered aloud. Outwardly, he let his attention appear to drift while inwardly he remained alert, and this time he saw the real kindness in the curve of the mouth that spoke of sorrow and regret. "Strength of purpose, humor, kindness," he muttered. "That will have to do." And walking forward, he touched the three hunters in turn with the ring.

Each time Kalan reached out the pearl flared in smoky incandescence, but when he finally stepped back, expecting the hunters to move or take action, nothing happened. Kalan frowned, wondering if he needed to touch them again, but a gloved hand closed over his arm.

"You have done enough," the Huntmaster said, "and done well. There are not many who can see to choose at all, let alone rightly or wrongly."

"But surely," protested Kalan, "they should do something now, act in some way."

The Huntmaster shook his head. "It is as I told you." The harsh voice was almost patient. "The hunters as you see them here are only a metaphor, a reflection of the people and forces at play in your world beyond the Gate. Now we must wait to see how well you have chosen. But even if we cannot act on that plane ourselves, we can at least let this worm see us, perhaps even distract it a little!"

Kalan turned, and saw that while he had been concentrating on the hunters, the Huntmaster had brought the hounds under his control. The hooded spear was rammed butt-down into the grassy hillside alongside the veil of shimmering air, and the hounds were gathered in a knot around it. Their eyes still glowed red but they were fixed on the Huntmaster now, and the line of their bodies and the angle of their heads showed that, however reluctantly, they were obedient to his will. When he walked back to them they came pressing and crowding around, and although they continued to growl deep in their throats at the siren worm, they no longer hurled themselves at the barrier. Kalan kept a wary eye on them, all the same, and stood as close as possible to the Huntmaster.

The tall black-cloaked figure raised his hand and placed it against the veil, which rippled and then grew clear as water. Kalan felt that if he, too, stretched out a hand he would be able to reach through and touch the red and white furnishings. For the first time, too, he could hear the sweet, cloying song of the siren worm. There was a hint of rankness beneath the sweet tone; it reminded Kalan of fruit that appeared sound but had turned to rot beneath the skin.

Despite that, the tune was alluring, mesmerizing . . . Kalan felt his concentration begin to drift, and a lethargy crept over him as the song whispered of the infinite desirability of ruin and decay. He longed for the slow demise of hope and life, and although the silver fire still burned, it seemed paler: forlorn, pathetic, futile. "It is doomed," Kalan muttered. "She is doomed. There is no hope."

The crow on the Huntmaster's shoulder bated, cawing: a discordant cry that cut through the muzziness in Kalan's head. "Stand firm, boy," the Huntmaster said, his voice even harsher than the crow's. "You need to think of wholesome things: the friend standing at your shoulder in hard times, and the unexpected kindness of strangers. Hold on to them against the seduction of the song. Trust in the Token as well, for like the armring, it has the power to resist such evil."

Kalan raised his head, shaking away the dullness and confusion. But he was not the only one who had heard the Huntmaster's voice. The flat head of the siren worm whipped around, hissing defiance. "Why are you here, Hunter?" the worm demanded. Its voice was half the sibilance of the hiss, half the cloying sweetness that characterized its song. "We both know that you cannot pass the Gate into the realms of the living, you who are less than a ghost, the very shadow of a shadow, clinging to the tattered edge of Derai dreams."

"Believe what you please, little crawler," the Huntmaster answered, "if it comforts you. But even dreams can be potent, and nightmares, too, if you get caught in them."

The worm hissed again, its head darting toward them, then swung back to the bed where the protective fire still burned. The woman by the hearth remained unmoving, her face turned away. "Do you threaten me with your nightmare pack?" the siren worm jeered. "They too are impotent, bound into Mayanne's web."

"Is that so?" the Huntmaster said softly. "Yet you, I think, have passed the Gate of Dreams in pursuit of your quarry and now the Hunt is roused. So will you be able to pass back again after—that is the question."

The siren worm looked momentarily uneasy. As well it might, thought Kalan, looking at the avid, blood red stare of the hounds. Then the flat head hissed, swaying higher. "I do not need to escape, Hunter, so long as I slay the girl—and you cannot step out of your tapestry to prevent me! Watch, then, and despair, while I free her ghost to wander with you forever in the limbo between worlds and time."

The worm whipped back on itself and began to slither around the circle of silver fire, wrapping it in an even thicker band of smoky shadow. As the worm moved it sang, the siren song swelling in strength and power. The silver fire sputtered and sparked, the hounds slavered and howled, and Kalan howled, too, his voice rising above theirs as he reached for the hooded spear. "I don't care! I'm going to stop it. Now!"

The Huntmaster's right arm was a steel band, holding him immobile. "Do you want to destroy your world?" the hard voice snarled, low into his ear. "Do you think that will save your friend?"

"But nothing's happening!" Kalan screamed back at him. "You and your Nine-cursed Token have killed her anyway!"

"Be still." The faint rasping voice was a whisper in Kalan's mind, slipping through his turmoil. *"Trust, and you will see how well you have wrought, with your power of three."*

Kalan barely heard. It's too late, he thought, all too late. I've failed. Nothing will save Malian now. And he slumped against the Huntmaster's arm, despair ragged in his throat.

21

Pieces on the Board

The hour was already late as Asantir made her rounds in
the New Keep, but the lamps along every corridor and
hallway blazed like jewels, washing the Honor Captain's
face with rose and copper and gold. Yet despite the light,
shadows remained, pooled in every corner and recess.

Lights against the darkness, thought Asantir, stalking soft
footed along the silent halls. We are like children, making
their nurse leave a candle to hold back the dark hours. And
this from the House that has taken Night for its very name.

Asantir's mouth thinned, but her responsibility was to
deal with the world as it was, so she pushed the thought
aside and concentrated on the shadowed corners and dark
alcoves. She was deeply weary, her wounded shoulder a
dull, throbbing ache, but still she kept her eyes and posture
alert. Both during and immediately after the excursion into
the Old Keep, she had chewed on dulkat leaves to deaden the
pain, but there was a limit to how long the leaves could be
used and their effect had long since worn off. Now there was
nothing to be done except grit her teeth and endure.

The chief healer, Akerin, had looked at the shoulder as
soon as she returned from the Old Keep, hissing under his
breath. "What folly is this, Asantir?" he had demanded. "If

you had left this wound much longer and infection had taken hold, then not only the shoulder but also your life might have been past our ability to repair. And where would that have left us all? Night cannot afford to lose both Keep Commander and Honor Captain at the same time!"

She had reached out with her good hand and grasped his. "Sometimes desperate need requires desperate measures. And you would still have the Earl and all the other captains serving in this keep."

Akerin, as experienced a campaigner as any guard in the keep, had shaken his head. "Losing Gerenth was a grievous blow, but losing you . . ." He had stopped as an orderly came into the room, waiting until the man left before speaking again. Even so, he had kept his voice low. "You will have to choose, you know, between the keep command and being Honor Captain. It leaves Night too vulnerable having one person, however able, trying to do both jobs for any length of time."

Akerin was right, Asantir thought now—particularly when we are already under pressure.

The Earl, she knew, was fully aware of the need to replace Gerenth as soon as possible. But it was not a job that just anyone could do and Gerenth had managed to get his two most senior lieutenants slaughtered with him. "So you," the Earl had told her, frowning across a worktable covered in dispatches and reports, "must do both jobs a while longer, Asantir." She had nodded, accepting this, and they had then talked long and hard about the implications of the battle for House and keep, and their options for dealing with its aftermath.

It had not been an easy discussion. The bitter reality was that their vulnerability had been laid bare and Asantir dreaded the keep's defences being tested again before the garrison could be brought back to full strength. Much would depend, she thought, on whether the attack had been simply a boldly conceived raid or the opening move in a more complex campaign. If the latter, then Night might well be doomed, for neither House nor keep were ready to fight a sustained campaign, let alone win one. The truth was that Night had grown weak and now she must expect their enemies to try and exploit that weakness, just as she would do in their place.

Asantir stopped, throwing out a silent plea to Mhaelanar that the attack did not signal a campaign. "Not yet at least, O Lord Defender," she prayed, using the ancient form. "Shield Night now, Shield of the Derai."

Although in all likelihood, Asantir thought, watching the storm draughts stir a lamplit hanging, the god has given up on the Derai. Why, after all, should the Defender exert himself for a people who had undermined their own defences so effectively—the sum of five hundred years of neglect and downright sabotage of the psychic powers and defences that were so necessary to combat the Swarm?

Asantir shook her head, knowing that the remedy was unlikely to be palatable to most in the keep, let alone the council. Even the Earl had looked more than usually grim when she told him what she believed needed to be done. She had watched the telltale tightening of the muscles along his jawline and wondered if she had lost him already, before her work had even begun. But in the end he had nodded, although his expression remained as bleak as the Wall. "Do what you must," he had said, knowing that she would.

She had implemented some of the smaller remedies immediately, such as doubling the guard throughout the keep and posting priests and guards together to watch the portals between the Old and New Keeps. Even that small act had caused a furor and Asantir grinned, wryly, as she remembered it. The outrage had not been confined to the barracks either. There had been plenty around the council table as well, although the councilors had stopped short of open challenge, a circumstance that reflected the uncertainty of the attack's aftermath as much as her authority in the keep.

"We have," Asantir had told them flatly, "allowed the Old Keep to become a breach for our enemies. I will not

compound that folly by continuing to leave its perimeter un-
guarded at our backs."

Their protests had died away, but she knew the resentment would linger on. Many councilors did not wish to con-
cede that it had been a Swarm attack, let alone admit that
the so-called old powers had been used against Night with
such devastating effect. Asantir paused again, her eyes narrowed on the soft light from a cresset, while another and far
brighter fire flowered in her mind's eye, blazing through the
darkness of the Old Keep. Even now her breath caught in
sheer wonder at the memory.

The Earl, however, had decided that they should not
share the news of the Golden Fire's return. "This is not a
time when we want House and keep relying on the hope of
rescue by an external force," he had said grimly. "And even
the Golden Fire, it seems, is not as it used to be. Until we
know what this really means for Night, we must continue to
rely on ourselves and assume that we stand alone."

Futile, Asantir reflected, because of course there were
already rumors. And perhaps the keep needed a measure
of hope to counteract the fear and uncertainty that swirled
around it, darker than the storm. It had not helped, either
with the rumors or the fear, that she had had to leave immediately after the return from the Old Keep in order to
escort the heralds to the borders of Night. She had protested
against that decision, but the Earl had been adamant.

"It is a matter of my honor," he had told her starkly.
"There are those, unfortunately, who believe that both Night
and my honor would be served best by ensuring that the heralds never return to the River lands, to report on what they
have seen here."

Their eyes had met then, in an understanding that was
as sour as the taste of dulkat leaves. "Even if they were not
your guests," she had said slowly, "they risked their lives for
the House of Night, going into the Old Keep. Murder would
seem a poor way to repay that debt."

"Apparently," the Earl had replied, his face so closed

that she still wondered who had made this argument to him, "such a deed would not violate all the laws and codes that I have vowed to uphold—as I might otherwise have thought—because the heralds are not Derai. Our laws, therefore, need not apply to them."

Asantir's mouth had twisted, quick and hard with the depth of her contempt. "Murder is murder, however one tries to dress it up." She had not added that the heralds might prove harder to kill than many in the Keep of Winds suspected; that was not the point, either for the Earl or herself. "Such a deed would blacken both your name and that of Night."

"And that," the Earl said grimly, "is why you, personally, must see them safely on their road while I keep their ill-wishers busy here. I am relying on you, Honor Captain."

It had been an eerie journey, threading through the deep clefts in the mountain walls that were the only safe path when a Wall storm shrieked and howled far above. The heralds, wrapped in deep silence, had rarely spoken and everyone except the golden minstrel had been subdued. Haimyr had seemed as impervious to the austere silence of the heralds as he was to the glum looks of the guards, including their captain. At one stage, Asantir had even feared that the guards might be tempted to regain their own good cheer by silencing the Earl's minstrel for good. But in the end she had managed to see the heralds safely to the borders of the Wall, and the beginning of their long road south, and return to the Keep of Winds without incident.

She had reported to the Earl immediately and then begun her rounds, checking the guard posts and the work that had been done in her absence. All seemed secure, quiet, ordered: Even the mixed watches of guards and priests on the Old Keep portals were working well enough together, at least to the extent that their duty required it. Sarus's influence, she knew, and Garan's—for wherever those two led, the others would follow.

All the same, Asantir could not shake a sense of disquiet. It feathered her spine with cool fingers and she felt that there was something she should have seen or heard, some sign she should have recognized, that would fit that uneasiness. Yet no matter how she ran her mind back over people, places, and events, she could find nothing that was wrong, nothing out of place.

She shook her head, trying to clear it. "Just tired," she muttered, "and jumping at shadows like a raw recruit." What she needed was a good night's sleep, and the sooner the better. Yet the uneasiness persisted, ghosting with her on silent wings down the corridor and into the well-worn office that was hers by right, as Captain of the Honor Guard.

Even now, after nearly five years as captain, Asantir still entered the Honor room with a sense of satisfaction, although there was little enough in it that was her own. The furniture, scuffed and worn with use, came with the office, and the gaily striped rug that lay before the desk had belonged to the captain before her. Nhairin had given her the wooden writing stand, and the delicately carved silver lamp had come from Haimyr, a gift from his native Ij. The twin swords that held pride of place on the war chest were unquestionably hers, but the weapons on the wall, the javelins and bows and mirror-bright shields, were a mix of her own and those left by her predecessors—just as the black spear had been handed down from Honor Captain to Honor Captain for many generations.

How many generations, Asantir wondered now, staring at the blank space where the spear had been. There was a mystery to it, there had to be, for so potent a weapon to have hung there, overlooked and unused for so long. She supposed she would have to find something to fill the space eventually, but for the moment she was content to honor the spear's memory by leaving its place empty. Even now she could hear its song, low and vibrant and fierce as it hungered for battle, then exultant as it flashed through the air. She saw again the terrible beauty as it caught fire and plummeted into the heart of its enemy: A fine way to go, if go one must, taking one's foe with you, down into the dark.

Asantir shook such thoughts away and went to study the chessboard on the corner of the desk. The set was hers also, with small campaign pieces in the traditional black and white, each one intricately and beautifully carved into a representation of the Derai world. The Earl was the king-piece that must be taken in order to win, the heart of the game, while the Heir was always the most powerful and versatile piece on the board. The High Priest and Priestess flanked the Earl and Heir on either side respectively, while the Honor Captain and the Keep Commander rode beside them on their fiery-headed steeds. The Keeps held either side of the board, while a row of eight stalwart Guards lined up in front of the major pieces.

Foot soldiers, mused Asantir, pawns of the greater players—except that a pawn on the chessboard might become Heir, with skill and Ornorith's favor, whereas that was impossible in real life.

The black and white pieces were spread out across the board, as though left in the middle of a game, and Asantir studied them thoughtfully. Her hand hovered over a piece, but then she shrugged and tossed her cloak over a chair, turning away to splash water over her hands and face. The washstand stood in the long, narrow sleeping room that opened off the office, a chamber spartan in its plainness and meant only for times of emergency and war. But after years of boundary patrols and living in barracks, the camp bed was more than comfortable enough for Asantir, who rarely slept in the comparative luxury of the Honor Captain's official quarters.

Even when she finished washing and came back into the office, Asantir did not unbuckle her sword belt or take off the armor shirt that she always wore on duty. Despite her tiredness and the pain in her shoulder, or perhaps because of it, she felt far from sleepy. The gnawing sense of disquiet remained and she drifted back to the chessboard, a slight frown between her brows as she studied it again.

"Interesting." Asantir sat down astride a chair and rested

her chin on her arms, along its back. She considered the disposition of the pieces, her eyes narrowed, but was not so intent or so weary that she missed the faint shimmer of bells in the hallway or the light footfall at her door. "Welcome, Haimyr the Golden," she said, without turning her head. "What brings you here so late?"

The bells tinkled softly as the minstrel strolled in and stood at her shoulder. "Interesting!" he observed, echoing her own comment. "Black and White seem very evenly matched." He paused, then added lightly: "Although Black should make better use of its Heir, rather than keeping it hedged about like that, especially with White dominating the center of the board."

"You are right," Asantir replied. "Black is playing too defensive a game. All its pieces are still intact but the understanding of positional play is poor. I will have to see if I can rectify that."

"Ah," said Haimyr. "Are you are playing both sides? That is poor sport. We really must play each other, you and I."

Asantir shook her head. "We shall, but I don't think it will be for some time yet."

"Ay, you have your work cut out at present. But one day, when you have more leisure . . ." Haimyr studied the game, his expression thoughtful. "Did you hope those two pawns would carry on unnoticed and reach the end of the board? Black may lose them if it is not careful, for White is pressing close and their position is unsupported."

Asantir turned away from the chessboard. "Even you did not come to talk about chess, Haimyr the Golden, not at this late hour. So what does bring you here to disturb my well-earned rest?"

The minstrel's eyes glinted as he, too, sat down. "Is this what you call resting?" he inquired. "If so, I will not beg your pardon. But the truth is that I find myself uneasy since our recent return, although I cannot say why. Perhaps it is simply the storm—but if so, I have never experienced such an effect before, despite many years living on your Wall. And I am not one to jump at shadows."

"No," agreed Asantir. "And you have no idea at all what has caused this uneasiness?"

Haimyr shrugged in a shimmering accompaniment of golden sound. "None. It's a feeling like—what was it Doria always used to say?—as though a Swarm minion had walked over the cold, lightless spot that will be my grave." He threw out his hands. "Which is to say that there is no reason for it at all! But the feeling has ridden on my shoulder for some time now, all the same. I could find no peace from it so I thought: Aha, I will take my disquiet and visit my old friend, Captain Asantir, who has the sharpest nose I know for sniffing out trouble."

Asantir considered him, a long, thoughtful look. "As it happens, I cannot assist you at all, except to say that I, too, feel uneasy and have done so since we returned from the Old Keep. But I have no better explanation to offer than you do." Her gaze swung back to the chessboard and her hand went out, hovering above the black Heir, her expression remote.

"Ever since we returned from the Old Keep," she repeated softly, then looked sharply around to the open door and the hallway beyond. The lamps shone as brilliantly there as elsewhere, but the shadows still pooled outside the light's bright circle. Asantir's eyes, fierce in their concentration, fastened on those shadows—and then she sprang to her feet, knocking over the chair with the violence of her movement. When she spoke, however, her voice was very soft. "What a fool I've been. We must hurry, Haimyr. Hurry!"

"Certainly," said Haimyr, as Asantir swung her cloak onto her shoulders and strode to the door. "But may I know where, and why?"

Asantir quickened her pace. "I have been a blind fool, my friend. Guards at every gate, guards at the Heir's door—but they need not come in a straight line or by the paths we know. We all saw that plainly enough, both when the Raptor returned and when Malian brought us back from the Old Keep."

"Asantir," he said, "you forget that I was not in the Old Keep. And the hour is too late for me to play at riddle games."

She shot him a quick sideways look. "This is no game, but the hour is indeed late and there is no time to explain for I must—" Haimyr, however, was never to learn what she must do for they rounded a corner and immediately had to jump aside to avoid the guard racing toward them.

"Lira!" said Asantir sharply. "What are you doing here? You are supposed to be on duty at the Temple gate."

Lira gave a hasty salute. "Both Garan and Nerys are still there, Captain, with the rest of our eight-guard. But I have an urgent message for you, from the Priestess Korriya." She hesitated, obviously uncomfortable, then added, "She bade me seek you out with all speed, Captain. She said it was a Matter of Blood."

"Again," Haimyr murmured, but Asantir's hand closed on his arm, compelling silence.

"Tell me!" she commanded Lira.

The guard frowned slightly, concentrating, then recited: " 'Sister Korriya, of the Temple of Night, salutes Asantir, Honor Captain and Acting Commander of the Keep of Winds, and greets her in the name of the Nine. Captain, know this: I have kept watch over the boy as I said I would and he has been dreaming a dreamer's dreams every night, although without discernible form. But now he has gone far deeper into the dream than even our strongest watcher can follow. All we know is that the occasional words torn from him speak of the Heir, of danger, and of fear. I, too, fear, Captain, for these are dreams of the now, not of past events. But without your help I cannot act.' "

"But act we must," Asantir said, as soon as Lira finished. "Lira, tell the priestess that I am going to the Heir's rooms now and she is to meet me there as soon as possible, with whatever strength she considers necessary." She paused, frowning. "Innor and Ter are to remain at the Temple gate, lest the Earl have my hide, but send Garan and the rest along with the priestess. Then you, Lira, must find Sarus, wher-

ever he is—wake him up if you must—and tell him I want
a backup eight-guard sent to the Temple with all speed, and
another to the Red and White suite. If Sarus demands expla-
nations," she added, "say only that I told you this: '*The eye
has passed and now we must run before the storm*'."

Lira saluted. "Ay, Captain. '*The eye of the storm*'. I understand."

"Then go!" said Asantir, her voice iron, and the guard
went, running as though there were storm demons after her.
Asantir strode on toward the Earl's quarter and the Red and
White suite, Haimyr silent at her side. They hurried along
the galleries that circled the Warrior's Court, past the High
Hall and the Great Chamber and the long corridors beyond,
and had just reached the main stair when there was a shout
from behind them. Asantir paused, one foot on the first step,
and turned to see Garan and Nerys jogging to catch up, a
small knot of guards and priests hurrying in their wake. She
remained where she was, her attention focused on the tall
figure of Sister Korriya in their midst. "Has there been any
change with the boy?" she asked, as soon as the priestess
was close enough.

Korriya made her a perfunctory bow, which Asantir suspected was to help regain her breath, then favored Haimyr
with an even shorter nod. "No. But it seems you were right,
Captain, when you suggested that he and the Heir have been
bound together in some way since the Old Keep. And it is
the Heir we must look to now."

Asantir looked at the initiate priests behind Korriya, nodding to Var, Torin, and Terithis, then took in the fourth with
a careful eye. He was a dark, thickset young man with an
open face and calm expression. "You weren't with us in the
Old Keep," she said, her tone making the words a question.

"This is Vern," said Korriya. "He is the best we have for
holding off a psychic attack. He would have gone with you
into the Old Keep except—"

"That he was still in the hands of your healers," Asantir
finished, and saw their quick surprise. "My sergeant, Sarus,

led the guards that relieved the Temple quarter. His report covered the condition of the priests that held the barriers of Mhaelanar's Temple against the Raptor of Darkness."

"Dead, unconscious, or mad," muttered Garan, who had been with the sergeant's company that night. "This lad was fortunate to wake at all, let alone to health and strength again."

"Not fortunate," said Asantir softly. "Strong." Vern colored, but did not look away from her scrutiny, and she nodded. "Strength we may need again now, if your priestess and I are right."

They hurried on up the stairs, Korriya falling into step beside Asantir, with Haimyr and Garan half a pace behind. "I don't suppose," the minstrel said plaintively, "anyone would tell me what is going on? Or what you all fear?"

"An attack," said Asantir over her shoulder, "on the psychic plane—or through it, since some of our enemies can open doors into the air." Her stride lengthened with her words so that she was almost running, and the others had to extend their pace to keep up. "An adept could open a portal directly into this keep, bypassing any watch that I've set!"

"But," Haimyr protested as they swept up the final flight of stairs, "if the Darkswarm raiders truly have that power, why would they have bothered with a physical attack at all? There would have been no need if they could simply open one of these doors into our midst."

Korriya shook her head. "To open a portal that large, and to hold it open long enough for numbers to pass through, would require extraordinary strength. Our histories suggest that even the Swarm has very few with such power."

"But what," said Asantir, "if it isn't numbers? What if it is only one, a solitary assassin? What then?"

"An assassin," Haimyr repeated, his golden brows drawing together. "Oh, yes. I do see."

"A wyr hound," the priestess said, without looking around, "might detect that. Although the beasts are far from reliable." Asantir nodded, knowing that the wyr hounds' instability, coupled with their ferocity, was the reason why the Earl would not have them in the Keep of Winds.

"Or—" Korriya's expression was suddenly haunted. "A strong dreamer might well detect such an intrusion." She shook her head. "I should have seen this sooner, thought through the implications of Kalan's constant dreaming days ago. I have been negligent, blind!"

Asantir lengthened her stride again. "Recrimination, whether directed at ourselves or others, will not serve us now. We can only hope that our eyes have been opened in time!"

And then they were all running, running as though their lives depended on it.

22

A Power of Three

On the other side of the Gate of Dreams a hound lifted its milk-white muzzle and howled a mournful, eerie sound that made every hair on Kalan's body stand on end. The Huntmaster's head turned, listening, although Kalan could hear nothing except the cloying sweetness of the siren song and the distant roar of the storm, muted through the veil between worlds. A quick look showed him no change in the red and white room: The silver fire was drawn in tight over Malian, the shadow of the siren worm pushing in hard against it. Around him, the entire pack was quivering, alert, and Kalan shivered as the hound howled again.

The fire in the red and white room leapt up with a snap, throwing out a cascade of sparks and the woman by the fire came to life with it, cursing as the sparks smoldered on her tunic and in her hair. The siren worm turned with a hiss as the double doors into the chamber burst open and the Honor Captain, Asantir, strode into the room. She was flanked on one side by the tall austere figure of Sister Korriya and on the other by a golden, fantastic creature who could only be the Ijiri minstrel, Haimyr the Golden.

"See?" the Huntmaster said, and relaxed his arm, letting Kalan step free.

Kalan nodded, all his attention focused on events unfolding on the other side of the veil. The woman by the fire was struggling to rise from her chair while Asantir advanced into the room with her swordsman's step, her blade drawn. Guards fanned out behind her as Korriya and a group of young priests formed a wedge inside the double doors. The Huntmaster shook his head. "Your heralds taught them how to work together but they will still be hard-pressed to match the worm's song, given their limited powers." He paused. "One of them, that dark boy, seems to have some strength—but they need to attack now, not defend."

He's right, Kalan thought. The siren song had not weakened as the worm moved swiftly to elude its enemies, blending into the half-light around the perimeter of the room. Asantir continued her soft-footed advance, but the worm still had too much room in which to maneuver its flexible body and venomous head. "A simple warrior will never corner it," the Huntmaster said, "not while the song holds your own power users back."

"Stalemate," Kalan muttered, wondering who would move to break it first. A flicker of gold caught his eye, but it was only the Ijiri minstrel tossing back his fantastic sleeves. No one in the room paid him any attention, but something about the movement and the minstrel fascinated Kalan. He stared at the golden figure and blinked hard, then blinked again, for there in the exact spot where the minstrel had stood before, sat a great, golden cat with lambent eyes.

"A powerful transformation," the Huntmaster murmured.

Kalan shook his head, puzzled. "But no one else seems to have noticed it at all." The cat began to pad gracefully around the perimeter of the room, in the opposite direction to the guards.

"Ay, they still see the illusion of the minstrel, standing by the door. Except," the Huntmaster added, with harsh satisfaction, "for the worm, of course."

The worm had indeed turned its head and was watching the cat with baleful eyes. The golden beast growled, a low rumble that reverberated in counterpoint to the siren song. The hounds pricked up their white ears, listening; their crimson eyes followed the prowl of the cat with intense interest. "How is it that we and the worm can see it," Kalan asked, still puzzled, "when the others can't?"

"Siren worms are masters of illusion," the Huntmaster replied, "so it is difficult to deceive them with such magic. And you and I stand very deep within the Gate of Dreams. It is hard for any illusion to withstand this place and harder still to cloud the eyes of one who bears Terennin's Token on his hand. But look to the worm!"

The rumbling growl of the cat had gained in strength and its tail began to lash as the siren worm struggled to hold the thread of its song. Kalan leaned forward. "It's not going to escape, is it?" he said. "Not with both guards and priests on one side, and the cat on the other." He glanced at the hounds, thinking that the worm would not dare risk the tapestry.

The growl of the great cat deepened until the room shook. Kalan wondered how the others there could not feel the vibration, even if they did not see or hear the cat. The siren song fractured into a series of harsh dissonances, finally dissipating altogether, and the silver fire sprang up again, incandescent. The worm shrieked.

"Bitter!" it wailed and there was no sweetness left in its voice. "Starbane!" These words seemed to finally release the woman by the fire from the remnants of whatever spell held her back, for she, too, stumbled toward the worm, grasping for her dagger. The silver light grew until its brilliance filled the room and any shadows that might have protected the siren worm fled. Asantir came coldly on and the worm darted away from her, closer to the tapestry.

"The silver light is anathema to it," the Huntmaster observed. "The worm cannot endure it, especially now that its own sorcery has been broken."

"But surely," Kalan said, "it cannot have forgotten the Hunt!"

They watched the worm hesitate, its head darting rapidly

between the tapestry and the half circle of its attackers. The golden cat sat back on its haunches, watching its prey with gleaming eyes. Suddenly, a slavering muzzle pushed its way through the fine membrane of the veil and snapped at the worm, missing it by inches. The Huntmaster snarled, hauling the hound back as the siren worm wailed again, a shrill cry of desperation and fury. The sound was abruptly cut off when Asantir—taking full advantage of the distraction— brought her booted foot down on the siren worm's neck, pinning its head to the floor. The worm's body thrashed, but it could not escape and the captain's blade swept down, severing head from body.

The Huntmaster gave a short, approving nod, but the hounds howled in outrage at being thwarted of their prey and surged forward as a pack. For the first time Kalan saw them straining in fury against the Huntmaster's hold, striving with all their strength to break free. The Huntmaster did not speak or move, but Kalan could sense the powerful ebb and flow of wills and for a few brief, terrible moments he doubted whether the Huntmaster would prevail. Slowly, however, the hounds were drawn back to the master, heads lowered and tails clamped, to stand at his side, resentful still, but defeated.

Kalan swallowed. "What happens if you can't control them?" he whispered.

The Huntmaster held up the stump where his left hand should have been. "There was only once when the matter hung in the balance. But it will not happen again."

Kalan shuddered and looked back at the red and white chamber, but the veil had already thickened and the people in the room could only be seen dimly, like figures through a mist. "The Gate closes," said the Huntmaster. "Our part here is done and now we must go." He turned and strode away, the black cloak flaring and the crow flying above his head. The hounds flowed at his heels like a white tide with the hunters gliding along in their wake. Reluctantly, Kalan trailed after them.

At least Malian is safe, he thought. Then, with a sudden

burst of pride: I saved her. I, Kalan, saved my friend, the Heir of Night—with the Huntmaster's help, of course!

He turned one last time at the edge of the trees and saw what looked like a wisp of mist detach itself from the main fabric of the Gate. As he watched, it drifted across the hilltop, toward the protection of the forest and the blanketing fog. "What is that?" he asked.

The Huntmaster stopped. "Well, well," the harsh voice said. "I had forgotten that siren worms have the power to detach spirit from body at death. That is what you see, the ghost of the worm or its soul, call it what you will, trying to return to its masters."

"What shall we do?" Kalan asked. He felt uneasily certain that something must be done, aware of all the information that such a ghost could pass on to the Swarm: about Malian and the silver fire, or himself and the Huntmaster, even the mystery of the great, golden cat. It could not be allowed to escape.

The black mask looked at him. "No indeed," agreed the Huntmaster. "But the remedy is easy enough. Here beyond the Gate it is safe enough for me to let the hounds slip their leash. The Huntmaster must still remain with the Hunt, but you dare not. You must go now, and swiftly, back through the woods to whatever portal you used to enter this place. Do not stay or turn aside for any reason, lest you be trapped here when the Hunt is loosed. Even I and the Token you bear may not be able to save you if that happens."

Kalan shivered, all too aware of the hounds' bloodlust, then hesitated. "I don't know your real name," he said, "but thank you for helping Malian. And me as well."

He was aware of a deep amusement behind the blankness of the mask. "You are the Token-bearer, boy—Kalan. It was you who roused the Hunt and once that happens then the Huntmaster must also wake and master it, lest Mayanne's binding unravel. As for my name, which concerns you so greatly, that goes with the ring, which should be clue enough for you. Now go! Time is pressing!"

He turned away with the white hounds pouring after him, their red eyes glowing. Kalan could just make out the pale ghost of the siren worm slipping into the woods, and thought for a moment that it might get away, after all. Yet even as he watched, the Huntmaster whistled and cried out to the hounds in his harsh voice. They answered with a deep, belling note and sprang away, streaming through the trees. The Huntmaster looked back. "Do not wait, boy—you won't like what you see. You must go, before the door closes again or the Hunt seeks new prey. So run now! Run!"

Kalan ran and the tangled forest of his dream closed in around him again. He had forgotten, when walking in the Huntmaster's shadow, just how dark and wild it had first seemed. Now the tree roots grew thicker and more contorted as he ran, conspiring to trip him, while the bare branches leaned down, clutching at him with twiggy fingers. He carried on, mindful of the Huntmaster's admonition, but the path grew increasingly narrow and the way ahead darker until the forest closed in around him entirely, hemming him inside a dense, impenetrable thicket. Kalan stared up at the tangled canopy through which no stars shone, his throat very dry, and swallowed hard.

"What do you want?" he asked, but his voice sounded thin and insignificant, lost in the pressing tangle of the forest. No voice answered, although the acute, listening quality of the silence deepened. Kalan drew a deep breath. "I know you can hear me!" he said defiantly.

Something moved in the darkness between the trees, slowly coming into focus. Kalan held his breath, both hoping and half expecting to hear the fierce hum of the great spear—but the movement resolved itself into the black mask of the Huntmaster. The mask floated amidst the tangled arms of the trees and the hollow eyes regarded him, fathomless and dark. "It is a wise person," the mask said, "who knows the face of his enemy."

"Not again!" said Kalan in disgust. "Why bother me with this now, when you yourself told me to begone?" But the mask was already fading back into the twisted web of branches. The trees shifted as though a secret breeze walked through them, the leafless branches creaking. A crow hopped onto a bough where the mask had been, preening its wings and turning to look at him with a small, bright eye. "Token-bearer!" it cawed. "Token-bearer!"

Kalan stared at it, exasperated. "What?" he demanded, but the bird only gave another caw and fluttered off. "What does it mean?" Kalan asked, only more softly this time, speaking to himself.

"Can you not guess?" a familiar voice asked from above his head, and he looked further up, meeting the down-bent gaze of Yorindesarinen. A crown of spring stars, misty and bright, gleamed in the dark coronal of her hair and her armor was burnished silver. She floated cross-legged in a space between two large trees and he could see clear sky behind her head, where only a few moments before there had been a tangled thicket.

"You're not really here either, are you?" he asked.

"Not really," she agreed. "Not in the way that you are here, at any rate." Her smile was as he remembered it—warm and friendly, a comrade's grin. "You have made your way very deep within the Gate, young Kalan, and this is not my wood. It is much wilder, older, and stronger; even I have difficulty imposing my will here."

Kalan rubbed a hand across his forehead. "But can you make it let me go?" he asked.

"Not easily," the hero replied, "unless it is ready to do so, but I think it could be persuaded. Besides, I have summoned help." She tilted her head, as though listening to something he could not hear. "Ay," she murmured, "I know. You are ancient and deep-rooted and you do not like to be disturbed. Yet now the Hunt has been loosed and the Huntmaster, too, has awoken." She looked down at Kalan again. "These things have not happened for a very long time and the forest sees that you have had a hand in them."

Kalan shifted. "The Huntmaster said that, too," he admitted. "He told me it was because of the ring that you gave me, which he called the Token. He said that Terennin himself made it, time out of mind ago." He met her dark eyes squarely. "Did you know that, when you gave it to me?"

"I knew," she replied, with the ghost of a smile, "that the ring was an ancient treasure, but not that it had a direct connection to the Huntmaster. It was given to me by a friend, as I said, and that, too, was a long time ago now."

"The Huntmaster," Kalan said abruptly, "also said that he was older than you, and much, much darker. But not," he added conscientiously, "necessarily stronger."

Yorindesarinen chuckled. "Did he really?" she asked. "Well, that is an admission indeed!"

"So do you know who he is, exactly?" Kalan asked. "I have never heard of him before, or read about him in the annals of the Derai."

"No?" Yorindesarinen replied. "But then, as you have already learned, not all the powers that walk beyond the Gate of Dreams are Derai. The Hunt and its master are an ancient power and a very strong one, whatever he said to you. They dwell deep within the layers of the Gate and rousing them has disturbed the peace of this forest, which is a thing not easily done."

Kalan looked around at the trees that were still crowding in on him. "So is the forest angry with me?"

"Angry? Not exactly," said Yorindesarinen, "but it associates the cause of its present unease with you, perhaps even resents you a little. You will have to be wary when you go walking in your dreams in future, my Kalan, for there are other forces like this forest, both ancient and vast, beyond the Gate. It is not wise to disturb them."

"Perhaps," said Kalan, very boldly, "I might be a less disturbing influence if I had not accepted the gift of a hero's ring."

Yorindesarinen grinned. "Indeed you might," she agreed. "Nonetheless, it would still be prudent to remember that the

Gate is a dangerous place for the unwary, however innocent their intentions."

Kalan considered. "How did you know I was in trouble? Or where to find me?"

"I gave you the ring," the hero said simply, "and you are still within the Gate, however deep you may have traveled."

Kalan nodded. "The trees showed me both the Huntmaster's mask and his crow, just before you came," he said slowly. "The bird called me the Token-bearer and the mask said that a wise person knows the face of his enemies. The Huntmaster said the same thing to me, too, when I met him in the forest."

The hero looked thoughtful. "As I said, you should pay attention to what this forest shows you."

"But why would it show me the Huntmaster's mask when you said that he disturbs it?" Kalan persisted. "What do you think it means?"

Yorindesarinen shook her head. "I do not know the mind of this wood," she said. "I will help you where I can, but there is still a great deal that you will have to work out for yourself. And it is right that you should," she added, "for your enemies are powerful and cunning, and you must be able to outwit as well as outfight them if you are to survive." He frowned up at her, perturbed, and she smiled a little. "Do not look so troubled. I have faith, Kalan the Young, that you will find both the wit and the strength of arm to make your enemies fear you."

" 'It is a wise person who knows the face of his enemy,' " Kalan repeated, still frowning. "Does that mean that the Huntmaster is really my enemy and I should know his true face? Except how can I, when he wears a mask? Or did he mean that I should be able to recognize who my enemies are, no matter what face they show me?" The frown deepened. "Or perhaps he is just playing a game with me?"

Yorindesarinen studied him, deeply thoughtful. "Sometimes, Kalan, it is necessary to change the way you listen, in order to better understand what you hear. The one thing you may be sure of is that the Huntmaster will not have spoken lightly, given that he spoke to you at all." She turned her head. "But it is time and more that you crossed back to the other side of the Gate—and see, the help I called is here."

Kalan looked around and saw that the trees had drawn back while they talked and a golden light was flowing down the path, lapping against the trunks of the trees. "Hello," he said. "You again."

"I might say the same," the fiery voice replied, dry in his mind. The advancing light halted a few feet from where Yorindesarinen floated amongst the trees. *"Summoned, I come,"* said Hylcarian. *"Greetings, Child of Stars."*

"In need, I called," the hero replied. "Time is short, old friend. This young dreamer must return to the other side of the Gate, but the wood has snared him. It will let him go now, I think, but he exists in both places at the same time, as do you—whereas my power is only in this world of dreams. He will find it easier to make his way back to his sleeping body if you lend him your aid, Hylcarian."

"Time is shorter than you might think," Hylcarian replied. *"They are coming for him now, in the New Keep, and I cannot remain here long."*

"I thought," Kalan said curiously, "that you were fully occupied shoring up the foundations of the Old Keep, and likely to remain so for some time?"

"So I am," responded Hylcarian, *"and must be, lest the whole Keep of Winds come crashing down around our ears."*

"Not quite the Fall of Night that we anticipated, eh?" observed Yorindesarinen, with a grin.

"Laugh then," said Hylcarian, but without heat. *"One cannot open portals into the void itself and expect there to be no consequences in the world on the hither side of that gate. Still, some good will come even out of that near disaster, for once I have sealed up all the rifts and cracks no enemy will penetrate the Old Keep again. I will make*

very sure of that. For now, just be thankful that I have done enough work to have some strength left over for running your errands, Child of Stars."

Yorindesarinen held up a hand, acknowledging the counter hit. "Forgive me, old friend," she said, very grave, but Kalan could see the smile lurking in her eyes. He suspected that Hylcarian could see it, too.

"I must go," the voice of light said, *"and take the boy, before we both get stranded within the Gate of Dreams."*

"Go, then," said Yorindesarinen, "and may the Nine go with you both!" She winked out like a star and the forest fell away from the Golden Fire as it flared through the trees like a sun track on water. Kalan began to run again, his feet flying along the path, faster and faster while the light blazed around him until he was not running at all, but arrowing up through a sea of light like a swimmer coming up for air.

At the last moment, on the very edge of breaking through the surface of light, the Golden Fire checked him. *"Wait! There are two messages that I would have you bear for me into your New Keep. The first is for the Child."*

"For Malian?" said Kalan. "I'm listening."

"The Child of Stars says that the Heir of Night must leave and go out into the wide world. I, too, see that it must be so, although it grieves me. Tell Malian of Night that she must seek for the lost arms of Yorindesarinen there: the sword, helm, and shield that were lost to us when the hero fell. I searched for them mightily, even after the others gave up, but found only darkness, silence, and death." The fiery voice paused. *"The one thing I learned in all that time was that the armring is the key to their finding. Tell the Child she must use that key, for she will need the arms to defeat her enemies and fulfill her destiny."*

"I will tell her," promised Kalan. "But where should she look?"

"I do not know," said Hylcarian. *"Even Yorindesarinen does not know and they were her arms once. The important thing is to look, for even now, I believe, the weapons will*

be rousing themselves to answer the Child of Night's need. But she must be very secret. No one else must suspect what she is doing. No one! So tell only the Child what I tell you now—and let no other overhear. Do you understand me, boy of Blood?"

"I understand," said Kalan, compelled by the Fire's urgency. "But what is the second message?"

"That," said Hylcarian, *"is for the Honor Captain, a warning to the wise, which is that siren worms always hunt in pairs. Where one is, the other will not be far away. They are cunning and patient, but not particularly courageous, except in pursuit of blood feud where they rival even the Derai. Your captain should be prepared for what will come. Now go, and swiftly, for they are coming for you."*

"Who—" Kalan began, but Hylcarian had already let him go; the golden light fragmented and soon it had vanished altogether. Kalan found himself safely back in his body, on the verge of waking, and with someone speaking his name.

23

Throw of the Dice

Malian sat up in her bed, wide-awake. The red and white room was filled with a clamor of voices; Nhairin was leaning one arm on the mantelpiece above the fire, her expression bleak; and a tall woman in a priestess's robes had taken the steward's place in the chair. Asantir was standing by the tapestry with her sword drawn, a pale green ichor dripping from the blade onto the floor, while the guards searched the room. Haimyr strolled over to the bed and perched himself on one corner, carefully settling the fall of his sleeves. Perplexed, Malian stared from him to the young priests at the door.

"What," she said, "are you all doing here?" She tried to take everything in, to work out what had happened, then shook her head. "I had the strangest dream," she muttered, as much to herself as Haimyr. "Kalan was in it, and the hounds in the tapestry had come alive." She shivered. "Their eyes were full of fire and their voices cried out for blood."

"Old tales to scare children with," Nhairin said, although she sounded shaken. "I should have known that Doria would fill your head with them, given half a chance."

The priestess in the chair glanced at Nhairin, her expression curious, but Malian shook her head again. "No," she said, "I've never heard of these hounds before. Or the masked huntsman that was with them." She frowned. "There was a cat, too," she added slowly. "It was as big as the hounds. But it wasn't in the tapestry. It was here, in this room."

Nhairin shrugged. "It was just a dream," she said, but Malian was looking at Asantir.

"What are you all doing here?" she asked again. "And your sword—What happened, Asantir?"

Everyone else stopped talking. "An attack," said Asantir. She indicated the severed head and the thick gray-black body that still twitched at her feet, then looked more closely at her sword blade. "Nine, this stuff must be caustic! It's pitting my sword." Carefully, she wiped the blade clean on the edge of her cloak.

"A vile thing!" Nhairin said, with some violence, while Malian leaned forward to peer at the body more closely.

"What sort of creature is it?" she asked, shaken.

"I believe," the priestess in the chair said calmly, "that this is the darkspawn known as a siren worm. Their song ensorcels all who hear it and their bite is death."

Malian shivered again, for although the details of her dream had begun to fade as soon as she woke, she was sure that she could remember a sweet, almost cloying song and finding it difficult to breathe. But Asantir was watching Nhairin. "What I want to know," she said, "is how it got so close to Malian without your seeing it, when you were here in the room?"

Nhairin frowned. "I cannot explain it at all, unless Korriya is right and that thing ensorceled me." She pressed her fingertips into the corners of her eyes as though they pained her. "All was quiet, all well, that is all I remember until the fire flared up and you burst through the door. But how did *you* know there was something wrong, enough to bring these others here with you?" She glanced at the initiates by the door with distaste.

Asantir shrugged. "I didn't know. It was just a feeling that kept gnawing away at me. Then Haimyr spoke of the same uneasiness and Sister Korriya, too, sent word that she was concerned. Reason enough, given recent events, to investigate further. Then when we got here . . ." She paused and looked hard at the tapestry on the wall. The others followed her gaze and Malian gave a little gasp. "What's wrong?" the captain asked her.

"It's changed," Malian said slowly. "Again. It did the same thing before I went to sleep as well, which is why I asked Nhairin to stay and keep watch. I knew it had changed, but it seemed so strange that part of me didn't really believe what my eyes had seen."

"Understandably," murmured Haimyr, to no one in particular, but Korriya remained grave, intent.

"How did it alter before?" she asked Malian. "And how is it different now?"

Malian glanced into the gray eyes and worn face and then as quickly away, because it was strange to think that this stranger was her only blood kin, aside from her father. "At first it always looked the same," she explained. "The white deer fled from the hounds with the hunters following behind, carefree and laughing. But earlier this evening the scene definitely altered. The prey looked more like a small unicorn than a deer, and the hounds were bigger and a lot closer to it. The hunters' faces had all turned aside, or were concealed in some way, and none of them were laughing—but now look. You can only just make out the unicorn, disappearing amongst the trees, but see how the hounds mill and swarm! Clearly they have run some other prey to ground—although there's only the one black-cloaked huntsman present, with no other hunters to be seen." She hesitated, puzzled. "The huntsman has never been in the tapestry at all, before this. But he was in my dream."

"I don't suppose," Asantir said, with some asperity, "that either of you thought to tell anyone else about this?"

Nhairin sighed. "As Malian said, she half thought she was being foolish. And to be honest, I couldn't see anything different about the tapestry. It looked very much as it always had."

"I see," said Asantir. She examined the weaving closely and then shook her head. "But Malian's tale does fit what I saw as we came through the door—not just the worm and a ring of silver fire around the bed, but the tapestry opening to Nine knows where!" A ripple of uneasy murmurs indicated that others had seen the same, or something very similar.

"I don't suppose," Haimyr said, pointing to the severed head and still twitching body of the worm, "that we can dispose of *that* before we go any further?"

Asantir regarded it indifferently. "I want to keep my eye on it for the moment," she said. "I assume," she added, speaking to Korriya, "that fire is the course you recommend for such vermin?"

The priestess nodded. "It is the only way to avoid contamination from any evil still clinging to their dead flesh. And we don't want such shadows to linger here."

"No," said Asantir, "we've had more than enough shadows lately." She turned back to Nhairin. "What more can you recall of what happened here? I want to hear everything you know or suspect."

Nhairin's tone was troubled. "I'm not sure how much more I can tell you." She spoke slowly, as though trying to clarify her recollections. "As I said, the room seemed peaceful enough and Malian soon went to sleep while I drifted with the play of the flames, half awake and half dreaming. I could hear a sweet, wordless song, but thought that was just the dream. I felt tired, my body weighted down, yet I felt no threat, no danger until the moment you arrived." She sighed. "The rest you saw for yourself."

Asantir said nothing for a moment, then looked across at Korriya. "What more do you know of these siren worms? Or about this tapestry and its properties?"

"These matters have not been my study," the priestess replied, "but I believe this may be the tapestry called the Web of Mayanne. It came into the possession of the Earls of Night shortly after we arrived on this world, but the records are ambivalent and its reputation uneasy, to say the least. We know that it is an object of power, but the how and why of that power are as mysterious as its origins." She shrugged. "We don't even know whether it is a Derai artifact or belonged to some other race."

Asantir pursed her lips. "What connection could there be between the tapestry and the worm?"

Korriya shook her head. "I would have said none, except that we all saw the veil where only the tapestry should have been, an opening that closed with the worm's death."

"So the question," Asantir said, frowning, "is whether they were in fact linked? And will the door in the web reopen?"

"Or perhaps," said Haimyr, smoothing out a wrinkle in his golden cuff, "*where* will another such door open, and when?"

"And how," finished Asantir softly, "can we possibly guard against it?"

Korriya shook her head. "We can't, not with any certainty. We had the power and knowledge to withstand such magics once, but now . . ." Her voice trailed off.

Malian straightened as Asantir turned, the keen eyes meeting hers, but then the captain shrugged and deliberately sheathed her sword. "As you say: now—which is all we can deal with. And deal with it we will." She nodded to the guards who had been stationed outside the door. "You may both resume your post, there's nothing more for you to do in here. Garan, Nerys, take the initiates and wait with them outside until we have finished talking with their priestess. Korin, you go to the end of the corridor and keep watch for Sarus: Let him know what's happened here. As for the worm—" She spurned it with her booted toe, her expression one of distaste and spoke to the remaining guards. "Tain, Ban, roll the head and carcass into a cloak and take them to the furnace. Make sure there is nothing left of either, lest the worm's shade comes back to haunt us." She did not smile as she said this and nor did anyone else. "And stay alert, all of you. This may not be over yet."

Silence flowed into the room as the last of the guards filed out and the doors clicked shut. Malian watched Asantir closely, sure that something important was about to happen, and saw the same focus reflected in Nhairin's face. Well, she knew Asantir, too, probably better than anyone; she should know the signs. Of them all, only Haimyr seemed unconcerned, still absorbed by the set of his cuff.

"The time has come," Asantir said, "for hard decisions." She nodded at Korriya. "After the attack, you told the Earl that we would pay a bitter price for the schism fostered within the Derai—and already we are forced to admit that we cannot protect Malian against another attack, or predict when it will come, or how, or where." Her gaze challenged them all. "Can any of you deny it? Dare you?"

No one answered, although Nhairin's expression grew dark. "It seems likely," Asantir continued, "that the situation will be little different in any other keep along the Wall. Given this, I cannot see how the old, bitter answer to Lady Nerion's power, twelve years ago, can be the right answer to Malian's power now."

"Any more than it was to Nerion's then," murmured Korriya, but Nhairin's dark look sharpened.

"What are you proposing?" she demanded.

"The Earl," said Asantir, "intends sending Malian to the Sea Keep. One of his reasons, amongst others, is that he, too, fears for her safety here." The Honor Captain paused as Malian nodded, but it was Korriya who spoke.

"The Sea Keep has always been more tolerant of the old powers, which is one reason the Old Earl disliked Lady Nerith so much. But I doubt even they have sufficient strength, these days, to protect against concerted attacks of the kind we have experienced."

"None of this," Nhairin said pointedly, "will change Tasarion's mind. You must know that!"

Asantir nodded, but when she spoke it was to Malian. "When the storm blows, one must either battle into its teeth or run before it, looking for safe harbor. I believe that you must run—must disappear into the realms of Haarth like a stone dropping into a pool."

"Leave the Wall?" demanded Nhairin, before Malian could reply. "Send the Heir of Night amongst outsiders? You must be mad, Asantir, or bewitched by those heralds!"

Asantir shook her head, while Malian looked from one to the other, a little dazed by the unexpected turn of events. "Neither mad, nor bewitched," the Honor Captain said calmly, "and certainly not by the heralds of the Guild. Think, Nhairin! How much longer can we hope to thwart attacks by Swarm powers such as the Raptor of Darkness and this siren worm? We have only prevailed through Ornorith's own luck so far, but it has never paid to rely on the Two-Faced Goddess." Asantir shrugged. "It seems clear that Malian is their main target. I believe her best hope is for us to send her somewhere they will never think to look—a place far from the Wall, where she can learn to use her powers in safety." Malian caught her breath at the hard look Asantir bent on Nhairin. "We are talking survival. No other consideration must be allowed to weigh against that."

"So long as the choice, whether to go or to stay, is Malian's," Haimyr put in quietly. He reached out and gave her hair a gentle tug. "You had best speak up, my dear, lest Asantir bear you away by main force."

Malian nodded, but she spoke to Nhairin rather than the Honor Captain. "Asantir is right. We don't have the strength to keep thwarting these attacks. And I don't want to die, or to be sent away like a criminal or a traitor as my mother was, to live in captivity for the rest of my life. I think leaving the Wall may be the only way for me."

Nhairin's face twisted. "But where will you go? Who will befriend you and keep you safe?"

"Who will keep her safe here?" Asantir asked. "Or in the Sea Keep? Can you do it, Nhairin?"

The light caught the scar on Nhairin's face as she shook her head. "You know I cannot. But you, Asantir—" Her face hardened as she met the Honor Captain's eyes. "Tell me," she said, her voice bitter, "how does this course sit with your honor and sworn oaths? I recall a guard, only twelve years ago, who thought me forsworn for even proposing such a flight!"

Asantir sighed. "People change, Nhairin. I have come to believe that you were right then, and I was wrong. As for my oaths as Honor Captain, one of them is to defend and preserve the Heir at all costs."

"And what of the Earl and the Blood Oath?" Nhairin whispered. "How does defying Tasarion and aiding Malian's flight sit with that?"

It was Korriya who answered, every plane and angle of her face sharp with conviction. "There *is* no conflict with the Oath, Nhairin. The law has been my study since I entered the Temple life and the words are plain. They state that no *priest* may live outside the boundary of the Temple quarter. In the past five hundred years we have chosen to equate the word *priest* with those who bear the old powers—but the two are not synonymous. To be a priest of the Derai one must take the seven-fold vows and Malian has not done so." She relaxed suddenly, sitting back in the chair, and her voice grew softer. "Nor has any other novice or initiate priest in the Temple quarter for that matter."

Nhairin frowned. "Surely," she protested, "that is using the form of the words to defeat the intent of the Oath, which has seemed plain enough for five hundred years."

Korriya's answering look was grim. "And look where it has brought us all! Regardless of that, it is what the law actually says, not what we believe it was meant to say, that counts. Thus spake Thiandriath, the Lawgiver, in the first times, and the edict has proven sound throughout our long history." She leaned forward again. "I thought you, for one, would be glad of this, Nhairin."

The steward unfolded and then refolded her arms, her face grim and troubled. Malian, watching them, realized that Nhairin would have grown up with Korriya, as well as with her father, and must have known the priestess well, once. "Why," Nhairin asked finally, "could you not have expounded all this twelve years ago?"

"She tried," Asantir said quietly, "but the Old Earl wouldn't even admit her into his presence, let alone listen to her. He said that if she were not of the First Kin he would have had her put to death for even trying. You were ill from your wounds when it all happened, and by the time you recovered it was already an old story."

"I see," said Nhairin, very bleak. Malian stretched out a hand to her.

"Don't you want me to go, Nhairin?" she asked softly. "Because I really don't think it's safe for me to stay."

Nhairin limped over and caught the hand in both hers. "I am being a fool, that is all, dwelling too much on old, bitter histories. I know that Asantir and Korriya are right: You must go, and quickly." She looked at Asantir. "So what do we do now?"

"We cast what dice we hold," the Honor Captain replied. "But we must be swift and secret, or the throw will be lost before it is even begun. That is why I sent the others away, even those who have sworn to protect Malian's life with their own."

"Ay," murmured Haimyr, "for it is here that betrayal will come, not from the outside lands."

"I agree," said Asantir, checking Nhairin's protest. "For what is one more girl amongst the millions of Haarth? One would do better to look for a single dust mote in a Wall storm. But what of Kalan? Shall we send him with you, my Malian?"

"Yes," said Malian, then swallowed, for now that flight was real and imminent it seemed a great deal more daunting.

Korriya rose and shook out the folds of her robe. "Very well. Go he shall, if we can bring him safely back from his dream." Her gaze, however, remained fixed on Asantir. "But perhaps Nhairin is right. Are you sure you want to take responsibility for this? It will sit more easily on my shoulders than on yours."

Asantir smiled, a flash that was gone as quickly as it came. "Nothing sits easily on my shoulder at present. It aches damnably." Haimyr laughed and both Korriya and Nhairin frowned at him, an identical reproving look. "As for the rest—" Asantir shrugged. "I will make my own throw in this game and live with what it brings. All I ask, Sister Korriya, is that you bring Kalan to me as agreed. But tell Garan and Nerys that I said to go with you, lest any challenge you between here and the Temple quarter."

Korriya inclined her head. "So be it," she said, and Malian shivered, thinking that the words had the formal ring of a doom. Even Haimyr seemed more serious than usual as the priestess left the room. When he spoke, however, his tone was light.

"And what of Nhairin and I? What part shall we play now, O Honor Captain?"

"If Malian's departure is to remain a mystery," Asantir replied, "then she must not be seen leaving this room. And there must be only one set of facts for the keep to learn once her flight is discovered. These, then, are the bones of our story. Firstly, Nhairin and I will leave now to meet Sarus and reorganize the watch while you keep Malian company until I return. This I will do shortly, bringing another two guards, ostensibly to watch over the interior of the room. Both you and I, Haimyr, will then leave, and that is the last part you will play in our tale. There is no reason, after all, since matters have been settled here, for you to leave your quarters again before morning. Too much suspicion will fall on you anyway, as an outsider amongst us—and unlike Lady Rowan you will not have the Earl himself for your alibi."

Haimyr looked sadly at Malian. "You see how it is. I am never allowed to be useful, or play a part in the adventure."

Malian could not help smiling. "You have been useful already," she said softly, "and you know it!" But she was frowning when she turned back to Asantir. "How will I escape unseen if there are guards in my room?"

The Honor Captain smiled. "You didn't think we'd let you go alone, did you?" she asked, in unconscious echo of Yorindesarinen. "The guards who come to your room will leave with you tonight. As for how you leave—your old chambers were not the only ones with a secret passage behind them. I will return again by the secret way and we will all leave together by the same route." She looked thoughtfully at Malian. "It would be best not to make it immediately obvious that you have fled the keep altogether, so don't take anything from this room except the clothes you wear. Nhairin and I will organize everything else that you'll need. If all goes well, the keep will be turned upside down before a wider search is ordered."

"And what of you?" asked Nhairin, the edge back in her voice. "Surely, given the missing guards, you are the first person on whom suspicion will fall?"

"Perhaps," Asantir said blandly, "people will believe that the door in the tapestry reopened. And there are these rumors of the Golden Fire as well . . ." She smiled faintly as Nhairin snorted. "You are right; it is inevitable that suspicion will fall on everyone associated with the Heir. I will have to take my chances, but I think it would be better if you did not. You, old friend, shall go with Malian and the others, which should help direct a good deal of suspicion away from me."

Nhairin's eyes narrowed. "Why, you cunning—!" she began, breaking off as she caught Malian's eye. "Very well," she said tersely. "At least in going with the Heir I will be doing as the Earl wishes. But may the Nine preserve us all!"

"We must ask Sister Korriya to look to that aspect of the matter," said Haimyr lazily. He winked at Malian. "While you and I wait patiently for the captain's return."

"Not very patiently," Malian muttered, and Asantir's brows flicked up.

"We had best get on, then," she said briskly. "Are you with me, Nhairin?"

The steward looked dark and seemed about to say something more, but instead she nodded, turning abruptly away, and together they left the room.

As soon as they had gone, Malian slid off the bed and ducked behind the red and white billow of its curtains. "I suppose," she said, her voice muffled, "I could go out into the world in my nightgown but—" There was a brief silence and then she continued, her voice much clearer, "—I'd rather not!"

A few minutes later she reappeared, wearing a dark tunic and hose with soft boots, her hair twisted into a rough plait. "Do I look ready for adventure?" she asked Haimyr, setting her hands on her hips.

"As any hero of song and story!" he assured her, and she tossed her head, blinking back tears at the same time.

"Except," she said, "that I go forth without either my father's blessing or a sword of power on my hip."

The minstrel shook his head. "Not all hero tales are the same, my Malian."

She paced restlessly, then paused to frown at the tapestry. "Are they not?" she said, speaking over her shoulder. "I thought they were, in their essential parts. It's real life that twists and turns. The hero tales are less . . . complicated."

"You are growing wise, Child. That would make a fine beginning for a hero tale, don't you think? 'The Earl of Night had a wise child and her name was Malian.'"

"Stop!" said Malian, then shook her head. Her apologetic smile was brittle as she turned, her expression strained. "I'm sorry, Haimyr. So much has happened in so short a time. It's not just this last attack, it's everything else as well. I can't believe it was only this afternoon that you and I first plotted an escape."

"And now Asantir has taken it out of our hands," Haimyr finished calmly. "Does that trouble you?"

Malian frowned and came back to sit cross-legged on the bed, facing him with her chin resting on her hands. "I suppose not," she said slowly, "but it is unexpected. Still, a great deal about this past week has been unexpected." She fell silent, listening to the roar of the wind. "How much longer do you think the storm will last?" she asked.

He shrugged. "Two days perhaps, probably not three. But you will have to travel by the narrow paths through the Wall itself, as we did. And you won't be able to cross the Gray Lands until it passes."

"No," said Malian, a little hollowly, and Haimyr stretched out his hand, covering one of hers.

"You will reach the Border Mark before the heralds leave, have no fear of that. They will then see you safely to the River."

And after that? Malian wondered. But she said nothing, just slipped off the bed and walked over to look at the map, turning the tabletop beneath her hand. She murmured the names under her breath: Ij, Terebanth, the Winter Country; Emer, Jhaine, and Ishnapur. "After Ishnapur, what?" she asked Haimyr.

"The great deserts," he replied, in his lazy way, "the sea of sands, perhaps even the very end of the world. Why, would you go there, my Malian?"

"I would like to see it for myself," she admitted. "To be something more," she added, not quite under her breath, "than just a vessel of ancient prophecy."

The golden eyebrows rose. "You must know that you are more than that—to me, to Nhairin and Asantir, even to your father."

"My father," said Malian shortly, frowning down at the tabletop. "And Asantir. At one level," she continued softly, "just two names, another two people—but think what they stand for. The Earl of Night, leader of the first and oldest House of the Derai Alliance, and Asantir, his Honor Captain, sworn to defend Earl, Heir, and keep with her life." She looked up at Haimyr, her expression deliberately fierce.

"Yes?" he inquired mildly.

"The Earl and his Honor Captain should be as one: That is our history. Yet now their two courses are at odds, or so it appears. How can the Honor Captain act against the Earl's express order, even if it is for the Heir's benefit? It seems to slice through the very heart of our Derai code."

"Do you think so?" inquired Haimyr. "To me it was as though the Derai Wall had cracked from top to bottom."

Malian smiled in spite of herself, then shook her head. "It's not funny, Haimyr."

He regarded her thoughtfully. "Yet what, in terms of your code, is the difference between the Heir plotting an escape in the afternoon and the Honor Captain executing it in the evening?" He shrugged. "But it is Asantir you must ask about these matters. I am neither Derai nor a warrior, and see the world very differently."

"Perhaps," Malian said softly, "it is that different view I wish to hear."

He flicked a bell on his sleeve with narrow fingers, his smile crooked. "Let me ask you another question. Do you trust Asantir?"

"With my life," Malian replied, without hesitation.

"Why?" Haimyr asked.

Malian frowned. "She is just one of the things I've been certain of all my life. I don't even think about why." She paused, then continued slowly: "She always seems like the Wall rock beneath one's feet. All those things we say about honor and giving one's life for one's House and the Derai cause—with Asantir you know it's real. But not," she added, "in a stupid way. Asantir thinks about things."

"Yes," said Haimyr.

Malian smiled, a small reluctant smile. "I see what you're saying, I suppose. If Asantir thinks that I should leave, even if it means going against my father's wishes, then I should trust her judgment."

"I feel compelled to point out," Haimyr observed, "that it is you who are saying these things, not I. Is it for a minstrel of Ij to advise the Heir of Night?"

"If the Heir of Night seeks his advice, then why not?"

Malian revolved the map table gently beneath one hand, watching the world turn before her eyes. Haimyr came and stood behind her, resting one long hand on her shoulder; after a moment she reached up and placed her smaller hand over his, holding it there.

"It is a wide world, my little one," he said softly.

"I trust my father, too," she said, in a voice so low he had to stoop to catch it. "I know that he will always uphold the laws and oaths of our people, although there have been many Earls less scrupulous. He will also do all that he can to hold both Night and the Derai Alliance itself together." Her small smile was rueful. "I trust him to be the Earl of Night, I suppose—and my father only when other considerations allow." She tapped her forefinger on the table, first on the sinuous vein of gold that was the great river Ijir and then on the vastness of the Winter Country. "He alone, of all our people, has traveled to both these lands and learned something of their ways. Yet now the people of Night will want certainty. They won't have confidence in an Earl who tries to turn the Oath, or their understanding of it, on its head. That," she finished simply, "is why he feels that he cannot temper the Oath even a little in my favor."

"I said that you were growing wise," the minstrel murmured, "if it is any comfort to you."

"Not much," she said. Haimyr smiled.

"No," he agreed. "I fear it may be easier to be happy if one is not wise. Life is so much simpler."

Malian smiled, too, then she sighed. "I suppose that if my father has given no actual orders concerning me, if he has only spoken of his intentions, then there cannot be disobedience. Not by the letter of the law anyway."

Restlessly, she moved away, trailing her fingers over the textured surface of the tapestry, feeling the myriad tiny stitches that made up the scene of hunt and hounds. Something rippled deep within it, a thread of awareness—*disturbance*—and she snatched her hand away. The scene had changed again, she noticed, reverting more to its previous form, although the white deer—or unicorn—was still half concealed by trees and the hunters' faces remained hidden. Malian shivered and turned on her heel.

"Where is Asantir?" she said, walking back to the fire and holding out her hands to the flames. "What if something's gone wrong? Maybe we should leave now, rather than waiting?"

"She will come." Haimyr strolled over and seated himself in Nhairin's armchair. "Time always passes slowly when you are waiting for something important to happen."

Malian frowned, wanting to argue that it had been too long, that something *must* have gone awry, but after a moment she nodded and sank onto the rug, cross-legged again. "So," she asked, to take her mind off the waiting, "what did happen twelve years ago, between Nhairin and Asantir? From what they said, it must have had something to do with my mother."

The minstrel shook his head. "My dear, that is not my story to tell."

"So you do know!" she pounced, then added slowly: "You would have known my mother, too."

"Yes, I knew her," he replied quietly. "But do not ask me to speak of her, my Malian. It is an old grief and we should let the dead sleep."

"What if she is not dead?" Malian asked, just as quietly.

The golden brows flared upward. "Who told you that?" he demanded. For the first time, she heard a flick of anger in the golden voice.

"My father." She fiddled with the end of her braid. "He didn't say that she was alive, for certain, but he indicated that it was a possibility. He also told me something of what happened here, twelve years ago."

"Did he now?" the minstrel murmured, echoing Nhairin when confronted with the same news. "But that still doesn't give me the right to speak to you of what Nhairin and Asantir have chosen to keep to themselves."

Malian sighed, exasperated. "I thought minstrels were supposed to pass on information and recount histories!"

Haimyr smiled. "We are also meant to be diplomatic and discreet."

Malian brooded over this, resuming her contemplation of the fire. They did not speak again, but both their heads turned as one at the sound of voices outside—and finally, Asantir was back, slipping into the room with Kyr and Lira behind her.

"Time for you to bow out, Haimyr, my friend," the Honor Captain said briskly, "for the reasons we agreed before."

"Did we agree?" the minstrel murmured, uncurling from the chair like a cat. "Now, there I was thinking that you commanded and I humbly obeyed, as always!"

He turned back to Malian, who had scrambled to her feet, and took her face between his hands. The golden eyes looked into hers and for a moment there was no laughter or mockery in them. "I will not say the long good-bye," said Haimyr the Golden, "for I believe that we shall meet again. But I will bid you take care and wish the blessings of your Nine Gods on your path and your cause."

Malian hugged him fiercely. "Farewell, Haimyr." She blinked back her tears. "Take care of my father for me."

The look he gave her was quizzical. "Your father has always had my friendship, my Malian. Never doubt that."

"I don't." She held out her hand to him, not as a child but in the clasp of equals, and for a moment it was as though their two hands melded: the smoke gray eyes and the golden met and held. "I am trusting you to do this for me, above all else," Malian said, and felt the power rise within her, weaving its note through her voice. She saw the recognition of it in Haimyr's face as he lifted her hand in his own, bowing over it like a courtier.

"As you wish, Heir of Night, so shall it be," he answered. "For are we not also dear friends? Farewell, my Malian, until we meet again."

"Farewell," she echoed, blinded by tears. She felt his

hand touch her head and heard his light, departing step. By the time her vision cleared he had already gone, leaving her with Asantir and the somber-faced guards.

Dour Derai faces, Malian thought, with a glimmer of humor that vanished as Asantir held out a cap of black leather and a plain, dark cloak.

"Hide your hair beneath the cap and wrap the cloak about you," the captain said. "Then even if anyone does see you, which I doubt on the paths we shall travel, you will simply look like any other page. Now I, too, must leave again while Kyr and Lira stay. But fear not—I shall return at once by the secret way."

Malian nodded, and both she and the guards drew closer to the fire, which was burning low. "Soon," said Asantir on a promise, and was gone again.

24

The Long Goodbye

"*K*alan, wake up."

The voice spoke very quietly, but it was also a command. Kalan groaned, stirring, and finally sat up, staring into Sister Korriya's face. Her eyes were shadowed and she carried one of the cone lamps shielded beneath her cloak. She held up the other hand to require his silence. "Get up and dress, Kalan. It is time for you to leave us."

The note of authority in her voice brought Kalan out of bed and fumbling for his clothes. Questions burned as he began to dress, but Sister Korriya had already turned and was standing in the doorway, her back to him. Kalan could see other people in the hallway; all were cloaked and hooded and they bore no lights. He wondered, as his fingers struggled to manage fastenings, whether he should be afraid, and the words of the Huntmaster circled again in his head: *"It is a wise man who knows the face of his enemy."*

Kalan longed to ask who had decided that he was to leave: the Earl, the ailing High Priest, or even Sister Korriya herself. But something in the stern, forbidding line of Sister Korriya's back precluded questions. He paused, halfway through pulling on his boots, and the priestess looked at him over her shoulder. "What, not ready yet? Time is short!"

"I'm dressed," Kalan said hastily. "Do I need to bring anything?"

"Not for this journey," she replied. She shone the light around the small room as though checking that nothing had been missed, then stepped into the corridor and gestured Kalan to follow. The cloaked and hooded figures closed around him as he stepped outside, but no one spoke. One of their number handed him a cloak, similar to their own, which he pulled around his shoulders, fumbling a little over the clasp. Sister Korriya pulled the hood forward over his face and nodded once, as though satisfied that he was indistinguishable from the rest, before turning away down the corridor. The others fell in behind her with Kalan in their midst.

He could not help glancing at the cloaked, silent figures surrounding him and remembering the hunters in the tapestry. Their faces, too, had been hidden, concealing both identity and intention. Kalan shivered, remembering how Sister Korriya had said that he need not bring anything with him on this journey—but he could not believe that the priestess would do him harm. Besides, it would have been too easy to have killed his sleeping body while he wandered beyond the Gate of Dreams. No, Kalan decided, this silent journey must lead to some other end. And despite the strangeness, or perhaps because of it, he felt a small thrill of excitement.

They descended a long flight of stairs and then there were more corridors and more stairs, each one caught between darkness and shadow. The hooded figures wove in and out of the dimness and Kalan, who had thought he knew every stone and step of the Temple precinct, now realized how strange even a familiar place could look when passing through it by night.

Finally, after so long a time that Kalan wondered if they had crossed the entire Temple quarter, Sister Korriya led them down a shallow flight of steps and stopped by a steel door. He felt the priestess's eyes rest on him as she turned, although her face remained shadowed beneath her hood.

When she spoke, she kept her voice low. "This is my journey's end, Kalan, but not yours. This door opens into a loft above the keep stables; there you will find another stair that leads down into the stalls. From the stable you must make your way to the undercroft below, where others are waiting for you."

What others, Kalan wondered? His mouth was dry, his heart beating fast and hard. "How will I know," he asked, "whether those I meet are friend or foe?"

"Two of our company will go with you," Korriya replied. "They know the passwords and the faces of those who await you." She stepped forward, resting her hands on his shoulders, and Kalan forced himself to remain still, meeting her searching gaze. He wondered what it was that she was looking for, and whether she found it. "Go well, Kalan," she said at last, and he heard both fear and hope warring in her voice. She shut off the cone light and pressed it into his hand. "May the Nine guard you, for the path ahead is dark and I am no seer, able to read your way."

Kalan's fingers closed around the light and his heart began to hammer as he understood that they really were sending him away—but why so secretly? Korriya held up a hand, forestalling questions, and nodded to one of her anonymous companions to open the door. Kalan followed the hooded figure through, before turning to look back at the anonymous company above him. "Farewell, Sister," he said softly, and Korriya inclined her head, signaling another of the cloaked figures to join him. The door closed, and the first of his silent companions reached back and locked it.

The loft stair was easy to find and led them down into the warmth and darkness of the stable, with its scents of straw and leather, and the shift and murmur of the horses in their stalls. The place was vast, thought Kalan, and he remembered that it was underground, carved out of the rock of the Wall itself. His companions had used the curved wall to guide them down and Kalan followed their lead, even though he could see perfectly well in the darkness. When they reached the bottom a firm hand rested on his shoulder and exerted a pressure that said, as plainly as words: *Wait.*

Kalan waited, and soon there was a slight scrape of wood against stone. A figure detached itself from the surrounding darkness, moving along the stalls and stopping about ten paces away. Kalan's companions remained still as stone on the narrow stair; the shadow figure began to whistle, a soft snatch of tune from the *Night March*, a song of the armies of Night. Still his companions waited, but when the same whistle came again, the one with a hand on Kalan's shoulder whistled the next bar back. The whistler's face turned toward them and Kalan saw that it was the guard called Lira, whom he remembered from the Old Keep. "The eye has passed," she said, very quietly.

"And now we must run before the storm," the first of Kalan's companion's replied—a man's low voice—and Lira relaxed, smiling.

"Well met, my friends," she whispered. "The others are in the undercroft." She turned and they followed her to a small door that opened onto another narrow stair. It was the door, Kalan realized, that must have made the scraping sound. The stair twisted down into the undercroft, where the grain and the other supplies necessary for so vast a stable were stored. Lira stopped at the foot of the stair and whistled softly, this time the even more famous refrain from the martial air known as the *Charge of the House of Night*. A lantern flared in answer, and dark figures materialized from behind barrels and grain bins. Kalan stepped forward with a glad cry as he saw Malian appear beside Asantir, but the Honor Captain checked him.

"There is no time," she said. "You and Malian need to leave at once, before the night grows old. You must take the narrow ways to the Gray Lands and cross as soon as the storm dies, aiming for the Border Mark and the road south." She turned as a tall woman with a scarred face led forward a string of horses. Lira moved swiftly to help and Kalan's companions also stepped forward, pushing back their hoods. Kalan whistled softly as he recognized Garan and Nerys, amazed that they had dared to pass through the Temple quarter, even in secret. But then he saw the horses clearly and forgot everything else.

There were five horses, all black as night and as beautiful, with spirited heads, deep chests denoting endurance, and legs built for speed. All five horses were equipped for a long journey, with a travel roll and journey bags strapped behind each saddle, and they snorted and stamped their hooves as they waited. "But—these are messenger horses!" Kalan exclaimed.

"I know," said Malian. Her eyes were blazing with excitement. "Asantir says they will outrun and outlast anything else in the keep."

"But—" Kalan protested. "Messenger horses!"

The scarred woman snorted. "Are you worried about what the Earl will say? Let me assure you, purloining messenger horses is likely to be the least of our worries if the Earl of Night catches up with us."

"Fear not," Asantir said quietly. "These horses will not be missed immediately, for they belong to those who come and go from this keep unseen and unknown by all but a close-mouthed few. Like the horses, the way that you will take now is made to serve such comings and goings."

The scarred woman snorted again, her mouth tight, and Kalan wondered why she was angry with the captain. He remembered seeing her before, when they returned from the Old Keep, and again later, from the other side of the Gate of Dreams. She was the one who had sat by the fire, caught beneath the spell of the siren worm. Her name, he recalled, was Nhairin. "Are you coming with us?" he asked.

"Ay," she replied. "The Earl said I was to go with Malian anyway, and I'm not staying behind now to tell lies or, worse still, evasive truths to his face." Her tone was sharp but her glance, sharper still, was directed at Asantir. "Besides," she added, more mildly, "we could hardly let two such babes ride out alone."

"Not entirely alone," the Honor Captain replied. Kalan could tell that she was aware of Nhairin's anger, but chose not to respond to it. "Kyr and Lira have volunteered to go with you as well. The Wall, after all, is still the Wall and you may need their weapon skills there as well as on the long road south."

"Hmm," said Garan, low voiced but grinning as he adjusted a stirrup for Malian. "We can all guess why Lira volunteered—eh, Lira?" he asked, looking at her across the horse's back. "Are you hoping to kiss the beautiful herald Tarathan again?"

"Just because no one wants to kiss you," Lira retorted cheerfully, but equally quietly, and Kalan exchanged a covert grin with Malian.

Asantir spoke beneath their banter. "Malian will need you, too, Nhairin, when she walks among strangers, both for your love and for your wisdom." The steward nodded but did not answer, busying herself with her horse. Kalan looked a question at Malian, who shook her head, so he turned instead to his own mount. The beautiful black head looked around at him with a kindly eye, and he hoped that he could still remember how to stay in the saddle after seven years in the Temple quarter.

A few moments later, they were all gathered around Asantir for her final instructions. "There is a way out of this undercroft," she told them, "into the paths that lead through the Wall itself and finally into open country. It is only used by those on the Earl's secret business and very few know of it, but both the High Steward and I are among those few. Garan and Nerys will accompany you to the gate, to let you through, but after that you will be on your own." She regarded them all steadily. "I will not say take care, for you ride with the threat of pursuit behind you and potential foes on every side. Speed and daring, not care, are your best hope now. But although your steeds are swift and have great hearts, it is your own wit and courage that will bring you through."

Kalan felt his throat tighten with a mix of excitement and fear, but pride as well, as the Honor Captain saluted Malian. "My honor for your honor, Heir of Night," she said, "until the end. Learn, and grow strong, and return to us soon!"

"I will do my best," Malian replied. "I give you my word, Asantir." She paused, and Kalan saw her gaze flick to Nhairin's impassive face before she added: "If there is wrong in what we do, to Earl or House or to the Derai Alliance itself, I take it now on my own honor. It need not lie on yours, Asantir."

The Honor Captain smiled. "Even the Heir cannot come between a warrior and her own honor, although I thank you for the offer, my Malian." She nodded to Kyr, who would lead the way. "Go now, for it is time and more. And may the Nine go with you!"

They went, leading the horses single file into the tunnel that led out of the undercroft. The guards went first with Nhairin behind them, while Malian and then Kalan brought up the rear. The cobbles underfoot gave way to sand that muffled the horses' hooves; a breath of cold and dusty air came stealing to meet them. Kalan stumbled over a small stone and on a sudden impulse he stooped and slipped it into his pocket.

A piece of the home earth, he thought with an ironic smile. But the Keep of Winds *had* been home to him, however reluctantly, for seven years, just as Night had, in their own way, taken him in when Blood threw him out. Kalan wondered what Malian was feeling now. He had longed for years to escape but it was different for her; she was the Heir of Night and so this flight must seem like the bleakest of exiles. Even he felt qualms, for in his daydreams he had always ridden out to combat the enemies of the Derai, not crept away as a hunted fugitive. Kalan thought of wyr hounds and shuddered, then clapped his hand over his mouth. "Oh, I forgot!" he exclaimed.

"What?" asked Nhairin, impatient.

"I have to tell the captain that siren worms hunt in pairs!"

he said urgently. "She needs to know that there'll be another one."

Nhairin's expression, as she looked back at him through the darkness, was very strange indeed. "How do you know about the siren worm?" she asked.

"Sister Korriya will have told him," said Malian. "She was there, after all."

Nhairin continued to stare at Kalan with narrowed eyes, a kind of weighing-things-up twist to her mouth, but eventually she shrugged. "Tell Garan and Nerys, then, and they can tell Asantir."

Now that, thought Kalan, as they moved forward again, was careless. He looked across and met Malian's gaze, which was as speculative as the steward's had been.

"How did you know?" she whispered. "*Did* Sister Korriya tell you?"

Kalan shook his head. "Later," he muttered back, feeling far from easy. He was remembering Hylcarian's message to Malian, bidding her seek out Yorindesarinen's long-lost sword, helm, and shield—and the warning to be very guarded.

There would, he decided, be plenty of time in the days ahead for more private talk. He smiled, too, because the arms of Yorindesarinen were the stuff of legend and almost as famous as the hero herself. Even the thought of them sent a shiver down his spine, and it would be a marvelous thing if all three could be found and brought back to the Derai Alliance.

Now there, thought Kalan, his heart lifting, is a true quest—a worthy Derai adventure.

A few paces more brought them to the door that opened into the Wall itself. It appeared, Kalan thought, staring at it, to be made of stone; the metal crossbars were so heavy that it took both Garan and Nerys, working together, to lift them down. Kyr gave the quiet order to mount up and they all swung into the saddle, Kalan thankful that he managed successfully on his first attempt. His black horse walked calmly forward, following Malian's, but Kalan drew rein at the gate, bending to speak with Garan.

"I have a message," he said, "for Captain Asantir." He repeated what Hylcarian had told him about siren worms hunting in pairs, while keeping the source of the information to himself.

"In pairs, eh?" Garan said, rubbing at his jaw. "That's not good news. But thanks, lad. I'll make sure the captain knows."

"Don't forget," said Kalan, although already he was thinking more about what lay ahead. He looked up to find that Nhairin had stopped as well and was watching him again. She shrugged when he stared back, but said nothing, just turned and rode on.

Malian had stopped just beyond the gate and was looking behind her into the dim corridor that was the last of the Keep of Winds. Her hood shadowed her face, but Kalan sensed her sorrow and loss as Garan and Nerys began to swing the doors closed.

"Farewell, Keep of Winds." Malian bowed deeply from the saddle. Her voice was soft, but Kalan's keen ears heard both the words and the longing and regret with which they were spoken.

"Farewell, Child of Night." The reply rippled in Kalan's mind—and he assumed in Malian's—unheard by anyone else. He recognized the voice at once, even though it was muted by distance. *"I will not forget you. I shall be waiting for your return."*

Malian straightened out of her bow, and Kalan saw her hands tighten on the reins. "I will not forget you either," she said. "I, too, long for the day of return."

"Soon," said the light-filled voice, fainter than an echo.

"As to that," Malian replied, "it is as the Nine will, and not I." She raised her right hand, palm turned outward in formal salute "Farewell, Hylcarian."

And with only Kalan of the House of Blood to ride behind her, Malian of Night turned and rode away from the Keep of Winds, which had been her home and her inheritance. She did not look back again.

PART III

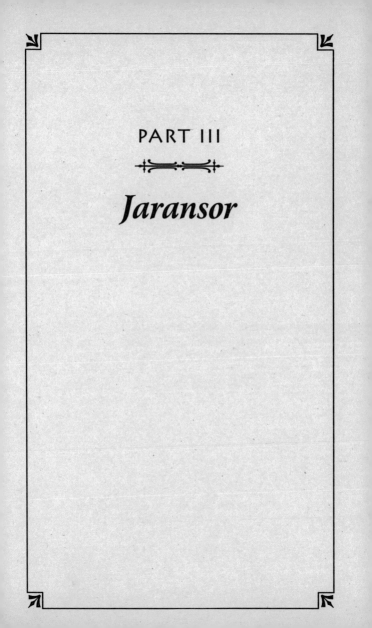

Jaransor

25

The River of No Return

The wind was blowing again, no longer a full Wall storm but driving in gusts, bringing dust and grit from the jagged peaks that towered above the Gray Lands. It blew under the bivouac where the small band of fugitives lay hidden and shrilled around its perimeter. Malian shifted uneasily on the hard ground, feeling the stone beneath her hip and a pebble that was pushing into the small of her back. Rest eluded her, despite her weariness, and she envied Kalan who lay curled in exhausted sleep at her side.

They had been traveling by night and resting by day in an attempt to avoid detection, with Malian falling asleep as soon as her head touched the stony ground. Even the full daylight had not been able to keep her awake, but now her eyes refused to close and she could see Kyr, Lira, and Nhairin crouched close together by the entrance to the small bivouac, their voices an anxious thread beneath the wind.

It was the fourth day since they had fled the Keep of Winds, traveling through the narrow ways of the Wall while the storm raged above them. It had taken two full days to blow itself out, just as Haimyr had predicted, and they had reached the western rim of the Wall by the end of the second day. The evening light had been in their faces when

Kyr pointed beyond the rock-strewn foothills to the vast, flat emptiness that was the Gray Lands. "That is the way we must go," he'd said. "We shall travel by night to avoid prying eyes, although it will make our progress slower."

They had kept to this plan, making their way down through the foothills and only setting out across the Gray Lands once it was full night. The rocky plain was full of sudden dips and dry streambeds that kept their pace slow, but at first Malian had enjoyed the journey, the smooth stride of the horse and the breeze at her back that raised small dust devils across the plain. After hour on hour of silent riding, however, only stopping for short rests and to snatch a hurried mouthful of food, the ride became a matter of simple endurance. Only the paling of the eastern sky had finally signaled a halt, and their hiding place that first day out had been little more than a scrape in the surface of the plain. Even the horses had lain down to rest, while Kyr and Lira had stretched a tarpaulin, as gray and dreary as the land itself, from one side of the hollow to the other. They had all huddled beneath it, first to eat the dried rations from their saddlebags, and then to take turns sleeping. "For only a fool," Kyr had said, "would fail to set a watch in these lands."

This was their third cold camp, for Kyr would not allow a fire. And although he insisted that they wait until full dark before striking camp, Malian, who was used to a world of stone walls, still felt overwhelmed by the openness of the plain. It was full of unexpected noises, the voices of birds and insects, and the stealthy movement of animals by night; even the gray light filtering through the tent seemed strange after the brilliant illumination of the keep.

The voices near the entrance quietened and Nhairin moved back toward Malian. "Still awake?" the steward said. Her scarred face was drawn, her hair filmed with gray dust.

Malian raised herself on one elbow. "What's happening?" she asked in a low tone, so as not to wake Kalan. "Something's wrong, isn't it?"

The steward hesitated, then said reluctantly, "We're not

sure. We think there's something out there that shouldn't be, but we don't know who, or what. It could be a hold patrol, but we're a long way off their usual routes." She hesitated again. "Lira's going to check it out."

Malian looked past Nhairin to where the two guards still squatted on their heels by the entrance. Kyr looked grim, but Lira gave her a reassuring smile and a wink as she looped a water bottle onto her belt and checked her knives. "A horse would be too obvious by daylight, in this terrain," she said, picking up her rider's bow and pitching her voice just loud enough for Malian to hear. "I'll scout this one on foot."

"Be careful," Kyr growled, and Lira gave him a quick nod and the ghost of a smile. "Of course," she said, and slid out through the entrance.

Malian thought that she would never sleep then for worrying about Lira, out there alone on the hostile plain. She watched Nhairin settle down beside her and wondered how long they would have to wait before the guard returned. Kyr remained by the entrance, carefully whetting the blade of his sword; the sound was sinister beneath the gusting wind. Malian stared up at the tarpaulin, listening to the wind's voice—and the next thing she knew the shadows were thick under the bivouac and she was blinking her eyes awake. Voices murmured by the entrance and she sat up quickly. Lira was back, dust coated from the plain, but she seemed unusually subdued and both Kyr and Nhairin looked bleak.

So, thought Malian, not good news. She saw that Kalan was awake and listening, too, although he had not yet moved. "What did you find?" she asked Lira.

Lira sighed. "There's a large band of riders out there," she replied, "and they're definitely not Derai. Their harness is similar to that of the warriors we fought in the Old Keep, so they may be Darkswarm. But whoever they are, they're on our trail—and it looks like a second group's split off to get between us and the Border Mark."

Nhairin muttered an imprecation. "How long have they been following us, do you think?" she asked.

Lira shrugged. "I'd say they've been searching for our trail since we left the Wall. Now that they've found it, they'll be pushing hard to catch up. Fortunately for us, they don't seem to like traveling by day much either."

They were all silent for a moment and Malian got up and moved to the entrance. "Can't we outrun them," she asked, "since we have messenger horses?"

"They're good horses," Kyr said gruffly, "swift and enduring, but it's too far to the Border Mark. And if we tried to gallop across terrain this rough, even by day, they'd end up with broken legs."

"Besides," said Lira, "as soon as we forsake stealth and run for it, the dust alone will tell our pursuers exactly where we are."

Nhairin's frown was heavy as she looked from Lira's dusty face to Kyr. "What other options do we have?"

Kyr cracked his knuckles, one by one, until Malian felt like shaking him. "If we keep on going as we are," he said, "they'll catch us pretty quickly, now that they've found our trail. So we need to try and outwit them, if we can, do the thing they won't expect. I say we turn west and head for Jaransor."

The wind gusted hard into their silence, blowing grit through the bivouac entrance. "The Jaransor hills." Nhairin's voice sounded odd, flattened. "That is an ill-omened place."

"It's what the captain would do," Kyr responded, "the thing no one would expect."

"I don't think anyone would expect Jaransor," Nhairin answered, still on the same odd note. Her eyes were shadowed as they met Malian's and the line of her lips had thinned.

Kyr looked at her curiously. "What do you know of Jaransor?" he asked.

Nhairin shrugged. "Only what anyone does. Those hills have long been forbidden, off-limits, because too many of our people have foundered there. And the old records say that Jaransor is hostile to both the Derai and the Swarm.

They claim that it is one of the ancient places of this world, possessed by a power that sleeps but lightly and is dangerous if woken. They also say," she added, "that Jaransor is ghost-ridden and drives people mad."

Kyr looked at her from beneath his brows. "People say that the Old Keep is infested with ghosts as well, full of their old hatreds. But we didn't see any when we went in there, did we Lira?"

The other guard shook her head but said nothing, apparently content to let Kyr and Nhairin resolve the matter between them. Malian looked at Kyr. "I haven't heard of Jaransor or these tales," she said. "Is it as dangerous as Nhairin says?"

"Ay," he replied, "it's dangerous. But I am hold born, as you know; raised in Westwind, which is the closest of Night's holds to Jaransor. Westwind folk still go into the Jaransor hills, despite the ban, and return to tell the tale. The real question is, can we escape our pursuers if we carry on as we are? And the answer to that is no."

There was another brief silence while they absorbed this. "So what happens when we get to Jaransor?" Kalan said eventually, sitting up. "Can we still reach the Border Mark by that route, or will we have to find another way south?"

Kyr drew a map in the dust and they all crowded close to look. "The main Jaransor ridge, here, will bring us back down to the Border Mark, if we can shake our pursuers for long enough. Jaransor has never been friendly to the Darkswarm and its minions, so I am hoping that going into the hills will buy us the time we need."

"And if not?" Kalan asked. "What lies the other way?"

"Eventually," said Kyr, sketching more lines in the dirt, "the main ridge splits into two. One spine angles back toward the Wall until it finally peters out in the northern reaches of the plain. The other arm carries on, league on weary league, until eventually you come to the Winter Country, or so they say. West of Jaransor there is just wilderness. I have never heard what, if anything, lies beyond that."

"So," Malian said carefully, "you are saying that we have a choice between possible danger if we enter Jaransor, and certain danger if we don't?"

"Oh, we'll definitely be in danger if we go into Jaransor," said Kyr grimly. "But at least it should give us an even chance of eluding our pursuers, whereas out here on the plain . . ." He finished his sentence with an expressive shrug.

"I still don't like it," muttered Nhairin.

"You'd like it even less if we were dead," observed Lira, getting to her feet while Kyr brushed the map away. "And believe me, we will be if we stay here."

They rode out as soon as darkness fell and turned their horses west, toward Jaransor. Kyr pushed them hard, setting a faster pace and allowing fewer stops. He rode slightly ahead of their small company, while Lira was rearguard and frequently dropped behind, checking their back trail. Malian and Kalan rode close together, sometimes knee and knee, sometimes one horse behind the other, but they did not speak. An air of palpable tension hung over them all, but although Malian listened for the sounds of pursuit, all she heard was the wind and the steady thud of the horses' hooves on earth and stone. The night stretched out, cold and black and seemingly endless, while she rose and fell in the saddle, fell and rose until it was all she could do to remain upright.

This time they did not stop with the dawn but carried on toward the range of hills that rose up before them, rough and wild in the gray light. The ridges were far lower than the Wall of Night, but still very rugged, with stony outcrops along their tops. "We'll have more shelter once we're in amongst the hills," Kyr said. "We can stop, then, and find a safe place to rest." So they pressed on again and eventually came to a wide river that comprised several braided channels flowing between shingle banks. The water was a pale blue-green in color and looked cold.

"The river Telimbras," said Kyr. "It marks the boundary

between the Gray Lands and Jaransor. In Westwind Hold," he added, his expression impassive, "we call it the River of No Return."

Malian glanced quickly at Nhairin and saw that the steward's face was set, although she made no reply to Kyr's remark. Kalan grinned. "Well," he said cheerfully, "this is the river for us, then, since going back is not an option."

That surprised a laugh out of Lira and a reluctant grin from Kyr. Even Nhairin's countenance eased a little. They clattered and splashed their way across the riverbed, throwing up clouds of glittering spray as they rode through the deeper channels, and then climbed steadily, following narrow trails up rocky ridges and across steep slopes. The focus of Malian's world closed in again: to the black neck of her horse, to staying in the saddle, and to gritting her teeth and keeping going.

Despite her weariness, she began to notice small details about the landscape around her. The herb thyme grew wild and its scent rose, heady and aromatic, whenever the horses' hooves crushed it. Small yellow flowers danced amongst the rocks and the higher slopes were covered in a mix of scrambling green—sweetbriar, said Kyr, when she roused herself to ask—and dark, twisting thorn scrub. Eventually, Malian began to see the green shimmer of trees growing along small precipitous creeks, and they stopped at last in a narrow ravine where the trees formed a green roof and a stream ran clear over brown pebbles. "A short rest only," Kyr warned. "Just to eat. We need to get further into the hills and keep pushing south."

"Without killing either ourselves or the horses," murmured Lira. Malian wondered how the guard could keep going when she had had no rest for a night and a day. She herself was so stiff and sore that she practically fell out of the saddle, and Nhairin's limp was pronounced. But the tranquil green was pleasant and both horses and riders drank gratefully from the clear water. A large rock with a smooth, flat top was set into the steep sides of the creek bed; they all sat there, either cross-legged or swinging their feet over the edge, and chewed their rations in weary silence.

"Time for a nap?" asked Lira, when they had finished eating.

Kyr shrugged. "Only a short one. We need to keep moving."

Nhairin stood up, brushing the dust from her coat. "I'll keep watch," she said. "I think I'm too weary even to catnap."

Malian watched her limp to a small tor that overlooked their back trail, pausing only for a pat and a word to the horses. Lira already had her eyes closed, lying flat out on the sun-dappled rock, while Kyr and Kalan were sitting with their backs against a tree, both staring at nothing in particular. Malian felt her own eyes growing heavy and she allowed her head to nod forward.

She woke to find the sun a little higher in the sky and Kyr shaking Lira awake. Malian sat up groggily and decided that she felt worse after an hour's sleep than she had before. "Ugh," she muttered, and Kalan grimaced in reply.

"I feel awful," he said, smothering a huge yawn. They staggered to their feet and over to the horses, where Nhairin was strapping on their refilled water bags. She slanted a small smile at Malian, who smiled back—then reached out and placed her own hand over the steward's. "I'm glad you're here," she said.

Nhairin's hand stilled momentarily, then grew busy again as her smile twisted. "Are you?" she asked. "I must confess to feeling singularly useless, as well as ten years older than when we left the keep."

Malian peered up at her. "Are you serious, Nhairin?" she said. "You must know that we need you."

The steward shook her head. "Do you? How can that be, half crippled as I am?" But her bleak expression eased when she looked around. "Nay, don't look so worried. The leg's not used to being pushed like this, and I'm tired and out of sorts, that's all."

Kyr now led them higher into the hills, using the folds in the terrain to conceal their progress from any watchers below. He kept well beneath the tor-dotted ridgelines, but occasionally they would come to a natural gap where they could look back over the Gray Lands without being seen themselves. The plain lay far below them, with a milky haze across its face and the Wall of Night marching along its far side, blue with distance. The only movement besides their own was a falcon high overhead, and Malian found herself caught by its effortless mastery of the air. She had seen falcons before in the keep mews, but never like this, wild and free in the empty sky.

"We saw birds sometimes, in my home hold," Kalan said, when she admitted this to him. His face was tilted to watch the hawk's flight. "It was close to the border, with a creek that ran out of the Wall into the Gray Lands; that's why the birds could live there. But they were only small, nothing like this."

"You get a lot of hawks here," Kyr put in unexpectedly, "up amongst the higher peaks." His eyes, too, were fixed on the hovering falcon. "The tor hawks in particular are famed for their size, their courage, and their speed."

He loves them, thought Malian, watching the guard: both the land and its hawks. And it's obvious that he's been here before.

She let her mind soar, following the bird, and suddenly the whole world was sharper, clearer, every rock and ridge outlined as though she saw it through the falcon's eyes. That gaze swung wider, out over the plain, and Malian felt certain that her enemies were there, hidden beneath the milky haze. Their presence buzzed at her, sharp as a wasp along the outer edge of her mind. She could sense an inexorable quality to their pursuit and did not think the river Telimbras would stop them for long.

Malian peered down, catching a glitter behind the veil of dust and wind. She shook her head, trying to focus, and her hand crept toward the armring beneath her sleeve. The opacity of the haze grew clearer—and then vanished altogether as her fingers clasped the silver band. She saw the flash of armor and the glint of light on spearpoints, and drew her breath in sharply. But when she blinked and looked back again, her vision was obscured once more by the haze. Her horse moved, tossing its head restlessly, and she looked around to meet Nhairin's dark, searching stare. "What do you see?" the steward asked.

Malian shook her head. "Something. Nothing. It's hard to see because of the heat haze and the dust, but there is definitely something out there. I can feel it."

They rode on, circling below the gap to avoid being outlined against the sky and then climbing again. As soon as an opportunity arose, Malian urged her horse alongside Kalan's. "Do you think you could shield us like you did in the Old Keep," she murmured, "so that we disappear from their psychic view?"

Kalan frowned. "Jehane Mor might be able to do it, but I would find the numbers difficult, particularly with the horses—also because we're always moving and our surroundings keep changing so much. I suppose," he continued slowly, "I could try something like a shield of opaque air around and above us. Yet I can't help feeling that would be a bit obvious, too much of an anomaly in the natural pattern of things."

Malian nodded, seeing that what he described might be like a beacon for their pursuers, rather than throwing them off the trail. Kalan pushed his hair back from his forehead, leaving a track of sweat and grime. "But perhaps, when we make camp and everyone's settled," he said, still frowning. "I might have a better chance then."

Malian kept her voice low. "They seem to have found us so easily. You don't think that's because of me, do you, the same way the were-hunt followed my light in the Old Keep?"

Kalan shook his head, a quick negative. "I don't think so. You're keeping it well damped down now. Besides, it's not the same out here. There's so much light everywhere, so much life and activity, that your light is almost lost in it." He leaned closer to her. "What did you really see, down there on the plain?" He shrugged as Malian looked back at him, her expression blank. "You know there's been an empathy between us since the Old Keep, so I know when you're being evasive. I just wondered why."

Malian shifted in her saddle. "I'm not quite sure. It's just a feeling that I should be careful." She frowned down at her hands. "That I shouldn't give too much away. I keep asking myself how our pursuers could possibly pick up our trail so quickly—unless they already knew where to look. And Nhairin is not herself, and Kyr has plainly been to Jaransor before, despite the ban." She paused, then finished softly, "I don't feel inclined to trust anyone too readily."

Kalan nodded, staring at the unknown land all around them and then at Kyr and Nhairin's backs, only a few horse lengths ahead. "Lira does seem certain that we've been hunted ever since we left the Wall," he said at last. "You're right—as though they were expecting us." And Malian watched the light of adventure that had shone in his face for the past few days, even when exhausted, fade into something harder.

It was midafternoon when they crested the main Jaransor ridge. Even tucked into the cover of rocks and thorn scrub it felt like sitting on the top of the world itself, with the haze of the Gray Lands far below and ridge on ridge of wild country stretching into the west. Malian could not help drawing a deep, satisfied breath before her attention was caught by what she had thought was just another tor. Now, closer up, she realized that it was the jagged remnants of a tower. "What is this?" she asked Kyr, surprised.

"One of the ruined towers of Jaransor," he replied, wiping the sweat from his face. "There's a line of them along these hills. They say they were watchtowers, built to mark the border of the Old Empire that once stretched from Jaransor in the north to Ishnapur in the south."

"I've read a different account," said Nhairin. Her face was still drawn, but she studied the crumbling watchtower with interest. "It said they were built by another people, long before the Old Empire rose, who wished to dwell remote from others and watch the stars. No one knows why their towers fell, but it is written that the land is imbued with their ancient power."

"How do you know such things?" Malian asked curiously.

"I have always liked old histories," Nhairin replied, "and a steward has more time than a guard to indulge such interests. We Derai collected such stories when we first arrived here, even though few read the old books now."

Kyr shrugged. "Who knows which of the two accounts is true?"

"They could both be true," Kalan said, then flushed when they all stared at him. "Brother Selmor's an historian and he says that it's possible to get layers of history in one place, particularly where one civilization has succeeded another."

"And so much for the past!" Lira said impatiently. "I am more interested in the present and keeping our Heir from becoming part of history for a while longer. Do we stop here, Kyr, or keep moving?"

"More importantly," said Nhairin, "dare we risk pushing further into this place, despite our pursuers?"

Kyr frowned. "We can't stop here," he replied. "It's too open and we still have a few hours of daylight left. We should use them to find the old road that runs along the western side of the ridge, linking all the towers, and follow it south to the Border Mark."

"Assuming the road's still there," Nhairin said gloomily.

"It will be." Kyr was very certain. "The road is like the watchtowers. Their builders made them to last."

It took them some time to find the old road, for it was closed in by creeping vines, and scrub that stood shoulder high to a horse. Yet once found, there was still a discernible pavement beneath the encroaching green, and even old milestones sunk into earth. And wild as the path was, they followed it until the sun dipped toward the western horizon and shadows lay thick in the deep gorges below the main Jaransor ridge.

Kyr finally called a halt beside a small plateau, where they found more ruins crumbling amidst grass and trees. The guard led his horse amongst the remnant foundations until he found a piece of upright wall; the surrounding foliage was so dense that it was like being in a cave. "We can use the wall for shelter," he said, "and no one will find us easily back here, not unless they know where to look. But no fire," he added, when Kalan started to pick up dry wood. "That's a comfort we still can't afford."

He sent Malian and Kalan to look for water instead, and they followed their ears to a small stream that purled its way down the hillside through a series of stone channels. One of these diverted water into a square tank, which was also faced with stone. The water in the tank was deep, but not murky, with only a few leaves floating on its surface.

"This place is peaceful, isn't it?" Malian said, when they had splashed the dust from their faces and hands, and drunk from their cupped palms. "I wonder what it used to be? It seems quite different from the watchtower."

"A house perhaps," Kalan replied, "or a Temple? I saw fallen colonnades back there amongst the long grass." He drew one finger along the tank's worn coping. "It's amazing that the irrigation channels have remained intact when these ruins are so old."

Malian nodded. The wind was teasing out wisps of her dark hair and she tucked the strands back behind her ears. "It seems very strange," she said, "to build such high towers simply to watch the stars." She walked on alone to the edge of the trees, staring out over the wild terrain to the west and the steep, bush-clad heights bathed in evening amber—and was struck again by the immensity of the land, and a sky that held nothing except the falcon's hovering speck.

We came from the stars, Malian thought, staring up at the

hawk. Or so the histories say. I should not feel intimidated by this country, however vast it seems.

Nevertheless, she was intimidated. "Jaransor," she murmured, as if saying the name aloud could empower her. "The hills of the hawk." Leaves rustled and there was a footfall in the grass, but it was not Kalan who came to stand beside her. "I feel like I am standing on the very edge of the world," she said to Kyr.

"It is high up here," he agreed, looking out over the great sweep of country with an expression very like content.

"And rugged," Malian said, hearing the terrain's remoteness in her voice. "Wild. But less harsh than the Wall."

"Don't be fooled by it, Lady," Kyr squatted on his heels. "It may seem softer, more worn down by time, but it's a hard country for all that. You could lose yourself among those hills and valleys and no one would ever find you—or you find your way out again either."

"Does anyone know what lies beyond it?" Malian asked.

"No one has ever traveled there that I have heard," he replied, "or returned to tell the tale if they did."

Malian nodded, studying his dour profile. "You love this place, don't you?" she said. "Even if it is dangerous."

The guard shrugged. "What is dangerous? Other folk might well say that we Derai are dangerous, warlike and chancy to deal with, with our blood oaths and warrior codes. There are not many who'll dare the Derai Alliance and the Wall of Night." He turned his head and looked at her, a gleam of genuine amusement in his dark face. "Besides, just because something's dangerous doesn't mean you won't love it. Sometimes the more dangerous it is the more you love it, like warriors who live for battle glory, and youngsters like yourself and the boy there who dream of adventure. Wouldn't you say?"

Malian nodded.

"Well," he continued gruffly, "Jaransor's like that, especially for all the hold brats growing up in Westwind. You can see the hills, blue with distance but still clear, from the hold's battlements. And the ban only makes the place more alluring, more of a challenge. All the young ones naturally head this way as soon as they're old enough to go hunting. My friends and I usually stayed around the foothills and the river, but on one trip I ended up going much further in and discovered the old road that we're following now—mainly because the deer I was hunting went to ground in the thick scrub of the escarpment." He shrugged. "I went hungry that night, but I had my fill of adventure."

"And you came back safely," Malian said.

"Yes," Kyr agreed, "I did. But not everyone does. Some never come back and some—well, it is as though something in here drives them mad." The gleam of amusement crossed his face again. "Perhaps I have too little imagination for the madness to take hold."

Malian did not think he really believed that any more than she did. She turned her eyes back to the evening hills. "Yet you still see Jaransor as being the lesser of our current dangers?"

Kyr nodded, his expression grim again. "I do," he said heavily, "for we are few and far from help, and our enemies, from what Lira's seen, have numbers. Jaransor has been kind to me in the past and I hope it will aid us now, the Nine willing. Nonetheless, I want you to promise me something, Heir of Night, should matters go badly."

"What?" asked Malian cautiously.

"If I give the order," said Kyr, "or Lira does, I want your promise to flee at once. Do not hesitate, or wait for anyone, or look back, just go as swiftly and secretly as possible. The others and I—we will follow if we can. If not, you must do your best to survive on your own and reach safety."

"And where," Malian asked soberly, "should I look for safety in these hills?"

Kyr's reply was unhesitating. "You must get to a watch-tower, for there is power in them. I felt it often when I hunted here as a youth. If there is any strength in this land to protect you, you will find it there."

"If there is strength," said Malian, "and if it will aid me. And if not?"

"Your goal is the Border Mark," the guard replied, "but if you can't reach it then you must turn north again and run for Westwind. It's better than being caught by the Darkswarm," he said, seeing her expression, "and at least you will be amongst our own people. So, do I have your promise, Heir of Night?"

Malian hesitated. "I don't like the idea of leaving the rest of you in danger while I run away. It doesn't seem right."

Kyr snorted, a short grim sound. "I'm afraid that is what it means to be Heir, Lady Malian. It's you they want, so that makes it both our duty and yours to make sure they don't get you."

"And what of Kalan?" asked Malian, conscious that he could overhear, even though he had moved away. "He's at risk, too."

"But he isn't Heir of Night," Kyr told her. "I said that you must not wait for anyone and that's exactly what I meant. The boy will just have to do his best, like the rest of us. Still," he added, with a glance toward Kalan, "I doubt you'll have to worry about that one. He'll stick close."

Malian nodded, knowing he was right. "Very well," she said. "You have my word, although I hope you won't need it."

Kyr stood up. "We all hope that," he said. "But remember what I told you—do not wait or turn back for any reason. Flee as fast and far as you can."

Malian looked up and saw that his mouth was shut hard, his eyes cold. She stood, too, and placed her hand on his forearm. "Kyr," she asked quietly, "have we been betrayed?"

She felt a muscle jump beneath her hand, but when he spoke his voice was uncertain. "I don't know, Lady Malian. But given the circumstances, it doesn't look good."

"No," agreed Malian, "it does not look good." She felt lost again, hollow and empty, but this time it was not because of the vastness of the land.

Kyr gripped her shoulder. "We are not done yet, Heir of Night." He looked around him slowly, an expression in his face that Malian could not remember seeing there before, and which she struggled to name. "Neither is Jaransor. That is something I do trust in, no matter what they say. It always felt like a good place to be, when I was young."

He turned back toward their campsite, but not before Malian had managed to put a name to the expression that did not quite fit with the Kyr she had always known. "Mystery," she murmured, and wondered what this Jaransor truly was, that it could touch even the Derai.

26

Nightfall in Jaransor

Malian stood motionless for some time after Kyr left, the taste of suspicion bitter in her mouth. She did not know which was worse: the thought that the traitor might still be in the Keep of Winds, close to her father and all his councils; or out here, wearing a familiar face and riding close beside her.

But not Kalan, she thought. Him I can trust. I think.

She drew a deep breath and caught his eye as she turned back to the water tank. "Just watching?" she inquired ironically. "Or listening?"

"Both." His shrug was apologetic. "I really can't help it, you know. I hear exceptionally well and the empathy seems to enhance that."

"Which could be useful, I suppose," Malian said thoughtfully. "Although it would be better if it were more of a two-way process."

"That may still happen," Kalan said, "if it really is the old empathic bond. From what I've read, it often took longer for one partner to develop than the other."

"But sometimes it just stayed one way. I've read about that, too," Malian replied. Her voice became a half chant. "Telemanthar and Errianthar had the bond, and Kerem and

Emeriath did as well, after their flight from the Swarm. But the link between Antenor and Maron was only one way, even though they were sworn closer than brothers."

"And so," finished Kalan, "Maron did not know to turn back when Antenor was ambushed. Sister Korriya says that their story teaches us that gifts are exactly that, an extra tool to aid us—not a replacement for everyday common sense and intelligence."

"My First Kinswoman," said Malian, "and yet you know her better than I do. She sounds a little daunting."

Kalan grinned. "She can be very daunting, but she is pretty fair, too, most of the time."

They were both silent, then, until Nhairin came limping over with the water bags. She did not stoop to fill them, but stood with her head tipped back, studying the last of the sunset and the black speck that still hovered in the sky. "We have ridden all day beneath the shadow of that hawk's wings," she said. "Under the circumstances, I question whether that's a coincidence."

Kalan and Malian's eyes flew to the sky and then to each other, startled and worried. "Kyr did say that hawks live in these hills," Kalan said slowly.

"But," said Nhairin, "you'd have expected it to have dived after prey or drifted away at some stage, wouldn't you? Yet it hasn't left us at all. I didn't question it either," she added, as though someone had queried her silence, "not until I realized it was still up there, even at this late hour."

"It could be just chance," Kalan said. "All the same—"

"Indeed," agreed Nhairin. "Whose is it?" she muttered, frowning up into the sky. "Whom does it serve?"

"Why would it serve anyone?" Malian asked curiously.

The steward started. "I don't know," she said, "but there is power here. I feel it, bound into the roots of the hills." She shuddered, turning her face away from them. "It eats at me," she whispered. "But the hawk—I do not know."

Malian stepped closer to her. "Are you all right, Nhairin? You look very tired."

"I am tired," the steward said, still in that same low voice as though speaking to herself. "So very weary."

"We'll help you with the water bags," said Kalan, reaching for them. "You shouldn't be carrying so many, not with your bad leg. And we should all go back, get some food."

Nhairin smiled wryly, her full attention caught. "I'm not done yet, young man," she said, but she let him help anyway.

Malian watched her covertly during their quiet supper and thought that Nhairin did seem exceptionally tired and drawn. It's this journey, she decided, feeling her own fatigue. It's wearing us all down.

As soon as it grew dark, Kyr and Lira slipped off to scout their backtrail again, while Malian, Kalan, and Nhairin waited by the vine-hung entrance to the small camp. The wind that had followed them out of the Gray Lands had died away and the first stars were out, white and clear. There was still a very faint wash of color along the western rim of the sky, but that was all. Night had fallen on Jaransor.

So this, thought Malian, peering up, is what we mean by night's beauty—what the House of Night swears to in the Keep of Winds and all our holds along the Wall.

She made no effort to speak and the silence stretched until Kalan broke it, his voice diffident through the darkness. "Do you mind very much," he asked Nhairin, "being the Earl's High Steward rather than a warrior anymore?"

Nhairin sighed and stretched her leg, as though considering her answer. "I am not precisely the Earl's High Steward anymore," she said dryly. "But no, I don't mind. I was only ever a moderately competent soldier, but I am a good steward. To be honest, I only became a guard because it was expected in my family. What I do mind," she added with sudden intensity, "is being lame and disfigured, and the pain that has gone with both those things. At times like these, one cannot help but feel that even a moderately competent soldier would be more useful than a lame steward, however able."

Beside her, Malian felt Kalan shift. "I'm sorry. Perhaps I shouldn't have asked."

"No," said Nhairin, "I think you should ask. You are young and dream of battle glory and the warrior life, I can see that. It is only right that you should know the truth of what you wish for. The songs and stories never tell you about the agony when steel slices through your flesh, or the long, weary years afterward for those who survive, living with their pain and trying to eke out an existence on the fringes of keep and hold life. I was one of the lucky ones. I had the use of my limbs still and a place of honor in the Keep of Winds. It might have been very different, though."

"Why is that?" asked Kalan. His voice sounded remarkably sober, as though he, like Malian, was digesting the bleak picture conjured up by Nhairin's words. Malian's thoughts had flown to all the wounded veterans in the keep, recalling the menial make-work they did around stable and hall, and how they always sat furthest from the feast tables and the great fires.

Nhairin is quite right, she reflected uncomfortably. I have never even considered their situation before, let alone questioned it. "Why might it have been different?" she asked, echoing Kalan's question when the steward remained silent.

She felt Nhairin's hesitation. "Well, why shouldn't you know the story?" the steward said finally. "Everyone else does, although no one speaks of it. It was the Old Earl himself who wounded me in his rage, because I was standing guard outside the Heir's quarter on the day he tried to slay both you and your mother. He cut me down because I held to my post and would not obey his order to stand aside."

The air in their small camp was suddenly tense and the beauty of the stars seemed colder, remote with distance. Malian spoke carefully into the charged atmosphere. "I thought you said that it was my father who stopped him from killing us?"

"That was later," Nhairin replied. "He was out with the guard when it all blew up, training in the mountain country around the keep. I was part of the Heir's Guard at that time, as was Asantir, and we were both on duty outside his quarters that day. One of the pages came running to tell us that the Earl had gone mad and sworn to slay his daughter-in-law and grandchild. I wanted to flee at once with both of you, but Asantir argued that doing so would be contrary to our oaths and honor. Her solution was to find the Heir with all speed and bring him back, in the hopes that he could restrain his father, while I stayed and tried to reason with the Earl. Not," she added, "that he was ever susceptible to reason, even at the best of times."

"So that is what you meant the other night, with Asantir?" Malian murmured.

"Yes," agreed Nhairin. "It was what you might call an old argument."

"I take it," Kalan said cautiously, when the silence stretched out again, "that the Old Earl was not open to reason that time either?"

Nhairin gave a hard laugh, almost under her breath. "That is one way of putting it," she said, "although he did take the time to curse me as a traitor and an oath breaker before he cut me down. Unfortunately, he was a formidable swordsman, so I was not able to hold him off for long."

Malian hesitated. "I can't help wondering, given your relative skills, why it was Asantir who went and you who stayed?"

"There were many reasons, in the end," said Nhairin dryly. "One of the more compelling being that if Asantir had held that door, then none of those who tried to take it by force would have survived—including the Old Earl. And even though Nerion was my dearest friend, neither I nor Asantir was brave enough to take the matter that far."

"You never told me any of this when we spoke of it before," Malian said quietly.

She felt rather than saw Nhairin's shrug through the darkness. "Your father forbade anyone to speak of it to you all these years, and when you did ask, well, it's hardly an edifying tale. And I suppose I became used to my situation.

As I said, I was a good steward. But now, when we are all in danger, it galls me to be so thoroughly useless."

"You aren't useless," Malian protested, but Nhairin cut her off.

"No? I am already worn down by the riding and I could not keep up at all if we had to travel on foot. Kyr and Lira know that I cannot help them with the scouting and very little with any fighting either, should it come to that." Her voice was flat and hard.

"Well," said Malian, "neither can we, Nhairin."

"True," agreed the steward shortly, "but I am not a child."

Malian sighed, and the silence grew tense and uncomfortable. "So what is the full story, Nhairin?" she asked finally. "What did stop my grandfather in the end? You may as well tell me."

"I suppose I might," the steward replied. The hardness was gone from her voice. "Although I don't actually recall very much after my encounter with the Earl. They told me afterward that Doria and the other maids had tied the doors closed with material torn from their dresses, barricading them with furniture, which held the Earl out for a time. Not for long, however."

Nhairin paused, staring straight ahead into the darkness. "The thing that checked him, when they finally burst into the Heir's quarter, was finding that the baby had gone. You, Malian, had vanished. No one knew how or when you had disappeared, except that it was while all attention was focused on events at the door. The Earl blamed Nerion, but she denied it and the truth was that she was very weak at that time. She had been ill after your birth, and the late flowering of her power compounded that. Anyway, the effort of trying to beat your whereabouts out of her servants stayed the Old Earl's hand long enough for Tasarion to get back and put a stop to the business."

Malian felt as though a band of pain had circled her heart, making it difficult to breathe. "Did he stop it?" she asked. "What did he do?"

She saw Nhairin's nod. "He did stop it. They told me later that he nearly killed his horse getting back to the keep, and then ran all the way from the outer courtyard to his own quarters, still in full armor. He found me fallen across the threshold and his father in a paroxysm, on the verge of finally killing both the servants and Nerion because no one could reveal your whereabouts. But although the Old Earl was terrifying in his rage, Doria told me that Tasarion, confronting him, was more frightening still. Apparently he did not draw a weapon or even raise his voice, but his father, for all his fury, fell back rather than confront him."

"What did he say?" asked Kalan breathlessly.

This is just a story for him, thought Malian, not personal and terrible as it is for me.

"What, still expecting some hero tale?" Nhairin inquired sardonically, "some declaration of weighty defiance or desperate glory? Well, there was none. According to Doria, he only uttered one sentence: *'The law of the Derai prevails in this keep, Earl of Night, and you are its upholder.'* Disappointed?" she asked, when Kalan stayed silent.

"Well," said Kalan, "it does seem a little dispassionate. I mean, the Lady Nerion was his wife."

And the Old Earl, thought Malian, was both his father and his Earl. She wondered if Kalan could see the terrible nature of that conflict—and wondered, too, why she had never asked the steward about her wound, even when she was younger. Was it simply that Nhairin the lame, Nhairin the scarred, Nhairin the steward, was something that she had taken as a given all her life, like the keep and the Wall itself? Or was it because she had sensed that she did not want to know the answer? Malian shivered, forcing herself to concentrate on Nhairin's soft, uninflected reply. "Childhood friend, the sweetheart of his youth, and then his wife—but no word of that was spoken."

"Because it would have done no good, and well you know it, Nhairin." Kyr's voice was pitched from just beyond the vines and they all started. Malian wondered how long he had been sitting there, listening to them talk, and whether Lira was with him or still scouting the Jaransor night. She leaned forward as the guard continued to speak.

"The Old Earl was as harsh and unreasonable a man as ever led the Derai, and any word of affection or loyalty for Lady Nerion would only have spurred him on. He would have called it weakness, and he despised weakness, almost as much as he hated and loathed the priestly kind. I was there, too, Lady Malian," Kyr added, "and your father did right to call on the law of the Derai, rather than any claim of emotion, or kinship, or common decency. He instantly put the Earl in the wrong of our own code, the laws and honor that he claimed to uphold. It may not sound like much, but your father turned the tide of events in that room, so that lives were saved and not lost."

Malian hesitated. "But Kalan is right. It does seem cold, just focusing on the law like that."

Kyr's reply, out of the darkness, was slow and thoughtful. "Well, now, Lady Malian, you're Heir of Night and so you've had a lot of lessons drummed into you, history and such that guards don't need to bother with. But we still know the old stories down in the barracks, and it seems to me that whenever things have gone wrong for the Derai—I mean really wrong, like the Great Betrayal—it's always because some great lord or leader thinks that he or she is above the law that's meant to bind us all. We've all heard tales from some of the other Houses as well, suggesting that a fair few of their lords and captains don't bother too much with the niceties of the law. Your father, though, the Earl Tasarion, he's not like that. With him there's only one rule, the same for him as for everyone under him, and no exceptions. If that makes him a cold man, then I'd rather have his coldness than his father's bloody-handed passions, any day." Malian heard him spit, as if to emphasize his words, and then he added, "Still, I wouldn't exactly call him cold, myself. Would you, Nhairin? You've known him longer."

The steward shifted as if to ease her leg again. "I wouldn't have, when we were young together, but now I'm not so sure. After all, the law may have saved Nerion's life that day, but she was still sent away and died of that exile as surely as she would have by the Old Earl's sword. A cold death, rather than a passionate one perhaps, but just as dead. And the only reason we're all here now is because the Earl intended upholding that same law again and exiling Malian, probably to no better end."

The guard grunted. "True enough. But I still say that back then he had no choice, given he had Lady Malian and the House of Night to think of. Besides, you could argue that it was the lack of law where Lady Nerion was sent that killed her. Any shame for that lies squarely with the House of Adamant." Kyr cleared his throat. "And he spared you, Nhairin, even if he couldn't save his wife."

"What does he mean, Nhairin?" asked Malian, when the steward did not answer.

"He is referring to the end of my sorry tale," Nhairin replied, although she sounded reluctant. "The Old Earl threw me into prison because I had stood against him at that door. I would have stayed there until either I died of my wounds or he had me executed as a traitor, except that he didn't live much longer himself—finally worn out by the violence of his passions, no doubt. When Tasarion became Earl in his turn, he released me and made me High Steward, and the rest you know."

"Not quite all of it," said Kalan. "Where was Malian found, in the end?"

"Ah," said Nhairin, "that turned out to be a genuine mystery. The whole keep searched high and low, but Malian could not be found. Until that evening, when the duty priest went to renew the holy fire on Mhaelanar's altar and found her lying on the Defender's sacred shield as though it were a cradle. There was a huge outcry about it at the time. Warriors and priests alike said that it was a sign from the Nine, that you, Malian, must be favored of the gods. Some even said that you must be the long prophesied Chosen of the De-

fender himself. It was all such a business that even the Old
Earl was forced to put a good face on things. But no one has
ever been able to say how you got there."

Kalan whistled softly and Malian shook her head, remembering what Garan had said when he knelt and swore to
her, in the Hall of Mirrors: *"Chosen, Shield of Mhaelanar,
beloved of the Nine."* So many of those around her must
have known the story yet said nothing, bound by her father's command of silence—but that knowledge would have
shaped their response to the revelation of her powers in the
Old Keep. "It makes my head ache," she said, "just thinking
about it all."

"Of course it does," said Nhairin. "Why not, when it has
made both my leg and my face ache all these years?"

They all chuckled, but no one argued when Kyr suggested that they get some sleep while he took first watch.
Lira was still not back and Malian could not sleep, not with
her thoughts churning around everything Nhairin and Kyr
had said. She knew that Kalan, too, would be lying awake,
waiting for Lira to return so that he could try and build his
shield.

Does he pity me, she wondered, for having so grim a
heritage: a grandfather consumed by hatred and unbridled
passions, my mother's disgrace and exile, and a father who
upholds the law at the expense of family love and loyalty?
Malian hunched a shoulder and turned away.

I don't need pity, she thought, especially not from a
novice priest who has been cast out by his own family as
well as by his House.

*"Ay, that is what your grandfather would have said,
wanting no one's understanding and despising anyone who
showed compassion or mercy."* The thought drifted into her
head, delicate as the starlight, and she realized that one hand
was clenched tight around the silver armring.

Yorindesarinen? Malian asked silently, but the voice
did not speak again. After a moment she realized that other
voices were talking softly, the words drifting back from

where Nhairin had gone to sit with Kyr on the other side of the vines. Their speech was accompanied by a soft chirring sound, and she realized that one of them must be sharpening a blade.

"I thought you were hard on the Earl before," Kyr was saying. "He did his best in a difficult situation, I always thought."

"Well," Nhairin answered, with a curious little edge to her voice, "you should know."

Malian heard the pause before Kyr replied, a touch of anger in his voice. "I tried to do my duty then, as I do now, to House and keep."

"Still," Nhairin said, "I notice that you didn't tell Malian where you stood on that day."

"What's the point of raking over cold ashes?" he asked, weariness replacing the anger. "The Old Earl and Lady Nerion are both dead; let the past die with them. Still," he continued, when she said nothing, "I don't think Earl Tasarion adheres to the law because he's passionless, but because he sees that's what the Derai need. It's one reason why he's finally been able to start rebuilding the old allegiances. The Alliance is beginning to realize that he stands for more than just his own personal interest, or even that of Night. And he seems to love the Winter woman well enough, for a so-called passionless man." Kyr paused and Malian imagined him shaking his head. "Although I admit that doesn't help his cause with the other Houses."

The weight of Nhairin's silence was an answer in itself. The quiet lengthened, and Malian felt her mind turn to the murmur of the night breeze and the slow movement of the stars. She could follow the breeze, she realized, her fingers clasped around the armring, just as she had followed the vision of the hawk earlier in the day. She flowed with it across the hillside, letting the little wind show her the fallen stones beneath the grass and the scurrying path of some small night creature. Malian could hear Lira's footsteps, almost lighter than the breeze, as the guard made her careful way back to them. And she could sweep high, too, far above the hills, and make out the whole length of Jaransor stretched out below her, just as the hawk must have seen it spread beneath its wings.

There *was* power in the land. Malian could see it flowing like a river—but deep, far down in the earth. The hidden river only bubbled up at intervals along the crest of the hills, in a series of evenly spaced springs. The springs, she realized, matched the ruins of the watchtowers that had once stretched the length of Jaransor: Kyr was right, the ruins were centers of power still. And then she sensed the chill of another force, alien but aware as it probed the night.

Where? Malian wondered sharply. She drew back and waited for the wind to tell her, which at length it did, showing her the wide braids of the Telimbras, shrouded in night. Darkness seemed to pool by the western bank of the river, impenetrable even to the little breeze, which took fright and fled away.

They have already crossed the Telimbras, Malian thought, her awareness drifting beneath the white glitter of the stars. They are here in Jaransor.

She shuddered, hovering between her mind's flight and her grounded body. In that one, brief moment she sensed another presence hidden behind the wind, concealed in the swirling dust of the Gray Lands. The impression was so fleeting that Malian almost missed it—but not quite. The afterimage of a solitary, cloak-wrapped figure, its pony's tail and mane blown forward by the wind, burned behind her eyes in the darkness. "Who?" she asked on a half breath, then realized that Kalan was up on one elbow, staring toward the entrance.

"Lira," he said. "I think she's back."

No, thought Malian, not Lira. There is someone else, someone who follows the followers.

She strove to restore the fragile link, but any sense of a hidden presence was gone. After a moment she let it go, for at least Lira had returned safely and Kalan could begin to build his shield. For now, the rest could wait. Sighing, Malian pulled her blanket close.

An unearthly shriek split the night, distant but piercing as it spiraled upward to a knife-sharp point, then fell away again in a long, bubbling wail. The black horses plunged, terrified, and Malian jerked upright, her heart pounding in rapid hammer beats of fear.

"The Nine preserve us all!" Nhairin cried in a hoarse, strained voice. "They have brought some sort of demon with them!"

27

The Border Mark

A thin, shrill wind had risen in the night and was blowing steadily from the north. It brought a cold dawn with it, creeping across the Gray Lands and around the Border Mark. The pillar of weathered stone had been standing long before the Derai ever came to the world of Haarth and the inscriptions on its surface were worn down by time. No one could read them anymore, just as no one knew who had placed the pillar there. It served now to mark the boundary of Derai influence and the end—or beginning—of the road that snaked south into low, rounded hills, toward the River lands.

The country was both lawless and desolate, but there were way stations all along the road's length, established by the River merchants who traded with the Derai. The last—or first—of these was tucked into the low hills around the Border Mark and comprised little more than a wood pile and a ring of blackened fire stones. The dawn light, stealing into this camp, revealed a fire's cold ashes; two great gray horses were tethered amongst the wind-stunted trees, with their saddles and a modest amount of equipment trussed into the branches overhead.

The riders were harder to detect. They were cloaked

in gray and sat as still as stone amidst the tree shadows, looking out toward the morning. The wind caught at their cloaks, but otherwise only their eyes seemed alive, snaring the sun's light when it finally crept up and over the horizon. Its warmth was muted, veiled behind a baleful haze, and the horses moved uneasily, tossing up their heads. The cloaked figures stirred as well, standing up and stamping their feet against the morning chill. One walked to the edge of the camp and looked out over the Gray Lands while the other remained hooded in shadow, reverting to stillness while her companion quartered the plain with his eyes.

"*Well,*" Jehane Mor said, using mindspeech so that no sound broke the night's silence, "*what news does the dawn bring?*"

"*None out of the Gray Lands.*" Tarathan did not turn his head. "*I can see nothing except a hawk, climbing high toward Jaransor. Yet, there is something stirring all the same—in the hills, and hidden behind the wind. I can feel it.*"

He stared toward the dark bulk of the Jaransor hills and Jehane Mor's gaze followed his. "*Jaransor,*" her mindvoice murmured. "*Is it part of this?*"

"*I fear,*" Tarathan replied, "*that it may be. The power that slumbers there is waking. I sense confusion and an ancient wrath burning in the land itself. It is slow as yet, but it is moving.*"

The first sunlight touched the top of the hills, separating tor and outcrop from the shadows below. "*Dare we risk that power?*" Jehane Mor asked reflectively. "*Do we even need to? It may have nothing to do with our business here.*"

Tarathan shook his head. "*It does. Every time I seek for Malian and Kalan I am drawn to Jaransor, like a compass finding north. I suspect they have been lured into those hills, or driven. They may even be part of what is rousing there. But they are also in grave danger. The awareness of it presses in on me—and the danger is growing.*"

"*Are they caught up in what is happening there?*" Jehane

Mor was thoughtful. *"Or are they the catalyst, the pebble that has started the avalanche? They are Derai, after all, and Jaransor has little love for their kind."*

"The Madness?" Tarathan frowned. *"Perhaps. But I don't think Jaransor needs to wake for that particular curse to fall."*

Jehane Mor's slim brows drew together. *"So where does this leave us? We could wait out the month here, in accordance with our agreement, then return quietly to Terebanth without shame or dishonor. That is one option."*

"It is." Tarathan turned back to the plain. *"There is something concealed behind this wind,"* he said again. *"But what?"* The wind riffled the braids of his chestnut hair. *"Is there another option?"*

"Of course," she told him. *"The one that you prefer. We can follow your seeking into Jaransor and see what we find there."*

His lips curved in a brief, fierce smile. *"I do prefer that option. But what does the voice of caution advise?"*

Jehane Mor's answering smile was slight. *"That doing so will be extremely hazardous—and is not required by our herald's oath."*

He turned, his eyes very dark in the early light. *"But are we willing to abandon Malian and Kalan to whatever fate has drawn them into Jaransor? Shall we do only what is required of us and no more?"*

Her smile deepened. *"We never have before, that I can recall."*

"It is good," he said simply, *"that we are of one mind."* A gleam from the rising sun caught in his hair and in his eyes, turning both to fire. *"But we should not ride blindly into whatever is brewing in Jaransor. First we must pinpoint Malian and Kalan's location, if we can."*

Jehane Mor looked resigned. *"You intend seeking for them through the Gate of Dreams. Is that wise, given what we know of Jaransor?"*

Tarathan shook his head. *"Almost certainly not, but we*

need to find them quickly. And if what we have been taught is correct, Jaransor is one of the few places that exists both here and beyond the Gate of Dreams at one and the same time."

"Which makes seeking the logical choice." Her gray-green eyes met his, grave and very level. *"But if Jaransor is indeed rousing, that could make the risk of using the Gate far greater. We know so little about Jaransor's power, but what we do know is a litany of unpredictability, terror, and madness. It may very well overwhelm us both."*

"Jaransor is a danger," Tarathan agreed soberly, *"but one that may be lessened if only I pass beyond the Gate, while you hold your shield on the border between this plane and the dream realm."* His glance swept the small, exposed campsite. *"It might be best, in any case, not to leave ourselves unprotected here."*

Jehane Mor's look was still grave. *"If I remain on the border between realms that will also lessen the strength of my shielding once you pass the Gate. I should still be able to screen out unwanted scrutiny from the Swarm, but as for Jaransor itself . . ."* Her shrug left the outcome hanging. *"You will have to be wary."*

He grinned, then. *"When am I anything else? Besides, do we not have a destiny to fulfill? I do not believe that I am fated to die in Jaransor."*

She shook her head, glancing out over the brightening plain. *"Destinies may change, you know that as well as I. But we had best make haste, for neither the day nor Jaransor will wait for us."*

They ate quickly while the wind strengthened and grew colder, then saddled the horses and led them further into the trees. *"Best to stay out of sight of prying eyes, and be ready to leave quickly."* Tarathan's horse danced a little, scenting the wind, and he patted its neck. "Gently there, my brave-heart," he said aloud. "Although you are quite right about this wind. I don't like it either."

"Nor I." Jehane Mor frowned, studying the sky. *"If it*

were not too early in the year, I would swear that I smelt winter at its back."

Tarathan nodded. *"There is snow behind it, which is even more reason to make haste."* He spread his long cloak beneath the densest tree cover and lay down, his two swords naked across his breast. Jehane Mor sat cross-legged at his head, her eyes and face very calm within her gray hood.

"I am ready," she told him, her mindvoice calm.

"And I," he replied—and sent his spirit forth, past the Gate of Dreams and into Jaransor.

28

Flight

*F*ar to the north, Malian stood with a hand on her horse's rein, her face hidden by the curve of its neck while Kyr and Nhairin argued. Lira sat to one side with her hands lying loosely over her knees. Her bow was already slung over her shoulder, the quiver on her back was full, and two knives were sheathed beside her sword. Her normally lighthearted face was grim and she seemed removed from them, her mind fixed entirely on what lay ahead.

She already knows what she has to do, thought Malian, and leaves Kyr to argue with Nhairin, who does not.

It had been a long, long night since they first heard the terrible scream that Nhairin had identified as one of the demon creatures that hunted with the Swarm. Malian had felt Kalan's shield slam up, surrounding them with the color and shape of night, a pattern comprised of leaves, stars, and the night breeze. None of the others seemed to notice it, although Malian had caught Nhairin looking at Kalan once or twice with a puzzled frown. They had all stayed awake for a long time, waiting to see if the demon would hunt out their trail. But whether because of Kalan's shield, or simply through luck, no Swarm demon had appeared and eventually they took turns to sleep. Only Kalan had remained awake all night; he had whispered to Malian that he was afraid that his shield would dissipate without his conscious will holding it in place.

Kyr had roused them before first light. "I would not have thought that a Swarm demon could have missed us," he had said. "If that is what we heard. But the pursuit will be hard on our heels anyway, since both Lira and Lady Malian believe that they have already crossed the Telimbras." He had paused, shaking his head. "Only speed and luck will save us now. The way Lira and I see that, Heir of Night, is that we must try and make some luck, while the rest of you flee as far and fast as possible."

"What do you mean make some luck?" Nhairin had asked sharply.

Kyr had looked back at her, heavy browed. "Why, even the odds a little, slow them up with a few losses. Who knows, we may even persuade them to turn back."

"What folly is this?" Nhairin had protested. "You know we are hopelessly outnumbered! What you are proposing is certain suicide, when our best hope, surely, is to stay together!"

Kyr had grabbed her by the arm then, pulling her away from the others, and they were still hissing at each other on the far side of the small plateau. Malian looked an enquiry at Kalan, but he only shook his head, either unable to hear or unwilling to reveal that he could, with Lira there. Malian sighed and led her horse over to the other guard.

"Is Nhairin right? Is it suicide?" she asked.

Lira shrugged. "It's a fighting chance, to slow them down a bit, not to stop them. It's true the risks are high, but it's the only way, Lady Malian. If we stay together, as Nhairin suggests, we'll all be caught together—sooner probably, rather than later. This way, there's a better chance for the rest of you to escape."

"I see," said Malian, and she did see, all too clearly. Before she could say anything else, Kalan spoke quietly from behind her.

"So why does Nhairin advocate a different course?"

Lira shrugged. "She speaks out of her fear that she, on her own, will be unable to protect you. She doesn't look at what she can do, even now, but sees only what her leg prevents her from doing." The guard slid a sly smile at Malian. "That is not my wisdom, it is what the captain warned us of before we left. But I think that she saw truly. And this is no time for arguing. It is a time for doing."

She is right, thought Malian, so now I must act as Heir of Night and settle the matter.

She led her horse over to Kyr and Nhairin, who both looked around at her in surprise. Kyr's expression was grim and exasperated, while Nhairin looked both angry and upset.

"Nhairin," said Malian, meeting the steward's eyes squarely, "I don't like what Kyr is suggesting any better than you do, but Asantir put him in command and we have to do as he says."

"Even though it means their deaths?" Nhairin asked deliberately.

Malian sighed and folded her arms across her chest. "It's a risk that they are prepared to take," she replied. "I do not like that, but as Heir of Night I have to accept it. Things have gone awry and now we all have to do what our duty requires. Kyr and Lira believe that they have one duty, while you, Kalan, and I have another—which is to do everything that we can to evade our enemies."

Nhairin stared at her, and when she spoke her words were slow and heavy. "I have never before seen how truly you are his daughter."

"She speaks as Heir of Night," Kyr said tersely, "and with more wisdom than you are showing. We have wasted enough time, Nhairin. We have to go."

"Don't be angry, Nhairin," said Malian, as Kyr walked away. "It may be that they will be successful in what they do."

The steward turned her face away. "Do not delude yourself," she said. "Still, if this is the course that you are all determined to follow, we had best get on."

Malian shivered. The wind that had risen in the night was stronger and colder now, with clouds scudding high and fast out of the north. Lira came to stand beside her, casting a thoughtful look at the sky. "There's nasty weather coming," she said. "It feels like snow, even though it's at least a month too early for snow here."

"As Lady Malian said, things have gone awry." Kyr laid a hand on Malian's rein as she settled herself in the saddle. "Remember what I told you," he said, "and do not stop or hold back for anyone. Most particularly, do not wait for us. Lira and I will follow if we win free."

"I have given you my word," Malian replied. She held out her hand to him, her throat tight. "The Nine be with you, Kyr—and you, Lira." Quickly, she turned her horse away, and although she looked back once, just before losing sight of the camp, the two guards had already disappeared into the trees.

If this is what it means to be Heir of Night, Malian thought drearily, then I do not want it. She blinked back tears, staring hard at the fast-moving sky.

They headed south with the wind driving at their backs, listening hard for any sound of conflict or pursuit from behind them. At first Nhairin preserved silence, her expression set, and it was Kalan who kept a watchful eye on their backtrail and on the sky, where a black speck shadowed their path. After a time, Nhairin began to cast frequent, sidelong glances at him and mutter to herself, an indistinguishable murmur below the voice of the wind. Oppression, sullen as the weather, hung over their small party.

They stopped for a brief midday meal in the shelter of a jagged tor, torn between their need for food and rest and the compulsion to keep going. Nhairin chewed her lip as she studied the terrain ahead, which was becoming rougher, full of jumbled rocks that hampered the horses. The sky was gray as iron now, the clouds pressing lower onto the hilltops and shrouding the higher peaks. "We'll have to stick close together," Kalan said, "or we'll lose each other in that cloud."

"Could we leave the old road and go further down?" asked Malian. "I mean, as far as we know our enemies are behind us, not below."

Nhairin frowned deeply over that. Her face was still shadowed, but her eyes seemed clearer than they had earlier in the day. "We don't know that for certain, though," she said slowly. "They might have split their party again. Besides, it's very rough country further down. The valleys are so clogged with brush and rocks that we would risk getting hopelessly lost. It's always best to keep to the path in this sort of country, so I think we'll have to chance the cloud."

Malian nodded, recalling Kyr's advice about the watch-towers and deciding that it might, after all, be best to stick with the main ridge. She shivered as a sharp gust of wind caught them. "We had better press on."

Press on they did, with the wind prying through the warmth of their cloaks. The clouds, too, conspired against them, rolling lower and lower so that the path ran through banks of gray, moist air with increasing frequency. The world darkened every time they entered the fog so that Nhairin, who was riding immediately ahead of Malian, became little more than a dimly seen shadow. She seemed to fall deeper into her abstraction with every passage of the clouds, but roused herself at their next halt. "I don't like this weather at all," she muttered, "Lira was right, there is snow in the wind. I think we'll have to find shelter soon."

"Does that mean we won't make it to the Border Mark before the storm breaks?" Malian asked, trying not to let either fear or disappointment sound in her voice.

Nhairin shrugged, her expression weary. "We're still at least a day's ride from the Border Mark, perhaps more. Whatever's behind this wind will be on us long before that."

Kalan frowned into the wind. "We don't have the equipment or supplies to survive a snowstorm," he said slowly.

Nhairin looked at him, her expression dark as the cloud-wracked day. "Death behind us," she muttered, "and death ahead. So where now does duty lie?"

"Exactly where it did this morning," Kalan said sharply. "If we can't outrun the weather, then we must find shelter—as you just said—and do our best to survive. That is our duty, Steward Nhairin."

Nhairin continued to stare at him, her eyes narrowed. "Is it?" she asked, in a strange high voice that reminded Malian, uncannily, of the rising wind. "Who are you, little priestling, to tell me my duty? You grow presumptuous—or perhaps you always have been? Ay, that's it," she mused. To Malian, watching, it was as though the darkness in her face deepened. "I knew there was something more to you than met the eye."

"Nhairin," said Malian uneasily, "are you all right?"

"Is he?" Nhairin countered, not taking her eyes off Kalan. "I knew he was Temple raised, but that could mean anything or nothing these days. No one told me anything about this boy, except that you wanted him along. There's more to it, though, isn't there?" Her voice developed an odd, crooning note. "I see the boldness in him now and the power, too, strong as earth and hard as stone. He's more important than we thought."

"*We?*" Malian leaned forward. "What do you mean by *we*, Nhairin?"

The steward shifted slightly, shaking her head as if to clear it. "Why—Kyr, Lira, and me, of course," she said, after a slight hesitation.

Malian stared at her. "We're all important, Nhairin, you know that. And you've always been important to me."

Nhairin gave a bitter laugh. "Have I? More important than Kyr and Lira? You seemed quite ready to send them to their deaths. I have always thought you your mother's child, but I saw Tasarion in you then."

Malian gripped her reins tightly, but it was Kalan who replied. "Malian didn't send them, Steward Nhairin. It was Kyr's decision. And their deaths are not certain."

"Aren't they?" Nhairin's lip curled. "Who will be next, my boy, have you asked yourself that? Will it be you or me, sacrificed for her Blood?"

"Why are you speaking this way, Nhairin?" Malian was beginning to feel alarmed. "Are you ill?"

Nhairin shrugged. "I am well enough. But what of him, this priestling who rides at your back? Does he mean well?"

"Of course he does," Malian answered, as steadily as she could. "All he said was that we must find shelter, if necessary, from this storm that's brewing. You know that's sense, Nhairin!"

"Shelter, ay," Nhairin muttered, looking away from Kalan at last. "Yes, yes, you are quite right, we'll have snow before nightfall." She shook her head again and her eyes cleared. "But why are we sitting here talking about it? We need to keep ahead of our pursuers and find somewhere safe to sit this weather out."

"Yes," agreed Malian relieved, "and the sooner the better!" But she exchanged a doubtful look with Kalan as the steward urged her horse forward.

"Is she often like this?" he asked.

Malian shook her head. "Never. She's not acting like herself at all."

Kalan looked grim. "She's been getting stranger ever since we crossed into Jaransor. And she knew that I was using power last night, with the shield, even if she didn't know exactly what I was doing. She kept looking over at me in a measuring sort of way."

Malian bit her lip. "Both she and Kyr said that Jaransor can drive you mad. But we'd better stop talking now before she turns on us again."

Nhairin did indeed give them a sharp look, back over her shoulder, but she said nothing and they continued on in silence. Soon they rode into cloud again, and this time it surrounded them for some time before lifting. The path dropped steeply away in front of them and they sat looking out over what seemed like a vast sea of fog. Kalan pointed ahead to where the land finally rose out of the cloud again. "There's another watchtower there," he said. "That may offer the shelter we need."

"You have keen eyes," Nhairin observed, and Malian's heart sank as she saw that the shadow had flowed back into the steward's face and eyes.

Kalan nodded, his expression wary, and Nhairin's horse sidled a few steps closer to his. "What other gifts do you have?" the steward asked. "What else have you been hiding so that you can spy on us?"

"Nhairin!" exclaimed Malian. "Stop this! Kalan is our friend, not a spy."

"Your friend perhaps, but not mine," Nhairin replied. "He means me no good, do you boy?" Her horse danced nervously as she turned it toward Kalan, ignoring the long fingers of cloud that were already curling around them. She stared at Kalan with dark intensity. "The little priest said yesterday that going back is not an option. Perhaps," Nhairin crooned, "he would even prefer death. Well, that can be arranged!"

"No!" shouted Malian, kicking her horse forward as a long knife appeared in the steward's hand. Nhairin's mount reared, neighing shrilly as the steward tried to pull it back down with one hand. The other hand still held the knife, its blade sharp and dangerous; the black horse shied sidewise, away from Malian, as it came down. Kalan urged his horse into the gap, shoving Malian away.

"Run!" he shouted.

Malian tried to cry out a protest or a warning, but her horse was already lunging forward. She heard a shout from Nhairin, and an answering cry from Kalan as she tried to turn and see what was happening. But all she could make out was a blur of black—and then Kalan was tearing after her, crouched low on his horse's neck. They thundered down into the sea of cloud, which was so dense it quickly turned into impenetrable blankness, forcing the horses to check their headlong pace. The fog blew past them in great strands, but it did not dissipate or roll away; eventually, the horses stopped altogether. Malian and Kalan sat very still, listening, but they heard nothing except the soughing of the wind among the tors. "What happened?" Malian whispered. "Why didn't she follow us?"

"I threw my cloak into her horse's face," Kalan whispered back, "so it shied and then stumbled off the edge of the path. I didn't wait while it scrambled to find its footing. I just charged after you."

Malian shook her head from side to side. "I can't believe that she would try and kill you."

Kalan huddled his arms around his body. "I think the old madness must have taken her."

"I suppose so," Malian said miserably. She wanted to throw back her head and howl, but she forced herself to remain calm, to concentrate on what they needed to do next. Kalan was hunched down in the saddle and she leaned toward him through the murk. "You're hurt, aren't you? Was it the knife?"

"Under the arm," he said faintly. "Nhairin slashed with the blade at the same time I threw the cloak. It's just a glancing blow, not a deep wound. But it really hurts."

"We have to get you under cover," Malian said. "We'll make for that next tower; there's bound to be some kind of shelter there. But you'd better take my cloak."

Kalan nodded, his face white and set with pain, and did not argue about the cloak. Malian handed it over quickly, before she could change her mind, and shivered as the cold struck sharply through her jacket.

They moved forward slowly, and this time the cloud showed no sign of lifting. Kalan was swaying in the saddle, his left hand clamped under his right arm, so eventually Malian dismounted and led both horses, always peering ahead to find the next few feet of path. For a long time she felt as though they were moving through the mist between worlds again, only this time there was no hope of rescue: no Yorindesarinen sitting by her small fire, no herald to come walking out of the flames, or Asantir waiting on the other side of a door in the air.

And no Nhairin. But Malian pushed that thought aside. She could not think about Nhairin now, would not, until she had Kalan safe. The day and the cloud stretched on, interminable, and she had almost given up when the path rose steeply and a darker mass of shadow bulked through the gloom. When Malian drew closer, almost dreading to hope, she saw that it was indeed one of the ruined towers—a mass of jumbled foundations with wing walls falling away on either side. The tower itself rose smoothly to about thirty feet above her head, then ended abruptly in broken stone. The location was very exposed and the low, scrubby vegetation offered little shelter. Malian hesitated, biting her lip, while the wind and the cloud swirled around them.

"You'd better get down and stay with the horses," she said to Kalan. "There's a bit of protection in the lee of this wall. I'll scout around and see if I can find anything better."

The tower was larger than she had realized and it took some time for Malian to work her way around its base, especially with the thorn scrub growing right up to the walls. She found the archway on the tower's far side, a span of stone curved above gaping darkness, and peered through the entrance, expecting to see a circle of ragged stone with cloud above. Instead she found a tunnel that angled down, further into the dark. Malian hesitated, thinking that wild beasts might lair in such a place, then shook her head sharply; at least it was out of the weather. Turning, she made her way back to Kalan, feeling every stumble and thorn stab more now that her mind was no longer focused on finding shelter.

Kalan was sitting against the wall and holding on to the horses' reins with the hand that was not pressed against his wound. He got up without complaint when Malian told him what she had found, but he had to lean heavily against her while they made their slow way back around the tower. It was only when they got there that his attention sharpened as he stared up at the weathered arch. "Why," he said, "it's the Hunt."

Malian looked—and wondered how she could have missed seeing it before. There, etched deeply into the stone, was the fleeing hind and the pack of hounds pouring in pursuit, with the hunters close behind. There was the horn lifted merrily to the sky, the unfurled cloak, and the shaded eyes following the progress of the hounds, just as she had seen it all before in the Red and White Suite. The only difference was the hawk that flew high above them all, its wings spanning the sky.

"The Huntmaster," Kalan said, speaking just a little thickly. "He should be there, too, with his crow."

Malian shook her head, not quite sure what he meant and hoping that he was not going to turn as strange as Nhairin. "We need to get out of this wind," she said bracingly, "and take a look at your wound." She frowned. "Although I'm not sure how the horses will like going down into this place."

The horses, as it turned out, had considerable doubts but were willing to be persuaded—particularly, Malian supposed, given the weather and that they were used to the subterranean stables of the Keep of Winds. Nonetheless, they shied as they passed beneath the arch, and stamped and laid back their ears when she began leading them down the curved tunnel. Kalan followed with one hand clutching a stirrup leather for support; the other was still pressed under his arm.

Malian had been afraid that the tunnel might take them deep underground, but in the end its curving descent was only about one floor. As it broadened, she felt a sense of space above her, as though the roof arched. The air was dry and a little musty but not unpleasant. "What is this place, do you think?" she whispered to Kalan, not yet daring to speak in a normal tone.

"It looks like a cave," Kalan replied, looking around, "or a cellar. Oh, I forgot! Sister Korriya gave me one of those cone lamps. It should be in my saddlebags."

"Now he tells me," Malian muttered, and rummaged until she found it. She fumbled for a moment until the lamp ignited, flowering into a small steady glow, then looked around. She saw walls of stone and earth with a heavy layer of dust and leaves on the floor, but no litter of bones or dead animals—*not* a predator's lair, then, after all. "Is it a cellar?" she asked, turning slowly and watching light and shadow chase across the walls. "If so, why are there pictures on the stone?"

Kalan moved closer. "It's another hunt," he said. "See, here are the hounds—and there are the hunters following them. But these drawings are much more primitive than the depiction over the arch. They must come from a very early time. It's not exactly what you expect to find in a cellar, though."

"No," agreed Malian, "but it's dry and out of the wind. I vote we stay."

Kalan nodded and sat down heavily against the wall. He was still very pale, and Malian looked at him worriedly. "I'll see to the horses," she said, "and then have a look at that wound, if you think it can wait."

He nodded again, his eyes closed, so she tended the horses and hoped the place was as safe as it appeared. Malian shivered, thinking of the Night Mare's blood-curdling shriek, and wondered if it could continue to hunt regardless of the storm, or whether it, too, would need to seek shelter. She hoped the weather would deter all their pursuers—and that Kalan would recover enough strength to build another shield. "We need a fire," she said.

Kalan opened his eyes. "Dare we?"

"Feel how cold it is already," Malian answered, "even out of the wind. It'll be worse tonight. And glancing blow or not, that wound should be cleaned." She tried to remember what the guards had always told her about making fires in the wild. "The roof's high, so it shouldn't get too smoky, not if I keep the fire small and can find dry wood." She turned toward the tunnel entrance. "I'd better go now, before it gets dark."

"Be careful," Kalan said, but he did not try and stop her.

It was bitterly cold outside, and Malian's heart jumped in her chest every time the wind whistled through the rocks or howled amongst the ruins. But nothing untoward happened, and she found plenty of dry wood under the thick scrub cover. It took several trips to get all the fuel from the arched entrance down into the cellar, but Malian did not grudge the effort once she had coaxed the first small blaze from a meager beginning of twigs and leaves.

It was remarkable how cheering that fire was—and it meant she could boil water to clean and bandage Kalan's wound. Malian winced in sympathy as he removed his jacket and fresh blood seeped through his already bloodstained shirt. He had been lucky, she saw, when she helped him ease the shirt off, for the knife had scored the fleshy area below the armpit, but had not cut deeply. Being the child of a warrior House, she knew enough to worry about the dangers of infection and cleaned and bandaged the wound as carefully as she could. Afterward they both huddled close to the fire, knowing that overhead the cloud-hung day would be darkening into a freezing, windswept night.

"I'm glad we're not still up there," Malian said, listening to the wind shriek. She propped her chin on her drawn-up knees and looked across the fire at Kalan. "Will you be able to build us a shield?"

He nodded, and she watched his expression focus, his eyes concentrating on forces that she could not see. She tried to imagine what it would be like, reaching for a sense of the tumbled-down stone of the tower and the dark air that stretched across the entrance—then building an illusion of stone on stone to fill the empty archway with a semblance of wall. Kalan would have to shape thorn scrub across it, too, so it looked no different from the rest of the tower, and set an invisible perimeter around the top of the hill.

Kalan collapsed back, sweat standing out along his forehead and upper lip. "Done!" he said, but Malian could see he was exhausted. She unrolled his blanket and placed it over him, on top of her cloak, then lay down on the other side of the fire, her arms crossed beneath her own blanket. The firelight played across the archaic drawings on the wall and she thought about Kyr and Lira, who might be dead, or wounded and trying to survive in the storm. Her fists clenched, thinking about Nhairin.

"I don't know which I hate more," she said slowly. "The thought that Nhairin really was our enemy and might have betrayed us, or that she isn't and is lost somewhere out there, in this weather."

Kalan was silent, and she wondered if he was asleep. When he did speak, she guessed that he must have been weighing his words. "There was always something in her, gnawing away, but I didn't see it until we came into Jaransor." He hesitated. "I think she really was mad, in the end."

Malian shivered, not just because of the madness, but because she felt that Kalan was right and the influence of Jaransor had revealed a condition that was already present in Nhairin, however well concealed. She could not bring herself to mention Kyr and Lira out loud, even to him, as though speaking of what might have happened could make the worst real.

All we can do is hope, she thought, and try to keep faith with them by surviving, which is what they wanted us to do.

Very slowly, despite the fears and dangers of the day, Malian began to relax—until another thought brought her up on one elbow. "Kalan, what about the shield? Do you think that it will still hold if you fall asleep?"

There was no reply, just the even rhythm of Kalan's breathing and the murmur of the fire beneath the voice of the wind. Malian sat up and fed the small blaze. "Well," she said, to the flames and the dozing horses and the Jaransor night, "I guess we'll find out. But one of us had better stay awake."

29

Shadow Journey

A day's journey away, the ruins of another watchtower rose from a murk of low-lying cloud and intermittent sleet, but the dark shape of the man standing beside it cast no shadow against the crumbling stone.

For Tarathan, standing within the Gate of Dreams, it was as though a great storm of power was building over Jaransor. It might not have broken fully in the physical realm, but here in the world beyond the Gate, Jaransor was thrumming. He could sense the Swarm minions, like a darkness moving on the face of the land, as well as the aura of the psychic predator they had brought with them. Its hunger and thirst for blood were palpable, but it left no track that he could follow. Above all else, he felt the brooding presence of the storm, which he now knew was something more than a natural force. Any disturbance that was entirely of the physical world would not leave any footprint beyond the Gate of Dreams.

The tremendous buildup of energies had made his passage beyond the Gate both slow and dangerous. He had been tossed around like a leaf bobbing on the surface of a flood, buffeted from one current of power to another. Tarathan thought it quite likely that he would have been lost in the turbulence if it were not for two factors: The first was that he was still connected to Jehane Mor's steadfast presence a very long way behind him. The second was that the watchtowers themselves provided a refuge, like islands in the torrent of power.

Tarathan was not quite sure whether he had made his own way to this one, or whether it had extended its influence and plucked him from the flood. For one dangerous moment he had felt the integrity of his spirit presence beginning to fray; the next he had been standing in the shadow of the tower and looking out, as though through a shroud, into the physical world of Jaransor.

The herald had waited for some time, recovering his strength, before extending his awareness again. He could see the fragile thread of his connection to Jehane Mor running from island to island behind him, providing a clear path back—and could observe how the two landscapes of Jaransor, one on either side of the Gate, reflected each other.

So it is true what the loremasters say, Tarathan thought: These hills exist simultaneously in both the physical and the metaphysical realms. He frowned, wondering whether this meant that events in the two realms would mirror each other exactly, or whether it was possible to act in one without creating an effect in the other. As if in response to his thoughts, the murk that surrounded him began to clear, revealing a narrow path that looped around the tower and ran almost to his feet.

He knew, then, that there must be somewhere nearby that he was meant to go—or something that he was meant to see.

The moment Tarathan stepped onto the path, he received his first sense of Malian and Kalan. The impression was very faint and overlain with what he guessed must be the auras of their pursuers. But he was sure, now, that they must have passed this way in the physical realm.

He found the shadow of the first body several hundred yards from the watchtower. The actual body must be lying on the same hilltop in Jaransor and could not have been dead long; its shadow retained too much substance. The shadow body wore black armor with a visor closed over the dead face, and the cause of death was a Derai arrow in the throat, a precise shot into the narrow gap between gorget and breastplate. Tarathan considered it, narrow-eyed, before moving on, every sense alert for hidden danger.

The next bodies were only a short distance further along, one sprawled on the path, the other fallen forward over a rock; again, both had been shot by Derai arrows. Tarathan walked on until he found the shadow of a horse collapsed across the path, its dead rider trapped beneath it. There was the faint impression of tracks—the very shadow of a shadow—around the bodies, and Tarathan knelt to examine them more closely. The tracks told him that a number of riders, perhaps as many as twenty, had gathered around the fallen horseman before fanning out again. They would, he knew, have been hunting in earnest by then, determined to end the depredations of the Derai archer, or archers. He could detect no track that might have belonged to the psychic predator, or sense any other hint of its presence with the riders. Tarathan frowned, wondering whether this absence might mean that the predator was hunting on its own account, an ally rather than a servant of the Darkswarm warriors.

There were no more bodies for nearly a mile, then Tarathan rounded a rock outcrop and found a man's body spread-eagled between two down-bent saplings. The shadow of a man, he thought automatically, strung between shadow trees—except he knew that what he saw was real, in Jaransor. This man was no Darkswarm warrior, but clothed in the leathers and somber cloth that a hunter or a traveler might wear. What was left of his face had been smashed in by a blow from what had almost certainly been a mace or morningstar, but Tarathan still recognized him. He had been one of the guards who accompanied them into the Old Keep. Kyr, that was his name: a dour, grim sort of man, but a competent soldier.

Tarathan studied the shadow of the body with care, trying to read the story of Kyr's death. The blow to the head had undoubtedly been the finishing stroke, but the man had already taken an arrow in the knee and a spear in the back, probably trying to break away.

So then they strung him up, Tarathan thought grimly, for the macebearer to finish the job in style. He sighed. It was the nature of wars to brutalize those who fought in them, and the Swarm and the Derai, if the accounts were true, had been at war for a very long time. But it went against the grain to leave anyone like this, especially one who had, however briefly, been a comrade in arms.

Tarathan drew his knife and cut through the shadow bonds, unsure whether his action would have any effect on this side of the Gate. But the two Jaransors, it seemed, were close enough for that. He had to move quickly to ease the weightless body down onto the hillside, turning Kyr's broken face to the sky.

"May you find peace with your Nine Derai gods," the herald said, and turned away.

Two more armored warriors had fallen to Derai arrows on the edge of a small plateau where old ruins lay exposed to the sullen sky. A third was sprawled a little distance away beside another dead horse. It was clear that someone had been using the ruins to play a game of hide-and-seek that disadvantaged mounted pursuers—but they had caught her in the end.

She must have turned to fight at the last, Tarathan decided, for she lay on her back with a lance impaled through her stomach. It looked, from the limp twisted body, as though a horse or horses had trampled over her. He could see the shadow of her blood, pooled on the ground, and he thought how sharp and clear her image looked, almost substantial for the world of dreams. It was only when he knelt beside her that he realized that the guard called Lira was still alive.

Only just alive, Tarathan thought, looking at the slick

of almost black blood that trailed from the corner of her mouth, and the terrible wound in her stomach. He knew that there was nothing, either in Jaransor or beyond the Gate of Dreams, that could be done. But slowly, incredibly, her eyes opened; the herald watched them focus on his face. He was not surprised that she appeared able to see him, not only because they were in Jaransor, but because the Gate of Dreams was a spirit realm and Lira's spirit was very nearly all that was left of her. Even so, he had to bend close to the shadow of her mouth in order to hear what she said.

"Malian . . . south . . ." It was barely a thread of sound. Lira's eyes remained locked on his face as though to a lifeline and she struggled on, dragging each word out. "Save . . . Heir . . . 'ware . . . treachery . . . save . . ."

The thread of her voice died and her gaze lost focus, drifting beyond him. Tarathan covered the shadow of her hands with his own. "Be of good heart, Lira of the Derai," he said. "We will do all in our power to find your Heir and save her."

Her gaze returned to him, holding his eyes with painful intensity. ". . . your word . . . herald . . . give . . . your word . . ."

"You have my word," he replied steadily, "so be at peace. Is there anything else I can do for you?"

The ghost of a smile caught at Lira's lips, but he had to bend even closer now to hear her whisper. ". . . kiss . . . farewell . . ."

"I would be honored," Tarathan replied softly, "to kiss one so valiant and so true." The ghost smile deepened for a moment as he kissed her, very gently, on the shadow of her cold mouth. Her lips parted as though to speak again, but no more words came.

Tarathan reached out his hand and rested it briefly on the shadow hair. "Farewell, Lira of the Derai," he said quietly. "You died well. Now I must honor my word and both find and save the Heir of Night—if I can."

"Fear not," said Jehane Mor's voice, clear in his mind. *"We will find them one way or the other, in life or in death."*

Tarathan swung around, but all he could see of her was the glow of the filament that joined them, fragile as a cobweb. He turned to follow it back, but the connection began to reel in far faster than he was expecting. The watch-towers rushed past below and Tarathan wondered whether it was the Gate of Dreams that was done with him for now, or Jaransor itself. He could feel the substance of Jehane Mor's presence growing, grounding him—and almost missed the glimmer of power below, no more than a firefly spark in the vastness of the hills, before he stepped back into the anchor of his body.

He opened his eyes to a cloud-wracked sky and Jehane Mor's quiet gaze. "I think I found them, there at the end." He spoke aloud just to hear his own voice, and hers, after so long in silence. "It was just a flash, no more, but they are alive and closer to us than before."

She nodded. "You were gone a long time, but we can make some of that up if we cross the river now and ride until either night or the weather stops us. Although the storm, I think, will not reach this far south until tomorrow." Tarathan saw that she had already brought the horses close, ready to leave. He took the hand she held down to him and came swiftly to his feet, holding both the hand and her eyes with the question in his own.

"I heard what you said when Lira died. I thought that you stood at my side."

Jehane Mor's expression was thoughtful. *"It was some trick of the Gate, I think, or of Jaransor. I felt as though I walked with you, step for step, once you left the shelter of the watchtower. And I heard you pledge your word."* She shook her head. *"I was—a little surprised. I felt a change then, too, in the pattern of events."*

His answering look was somber. *"She died hard, they both did. I did not think you would object."*

She smiled faintly. *"Would it matter if I did?"*

Tarathan's eyes did not leave hers. *"You know that it would. But we embarked on this path long ago. Pledging my word to the dying only reinforces what we had already begun. As for a change in the pattern—"* He shrugged. *"With such power at play in there, how could it be otherwise?"*

"Change lies at the heart of every pattern, in any case," Jehane Mor observed, her face calm, if not untroubled. *"And we are still one in this endeavor, as we have always been."* She withdrew her hand and turned, stepping into the saddle. *"So now we must ride. I will do what I can to shield our passage into Jaransor, but I think our best hope now is speed if we are to find them before the storm breaks—or worse occurs."*

As if to second her words, her horse flung up its head and trumpeted a challenge to the sky. She spoke softly to it, soothing, steady. And then Tarathan, too, had mounted and brought his horse alongside hers, facing north toward the Telimbras and Jaransor. While she watched, he slid his horseman's curved bow from its covering behind his saddle, strung it, and slid it across his back. *"Ready?"* he asked.

The gleam of her smile answered his, steel meeting steel. *"I ride in your shadow,"* she said, and both horses leapt forward as one, into the face of the wind.

30

The Shield Ring

S now fell softly out of a shadowed sky, dusting the midnight world of Jaransor with white. It touched the still, upturned faces of Kyr and Lira where they lay, unmoving beneath the sky, and floated, delicate as lace, into a perfect circle around the hilltop where the broken watchtower stood. The snowflakes swirled more thickly around the jagged rim of the shorn-off tower, spiraling across its shadow, which stretched black and unbroken on the wintry ground. Hounds gave tongue, calling to each other in a wild baying that circled between earth and heaven.

Kalan tossed fitfully, half asleep, half waking, caught between the pain of his wound and a sense of danger pressing in. He was aware that the pearl on his hand was glowing and he heard the voice of the hounds again, belling through his dream and calling him to rouse himself, to take action. Slowly, he got to his feet, wincing at the pain beneath his arm—whether awake or asleep, that at least was real. A glance at Malian showed her sleeping where she sat, propped against the wall on the far side of the fire. But the glow of the ring tugged at his attention, drawing his eyes toward the tunnel. Kalan hesitated briefly, then followed its pull, making his slow, determined way up the curving corridor, one hand against the wall for support.

He paused in the shadow of the arch and saw that the world was filled with softly falling white. There was something else out there, too, prowling beyond the perimeter of his shield ring, baffled still, but questing, seeking. Kalan could see the feral gleam of its eyes, like two viridian lanterns in the heart of a greater blackness. It did not call or make any sound, not yet, but he *knew* what that sound would be when it came—and the picture to match it was *there* in his mind as well, gleaned from one of the many Darkswarm bestiaries that he had pored over in the Temple quarter. "Night Mare," Kalan whispered.

"Careful, boy!" A heavy hand rested on his shoulder. "Do not name such a creature aloud, lest the very act of naming bring it to your side."

Kalan jumped violently and twisted round, staring up into the masked face. "You!" he exclaimed. "What are you doing here?"

"How could I not be here," the Huntmaster inquired, "when you yourself observed that both I and the crow should be present? This is our place."

"I saw the Hunt over the door," said Kalan. His eyes slid to the crow, sitting on the black-cloaked shoulder. "I thought I was awake, but I'm not, am I? This is the world of dreams."

The Huntmaster shook his head. "Do you know nothing of Jaransor, having walked into it so blithely? It is one of the few places on Haarth that exists simultaneously in both the waking world and the realm of dreams. This archway is one of the crossing points between the two, which is why I can come to you here unbidden. It is also the reason why you can perceive the demon that hunts for you on the physical plane, even though you stand within the Gate of Dreams. Your barrier," he added dispassionately, "holds against the demon, for now."

Kalan shivered. "I can feel it probing at the shield, but I don't know what more I can do to stop it getting through."

The black mask stared out through the lightly falling snow. "Probably very little, on your own. Its psychic power is considerable." The hand on his shoulder tightened. "Yet you are the Token-bearer. You may summon the Hunt to your aid, so long as you are confident that your shield will contain it."

Kalan stared at him. "But—isn't that too dangerous? Whatever's out there is on the physical plane, just like the siren worm in the keep. I thought you said that the Hunt had to be contained within the Gate of Dreams?"

The black mask looked back at him, inscrutable. "So it must. But your enemy is a psychic as well as a physical hunter and this is Jaransor, where you stand on a bridge between the two realms. Here, you will be able to call on the Hunt to act against the demon on the other side. And you can be sure of this, the demon *will* perceive the hounds."

"So long," Kalan whispered, "as they don't break through into the everyday world." He shivered again. "If Jaransor exists in both realms at once, then the barrier between the two must be very thin here."

The smile beneath the mask was grim. "If the Hunt is roused, then the Huntmaster must master it. But only the Token-bearer may summon the milk-white hounds with their eyes of blood."

Kalan hesitated, remembering the terror and power of the hounds—and what Yorindesarinen had said about the Hunt and its master being both an ancient force and a very strong one. He wondered, too, what the Huntmaster's coming to him unbidden might signify. Like Jaransor, the Hunt was not a Derai power and that could mean there was some trick to this, some hidden purpose that Kalan could not see.

But, Kalan reminded himself, the Huntmaster did help save Malian from the siren worm.

He could feel the pressure of the Night Mare's power building, icy cold and compelling, as it probed at his shield. The viridian eyes were brighter than before, and a great darkness bulked behind them. Soon, Kalan knew, he would require all his strength to hold the demon at bay—and it would not be enough.

"Use the Token or be lost anyway." The Huntmaster's voice echoed his fear. "Trust in yourself, Kalan. Summon the Hunt!"

Letting go of his fear, Kalan found, was like stepping off a cliff with the ground rushing up to meet him. He could feel the wild beating of his heart, his eyes wide open as the air streamed past him, and he felt ill and exhilarated at the same time. The moonglow of the pearl flared into the snowy night and formed a perfect circle around the crown of the hill, ending at the outer edge of the mindshield he had built before he slept. The pack of huge, milk white hounds materialized inside it, lunging and fretting at the perimeter of the shield ring. They were even larger than Kalan remembered, their scarlet eyes burning like watch fires in the wintry night. He could feel their hunger, avid for the hunt and the kill, as well as their strength, sliding like a second shield between himself and the compelling force of the Night Mare.

The dark figure of the Huntmaster picked up his spear from where it rested against the shadowed archway and stepped forward, standing tall and straight before the entrance to the ruined tower. Kalan let his breath out slowly and steeled himself to confront the demon, but the Huntmaster extended an arm, holding him back.

"Do not step beyond the arch. You must not let your enemy see that it has tracked you here. Let it believe that it has triggered one of the ancient powers of this place."

It was only afterward that Kalan realized that the Huntmaster had spoken into his mind. All the Night Mare would have seen or heard was the straining, snapping hounds and the silent, black-clad figure with the ruined tower behind it. But there was no time to think about that as a force like a black wind beat in against the edge of his shield barrier and tested it; the sweep of power was cold, malevolent, and hungry. The hounds howled their reply, and all along the boundary they leapt and snarled at whatever assailed them from beyond the shield ring. The cold, deadly pressure lifted, drawing back.

The wind rose again beyond the protective circle, screaming in toward the hilltop—and the demon screamed, too, a long, heart-chilling cry, and came riding in on the wind's back. Kalan flinched, but the hounds did not hesitate. They surged forward, baying their own thirst for blood, destruction, and death—and the flame-filled blackness stopped, hovering just short of the shield's rim. The hounds growled, a menacing rumble that shook the earth, and the Huntmaster strode forward, his cloak swirling at his heels. "Begone from this place, Night Mare!" His voice was strong and cold, and the crow raised its wings and cawed in fierce counterpoint from his shoulder. "This ground belongs to the Hunt of Mayanne. You cannot hunt here!"

There was no answer out of the darkness, but after a long, long moment the viridian eyes winked out, one after the other; the mass of black on black that surrounded them retreated slowly, then vanished. The hounds began to relax, sitting or lying along the shield perimeter, the soft pearl-light glowing around them. The Huntmaster stayed where he was, his head turned slightly as though listening to the wind, or for some other sound beneath its voice, before walking back to Kalan. "Whoever called it Night Mare," he said grimly, leaning the hooded spear against the arch, "named it rightly."

"What do you know of it?" Kalan asked. Even beyond the Gate of Dreams, the wind was cold, and he folded his arms against its chill.

The Huntmaster shrugged. "Other than that it hunts with the Darkswarm?" The black mask, if it could be said to have expression, appeared sardonic. "You could say that the Derai themselves brought the demon to Haarth, for your Alliance dragged the Swarm here with it, caught in the vortex of their great portal that tore apart the fabric of worlds."

Kalan stared at him and the sardonic regard was replaced with a certain grim amusement. "Did you not know that, boy? Ah well, it may be that some histories have too bitter a taste, even for the Derai. But the Night Mares are powerful predators, however they came here. Their powers are greatest by night, since they are almost blind in daylight—but do not be lulled by that. Their sense of smell is remarkably keen, sharp enough to hunt by scent alone. But night predator or not, I do not think the demon will dare this place again, not while the Hunt is here. My guess is that it will retreat and seek out allies, those who accompanied it across the Telimbras, and hope to pick up your trail again by day." He shrugged. "And even in Jaransor, the Hunt cannot protect you in the daylight world."

Kalan nodded, because he already knew that they could not stay here, that this respite was only for a night or until the snow stopped. He studied the hounds, watchful along the shield perimeter. "They seem different," he said slowly. "Not so wild as when we first met." He thought about what the Huntmaster had said, about this being the Hunt's place. "You knew that's how it would be. That's why you allowed me to bring them here."

The mask was unreadable. "Your need called us," the Huntmaster said at last, "and we answered, for you bear the Token."

Kalan was still not sure he understood the real reasons that the Huntmaster was helping him, but was grateful that help had come. He shivered and the black gauntlet clasped his shoulder. "You have overreached yourself, have you not?" the harsh voice said. "Well, it is never too soon to learn that psychic powers are no different from physical aptitudes. You may train and strengthen them, but you can exhaust them as well. So be wary, boy—Kalan—of your own limitations as well as the strength of your enemies."

The crow cawed as Kalan nodded again. "Ay, he should indeed rest," the Huntmaster said, as though answering someone that Kalan could neither see nor hear. He grasped the spear, turning back toward the snowy hillside. "You go, boy. Sleep. I will keep watch here."

Kalan blinked, feeling the physical weight of his body drawing him back into the cellar, toward the warmth of the fire. The deeper layers of sleep pulled at him and he let himself follow, slipping beneath the tide. It was only at the last that he heard the harsh voice again, deep within his mind.

"It was well done, Token-bearer, building a shield that could hold the Hunt of Mayanne."

31

The Hidden Tower

Hounds bayed in the deeps of Malian's dream but another voice spoke through them, filled with both darkness and light: *"Chosen of Mhaelanar, Beloved of the Nine."*

"I am here," said Malian. "Who calls?"

Only the night replied, the sigh of wind amongst the tors and the whisper of the falling snow, soft as death and as quiet. In the tunnel beneath the hilltop there was only darkness and the relentless, grinding voice of rocks within the earth. Anger turned in that voice, a slow, burning rage that echoed the belling fury of the hounds as they pursued a shade through shadows. Malian ran with them, keeping pace with their red-eyed flight, and the tunnel changed into the hallways of the New Keep. Everything she saw was at odd angles, as though she hung from ceilings or moved through walls, hating the light and thirsting after blood and death with a hunger that was not her own.

Retribution. The word reverberated down halls and along corridors as the hounds bayed again, scenting destruction and ruin. A miasma of fear crept through the silent courts and Malian saw stewards and pages looking back over their shoulders, starting at shadows and fearful for their lives. *Revenge.*

The hounds howled and raced through the shadows but their quarry eluded them, slipping away into darkness. *Blood*.

Malian drifted, silent as a fallen leaf through the familiar halls, and saw the trail of the fallen: Two guards lay in a pool of their own blood in the Warrior's court, and a third on a lonely stair down into the stable yard. A young priest sprawled, rigid in death, on the threshold of Mayanne's Temple, and the expression on his face was dread.

All the dead, Malian realized, as she looked down from vaulted roof-trees and ghosted through arched doors, were those who had fought the siren worm. Images flicked across her mind in quick succession: rooms, people, voices speaking.

"Retribution and revenge," said Sister Korriya, staring down at an ancient tome. "It will come for us all as it did for Torin and the guards. Even the wyr hounds cannot find it." The faces that looked back at her were mute and frightened, all young: all those who had gone with the priestess to the Red and White Suite—all except for Torin, who was already dead.

The Earl of Night lifted a bleak, hard face in the Little Chamber and stared at Asantir with eyes like chipped stone. "Find me this demon and slay it! How many more must we lose?"

In another room, at a later hour, Asantir stared down at the play of black-and-white pieces on a chessboard. "Blood feud," she said softly. She turned her head and looked long and hard at the war chest against one wall. *"Death my song,"* she murmured at last—and took down the two swords from their stand on top of the chest. Her mouth set in a grim line as she studied the patterns on the black scabbards, and then she thrust them both into the loops on her belt.

Night followed day, and the stars wheeled above the earth. In the Temple of Mhaelanar someone screamed in terror and despair. Voices shouted, feet ran, and a sinuous form slipped between darkness and shadow near the sanctuary where Korriya and Vern had taken refuge. The sacred flame burned on the altar and cast the silhouette of a flat, narrow head onto the wall, reared above a robed body. The head and neck were armored with chitinous scales; the long, lidless eyes regarded the priests with contempt. "Blood demands blood," it hissed. "Your puny defences will not save you, even here in the sanctuary of your great god. Where is your Defender now, servants of Mhaelanar?"

The sinuous body wove through air and shadow toward the trapped priests. Malian could see the wave edge of its power bearing down on the rim of Vern's psychic shield. Sweat gleamed on the young priest's forehead; beside him, Sister Korriya picked up the torch that held the sacred flame. The light illuminated her face, expressionless and austere as the mask of the god.

They are brave, thought Malian, filled with a remote regret, but they will never hold. Even the baying of the distant hounds fell into silence, waiting.

A dark figure stepped out of the shadows by the Temple door. "Will you dance with me, Worm?" the newcomer asked softly, and drew a long, curved sword from a black sheath. The blade snared all the light in the Temple into itself. "Darkness," said Asantir, "draws darkness, after all."

The worm, larger, swifter, and more powerful than the comrade it sought to avenge, hissed and looped back on itself, flowing across the darkened hall with frightening speed. Asantir and her sword slipped sideways into shadow again, away from that silent, deadly rush. The worm rippled, becoming one with the night—then the flat head burst through the fabric of air, its jaws wide, darting toward the black-clad figure that spun out of darkness, the curved blade slicing at the worm's neck. The worm rolled away, its powerful tail sweeping around in a counterstrike, but the black figure somersaulted out of danger in a movement that was almost too quick to follow.

Sound spun across the blackness of Mhaelanar's hall: a song of death and drought, of the first grass shriveling in a black frost, and topsoil blown away by incessant winds. The tune swelled, singing of harvests rotting in the fields and loves gone to ruin, an eternal promise of darkness, desolation, and grief that numbed the heart and vanquished hope. So powerful and persuasive was that siren voice that even Malian, watching and listening unseen, struggled to find an answer to it. "Who can possibly withstand it?" she whispered, knowing that no one would hear her. "This worm is too powerful. They will all be lost!"

But it seemed as though someone did hear her, for another voice rose in answer to her despair. As cold as death and black as the void between the stars, it soared across the lightless hall. A thread of unease crept into the siren voice, and the gleam of a lidless eye, quickly hidden again, peered through the gloom.

Malian glimpsed movement in the darkness beneath the latticed gallery that circled the great nave of the Temple. The shape of warrior and sword slid out of the blackness between the pillars, and the worm's head whipped toward it. This time, however, the worm checked, drawing back as it— like Malian—realized that Asantir's sword was the origin of the countersong.

Black blade. The name cut through the lightless air. When the worm eventually slithered forward it moved far more slowly, watchful, as the cold song pushed back against its own paean of doubt and despair.

Malian frowned, both fascinated and perplexed, for how *could* this sword be another black blade? It seemed impossible that there should be two such weapons in the Keep of Winds without anyone knowing. Could Asantir have lied, in the old High Hall, when she said that she had not known what the black spear was? Malian shivered, her doubt colder than any fear spell cast by the siren worm.

She remembered the Red and White Suite, and how the ichor from the first worm had corroded Asantir's sword. One would want a blade one could rely on, the next time one went against such an enemy—and some defence against its sorceries as well, not just a strong sword arm. And she had *seen* Asantir study the swords on the war chest before lifting them down, had heard her quote Kalan's saying about the black blades.

Malian shook her head as the combat became a deadly contest of strength and power. Warrior and worm flowed in and out of the darkness beneath the pillared gallery: the one luring and retreating, the other pursuing, seeking to bite or crush. Korriya and Vern watched from the sanctuary, making no move to intervene, and Malian saw what the worm did not—the silent figures creeping along the gallery and mustering outside the Temple doors. She noted the curve of bows through the balcony latticework and the shuttered glow of a firepot; she watched black-clad figures slide, quieter than a whisper, through the Temple doors and into the shadows along its walls.

Ah, thought Malian, understanding at last: Now the trap is sprung. Yet she was also aware of the vast width and length of the Temple nave, the sheer distance between the newcomers and the two combatants.

The sword's song had continued to build, filling the lofty hall, and the voice of the siren worm began to falter. Perhaps it sensed the silent net closing around it, for it hissed suddenly and Malian felt the surge of its power, hunting its opponent out. Asantir spun out of the shadows, moving to attack again, and the worm's sorcery retracted, forming a rampart around its body. Asantir circled left, keeping the sword between herself and the worm. The flat head swung, following her movement, and a jet of power hurtled toward the Honor Captain. Malian opened her mouth to scream—but Asantir extended the sword and the assault rolled away on either side of the black blade like a wave breaking, its energy dissipated.

This time, the worm did not stop but followed the wave of power forward. It was fully visible now, a sinuous coil of potency and strength, and Malian was astonished once again by the sheer speed of its attack. The figures by the door broke cover and raced forward; the archers in the gallery were bending their bows, but the worm's head was already stretched out, the jaws extended for the strike. Asantir came in from the left, cutting toward the worm's throat. The move was fast, very fast, but the worm pulled away from the strike and whipped around to come in again—except that Asantir had turned the sword cut into a roll, intercepting the trajectory of the worm's counterattack. By the time the beast turned she was already coming up, directly beneath its upreared head.

The worm hissed its surprise, but it was too late to evade or pull back again as the captain's left arm thrust up with the short blade that she had drawn as she rolled, extending it straight into the worm's chitinous throat. The blade pierced the armored scales like silk and the worm coughed, a guttural explosion of pain and rage. Asantir used the thrust and her own momentum to hold the head clear, simultaneously bringing the blade in her right hand around in a smooth, powerful cut that severed the siren worm's head from its body.

Malian's hands flew to her mouth as the head thudded onto the floor, ichor spraying around it. Asantir stepped back, her face dispassionate as she withdrew the short blade from the worm's body, which continued to writhe and thrash. "And death," she said, very softly, to the gaping mouth and glazed eye of the severed head, "demands death."

Deliberately, the Honor Captain wiped her blades clean and thrust them into their sheaths as the figures running toward her slowed. Malian noted, with detachment but no surprise, that the worm's caustic blood had made no impression on the somber gleam of either blade. Garan, Nerys, and the rest of the archer company in the gallery rose to their feet, quenching their fire arrows, but it was the Earl of Night who was the first to reach Asantir. The winged horse on his breastplate glittered as Korriya joined them, holding the votive flame high, but the Earl's stern gaze was fixed on Asantir. "Its neck was armored," he said harshly. "What sort of blade could cut through that so easily?"

What indeed, thought Malian—but if Asantir replied, she did not hear her, only Vern's rough, urgent speech: "I

can see no mark on Terithis. It may be that she is only ensorceled and will live if we fetch help quickly!" A clamor
rose, and feet ran again as the sacred flame blazed, burning
away the darkness of the New Keep. A voice, pure as silver
and cool as moonlight, spoke to Malian out of the fire: *"I
seek the Chosen of Mhaelanar, across time's divide."*

"Who are you?" demanded Malian. "What is the Chosen
of Mhaelanar to you? Why do you seek the One?"

"Ask, rather," the cool voice replied, *"what I am to the
One and why she should seek me."*

"Who are you?" Malian said again. "Where will I find
you?"

The moonlit voice rang in her mind, clear as a chime of
ice:

> *I lie outside of worlds and time,*
> *a-top a tower that isn't there:*
> *To find me here you must climb*
> *the shattered stair that leads nowhere.*

"What?" began Malian—and started up, wide awake.
The fire in the cellar was muted embers, but Yorindesarin-
en's armring had slid down to her wrist and was blazing with
silver fire, although the metal remained cool against her
skin. The horses stood with their heads up and ears pricked,
watching her; Kalan was fast asleep, sprawled on his back
with his left arm flung out.

Malian remembered the violence of her dream and shivered, wondering if it had been a farseeing and not a dream at
all. "It seemed so real," she whispered, and shivered again,
remembering the slain guards and Torin's face, fixed in a
rictus of death. She hoped, if the dream or seeing were true,
that Terithis would live.

"Child of Night!" The voice seemed to sigh out of the
ground itself. *"Come to me!"*

"Who are you?" Malian looked around, as if she might
spy out the owner of the voice. "What do you want? Are you

an enemy or a friend?" But there was no answer except the wind, crying around the broken tower. She frowned, knowing that she could not assume that the voice belonged to a friend or ally just because it had addressed her in the words of ancient prophecy. She could feel the summons still, reverberating in the quiet air, and thought how easily the voice had breached Kalan's shield—if, with Kalan asleep, his shield was even in place.

"Or—" Malian paused, her eyes narrowing. "What if whatever spoke is already here, inside the shield with me?" She thrust herself to her feet.

"Friend or enemy," she said, "I had better find you. Deal with whatever you want."

She cast one longing glance at the fringe of her cloak where it showed beneath Kalan's blanket, then picked up her own blanket and draped it cape fashion around her shoulders, careful to cover up the armring. Cold as it was beside the dying fire, she knew it would be colder still on the open hilltop with the wind and the snow and the Nine only knew what enemies lurking. One of the horses snorted gently, but she shook her head at it. "No, you stay here. You might as well be safe, and as warm as this weather allows."

The wind that pried through her draped blanket when she reached the tower entrance was bitter, but there was only a light dusting of snow. The quarter moon, appearing intermittently between clouds, cast a frail light. Malian could not see any tracks crossing the open ground, yet she still felt uncomfortable, as though she were the focus of unseen eyes. She drew back and waited, rubbing her hands together to keep them warm.

Wings fluttered and a shadow dropped through the dim moonlight onto the crumbling stone of the arch. Malian jumped back, throwing up an arm for protection, but no attack followed. Cautiously, she lowered the arm and saw a crow sitting on the keystone.

"Hello," said Malian, more than a little surprised. "Where did you come from?"

"It is less a matter of where I come from," the crow replied, speaking in a soft rasping voice that was half a caw, "but more of where you are going."

Malian gaped at the bird. "Did you, er, speak?" she asked finally.

The crow cawed softly, in what might have been humor. "Say, rather, that you heard me. How could you help it, with the hero's ring upon your arm?"

Malian stared at the crow a moment longer and decided to be bold. "How do you know where I'm meant to be going? Was it you who called to me?"

"Was mine the voice you heard?" the crow demanded, with a touch of asperity. "Nay, it was not I who called—although I may know who did." The bird fixed her with a bright, expectant eye.

Malian met that look and frowned, folding her arms. "Who does the voice belong to, then?" After all, given the strangeness of the whole business, she supposed she could do worse than seek information from a bird.

"You could," the crow replied calmly. "Much worse." It fluttered its feathers at her startled expression. "There are very few, child, who can understand me, and fewer still with whom I choose to speak."

Malian considered this. "The voice must be important. Or you think so, at any rate." She refolded the blanket around her in a vain attempt to ward out the wind. "So how does one find a tower that isn't there? What hint can you give me, O Wise Crow?"

The crow peered down at her. "You must look with the eye of your mind, the seer's vision, not just with those two orbs that you have for everyday use."

Malian frowned again, because Derai lore was full of tales of priests and heroes who were trueseers and farseers, able to look beyond the limitations of the mortal world. "Which makes sense, I suppose," she muttered, "if I'm looking for a place that isn't here." She let her mind drift as it had done the night before when she soared over Jaransor, although this time she floated no higher than the rough-shorn crown of the ruin, afraid of what might happen if she breached Kalan's shield.

How beautiful it must have been, she thought, when the towers stood straight and tall, and sages gathered to watch the heavens.

In the darkness behind her eyes the wheel of stars turned and Malian, too, spun in the heart of their vastness. Their voices sang to her, cool and brilliant, and another voice whispered beneath them, light turning to dark, then back to light again: *"Chosen of Mhaelanar."* Malian opened her eyes and saw the shadow of the watchtower stretching away, black and sheer in the fitful moonlight, with silver fire twisting along its length.

Excitement fluttered in the pit of her stomach. "The tower that isn't there," she breathed. "I was right; it *is* inside the shield already, both here and not here." She paused, her excitement fading. "But how, in Mhaelanar's name, does one climb a tower that is only shadow?"

"How indeed?" said the crow, fluttering down and landing on her shoulder. Its feathers tickled her ear. "You already have your guide and your talisman, Child. Don't you see?"

See what, Malian wondered, studying the empty hillside and the silhouette of the unbroken tower. Her eyes narrowed on the silver fire that spiraled around its shadowed length. "The armring," she said. "Of course." Her fingers found its cool surface—and she saw the glade between worlds again and a small fire that burned silver, with lilac and blue at its heart. Yorindesarinen's voice spoke to her out of the flames: *"Look inside the ring, Malian!"*

Malian blinked and slid the armring off, turning it to catch the fitful moonlight. The spiral of stars on its outer side blazed, but the inside remained dull, without either decoration or inscription. Malian tilted it another way and saw a line of fire flicker around the inner rim. After a moment the line brightened and the flow of letters became clear. "What does it say?" the crow asked.

"The lettering's archaic," Malian answered. "And some of the words are strange, but it seems to say: *'I move between worlds and time; I seek out the hidden, the lost I find.'* " She grimaced. "Is there nothing here that is not a riddle?"

"Very little," the crow replied dryly. "This is Jaransor, after all."

"Haimyr would like it," said Malian, with a small smile. "They play riddle games in Ij and he was always trying to test and trick me." Her smile became a frown. *"Worlds and time.* That's the same phrase as in the other rhyme, which suggests that the armring may be the key to climbing the stair to nowhere. A guide, as you suggested," she said to the crow. She cast her mind back, trying to recall the ruined watchtower as she had first seen it that afternoon, before she detected its unbroken shadow.

"There was a stair," she said, thinking hard, "and it was certainly shattered. It seemed to end just below the broken rim of the tower." She angled a sideways look at the crow. "And the silver fire is spiraling around the shadow tower, just like a staircase—" Malian struck one hand against the other. "Because the armring itself is a bridge between place and time! That has to be it!" Slowly, she drew the ring down onto her wrist again, clear of her coat's sleeve. "If I can make it work, that is. I will have to start with the stair, I suppose, and see what happens."

The crow remained silent but dug its claws into her shoulder, plainly intending to stay with her for the moment. Malian was glad of its company, for she still felt the pressure of unseen eyes as she left the shelter of the arch. She also felt the wind's full chill as she tried to make her way through the same scrub and crumbling stone that had challenged her that afternoon. Even with the silver light cast by the armring she stumbled several times, scraping her shins and bruising her knees. It was impossible to hold on to the blanket so she was forced to knot it around her chest, leaving her head and arms exposed to the freezing wind. "I hope you're comfortable," she said austerely to the crow, huddled beneath her hair.

In the end Malian fell over the collapsed first step, which had fallen askew from the tower, grazing her hands as well as her shins. She blinked away tears, and when her eyes cleared she saw the broken stairway circling up. The silver fire, too, danced merrily upward and Malian followed it slowly, her left hand against the tower wall for balance. She kept her head down against the wind as she tried hard to see with her mind rather than her eyes, which were still watering from her fall. But it was difficult to let her mind slip free when she had to resist the pull of the wind and keep her footing on steps that were often cracked and sometimes missing altogether.

Malian climbed like this for some time, until she began to think that she had been ascending too long given the height of the broken tower. When she paused and raised her head, she realized that the spiral of silver light must have thickened imperceptibly, for it was no longer a fine thread but had grown into a rope, curving around the outer edge of the staircase like a balustrade. Malian grasped at it with her numb right hand and huffed out her breath, relieved, when it felt solid beneath her fingers. Her feet began to move more freely and soon she was floating up the stairs rather than climbing. Some time later it dawned on her that she no longer felt cold and she found the courage to open her mind fully to her surroundings.

The balustrade still circled upward, but the staircase she climbed was made of darkness and silver fire, rather than stone, and a star-filled sky spun around her. When she looked down she could see nothing except night, not even the snow on the hilltop; above her head a full moon was rising, white and luminous over the tower's crown. Malian frowned, remembering the quarter moon over Jaransor. "Where am I?" she whispered.

"Outside of time," the crow replied from beside her ear, startling her. Its rasping voice was swallowed in the vastness of the night. "You will have to learn to make that transition with your mind's eye fully open," it added, when she did not answer.

Malian was not sure she liked the implication that shifting between place and time was something she might choose to do regularly. She craned to look at the top of the tower again and could just make out arched windows and curved eaves, with a sheer rise of wall between herself and the slender spire that seemed to pierce the moon. "Still a long way to go," she said, wondering how fast time was passing on the hilltop in Jaransor.

"Not for you," said the crow, "unless you choose to climb every step."

"What?" Malian was puzzled.

"You have taken yourself out of time," the crow replied. "Think about the armring and what it told you."

" 'I move between worlds and time,' " Malian said slowly. "But how can I do that if I'm already outside of time? I know I opened a portal in the Old Keep, but that wasn't like this. I was still part of the temporal world then."

The crow fluttered its wings. "Who spoke of portals? What has there ever been in this except you and your will, and the armring answering to it? It is your choice, Child. You can continue to insist on seeing the three that are yourself and the armring and the tower, or look again with the spirit's eye and see—differently."

"The oneness of all things," murmured Malian. Her voice came out in a sigh and the flames of Yorindesarinen's fire flickered in her mind, so that she was not entirely sure whether it was she who had spoken, or the hero speaking through her.

"Are you not One?" the crow asked. Its voice grew dreamy. "Long before the watchtowers stood, before empires and sages who studied the slow passage of the stars, this hilltop was already a place of power. Legend has it that the builders wrought the symbols of that power into the tower's stone, both at its foot and at its lofty crown."

"The Hunt," said Malian, thinking hard. "There was a hawk flying over it, too—or was it a crow?"

The crow shifted on her shoulder and its voice grew softer still. "This is Jaransor. These hills have always lain beneath the shadow of the falcon's wings."

Malian held on to the rope of silver fire and closed her eyes, visualizing the hunt and the hawk as she had seen them above the archway. The carved figures had been weathered, faded by time, but the details were clear in her mind—the fleeing hind and the pack of hounds pouring in pursuit, with the hunters close behind. Malian concentrated, seeing the curl of a hound's tongue and the foam that splashed the hind's flank; she noticed the curve of a horn, lifted to the sky. Cloaks spun from the hunters' shoulders and one shaded his eyes with his hand. The colors, she knew, came more from her memory of the tapestry in the Red and White Suite, but the fire and strength of the falcon flying overhead, the vast span of its wings, were all from the carving in the stone.

Malian sighed and opened her eyes. The stairs and the silver balustrade had disappeared and she stood on a mosaic in the center of a stone chamber, her feet on the falcon's wings. Moonlight, white and brilliant, poured through arched windows.

"Oh, well done!" said the crow.

"So which is the real tower," asked Malian, "and which the shadow? This one, or the one in Jaransor?"

She felt rather than saw the tilt of the crow's head. "Why cannot both be real?"

Malian opened her mouth, then closed it again, shaking her head. She looked around for the owner of the voice that had called to her, but the chamber was empty except for the mosaic on the floor. "Well," she said, hands on her hips, "here I am. What do you want of me?"

Only silence answered, but Malian sensed a presence all the same. Well, two could play at the waiting and watching game. So she waited, counting the stars in their slow dance around the tower. Her breathing slowed, became one with the immensity of the night while the spiral constellation of the armring stretched across the floor.

Like stepping stones across the void, thought Malian, but leading to what?

Her brows drew together, then smoothed out again. "Ah," she said. " '*I seek out the hidden, the lost I find.*' " Malian gave a sudden, soft laugh. "You told me who you were, didn't you, when you said that you sought the Chosen of Mhaelanar across worlds and time—and that you were my destiny, not I yours. The silver armring is indeed the key. I only need to ask who bore the bracelet before me, and what—connected to her—was lost or hidden a long time ago."

The crow shifted on her shoulder, while the moonlight listened. "How do you answer this riddle, Malian of Night?"

Malian lifted her arms wide so that the fire from the armring caught and glittered in the star pattern on the floor. "The arms of Yorindesarinen were lost when the hero fell, but of the three—helmet, sword, and shield—only the moon-bright helm ever had a voice." Her words became a chant, compelling. "I call you now by your name, Nhenir. Across time and worlds I summon you here!"

The tower shivered as the constellation on the floor blazed into fire. Malian opened her mind to the flare of power, absorbing it, but kept her eyes fixed on the small black plinth that had appeared on the last of the stepping stars. The helm on top of the plinth glowed and Malian caught her breath, for no song, no description, however detailed, could have prepared her for the beauty of Nhenir. The helm was made of black, adamantine steel and decorated with silver and pearl, like the bright and dark of the moon. Its visor was wrought in the shape of the dawn eyes of Terennin the Far-seeing, while the inlaid wings that swept up on either side and wrapped around the back of the casque were those of the phoenix. "Which hears all things," Malian murmured, knowing that the phoenix was also the symbol of the House of Stars. She stepped closer.

"The original helm shattered," the crow said softly,

"in one of Yorindesarinen's first great battles against the Swarm. She remade it in a forge lit by the Golden Fire of her keep. Some say she alone reforged it, others that Terennin himself aided her. All that is certain is that much of her own power and strength are bound into it, together with the residual power of the gods."

"I didn't know that," said Malian. "The stories about Yorindesarinen don't get told much in Night anymore. All I knew was that her arms were supposed to be magical and that the moon-bright helm could talk."

The crow cawed in her ear, a small, dry sound. "It is true that each one of the three weapons had power and gained more in the hero's hands. Nhenir was called the Helm of Secrecy by some and the Helm of Knowledge by others, because the wearer could pass by an enemy unnoticed and see through all enchantments intended to confuse and deceive. Of the three, it was always Nhenir that was the most . . . like a person, if you will. I suspect that came out of its remaking, but it does not surprise me that the helm has found you first."

Malian tore her eyes away from the fair and terrible beauty of Nhenir. "But you are wary of it?"

The crow was silent, almost as though debating whether it had already said too much. "You are very young, Child," the bird said at last, "and the moon-bright helm is long in years. And *like* a person is not the same as *being* a person. The helm is a valuable ally, but it has a will of its own. So although it is true that Nhenir is meant for you, Malian of Night, you would be wise to treat it with circumspection."

Malian nodded, but she still longed to reach out and take the glowing helmet into her hands.

"It is permitted," the moonlit voice said, *"but only to the Chosen of Mhaelanar. For any other, the price of wearing me is death."*

Malian almost took a step back. Yorindesarinen and the Swarm might both believe that she was the chosen One, and the hero's armring might have led her here, but what if they were all mistaken? She bowed her head, remembering the terror and excitement of the Old Keep, where Yorindesarinen had first spoken of her destiny and Garan and the others had pledged themselves to it. Shield of Mhaelanar, Garan had named her, then—and she had not refused his oath.

That's when I really made my choice, Malian thought now. I may have argued it to Haimyr later, but the decision had already been made and I knew it. He did, too, she added to herself with a wry inner smile, even if he wasn't with me in the Old Keep.

Malian lifted her head and bowed to the helm on the plinth, a grave, formal salute. "Nhenir," she said, "I accept my destiny and become yours."

Or die here, she added silently, somewhere outside of time.

She extended her hands, conscious of the sudden sweat along her palms and the high, fast thump of her heart, and lifted the helmet, placing it over her head. Something shifted within her, like two plates moving within the earth and then settling together. *"Found!"* said Nhenir, the moon-bright helm, on a long, long note of satisfaction.

Malian stood quite still. She could hear the movement of the stars and the snow falling on the ground, while far below that quiet surface she could detect the vein of anger rumbling through Jaransor, just as it had in her vision. She crossed to one of the arched windows and stared down at the world below. It did not seem so distant now as it had when she climbed the stairs. "What *is* Jaransor?" she asked. "Besides being dangerous and driving some people mad?"

Nhenir was silent, but Malian felt the crow's claws flex. "Jaransor," the bird replied, "is one of those matters the Derai have chosen to forget, although it is recorded in their histories. They came here in the early years, but the enmity of the hills preyed upon the minds of the vulnerable, particularly those with power, until they ran mad. That is why the Earls forbade their people to come here and why you would do well to fear it. Jaransor is not fully awake yet, it is only rousing—but the longer you stay here the greater your risk."

"Is that what happened to Nhairin, the madness of Jaransor?" Malian frowned. "Although she is not of the priestly kind."

"Perhaps not," said the crow. "But like these hills, your companion is filled with old anger. Her bitterness has divided her heart."

Surprised, Malian looked round. "How can you know anything at all about Nhairin?"

The bird shifted on her shoulder. "I am an old crow," it replied softly. "There is little I do not know about the dark and troubled places of the heart."

Malian hesitated, wondering exactly where the crow fitted in the legends and stories that were waking into life, and whether either the bird or the helm would tell her. Instead of demanding answers, she slid the visor down across her eyes and looked out over Jaransor again. A small circle of crimson jewels, pinpricks of distance, stared up at her from the hilltop below. Malian drew back, startled, when her curious mind encountered the power behind them.

"'Ware the Hunt," said the crow, "for even when you come into your full, adult power, Chosen of Mhaelanar or not, you would be hard-pressed to master it."

"The Hunt," echoed Malian. She glanced back at the mosaic, remembering how she had visualized the hounds and hunters in order to reach this chamber. "What are they doing here?"

"This is their place," the crow replied. "And as well that it is, since the night demon has already been here, hunting for you."

"The Darkswarm minion!" exclaimed Malian, and used the eyes of the helm to look more widely, but could neither see nor hear the Swarm predator. She shuddered, remembering its hideous cry, and looked wider still until she saw Kyr and Lira, both lying beneath the midnight sky with snow falling on their faces. "So they are dead," she said. She pushed up the visor and lifted the helmet off her head.

"Ay," said the crow, "the helm's gift of knowledge will

not spare you its bitterness. One must be strong of heart, as well as will, to engage with such powers."

"I suppose so," Malian said dully. All the excitement of finding Nhenir had leached out of her as soon as she saw Kyr and Lira's bodies. She frowned down at the inlaid patterns on the helm. "Do you think Nhenir will speak to me again? And how in the Nine's name will I hide it, once we leave here?"

The bird squawked, dry crow laughter. "Trust the helm to manage that for itself. It is powerful, Malian of Night, powerful—doubt it not!"

Malian did not doubt it. She tucked the helm into the crook of her left arm and visualized the entrance to the underground cellar, with the depiction of the hunt streaming across the archway. The circle of milk white hounds waiting on the snowy hilltop neither moved nor gave tongue as she stepped toward them, out of the hidden tower. They simply watched, their crimson eyes intent, as Malian steadied herself against the arch and looked around. The shadow of the tower was squat in the intermittent light of the quarter moon and ended abruptly in a jagged crown. The armring's fire died, leaving the silver dull.

"It's over, then," Malian said. The crow did not reply, just lifted itself and flew to sit on the shoulder of the tall, masked figure that watched over the hounds. He carried a hooded spear in his right hand, Malian saw; the left arm ended in a stump. The mask, dark and enigmatic, stared at Malian out of fathomless eyeholes.

Long before the watchtowers stood, she thought, hearing the words again in her mind. *But where does your shadow fall, I wonder?*

The tall figure did not speak, but the harsh line of his mouth curved very slightly as he raised the spear in formal salute. Wordlessly, Malian inclined her head in the Heir of Night's acknowledgment of an equal, but not a superior, and the smile deepened; the crow watched her with unblinking eyes.

As if I imagined it speaking, Malian thought. Discouraged, she trudged back down the tunnel. The horses were dozing again, and Kalan, too, slept on. Malian felt the deepening cold and every scrape and bruise as she built up the fire and then lay down, pulling the blanket around both her and the helm. She lay awake for some time, and when she did sleep her dreams were jumbled: A winged helmet pursued her along endless corridors, cawing with a crow's voice while invisible hounds belled, hunting through the folds of time.

Panicked, Malian fled the wild baying until a black-gloved hand on her shoulder made her spin around, expecting to see the Huntsmaster's mask. Instead she saw Yorindesarinen, smiling beneath a crown of spring stars, before the hero turned to the moon-bright helm, which hovered nearby on phoenix wings. Hero and helm looked at each other for a long time with their shining eyes, but if they spoke it was in a language that Malian could not hear.

The phoenix wings spread wide, beating the air, and the helm transformed into a crow. The hero held out her arm and the crow dropped onto it. "I am grateful," Yorindesarinen said, her expression both tender and very sad, "but I thought you had done with the Derai."

The crow lifted its wings and cawed, a wild, harsh cry that reverberated in Malian's head and down the dark corridor of her dream. She fled, but the cry pursued her: relentless as the knell of fate, inescapable as doom.

32

Passage of the Hills

K alan woke with a start to find that the night had already
become gray shadow and the ashes of their fire were
cold.

Only just dawn, he thought, sitting up. But we have to
get moving. We've got to keep ahead of the Night Mare.
The air was so cold that his teeth chattered as he combed a
hand through his hair, feeling the pull of his wound. A quick
glance showed him Malian's empty blanket, the wool full of
twigs and damp leaves. Kalan frowned at that, puzzled, then
yawned deeply.

She should have woken me, he thought. She shouldn't
have gone out there alone, not without making sure that my
shield still held.

The two black horses watched him expectantly, their
breath misting the air, as he got stiffly to his feet. "Ugh,"
Kalan said, as his own breath huffed out in a cloud. "It
must be really cold up there." His stomach growled and the
horses snorted, a reminder that they, too, needed to be fed.
Kalan hoped that there had not been enough snow to cover
the grass, because he knew they had little food left, either
for the horses or themselves. "And no idea how far it is,
still, to the Border Mark. I'll come back for you soon," he

said to the black horses, "but I need to scout outside first."

Kalan shivered as the colder air crept down the tunnel to meet him. He found Malian just beyond the entrance, sitting on a large block of fallen stone and surveying a morning that was lightly powdered with white beneath a washed-out sky. The wind had died away in the night, and there was no sign of either the Night Mare or the Hunt; even the carving over the archway was little more than a dim outline of hounds and hawk. Malian smiled as he came to sit beside her, but Kalan thought she looked tired, with dark shadows beneath her eyes. "How's the wound?" she asked.

"Better," he replied. "It's still sore and the arm's awkward to move, but at least the cut doesn't feel infected."

"You definitely look better than you did last night. Although we should check the wound again anyway, before we leave." Malian's fingers were busy as she spoke, braiding her hair. She smelled of woodsmoke and sweat, and Kalan regarded his grimy hands ruefully, supposing that he must smell the same. But Malian was looking out over the white and gray world, wonder in her eyes. "How beautiful it is," she said softly, "despite everything."

"Yes," agreed Kalan. Their breath clouded and mingled together on the still air.

I feel alive here, he thought. You can breathe and there are no walls, just the hillside falling away and the empty air. Almost empty air, he amended, his eyes finding the black speck that was the hawk, hovering far above them. Malian followed his gaze and frowned. "The shadow of the hawk," she murmured, still staring up into the pale sky.

Kalan was frowning, too. "It has to be some sort of spy," he said, and stood up. "We'd better get going."

"Yes. But we should eat first and check your wound." Malian finished pinning the braid around her head. "If you keep watch here, I'll fetch the horses." She half turned away, then paused, turning back. "We should cut our rations," she added slowly. "Try to make them last."

Kalan nodded, listening to her footsteps crunch away,

then frowned out over the snowy hills until she came back with the horses. The wound was clean when she checked it; afterward, they ate their scanty breakfast in silence, watching the horses pull at the rough grass. Kalan frowned again as they packed up their gear. "You didn't have that before," he said, nodding at the old-fashioned and rather dented pot helm that Malian was tying to her saddle bow.

"No." Malian hesitated, as though deciding how much to say, then she shrugged. "I had a very strange dream last night. Although maybe it wasn't a dream, it might have been a farseeing. I could hear hounds barking, and then it was like I was back in the keep again and the second siren worm was there. I watched Asantir kill it." She frowned, as though something about this memory bothered her, then shrugged again. "And then I woke up, but I could hear this voice calling me. It had been in my dream as well, but this time I was awake and I knew I had to answer it, to find out what it wanted. So I did. I went outside and found a shadow tower where the ruins are now." Malian paused and the look she shot him was defiant, as though she didn't think he would believe what she was about to tell him. "Yorindesarinen's armring showed me how to climb the shadow tower, but there was a crow here as well. It spoke to me, helped me work out what I had to do—" She stopped. "What?" she asked.

"Nothing," Kalan said quickly, then shook his head. "No, it isn't nothing. Are you sure the crow spoke to you? Was it all that you met out here?"

Malian crossed her arms. "I know it sounds strange, more like a dream than reality, but it was definitely real. And the crow was all I met at first, although later—" She broke off again. "But you wanted to know about the helmet. I should tell that part first."

Kalan glanced at the dented helm and nodded, then felt his eyes widen as Malian told him about what the crow had said to her, and finding the moon-bright helm at the top of the hidden tower. "It was the helm that had been calling to me," she said. "*Yorindesarinen's* helm, Kalan. I wish you could see it like it was then, both darkness and light, glowing on the black plinth." But Kalan was shaking his head from side to side and she stopped again. "What's wrong?"

"I am," he replied bitterly. "I was supposed to *tell* you that the lost arms of Yorindesarinen would be seeking you, and that the armring would help you find them. Hylcarian told me," he said, seeing the question in her face. "I was dreaming a lot in those days before we left the New Keep— because of the siren worm, I think, but it was all jumbled at the time. But I met Hylcarian in the dream and he gave me the message for you." Kalan wondered if he looked as miserable as he felt. "But I wasn't allowed to let anyone else know, so at first I didn't dare risk telling you. And then with everything else that's happened, I just forgot."

Malian was nodding as though pieces of a puzzle were falling into place. "So that's how you knew about the second siren worm! I saw you in that dream, although I thought that was all it was at the time, just a dream—probably because you were with the hunt that was on the tapestry in my room."

"The Hunt of Mayanne," Kalan said, and knew from her expression that she must have seen the hounds and the Huntmaster last night, as well as the crow. "The only times I've seen a crow, it's always been with the Huntmaster."

"It was last night, too." Malian looked around the hilltop. "It told me that this was the Hunt's place." After a moment she folded her arms again, tight across her chest. "When I put on the helm," she said, her voice very low, "I saw Kyr and Lira, dead in the snow."

Kalan nodded, feeling the sharp ache of her grief, answering his own. "I know," he said gently. "I saw them, too, in a dream."

Malian's eyes were fixed on the distant speck that was the hawk, but Kalan could see the glitter of her tears. "You're right," she said, not looking at him. "We should go. Carry on, like Kyr said."

They swung into the saddle, but Kalan looked back at

the faded carving over the archway one more time, trying to reconcile the ruined tower with the power and deadly beauty of the Hunt. "Come on," Malian said, a little sharply, and Kalan nodded, letting his horse follow hers.

She's upset about Kyr and Lira, he thought, and Nhairin as well. He was upset himself, about the guards, and knew they were both worried about the weather and their supplies lasting, on top of the Darkswarm pursuit. "What about a portal?" he asked abruptly, as his horse drew level with hers. "Could you open one to the Border Mark? According to the accounts I've read, power-wielders from the Blood didn't need to be in a keep to use those sorts of abilities."

Malian grimaced. "I've thought about that, but back in the Old Keep I knew my destination well. I've no knowledge of this country or the lands to the south. And there are too many stories of people who opened portals at random, without reference points, and never came out again." She shivered and Kalan did, too, thinking about the void that had swallowed the Raptor of Darkness. "Besides, I had help in the Old Keep: you, the heralds, the other priests. Opening a portal large enough to carry ourselves and the horses over that sort of distance—" Her look was apologetic. "I just don't know if I could do it on my own. It could act like a beacon for our enemies as well, who might have the power to follow it—unless you could shield them out?"

Kalan shook his head and Malian sighed. "I wish we could, though," she said. "Open a portal, I mean." Kalan just nodded.

The day, although windless, was still cold as they climbed higher into the pass beyond the watchtower. Snow-speckled hillsides rose steeply to the overcast sky, throwing deep shade across parts of the road; the horses' shoes rang loudly on every stone and rib of rock. Kalan could no longer see the hawk, but uneasiness prickled along his shoulder blades and the horses seemed nervous, laying back their ears and showing the whites of their eyes, although there was no sign of pursuit.

"I'll be glad to be out of this pass, " Malian said, her voice low.

Kalan nodded. "It's going to snow again, too, before long."

The pass snaked on through fold on fold of hills, but after a while the steep slopes pulled back and a creek twisted out across a narrow flat. Like the much larger Telimbras, it was wide and shallow, with braided channels that twisted between shingle banks. The ford was in the center of the flat, at the creek's widest point, and the rushing water looked very cold, although low enough to cross in safety.

"We should refill the water bags here," Kalan said, as they approached, "since we may not find another stream for a while." He heard his father's voice, an echo out of the past, telling him that a warrior always did the hard things first, lest they became too hard to do at all. "We should cross first, though," he added, looking down at the water's cold swirl.

The creek purled past the horses' knees as they waded through, but they crossed to the far bank without mishap. "I'll scout up past that first corner if you look after the horses and the water bags," Kalan said, as they dismounted. The path rose again toward the end of the flat, bending out of sight around a sheer bluff, and the trees on either side grew taller, making it difficult to see what lay ahead. A solitary snowflake floated down, settling on Kalan's nose as he walked forward.

Behind him, one of the black horses screamed, and Kalan whirled to see both animals rear high, tearing their reins out of Malian's hands. They came down in a lunging run, straight toward him, and he jumped for the side of the track as they thundered past. But his attention was all on Malian and the creature of nightmare advancing across the ford.

It was shaped approximately like a horse, only larger, with four legs, a mane, and tail—and it was black as the heart of night. The demon's eyes were no longer viridian flame but opaque and gray as pebbles; its nostrils flared scarlet as it quested the wind for scent. The mane was a mass of writhing serpents, each individual head darting at the air; the tail was a long supple lash with a spike at its tip, and the legs ended in claws rather than hooves. Instead of walking on those claws, the Night Mare drifted above the water like smoke, the horselike head swinging toward Malian. When the velvet muzzle opened, Kalan saw a double row of razor-edged fangs.

He could see five riders now, waiting a short distance back from the ford. Four of the riders wore armor and closed helms, each one shaped in the likeness of a grotesque bird or beast; the fifth, cloaked in black on a black horse, sat silently beside them.

The Night Mare, Kalan thought, must have used a con-cealing spell to hide them all. Far too late, he remembered the Huntmaster's warning about the demon's uncanny track-ing ability, even though it was practically blind by daylight. The blank eyes were fixed on Malian now, and the distance between the two had narrowed; the Night Mare looked as though it could reach her with little more than one bound off its powerful hindquarters. The hideous head snaked for-ward, the serpent mane twisting and snapping in anticipa-tion.

Kalan forced himself toward the creek, although his limbs felt like lead and nausea churned in his stomach as he caught the first rotten-meat whiff of the Night Mare's scent. He stopped, choking down a surge of bile, and stooped to pick up a rock. It was pathetic, Kalan knew—a rock against armed warriors and this Swarm demon, but he held on to the rock anyway, willing himself forward again.

Malian had stopped backing away from the Night Mare, as though she recognized that retreat would not help her. She stood very straight instead, her head high as she looked beyond the Swarm demon to the five riders. "What are you doing with Nhairin?" she demanded. "She is a retainer of the House of Night. Release her at once!"

Kalan wondered why he had not realized sooner that the cloaked, silent figure was Nhairin. Her messenger horse seemed restless and reluctant. Its head was being held on a close rein by one of the other riders and a line of foam ringed its mouth. Nhairin, however, did not move or react in any way.

"What have you done to her?" Malian said, her voice ragged.

"You are in no position to make demands, Heir of Night." A voice of smoke and terror, filled with echoes, boomed in Kalan's mind. He shivered, clutching his rock, and wondered how Malian could face the Night Mare without flinching, or retching at its stench. Yet her back, which was all he could see of her, remained resolute.

"Night is true to its own, Darkspawn! Whatever you have done to Nhairin, you may not have her!"

"Fine words," the mind voice sneered, *"although you may find there is little enough left to have. But first, shall we see what you can do against me, little Heir?"*

Malian's fists clenched. "Perhaps nothing," she said. "But I intend to try."

The Night Mare lifted its terrible head and the opaque eyes glittered. Power sliced into Kalan's mind like an ax and he reeled, almost dropping the rock. He heard the echo of malicious laughter as Malian swayed. A gray miasma billowed out from the Night Mare, creeping toward her across the water—and then everything happened at once.

Malian shouted defiance, snatching up the water bags that were lying near her feet and hurling them at the Night Mare. The demon growled as the bags smacked hard against its muzzle and exposed fangs; the miasma thickened and surged forward. At the same time, a harsh scream echoed Malian's defiance from above and a great falcon hurtled out of the sky, straight into the Night Mare's face. Powerful pinions beat at the serpent mane, and talons raked the opaque eyes.

The Night Mare growled, drawing back, and the watching warriors cursed and reached for their bows. One of them took aim at the falcon as it wheeled, circling to come in again. "No!" Kalan shouted. He ran forward, throwing his rock with desperate strength. It flew across the creek, smacking into the bowman's elbow, and the arrow went awry. The visored helm turned in Kalan's direction and the riders began to advance, joining the fight.

The Night Mare lunged, trying to spring clear of the water as Malian stooped for rocks of her own. The falcon shot past Kalan and closed with the demon again, but it was far from an even contest. The gray miasma swirled, reaching to entrap the bird, which strained to break free, evading a vicious snap from the fanged jaws and narrowly avoiding a flung javelin as it strove for height. Kalan looked around for another weapon as the hawk beat clear, knowing it was only a matter of time before arrows or the Darkswarm javelins found one or all of them. On the riverbank, the Night Mare's tendrils of smoke and shadow were beginning to curl around Malian, following her every time she twisted aside or backed away.

The falcon shrilled its battle cry above their heads, banking steeply as it turned to attack for a third time. Malian screamed, struggling against the Night Mare's power, while beneath them the earth rippled and then shook. The warriors' horses plunged, shying in fear as the air above the creek bed tore apart and two great gray horses came striding through. "Over here!" screamed Kalan. "Tarathan! Jehane! We're here!"

Tarathan's horse plunged through the creek and rammed the Night Mare's near shoulder, knocking it sideways. The Night Mare roared but the gray horse was already turning, charging the mounted warriors while Jehane Mor confronted the Swarm demon. The ground continued to undulate as the baleful head swung toward the second herald; gore from the falcon's talons oozed from one opaque eye. The gray miasma swept away from Malian and toward Jehane Mor, only to recoil from an invisible wall. It banked, trying to roll around the obstruction, but was pushed back onto the Night Mare.

Kalan crouched to pick up more rocks, his gaze darting back to Tarathan. The herald had loosed an arrow that punched through armor as though it were cloth, tumbling the nearest Darkswarm warrior out of the saddle, then dropped from his own saddle to hang by one leg while he shot another arrow from beneath his horse's neck. A second warrior reeled, pierced through the shoulder, and his horse shied, colliding with the riderless mount so that both scrabbled to keep their footing on the still-rippling earth. A crack ran along the ground and all the Darkswarm horses neighed wildly, struggling against their riders' hold. One warrior loosed an arrow, but his horse's plunge sent it clear of Tarathan, whose own mount closed the intervening gap in a burst of speed; the herald swung himself upright and struck at the bowman with one of his swords.

The rider collapsed sideways off his horse, while the warrior beyond him wrenched his struggling mount around and away. He pulled Nhairin's reluctant messenger horse along with him, the steward still silent and unmoving on its back— but the warrior with the shoulder wound had recovered control of his mount and drawn his sword. He charged Tarathan and the herald blocked his strike. The ensuing struggle was brief and fierce, ending with the Darkswarm warrior lying motionless, facedown on the edge of the creek.

Further out in the ford, Jehane Mor and the Night Mare were locked in a struggle where smoke and shadow were pushing hard against an invisible wall. Kalan moved toward Malian across the undulating ground, struggling to keep his balance as the shingle slid out from beneath his feet. Just as he reached her, the smoke and shadow rolled forward as though it had gained an advantage. Jehane Mor's hands rose in denial and the miasma was driven back, but not so far back as before.

The herald's expression was concentrated, her eyes narrowed, and her horse barely avoided the fire dart that shot at them from the smoke. The Night Mare sprang forward, its clawed feet and serpent mane extended, its jaws stretched wide. Jehane Mor twisted in the saddle, lifting her arms in an abrupt gesture, and the air between her hands spiraled into a funnel that pushed the Night Mare back—but for the first time since the day tore open, the creek bed between Malian and the demon lay unprotected. The creature howled and sprang sideways, a tremendous jump toward Kalan and Malian, and disappeared.

"Shield!" There was no remoteness in Jehane Mor's voice now and Kalan acted instinctively, slamming a mental wall around himself and Malian. He felt the Night Mare's flare of psychic rage as its unseen attack was thwarted, but it remained invisible. "Stealth hunter," whispered Kalan. "The Nine save us!" He focused on where the Night Mare had last been seen, straining all his senses to pierce the wall of daylight, but could detect nothing.

Jehane Mor's horse stepped out of the water, its ears flat and nostrils distended as it tried to smell out its adversary, but the rotten-meat stench had vanished with the demon. Tarathan, too, was urging his horse through the creek as Malian fumbled amongst the stones, straightening with the old pot helm in her hands. She jammed the helmet down on her head as Kalan's stretched senses caught something at last, the slightest bending in the light or whisper over stone. Air and rocks exploded outward as a force lunged through his shield barrier and Malian staggered back, sitting down hard on the rocky ground. The Night Mare rematerialized in midleap—and Malian's arms flew up, flame pouring from her hands.

The fire blast caught the Night Mare in the air and hurled it backward, roaring and twisting, before it reared skyward, its clawed forefeet raking at the sky. Yet even as it bellowed the gray miasma swirled thickly, smothering the fire.

"Nine!" cried Kalan. "It's going to recover from that! It's going to attack again!" Malian was already back on her feet and Kalan tried to rebuild his shield, to hold the Night Mare at bay. Tarathan was advancing, an arrow notched to his bow, but Kalan doubted that the herald could succeed where

Malian's wildfire had failed. Kalan groaned, trying to think of something, anything that he could do.

The ground cracked, a report like winter ice shattering, and one of the fractures beneath the Night Mare yawned apart. The predator dropped into the gap, its roar becoming a scream that echoed and reverberated between the hillsides as an updraft rolled it off balance, sucking the demon further into the earth. Kalan covered his ears, not quite taking in what was happening—then realized that the fissure was still moving, splitting the earth on a line aimed directly at Malian. She seemed mesmerized by its approach, frozen in place.

Another scream rang out, clear and wild as the falcon swept down, beating Malian away from the crevice with its wings. She stumbled back and the falcon soared up and away; the crevice, Kalan saw, had stopped moving.

What now, he asked himself numbly, staring at the yawning gulf and the frantically struggling Night Mare. Only a few moments before it had been terrifying, unstoppable: Now it seemed impotent as a fly, caught in the web of some ancient and unforgiving spider. The edges of the earth began to close, first creeping, then inching toward each other, and finally rushing together. There was one last despairing howl from the Night Mare, still fighting to lift itself clear, before the earth snapped closed and the world was still again.

"Nine!" Kalan heard his voice crack with strain and relief. "What *was* that?"

Malian stumbled to a boulder and sat down. She was shaking, and her hands trembled badly as she lifted off the helm. "Whatever it was—an earthquake, the enmity of Jaransor—it very nearly took me as well. It would have, if not for the hawk." She stopped, her teeth chattering together, and when she spoke again her voice was strained. "I pity any living creature a death like that."

Tarathan slung his bow across his shoulder. "I did not think the Derai wasted compassion on their enemies."

Malian lifted her drawn face to his. "It was very nearly my death, too. It was—terrible!"

Tarathan nodded. "It was," he said, his tone gentler. "But terrible or not, the intervention was fortunate. Even the four of us together were no match for that one Swarm minion."

"Five," said Kalan. "I thought the falcon must be spying for our enemies, but it turned out to be a friend."

"So it seems," agreed Jehane Mor. "But we should not tarry here, for the one who fled has friends as well and will return with them." She glanced at the sky. "There's more snow on the way, too."

"How can we go on while they have Nhairin?" Malian protested. "We must rescue her." She frowned when Tarathan shook his head. "We can't just abandon her to the Darkswarm!"

"You may be right to believe in her," Jehane Mor said quietly, "but it was by no means clear to me that Nhairin was a prisoner."

Kalan rubbed a hand across his hair. He had not noticed his wound during the fight against the Night Mare, but now it had begun to throb. "Malian," he said, "you know that Nhairin tried to kill me yesterday. Today she's with the Darkswarm warriors. You have to admit that doesn't look good. Besides, Kyr would say that your first duty is to elude your enemies."

Malian considered this, poking at the gravel with one booted toe. "I think it was the madness of Jaransor that took her yesterday, not treachery," she said at last, but he sensed the cold current of her doubt. "How can I believe that Nhairin would betray me, when she has been a friend all my life?"

"Someone did," Kalan said bluntly, then looked away from the desolation in Malian's expression.

"Whatever the circumstances," said Tarathan, "there is nothing we can do for Nhairin now. There are only four of us while your enemies are still many. We are in no position to attempt a rescue."

Malian said nothing, just stared down at the battered helmet between her hands as Kalan began to pick up the water bags. "I thought that was on your saddle," he said, nodding at the helm.

She shook her head. "It was, but I took it off. I just wanted to look at it again, to feel it in my hands, so I put it down by the bags while I watered the horses. When the Night Mare went invisible I knew the helm was probably my only chance. As soon as I put it on," she said softly, "I could see the demon. And I knew how to call the fire out of myself. The knowledge was just there, as though it was something I had always known." She stood up slowly, her voice stronger now, but bitter, too. "It's a recompense, I suppose, to set against losing our way, our companions, and now our horses."

"But you are still alive. That is worth a great deal." Jehane Mor took the water bags from Kalan and tied them behind the gray horses' saddles. "Besides, I think we may find your horses soon enough. Once their first terror has passed they are unlikely to push very fast, or far, into unknown country. In the meantime, our horses will bear a double load easily enough."

Kalan looked at the gray horses, really taking them in for the first time. "They are big, aren't they? I've never seen anything like them before."

Jehane Mor patted her mount's neck. "They are Great Horses out of Emer, bred to wear armor and carry the Emerian knights into battle. They are very strong, and with armorless heralds on their backs, tireless as well." She mounted and extended a hand down to Kalan, while Malian scrambled up behind Tarathan. Kalan caught her quick look up as the gray horses turned away from the ford, but although he, too, looked for the falcon, the sky remained as empty as the road ahead.

33

The Door into Winter

The day grew steadily colder as they rode, with snow-flakes floating intermittently out of the iron sky, and although they kept watch behind them, there was no sign of immediate pursuit. Malian frowned as the spray from another small stream flew up in their faces. "Why did the Night Mare make itself visible at all," she asked abruptly, "when it could have caught and killed us far more easily if it had stayed concealed?"

"I know why," said Kalan. "Many Darkswarm magics can't be sustained over running water. It had to relinquish its concealing spell to cross the creek."

Malian shut her eyes, then opened them again. "So it was only our crossing over before we stopped that saved us."

"It was almost pure luck," Kalan agreed soberly. He slanted a look across at Tarathan. "I suppose you found us by seeking, but what I really want to know is how you got here? It was like the air just opened and out you came."

"Some kind of portal," said Malian. If she craned, she could just see the curve of Tarathan's profile, but not his expression, so she looked at Jehane Mor instead. "I didn't think you had that power."

"We don't." Jehane Mor was rueful. "We were riding

hard, but even with Emerian horses we would never have reached you in time." She shrugged. "We are not entirely sure what happened, but it was as though Jaransor thrust us through from one part of itself to where you were."

Tarathan nodded. "The ground started to split and tremble, very like what happened at the ford, and then the air in front of us tore apart. A second later we were riding into your melee."

"It was utterly terrifying," Jehane Mor said simply, "which was fortunate in a way since we were already grabbing for our powers and our weapons when we emerged."

They had reached another rise in the pass, and the heralds drew rein in the shadow of the close-growing trees. All that could be discerned ahead, beyond an immediate fall in the road, was the pass swooping up again to meet the lowering sky, and Malian wondered whether they would ever see an end to Jaransor.

"I don't think our powers would have made any difference," Tarathan said, as they moved forward again, "if the one that seized us had been ill-disposed. The power here is elemental, drawn from the earth itself. Ours are puny by comparison, bound to the anchor of our physical bodies."

"Fortunately," agreed Jehane Mor, "it did not seem ill-disposed, at least not then. Yet it is volatile and unpredictable, as we saw when the crack in the earth almost took Malian along with the demon." She fell silent and Malian, looking across, saw that her expression was deeply thoughtful. "Jaransor is a strange place," the herald said at last. "Even the Guild knows little of it. The watchtowers were ancient long before your people came here; they are said to have been built from the roots of the hills themselves. That is why the ruins endure long after the builders, and those who came after them, have passed away."

"There is anger here," Malian said slowly, remembering the voice in the earth as well as the crack that had pursued her. "And the madness that attacks my people and took Nhairin."

Tarathan half turned his head. "The Madness, we call it. Yet how could the hills love those whose coming destroyed the towers, throwing down the knowledge and power of the wise?"

Malian exchanged a quick, puzzled glance with Kalan. "There is no record of any war between the Derai and Jaransor," Kalan said uncertainly.

Jehane Mor shook her head. "What need for war, when your coming caused devastation across this entire world? Haarth itself was shaken to its foundations when the heavens split and you descended upon us from the stars. Fire ran from the earth's core in molten rivers, cities were tumbled down in ruins, rivers changed course and the seas rose, drowning farmlands and cities, people and animals together. When the immediate devastation was over our ancestors found that a bleak and bitter mountain range had been flung up in the north of the world, with the blasted waste of the Gray Lands adjoining it. Mighty fortresses were strung along this mountain wall and they bristled with an alien and warlike race who called themselves the Derai. Later, we found that the Derai had brought their own dark enemy with them, one that consumed all life, and we needed both their Alliance and their Wall to hold its power in check. But Jaransor was closest to the cataclysm and did not survive it."

Kalan whistled softly, but did not speak. Malian, too, was silent, because although she had always known how the Derai reached Haarth, it had never occurred to her to ask how and why the Swarm had arrived at the same time. The constant presence of the enemy was simply a given in Derai history, the same history that never mentioned the impact of the Alliance's arrival upon the new world. Most annals praised those who had opened the gate in the stars, and Derai honor and dedication in continuing to hold to the Wall and protect Haarth.

From an evil, Malian thought now, that we may well have brought here ourselves.

She could tell from Kalan's expression that he was thinking much the same thing. Jehane Mor, looking around, seemed to read their faces. "It was a long time ago," she said, "and it was not the two of you, or any of the Derai who live now, who destroyed Jaransor."

Kalan shook his head. "I wonder if Jaransor knows that? Getting out of here seems like an even better plan than it did before."

"If we can," said Jehane Mor, "with the weather against us."

The gray horses strode on into a world that was whitening rapidly. Snow had begun falling in thick, soft flakes, and although Malian huddled deeper into her coat and closer to the warmth of Tarathan's back, the cold penetrated anyway. Soon, she thought, we will just be shadows moving through a curtain of falling snow, lost in Jaransor.

Behind them, a horn echoed in the hills. The horses snorted and Malian and Kalan looked at each other, alarmed, as another horn call answered the first—and then a third sounded, more faintly this time and further away. Tarathan and Jehane Mor exchanged a silent glance and the gray horses sprang forward as though the heralds had spoken aloud. Yet despite the horses' ground-eating stride, the snow was swifter. It swirled whitely around them, settling heavily on the ground, and Malian tried not to think about how many of her father's retainers had died in the storm that drove him into the Winter Country, three years before. Instead she peered ahead, trying to see through the whiteness. But there was nothing, just the snow and the looming walls of the pass—until she looked again and saw shadows clustered, waiting on the road.

Malian drew in a sharp breath, intending to call a warning, but the heralds were already stopping. They issued no challenge, simply walked the gray horses forward until the shadows became a single rider on a white horse, the two black messenger horses standing beside her. The falcon rested, still as stone, on the rider's left forearm, its feathers ruffled against the cold. The rider was wrapped in a robe of white hide that blended with the snow; it was stitched with patterns of sun and moon and wild animals that circled across it in whorls of russet thread. The peak was pulled well forward, shadowing the rider's face, and Malian wondered for a moment whether she was looking at a flesh-and-blood person or some apparition of Jaransor.

The heralds, however, did not seem to be in any doubt. "Hail, Lady of Winter," said Tarathan of Ar. "This is an unexpected meeting."

"Is it?" the rider asked, in a voice that Malian knew well. A gloved hand lifted the robe back, revealing Rowan Birchmoon's face. There was a glimmer of humor in her gray gaze, and Malian saw the same gleam lurking in Jehane Mor's expression.

"Perhaps not completely unexpected," the herald conceded. "The winter did seem very—unseasonal."

Snow swirled around the Winter woman, but her smile was warm. "Greetings, Heir of Night," she said. "My greetings to you also, Kalan, although we have not met before. I am Rowan Birchmoon."

Malian hurriedly closed her mouth, which had opened in her surprise. "Did you summon the winter?" she asked.

"Is that your hawk?" Kalan said at the same time. "Have you been shadowing us all this time?"

"Say, rather," Rowan Birchmoon replied, "that I asked, out of my need, and Winter answered. As for the hawk, he is not mine, but these are his hills and he has chosen to hunt with me for the moment." She turned her head and the snow around them drew back, so that they sat in a clear space where the air seemed warmer. "You need not fear this weather, so long as I am with you."

Kalan drew in a deep breath. "So you really are a witch," he said, then went bright red. "I mean, if you did summon the winter!"

Rowan Birchmoon smiled at him. "We do not use that word in the Winter Country, Kalan. I am called a shaman there."

"Yet even when there is need," Tarathan observed, "it is only the most powerful of shamans whose call will be answered by Winter."

Malian remembered how low the heralds had bowed to Rowan Birchmoon when they first met her in the High Hall, even more deeply than to her father who was the Earl of Night and lord of the Keep of Winds. "I take it," she said, "that it is a very great thing to be such a shaman, in the lands beyond the Wall of Night?"

"It *is* a very great thing," said Jehane Mor softly, "most particularly in the Winter Country."

Malian considered this. "So why is so powerful a shaman here? What is your business with me, Rowan Birchmoon, and with the Derai?" She did not add, *and with my father*, but the question hung in the air.

The gray eyes met hers. "You are my business with the Derai, Lady Malian, although I did not know it, or was not sure until recent events unfolded. I am here now to help you escape your enemies and reach a place of safety, if that is still what you wish."

Malian kept her face expressionless. "So you did not come to the Keep of Winds simply because you loved my father?" She paused. "Or perhaps you do not love my father at all?"

Rowan Birchmoon sighed. "Is there ever only a single thread to any pattern? My love for your father was one reason for my coming to the Keep of Winds. You need not doubt that. But it was not the only reason. Nor was it why Winter drove him into the Winter Country, where he met me."

"Why, then?" asked Malian, and the falcon stirred on the Winter woman's arm.

"Peace, brother," Rowan Birchmoon murmured to the bird, although her eyes never left Malian's. "It is a fair question." She paused as though finding the right words. "We of the Winter Country understand that there is a darkness assailing our world, and we have looked into the patterns of both smoke and stars to learn how we may combat it. Those patterns told us that we must look amongst the Derai for the key to turning back the darkness and so we tried to learn more of your people and their ways. We were not," she said, "very successful, for the Derai do not love strangers. We had almost given up when Winter itself brought your father to us. We knew, then, that he must be close to the heart of the pattern we sought to unravel. But you, Malian—I now believe that you lie at the very center of that same pattern, that you may even be the key itself."

Malian looked away. "So was it you I saw riding behind the wind? Following the followers?"

Rowan Birchmoon nodded. "Winter spoke to me, out of earth and sky and wind. It told me of your plight and that you must not be permitted to fall into the power of the darkness."

"You did not save Kyr and Lira." Malian met the Winter woman's eyes again. "Were they not part of your pattern?"

The gray eyes did not flinch from hers, although their expression was sad. "We are all part of the pattern, but Winter is of nature and so bound by natural laws. It takes time to call its full power—and in this case I was trying to bring it down early into the world. All I could do was trail you, and Winter came too late for Kyr and Lira. I am sorry."

Malian bowed her head. "I am sorry, too," she whispered.

Tarathan placed a gauntleted hand over hers where they clasped his waist. "We would all rather have them alive and back with us again," he said. "Your Nhairin, too, as she was before. But there are some things that cannot be undone, no matter how greatly our hearts may desire it." His hand squeezed hers, the lightest of pressures. "It was not the Winter woman who caused these ills."

Malian nodded, not wanting to look up and let him see the blur of her tears. "I know."

The white horse moved a step closer to her. "Malian," Rowan Birchmoon said softly, "my grief in this can never be as yours, but I, too, care for Nhairin. I have sought for her already, but it is not just the Madness. The Darkswarm have done something to her mind and I cannot separate her presence from theirs. But I am not your enemy—or your father's enemy."

"I know," Malian whispered again. She blinked hard against the tears and risked a look up. The Winter woman smiled at her; Kalan cleared his throat.

"Speaking of enemies," he said, "ours can't be far behind. We heard their horns, not long before we met you."

Rowan Birchmoon stroked the hawk's head with her gloved forefinger. "You need not fear. Even now the storm blows thick around your pursuers and it will not abate. They will need to find shelter, or perish."

Kalan glanced at the thickly falling snow behind them. "Can you really help us reach someplace that's safe?"

Malian straightened. "And if you do, what will you ask of us in return?" She thought Tarathan might have sighed, but the sound was so slight that she could not be sure.

"You are right, of course," Rowan Birchmoon said quietly. "There is always a price. That, too, is part of the pattern: cause and effect, action and reaction." Her gray eyes held Malian's, very steady, very clear. "For myself, I want nothing. But for this world, for Haarth, I want everything. I do not want the darkness to devour the sun and the moon and blot out the stars. I want many more generations to share in the beauty of the hawk's flight and hear the wind howl over the Winter plain. If you truly have power within you that can turn back the rising dark, then I ask that you use it to save this world, not retreat with your Alliance to another battleground."

Malian frowned, taken aback, and caught her lower lip between her teeth. But Kalan spoke up hotly, while she turned the Winter woman's words over in her mind: "The Derai have only ever retreated in the past when to do otherwise would be to suffer total defeat. We do not betray our allies or our oaths, even when keeping faith is not to our advantage."

Rowan Birchmoon's expression remained calm. "It does your heart credit that you think so, Kalan. But your histories suggest that the Derai Alliance have always used others' worlds to fight their war, retreating from them when the struggle required it. Perhaps that explains why the Derai have never become part of Haarth, holding our peoples at arm's length and shunning alliances with us. I will help you now anyway, but I would like to think that the path you follow offers hope for Haarth as well as for the Derai."

Kalan opened his mouth and then closed it again—reflecting, Malian guessed, on how rarely the Derai made compacts outside their own Alliance. And there was a ring of unpleasant truth in the reason that Rowan Birchmoon had suggested.

"It may be," Malian said, speaking with care, "that we lost the option of retreat anyway, when we lost the Golden Fire of the keeps. Even if the Fire returns, the Derai have fallen a long way from the old powers that enabled us to open gates between the stars." She saw, from the flicker in the Winter woman's eyes, that she knew this to be true.

Oh yes, thought Malian, you will have learned a great deal about the Derai in these past three years. And what of Haimyr? Is that why he serves my father, to learn our strengths and our weakness? If so, whom does he serve?

Her fingers touched the dulled silver of Yorindesarinen's armring and she heard the faintest whisper of the hero's voice: *". . . not all the forces that move and coalesce around you are enemies. There are many friends as well, some open and some still hidden from you."*

But am I their friend? Malian wondered. Will I keep faith with them? *That* is what the Winter woman is asking now.

"My father," she said slowly, thinking each word through, "has traveled beyond the Wall and the Gray Lands. He has brought both you and Haimyr to live amongst the Derai. I believe that he at least may see the other peoples of Haarth as potential allies."

"I believe he may," agreed Rowan Birchmoon, without

irony. "But it was not your father that I asked, Malian of Night, but you."

Malian nodded, acknowledging the point. "I have chosen the path of hope," she said, speaking more carefully still. "That is why I am here, having turned my back on my father and my House. I have pledged to come into my power and stand against the Swarm. I cannot promise you that I will succeed, any more than I can guarantee that I will live to make the attempt. But the Derai are part of this world now. I don't think it would be possible to save one without the other."

Something very like grief touched Rowan Birchmoon's expression. "Thus the Derai," she said. "Your words are always fair and carefully thought through, but you promise nothing—and in the end you hold only to your own, as you have always done. I can only hope, in the days to come, that you will think more on what I have asked. It may even be that you will find it in your heart to be as true to Haarth, then, as you are being to the Derai Alliance now."

"It is my hope," Malian replied stiffly, "that it will not be a matter of one or the other." Yet inwardly she was ashamed of the careful words that denied one who was helping her to escape from her enemies.

She helps me for her own purposes, Malian told herself quickly. But memories swirled: of Haimyr, comforting her childish griefs; and Tarathan and Jehane Mor coming to her aid in the Old Keep, then again here in Jaransor—where Nhenir, the moon-bright helm, had found shelter for years beyond count. The falcon screamed, a wild cry, and for one dizzying moment she saw all the lands of Haarth beneath her eye, exactly as they were laid out on the tabletop in the Red and White Suite.

Malian took a deep breath, meeting Rowan Birchmoon's eyes again. "I cannot promise for the Derai," she said, "only for myself. But I will do all that I can to save Haarth, whatever the future may bring."

Rowan Birchmoon sighed as though she had been holding her breath. "It is enough, for the moment," she replied.

"And time, in any case, for me to do as I said I would and help you vanish from sight and knowledge."

Kalan frowned. "Won't you be suspected, having been missing from the keep for so long?"

Mischief gleamed in the Winter woman's smile. "But I am not missing," she said. "I have gone out from the keep to hunt my animals, as I often do, accompanied by an escort of the guard." Her smile deepened at Kalan's uneasy expression. "My escort lies asleep in a cave not far from the Keep of Winds with all my beasts—my hawks, my hounds, and my wild cats—there to watch over them. When I return, the guards will wake and remember only that we have been hunting together. No one except ourselves will ever know what has happened here, or my part in it."

"So what is going to happen?" Malian asked.

"I will open a door through Winter," Rowan Birchmoon replied, "into my own country. My sister of Spring and brother of Summer await your coming and will ensure that you lose yourselves in the vastness of the Winter lands. From there, they will send you to a place that is hidden from your enemies. Even I will not know where it is." She looked from one to the other of the heralds. "But it would not be wise for you to disappear at the same time. You must return quietly to Terebanth by the expected road, and at the appointed hour—so it would be best if I returned you to the Border Mark."

Tarathan looked at her keenly. "Can you do such a thing, open a door into more than one place? Dare you even attempt it, with Jaransor rousing?"

The Winter woman's brows drew together. "Rousing, ay, and must be lulled to sleep again. Now is not the time to have Jaransor waking in the daylight world." Her expression eased. "But it is not I that does these things, it is Winter. And Winter's strength is at least as great as Jaransor's, once it has been called into its power." She looked from Malian to Kalan. "You will not be afraid to go amongst strangers, alone into the Winter Country?"

Kalan shook his head. "We crossed the Telimbras three days ago. For us, there is no going back."

Rowan Birchmoon smiled at him. "And now you must continue that journey." She held out the messenger horses' reins. "You had better take back what is your own. You will need horses in the Winter Country."

As soon as Malian and Kalan were back in their own saddles, she had them all turn to face the north. The snowstorm rose in strength, raging all around them, but Rowan Birchmoon still held it clear of their small group. For a moment Malian thought that nothing was happening, then the Winter woman began to sing.

It was more of a chant than a song, a resonance that spun into the deepening storm. The black horses flared their nostrils, as though the chant was a living thing and they could track its path. Perhaps they could, Malian reflected, since Derai legend claimed that messenger horses could see the wind itself. The rhythm of the song rose and fell around her until she should have felt sleepy, but instead was more alert than she had been in days.

She stole a look at Rowan Birchmoon's face and saw that every hollow and angle was stark, like a mask sculpted from bone. She looked the other way, toward the heralds, but their expressions remained as calm as ever. Only Kalan stirred and gave her a wry grin before looking straight ahead again—as though he, like the horses, could see that line of sound extending through the storm. The snow in front of them began to take on form, and soon Malian could make out the blurred outline of posts and a curved lintel, with a sliver of blue inside the frame.

The song went on, rising and falling but never faltering, and Malian began to hear other voices joining in from the far side of the door. The blurred outline solidified and the span of blue on the other side grew wider. Beneath it, Malian could see a white plain that seemed to stretch away forever, and fur-clad people with their hands raised in welcome as their voices wove through the chant. A tall man, thickset as an oak tree, and an equally tall but slender woman stood closest to the frame, their eyes fixed on Rowan Birchmoon.

"My brother of Summer and my sister of Spring, with others of our people," the Winter woman said, a world of longing in her voice, although the chant continued unbroken. Malian blinked, but Rowan Birchmoon reached out a gloved hand and touched her, very gently, on the cheek. "You and Kalan must go through now. Take great care, Heir of Night."

Malian clasped the Winter woman's hand, feeling a moment of connection between their power, just as she had with Haimyr. "I will," she said simply, then smiled as her eyes were snared by the unyielding gaze of the hawk. "Farewell, brother of air."

She turned to the heralds, impassive on their horses, but Jehane Mor forestalled her with a gesture. "Let there be no word of thanks between us," she said, "for are we not friends? Fare well, Malian, and you also, Kalan. May your Nine Gods watch over you both."

"Now go!" said Tarathan. "Both of you!"

Malian nodded, and she and Kalan urged the black horses toward the span of blue and the strangers who waited there. Kalan did not look back, but Malian turned once, to raise a final hand. The salute was not just for those who watched, but for Kyr and Lira with the snow falling on their dead faces, and for Nhairin, perhaps captive, perhaps mad, abandoned to an unknown fate in Jaransor.

The snow swirled behind the two black horses; when it cleared again the sky beyond the door was not blue but a patch of gray above a tall standing stone. "The Border Mark," said Rowan Birchmoon softly, "and the road to Terebanth."

"What of you?" asked Tarathan, his look searching as the hawk's.

"Why do you ask," she replied, "when you have already seen it, perhaps more clearly than I? My fate lies with the Derai and the Earl of Night."

"Nothing is written in letters of stone," he said. "The pattern can always be changed."

She shook her head. "Do not tempt me, Herald. I know the path I must walk and hold to it."

He bowed. "We bid you farewell, then, Lady of Winter. For your aid, we thank you!"

"Hold to *your* course, Herald," she said, "and that will be thanks enough for me."

"We will," Tarathan and Jehane Mor replied, their voices weaving together. They both bowed deeply, then let their horses step through into the gray world of the Border Mark. The snow blew wildly behind them and the door disappeared, leaving Rowan Birchmoon alone in the pass. The snow tugged at her, fraying the shape of rider and hawk and horse until they seemed half made of its whiteness. The Winter woman listened intently for a time and then began to sing again, but now the tune was more gentle, a lullaby.

"Sleep," Rowan Birchmoon sang, *"rest now, O Jaransor, slumber deep ye powers profound; sink back again into silence, drawn far down into earth. Sleep well, sleep soft, sleep deep, sleep long: sleep now. Sleep. Your time will surely come; it will come. But it is not now, it is not yet, it is not the season or the hour, so sleep—slumber long, slumber deep."*

She sang until a great stillness filled the hills and only the snow continued to flutter down: soft, steady, endless. "As it will," she murmured, "for a long time to come." Her task done, she simply sat, watching it fall.

"The rest," she said to the hawk at last, "I must leave to others. They will come again when the time is right, to walk in these hills and shake the power in the land awake. But what of you," she asked, as the bird turned its head to meet her gaze. "Will you stay here, or will you come with me for now?"

The falcon continued to hold her gaze a moment longer and then launched itself off her arm, beating a strong path up through the falling snow until it was only the shadow of a hawk flying, and then was gone. "Farewell, then, my brother of air," she said softly, "my braveheart, my valiant. Do not forget me, here amongst your hills."

The white horse stamped its hooves and snorted. "Ay," she agreed, "time to take our own road home and collect our sleeping friends on the way."

She turned the horse, and without undue effort—for the power of Winter still filled her—opened another door through the snow, this one into a quiet, sheltered place not far from the Keep of Winds. The keep's lofty towers and the bitter peaks of the Wall loomed together, high above her. "Welcome home," the Winter woman said to herself, and there was a twist to her mouth, half sweet, half bitter.

One last thread she spun, before departing Jaransor, a filament for the lost to find their way home by. "May it find you out, Nhairin, wherever you are," Rowan Birchmoon murmured. Then she bade the white horse take her through the door, leaving the snow to close in behind them and winter to obliterate any trace of her passing.

Here ends Book 1, *The Heir of Night*;
To be continued in Book 2, *The Gathering of the Lost*
The Wall of Night, Book Two

Glossary

Aikanor: the Heir of Night at the time of the Great Betrayal.

Akerin: chief healer in the Keep of Winds.

Alkiranth: maker of the black blades, in the deeps of time.

Alliance: a common term form the Derai Alliance; see also *nine Houses*.

Amboran: of the House of Night, second husband of Nerith of the Sea Keep.

Anarchy: the chaotic era that followed the ruin of the Old Empire.

Antenor: a figure of Derai legend, with a spirit bond to Maron, his blood brother and closest friend.

Antiron: Night's Master of Messengers.

Ar: a city of the River.

Armar: an initiate priest serving in the Temple of Night.

Artificer, the: see *Terennin*.

Artisan, the: see *Terennin*.

Asantir: the captain of the Earl of Night's Honor Guard. See *Honor Captain*.

Ban: a guard serving the House of Night.

Barren Hills: the uninhabited hills to the south of the Border Mark.

Belan: see *Brother Belan*.

Beloved of the Nine: see *Mhaelanar*.

Ber: a guard serving the House of Night.

Betrayal, the: see *Great Betrayal; Night of Death*.

black blades: weapons of power, commonly associated with the hero Kerem.

blood oath, a: a powerful binding used by the Derai where the one swearing draws their own blood; once sworn it can never be broken.

Blood Oath, the: an oath that has bound the Derai since the Time of Blood and institutionalizes the schism between the warrior and priestly castes; grounded in lifeblood drawn from every scion of the Blood of Night, the shades of the civil war dead, and in the secret names of the Nine Gods, it has endured beyond the deaths of those who first swore it. See also *Oath*.

Blood of Night, the: the direct bloodline of the Earls of Night. See also *greater line*.

Blood, the: includes the Earls of the Derai and any of their blood kin. Traditionally, the Blood have been closely linked to the power of the Golden Fire.

bond: see *spirit bond*.

Border Mark: the stone pillar that marks the boundary between the Gray Lands and the Barren Hills.

Brother Belan: an old priest in the Temple of Night, now dead, who was fond of storytelling.

Brother Selmor: a scholar priest in the Temple of Night.

chamberlain: an official of the Keep of Winds.

Chaos Worm: according to legend, the deadliest foe ever sent by the Swarm against the Derai. See also *Worm of Chaos*.

Charge of the House of Night: a war song of the Derai.

Child of Night: see *Malian*.

Child of Stars: see *Yorindesarinen*.

Chosen of Mhaelanar: the prophesied hero who will unite the Derai for the final victory and be born of both the House of Stars and the House of Night. Also known as *the Chosen, the One, One-to-Come,* and the *Shield of Mhaelanar*.

Chosen, the: see *Chosen of Mhaelanar*.

Citadel of Stars: the stronghold of the House of Stars.

Cloud Hold: a satellite fort of the Keep of Winds.

Commander of Night: the overall military Commander of the Keep of Winds and of the House of Night.

Count of the Rose: the hereditary ruler of the House of the Rose.

crow: companion bird of the Huntmaster.

Darkness of the Derai: see *the Great Betrayal*.

Darkness: the name given to the Swarm of Dark by the Winter people.

darkspawn: the minions of the Swarm of Dark.

Darkswarm: see *Swarm of Dark*.

Darkswarm Bestiary: a Derai book describing Darkswarm minions and their habits.

Darksworn: the vanguard of the Swarm of Dark.

Daughter of Night: a title given to a daughter of the Earl of the House of Night. See also *Malian*.

Defender, the: see *Mhaelanar*.

Derai Alliance: the formal alliance of the nine Houses of the Derai.

Derai-dan: ancient combat code of the Derai, including both armed and unarmed techniques.

Derai, the: warlike race, alien to Haarth, comprising nine Houses and worshipping nine Gods. They arrived on Haarth fifteen hundred years before and brought with them their traditional enemy, the Swarm of Dark. The Derai are fighting an eons old war to stop the Swarm obliterating the universe. The Derai are divided into three societies or castes: warrior, priest, and a third caste that comprises both warrior and priestly talents but are focused on some other skill, e.g. the Sea House are navigators and the House of the Rose are the diplomats of the Derai Alliance.

Doria: Malian's nurse.

dream: the power held by a dreamer.

dreamer: a person with the old Derai powers who can pass the Gate of Dreams in both their spirit and their physical body.

dulkat: a leaf that dulls pain when chewed.

Earl of Blood: the hereditary ruler of the House of Blood.

Earl of Night: the hereditary ruler of the House of Night.

Earl of Stars: the hereditary ruler of the House of Stars.

Earl of Swords: the hereditary ruler of the House of Swords. See *Sword Earl*.

Earl's quarter: sector of the Keep of Winds given over to the use of the Earl of Night and his household.

Earl, the: the hereditary title given to the rulers of the nine Houses of the Derai Alliance.

Eight-guard: the basic unit of a Derai guard, comprising teams of eight.

eldritch light: a sorcerous fire used by the Swarm to attack and overcome enemies.

Emer: a land of Haarth, located south of the River on the route to Ishnapur.

Emeriath: a figure of Derai legend, who appears in the songs and stories concerning Kerem the Dark Handed.

empathy: see *spirit bond*.

Ephor: a ruler of the River city of Terebanth.

Eria: an initiate priestess, serving in the Temple of Night.

Errianthar: the Priestess, an ancient hero of the Derai, twin sister of Telemanthar the Swordsman.

Falath: one of Rowan Birchmoon's hounds.

Fall of Night: the feared twilight of the Derai and then all worlds, should the House of Night ever fall.

farseer: a Derai with ability to see events across physical distance and time. See also *Terennin*.

Farseer, the: see *Terennin*.

Farseeing, the: see *Terennin*.

Feast of Returning: a formal feast held to mark the return of any Derai expedition, particularly those associated with the defence of the Wall.

fell lizards: creatures that serve the Swarm.

Fire, the: see *Golden Fire*.

fire-wielders: Derai with the power to bring fire with their minds and direct it through both eyes and hands as a weapon.

First Kin: the first degree of kinship to the direct or greater line of the Blood of any of the nine Houses of the Derai. See also *greater line*.

Garan: a guard serving the House of Night.

Gate of Dreams: a place between worlds and times that can be reached through dreams or via mind- or spiritwalking.

Gate of Stars: see *Great Gate*.

Gate of Winds: the main entrance into the Keep of Winds and a fortress in its own right.

Gerenth: military commander of both the Keep of Winds garrison and the House of Night.

God of Death: see *Hurulth*.

Goddess of Luck: see *Ornorith*.

Golden Fire: a power and strength of the Derai that once burned in the nine Keeps, until the Great Betrayal.

Gray Lands: the desolate plains that adjoin the Wall of Night.

Great Betrayal, the: refers to the Derai civil war and its intended end when the peace feast turned into a night of slaughter between House and House, warrior and priest, kin and kin. See also the *Time of Blood* and the *Night of Death*.

Great Chamber: the formal council chamber of the Keep of Winds.

Great Gate: the gate that Derai power-wielders opened between worlds to allow the Alliance to come through to the world of Haarth. See also *Gate of Stars* and *Great Portal*.

Great Horses: the destriers of Emer, bred to wear armor themselves and carry armored knights into battle.

Great One: the name given to one of the powers beyond the Gate of Dreams by the heralds of the Guild.

Great Portal: see *Great Gate*.

Great River: the Ijir, the major river that flows through the center of the land known simply as the River.

Great Spear: a weapon of power. See also *black blades*.

Great Strategist, the: see *Mhaelanar*.

Great Sundering: the legendary schism alleged to have split the Derai Alliance in the early years of the Long War.

greater line: the direct line of the Blood of a Derai House.

Guild of Heralds: a society of messengers, said to have special powers, based in the River lands. See also *Heralds*.

Guild, the: see *Guild of Heralds*.

Haarth: the Derai name for the world on which this story takes place.

Haimyr the Golden: a minstrel of Ij, which is the greatest city of the River. He is a friend and retainer to the Earl of Night.

Hall of Memories: the hall in the Temple of Mhaelanar that commemorates the dead of the House of Night.

Hall of Mirrors: a hall in the Old Keep.

Hall of the Dead: the main temple of Hurulth, the Silent God, the God of Death.

Halls of Meraun: the halls of healing, sacred to the god Meraun.

Halls of Silence: the anterooms to the Temple of Hurulth, the Silent God, the God of Death.

Healer, the: see *Meraun*.

Heir of Night: the designated successor of the Earl of the House of Night. See also *Malian* and *Aikanor*.

Heir of Stars: the designated successor of the Earl of the House of Stars. See also *Yorindesarinen* and *Tasian*.

Heir's Guard: a guard unit dedicated to serving and protecting the adult Heir of a Derai House.

Heir's quarter: sector of the Keep of Winds given over to the use of the Heir of Night and the Heir's household.

Helm of Knowledge: see *Nhenir*.

Helm of Secrecy: see *Nhenir*.

heralds: messengers trained by and bound to the Guild of Heralds, based on the River. See also *Guild of Heralds*.

High Hall: the main hall of a Derai fortress.

High Priest: the head of a Derai Temple quarter.

High Steward: the head steward, oversees most of the civilian affairs of a Derai keep. See also *Nhairin*.

Hills of the Hawk: see *Jaransor*.

hold: a satellite fort of the main Derai keeps on the Wall.

Honor Captain: the captain of an Honor Guard. See also *Asantir*.

Honor Guard: an elite guard specially sworn to protect the lives of Derai leaders, mainly the Earls of the nine Houses.

Honor Room: the office of an Honor Captain.

House of Adamant: a priestly House of the Derai Alliance.

House of Blood: a warrior House of the Derai Alliance.

House of Morning: a priestly House of the Derai Alliance.

House of Night: a warrior House of the Derai Alliance; claims to be the "first and oldest" of all the Nine Houses. See also *Night*.

House of Peace: a priestly House of the Derai Alliance.

House of Stars: a House of the Derai Alliance, particularly recognized for their mastery over the Derai powers.

House of the Rose: a House of the Derai Alliance, principally recognized as diplomats and peacemakers.

Houses, the: the name given by the Derai to the nine separate clans or peoples who comprise the Derai Alliance. See also *nine Houses*.

Hunt of Mayanne: a power that dwells beyond the Gate of Dreams.

Hunt, the: see the *Hunt of Mayanne*.

Hunter: see *Huntmaster*.

hunter-in-darkness: see *Raptor of Darkness*.

Huntmaster, the: a power that dwells beyond the Gate of Dreams, associated with the Hunt of Mayanne.

Hurulth: one of the Nine Gods of the Derai, known as the Silent God, the God of Death.

Hylcarian: the Golden Fire of the Keep of Winds. See also *Golden Fire*.

Ij: the Golden, the greatest city of the River, which is built on the delta between the river Ijir and the sea.

Ijir: see *Great River.*

Ijiri: a person or thing that is native to Ij.

Ilor: an initiate priestess serving in the Temple of Night.

Innor: a guard serving the House of Night.

Ishnapur: a fabled city and empire on the southern edge of the known world, which borders the great deserts of Haarth.

J'mair: a famed poet of Ishnapur, whose work has survived down centuries.

Jaransor: the range of uninhabited hills that lies to the west of the Gray Lands.

Jehane Mor: a herald of the Guild, from the Guild House of Terebanth, a city on the River.

Jhaine: a land of Haarth, located far to the south of the River on the route to Ishnapur.

Jiron: the Earl of Night's scribe.

Kalan: a novice priest in the Temple of the Keep of Winds, who was born to the House of Blood.

Keep of Stone: the stronghold of the House of Adamant.

Keep of Winds: the stronghold of the House of Night.

Kerem the Dark Handed: an ancient hero of the Derai.

Khorion: Lieutenant of the Gate of Winds, in the Keep of Winds.

Kin Right: the priority claim Derai may make on their blood kin; particularly inviolate in terms of the Blood. See also *Matter of Blood* and *Right of Kin and Blood.*

Korin: a guard serving the House of Night.

Korriya: a senior priestess in the Temple of Night and First Kinswoman to the Earl of Night. See also *Sister Korriya.*

Kyr: a guard serving the House of Night.

Lady Consort: *de facto* title given to Rowan Birchmoon by the Derai.

Lady of Winter: see *Rowan Birchmoon.* See also *Winter woman.*

Lannorth: Asantir's lieutenant, second in command of the Honor Guard.

Lieutenant of the Gate: commander of the Gate of Winds,

the main entrance into the Keep of Winds. See also *Gate of Winds* and *Khorion*.

Lieutenant, the: the second-in-command of the Honor Guard. See also *Second*.

lightless dark: one of the many terms for the Derai's great enemy, the Swarm of Dark.

Lira: a guard serving the House of Night.

Little Chamber: the Earl of Night's private council chamber.

Long War: the great and protracted war between the Derai and the Swarm before they came to the world of Haarth.

Lord Defender: see *Mhaelanar*.

Lord of the Dawn Eyes: see *Terennin*.

Madness, the: a condition associated with Jaransor.

Malian: only child of the Earl of the House of Night. See also *Heir of Night*, *Child of Night*, and *Daughter of Night*.

Mareth: a guard serving the House of Night.

Maron: a figure of Derai legend, best friend and blood brother to Antenor.

Master of Messengers: master of the House of Night's courier corps.

Matter of Blood: a matter of great importance, usually life or keep threatening, that concerns the Blood of a Derai House.

Mayanne: one of the Nine Gods of the Derai. See also *Spinner of Nets*.

Maze of Fire: a stronghold of the Swarm, from the legend of Kerem the Dark Handed and Emeriath of Night.

Meraun: the Healer, one of the Nine Gods of the Derai. See also *Healer*.

Merry Hunters: an aspect of the Hunt of Mayanne.

messenger horses: horses, usually black, belonging to the Derai messenger corps, famed for their endurance and speed. Legend has it that they can see the wind.

Mhaelanar: the Defender (or Defender of Heaven), one of the Nine Gods of the Derai. See also *Beloved of the Nine*, the *Great Strategist*, and the *Shield of the Derai*.

mindburned: a mindspeaker overcome by a psychic attack. See also *mindsweep*.

mindshield: a psychic protective barrier. See also *shielding*.

mindspeakers: Derai with the ability to communicate telepathically across distances, sometimes vast.

mindspeech: communicating directly from mind to mind, an old Derai power. See also *powers*.

mindsweep: a wave of psychic power, designed to sweep away any psychic obstacle in its path.

mindwalking: see *spiritwalking*.

moon-bright helm: part of the magical arms of the hero Yorindesarinen. See also *Nhenir*.

Nerion: Malian's mother, the Earl of Night's former wife.

Nerith: of the Sea Keep, mother of Nerion.

Nerys: a guard serving the House of Night.

Nesta: the most senior of the maids attending on Malian.

New Keep: the newer and inhabited stronghold of the Keep of Winds.

Nhairin: the High Steward of the Keep of Winds. See also *High Steward*.

Nhenir: the moon-bright helm, part of the magical arms of the hero Yorindesarinen. See also *moon-bright helm*, *Helm of Knowledge*, and *Helm of Secrecy*.

Night: common name for the House of Night.

Night March: a marching song of the armies of Night.

Night Mare: a stealth hunter and a powerful demon of the Swarm.

Night of Death: refers to the peace feast at the end of the Derai civil war, which turned into a night of slaughter between House and House, warrior and priest, kin and kin. See also *Great Betrayal* and *Time of Blood*.

Nine Gods: the nine gods of the Derai. See also *the Nine*, *Hurulth, Mayanne, Meraun, Mhaelanar, Ornorith, Tawr, Terennin,* and *Thiandriath*.

nine Houses: the nine Houses of the Derai Alliance. See also *Houses* and *Derai Alliance*.

Nine, the: the nine gods of the Derai. See also *Nine Gods*.

Nirn: a Darkswarm sorcerer.

Oath, the: see also *Blood Oath*.

Old Earl: the current Earl of Night's father, Malian's grandfather, now deceased.

Old Empire: an empire said to have existed prior to the Derai arrival on Haarth and to have stretched from Jaransor to Ishnapur.

Old Keep: the original Keep of Winds, now abandoned.

old powers: see *powers*.

One-to-Come: see *Chosen of Mhaelanar*, *Shield of Mhaelanar*, and *One*.

One, the: the prophesied hero who will come to unite the Derai and defeat the Swarm, predicted to be born of the Blood of the Houses of Night and Stars. See also the *One-to-Come*, *Chosen of Mhaelanar*, and *Shield of Mhaelanar*.

Ornorith: known as Ornorith of the Two Faces, one of the Nine Gods of the Derai, Goddess of Luck. She is depicted as having two, masked faces, looking in opposite directions.

outsiders: a Derai term for the non-Derai peoples of Haarth.

Place Between: a name for the space between worlds and different planes of existence.

power-wielders: Derai who wield the powers.

powers, the: the supernatural and magical powers of the Derai, which they once used to combat the Swarm of Darkness. Such powers include: the ability to command objects and forces, both natural and physical; understanding the speech of beasts and birds; acute eyesight and hearing, including seeing in the dark and hearing outside the normal human range; the chameleon ability to blend into surrounding materials and elements; dreaming; the empathic spirit bond; farseeing and foreseeing; fire calling; illusion working; mindspeaking; mind- and spiritwalking; psychic shielding; prophecy; seeking; truthsaying; and weatherworking. See also *old powers*.

Raptor of Darkness: a psychic vampire and eater of souls; a dark and terrible power of the Swarm.

Red and White Suite: a suite in the Earl's quarter of the New Keep.

Right of Blood: the right of the Derai Blood to speak directly with Earl and Heir. See also *Right of Kin and Blood*.

Right of Kin and Blood: a matter of great importance, usually life threatening to the Blood of a Derai House. See also *Kin Right*.

Rithor: a companion of Yorindesarinen, sent away before her final battle with the Worm of Chaos.

River: the lands along the Ijir river system, mainly comprising city states such as Ij, Terebanth, and Ar.

River lands: see *River*.

River of No Return: see *Telimbras*.

Rose, the: see *Tower of the Rose*.

Rowan Birchmoon: a woman of the Winter people, consort of the Earl of Night. See also *Lady Consort*, *Lady of Winter*, and *Winter woman*.

Saga of Yorindesarinen: the epic tale of the deeds of the hero Yorindesarinen.

Sarus: a sergeant and veteran of the Earl of Night's Honor Guard.

Sea House: a House of the Derai Alliance.

Sea Keep: the stronghold of the Sea House.

Second, the: the second-in-command of an Honor Guard. See also *Lieutenant*.

seeing: the power to foretell and see future events.

seeker: one with the power to seek out the hidden and find the lost.

seeking: the active use of a seeker's power.

seers: Derai with the power to foretell and see into the future. See also *sibyls*.

Selmor: see *Brother Selmor*.

Serianrethen: of the Blood of the House of Stars, first husband of Nerith of the Sea Keep.

Serin: an initiate priest serving in the Temple of Night.

Shield of Mhaelanar: see *Chosen of Mhaelanar*.

Shield of Stars: the shield of Yorindesarinen, said to have been made by Terennin in the deeps of time.

Shield of the Derai: see *Mhaelanar*.

Shield of the Nine: see *Mhaelanar*.

Shield-wall of Night: see *Wall of Night*.

shielding: the power to conceal objects or people from both physical and psychic search.

sibyls: see *seers*.

Silent God, the: see *Hurulth*.

siren worm: a powerful minion of the Swarm.

Sister Korriya: see *Korriya*.

Soril: a guard serving the House of Night.

Spearbearer, the: see *Tawr*.

Spinner of Nets: see *Mayanne*.

spirit bond: an empathic/psychic link between two Derai that can be either one or two-way. It usually occurs between two who are either blood kin, lovers, or very close friends.

spiritwalking: an old power of the Derai, allowing those with the gift to leave their bodies and act on the psychic/metaphysical plane. See also *mindwalking*.

Star of the Derai: see *Xeria*.

starbane: a term sometimes used for the silver fire associated with the hero, Yorindesarinen.

stewards: non military retainers of the House of Night.

Storm Hold: a satellite fort of the Keep of Winds.

Sundering, the: see *Great Sundering*.

Swarm of Dark: the enemy of the Derai; a vast entity comprising many fell and evil creatures. See also *darkspawn, Darkswarm, and Darksworn*.

Swarm, the: see *Swarm of Dark; Darkswarm*.

Sword Earl: see *Earl of Swords*.

Swordsman of Stars: see *Telemanthar*.

Tain: a guard serving the House of Night.

Tarathan of Ar: a herald of the Guild, from the Guild House of Terebanth, a city on the River.

Tarn Hold: a satellite fort of the Keep of Winds.

Tasarion: the current Earl of Night, hereditary ruler of the House of Night.

Tasian: the Heir of Stars at the Time of the Great Betrayal.

Tasianaran: the full name of *Tasian* (see above).

Tavaral: a Derai general at the time of Yorindesarinen whose name meant "faith-keeper." He brought up his wing to support the hero in her battle with the Worm of Chaos, but came too late.

Tawr: one of the Nine Gods of the Derai, called the Spear-bearer.

Telemanthar: the Swordsman of the Stars, an ancient hero of the Derai, twin brother of Errianthar the Priestess.

Telimbras: the braided river that runs the length of the Jaransor hills, separating them from the Gray Lands. It eventually becomes a tributary of the Ijir. See also *River of No Return*.

Temple of Mhaelanar: temple within the Temple of Night particularly dedicated to Mhaelanar, the Defender.

Temple of Night: the main temple precinct of the Keep of Winds, comprising temples to all nine Derai gods, but primarily dedicated to the god Mhaelanar, the Defender.

Temple of Stone: the main temple precinct of the Keep of Stone, the stronghold of the House of Adamant.

Temple quarter: temple complex in a Derai keep, comprising the temples and adjunct buildings dedicated to all of the Nine Gods, plus the living quarters of the priesthood.

Ter: a guard serving the House of Night.

Terebanth: a city of the River.

Terennin: one of the Nine Gods of the Derai. See also the *Farseer*, the *Artisan*, the *Artificer*, and the *Lord of the Dawn Eyes*.

Terennin's Token: see *Token*.

Terithis: an initiate priestess serving in the Temple of Night.

Teron: the Earl of Night's senior squire.

Thiandriath: the Lawgiver, one of the Nine Gods of the Derai. Also called the Merciful and Just.

Time of Blood, the: the civil war between the Houses of the

Derai Alliance, which terminated in the Night of Death. See also *Great Betrayal*.

Tisanthe: an initiate priestess serving in the Temple of Night.

Token-bearer: the one who bears the Token.

Token, the: the ring said to have been made by Terennin to bind the Hunt of Mayanne.

tor hawks: a breed of hawk found in Jaransor.

Torin: an initiate priest serving in the Temple of Night.

Tower of the Rose: the tallest tower in the guest wing of the Keep of Winds. See also *the Rose*.

trueseer: a seer whose visions come true.

truthsayer: a Derai with the power of truthsaying.

truthsaying: an old power of the Derai, allowing those with the gift to see through lies and to perceive the truth of hidden or concealed matters.

Two-Faced Goddess: see *Ornorith*.

Var: an initiate priest serving in the Temple of Night.

Vern: an initiate priest serving in the Temple of Night.

Vhirinal: an Ephor of the city of Terebanth, on the River.

vigil, the: denotes the Derai's long war against the Swarm, including their watch on the Wall of Night. See also *Long War*.

Wall of Night: the vast mountain range that protects Haarth from the Swarm and which is garrisoned by the Derai Alliance. It is said to have been created by the House of Night. See also *Shield-wall of Night*.

Wall, the: see *Wall of Night*.

ward fire: a protective fire, said to be used by heralds of the Guild.

Warriors' court: the hall that serves as a forecourt to the High Hall in Derai fortresses.

weatherworkers: Derai with the power to command the elements and natural forces.

Web of Mayanne: the tapestry in the Keep of Winds that depicts the Hunt of Mayanne.

were hunt: a power of the Swarm.

were hunters: the individuals that comprise a were hunt.

Westwind Hold: a satellite fort of the Keep of Winds.

Winter Country: the vast steppes in the northern regions of Haarth, which are inhabited by the Winter people.

Winter people: the nomadic peoples who inhabit the Winter Country.

Winter woman: see *Rowan Birchmoon*.

Worm of Chaos: according to legend, the deadliest foe ever sent by the Swarm against the Derai; slain by Yorindesarinen.

wyr hounds: hounds of the Derai, able to track psychic trails and those with psychic powers.

Xeria: a priestess of the House of Stars at the time of the Great Betrayal and reputed to be one of the greatest power wielders born to the Derai. See also *Star of the Derai*.

Xeriatherien: the full name of *Xeria* (see above).

Yorindesarinen: the greatest hero of the Derai; Heir of the House of Stars in her day, she slew the Worm of Chaos but died of the wounds received in that battle. See also *Child of Stars*.

Acknowledgments

Writing the first book in a series is always a major undertaking, and *The Heir of Night* has been no exception. I would particularly like to acknowledge:

My partner, Andrew, for his unstinting encouragement and support, as well as both our extended families.

My editor, Kate Nintzel, my agent, Robin Rue, and her assistant, Beth Miller, for loving the book and wanting to bring it to the world—and to the rest of the Eos team for backing Kate's call.

Peter Fitzpatrick for the wonderful map and Web sites.

Clare Davies and Grant Shanks, who were the first readers from within the professional writing field and who have remained generous with both their feedback and support.

All my readers: Irene Williamson, Janine Sowerby, Lou Stella, Elizabeth Kerr, Fitz, Sean Elvines, Robin Robins, Joffre Horlor, and Chris Whelan, for the time they gave to reading varying drafts and providing feedback. I am very grateful to you all.

I also wish to acknowledge Owen Marshall and the New Zealand Society of Authors/Creative New Zealand mentorship program. Although *The Heir of Night* was not part of the program, Owen's mentorship has assisted in the development of my writing.

Maggie Rowe, also for her mentorship and wise advice throughout the process.

My thanks to you all for everything that you have done, individually and collectively, to help me see *The Heir of Night* published.